Happy New Year

MALIN STEHN

Translated by Rachel Willson-Broyles

PENGUIN BOOKS

PENGUIN BOOKS

UK | USA | Canada | Ireland | Australia
India | New Zealand | South Africa

Penguin Books is part of the Penguin Random House group of companies
whose addresses can be found at global.penguinrandomhouse.com.

First published 2022

001

Copyright © Malin Stehn, 2022

The moral right of the author has been asserted

Set in 12.5/14.75pt Garamond MT Std
Typeset by Jouve (UK), Milton Keynes
Printed and bound in Great Britain by Clays Ltd, Elcograf S.p.A.

The authorized representative in the EEA is Penguin Random House Ireland,
Morrison Chambers, 32 Nassau Street, Dublin D02 YH68

A CIP catalogue record for this book is available from the British Library

ISBN 978–1–405–95303–0

www.greenpenguin.co.uk

For my parents

New Year's Eve, 2018

Monday

1. Fredrik

When Nina walks into the bedroom, I'm standing at the wardrobe.

'Does this make me look fat?' she asks.

I shoot my wife a hasty glance. 'You look great.'

My gaze returns to the wardrobe and the three ties hanging inside. Obviously the mint-green one from my high-school graduation is out of the question. The funeral tie matches my mood but not my shirt. With a sigh I take out the pale blue one with silver stripes, a Christmas present from my mother-in-law that felt outdated even when she gave it to me five or six years ago.

'You hardly even looked at me.'

Nina has moved over to the full-length floor-mirror. She twists this way and that as she examines herself, her forehead creased.

'It fits you perfectly,' I say.

Nina tugs at the green fabric of the dress. I join her at the mirror, smell her familiar scent. My wife has been wearing the same perfume for years now, so long that even I remember what it's called: Acqua di Giò. She tugs at the fabric again, snorting and muttering something I don't catch. I try to sort out the knot in my tie but don't get very far.

'You're wearing that one again this year?'

Nina is still facing the mirror, but her focus has turned to my tie.

'It's all I've got.'

She takes a long step over to the wardrobe but gives up when she sees the options left on the hook.

'You really need to invest in a new one for next year.'

I nod just as I hear the doorbell ring.

'That must be Jennifer.' Nina turns to the open door. 'Smilla! Will you get that?'

There's a sudden racket from upstairs; Smilla's feet thud down the stairs, and soon two voices reach us from the front hall.

Nina looks at me. 'What time is it?'

'Twenty past five.'

'Twenty *past*?' She hurries to the dresser and starts rummaging through her sock drawer. One pair after the next lands on the floor at her feet. 'Shit. Why do I always forget to buy nylons?'

A moment later, Nina leaves the room with something black in one hand.

'What's up with the boys?' she asks on her way into the hall. 'Are they ready?'

'I'll go see how they're doing.'

'Vilgot has to wear his dress shirt!' Nina calls from the bathroom. 'It's hanging on the chair.'

I button my pants, put on my blazer and inspect the result in the mirror. The tie makes me look like a clown. All that's missing is the red nose.

Vilgot and party clothes are a bad combination. Our six-year-old would be happy to live in sweatpants, and sometimes I wonder why we insist on dressing him up. Anton has become more compliant in this arena. He likes to wear nice clothes, and these days he spends time in

4

front of the mirror each morning, fixing his hair. The junior-high-school effect.

'Nice shirt,' I say as we go downstairs.

Anton shrugs but flashes me one of his rare smiles.

As we reach the kitchen, I stop short. I take in the two girls at the counter and try to calm my racing heart. Jennifer is not a monster; she is my daughter's friend. A perfectly ordinary teenage girl. I have to clear my throat more than once before my voice will work.

'Goodbye.'

Jennifer doesn't react; it seems like she's made up her mind not to hear me. She just keeps chopping lettuce, her back facing me. Her short, tight dress leaves very little to the imagination, and I do everything in my power not to let my eyes linger in the wrong places.

Still, I feel like I've been caught in the act when Smilla turns around. Her face lights up; she turns down the volume on the portable speaker and comes over to me.

'Bye.' I receive a firm hug. 'Thanks for helping talk Mom into this.'

As if I had any choice.

With my arms around my seventeen-year-old, a ridiculous but recurring thought pops up: how I wish it were possible to make kids stop growing when they reach the age of nine. Nine-year-olds are perfect beings. They are smart and reasonable, but they still have that unshakeable belief that their parents can fix anything. An afternoon at Leo's Play Centre is all it takes to appease the need for some excitement in their lives.

'You know the deal.' I take a step back and meet my daughter's eyes. 'Don't let in anyone who wasn't invited, no –'

Smilla covers her ears.

'I know!' She lets her hands fall. 'You and Mom haven't shut up about it for two weeks.'

I let go of her.

'We just want you to be safe.'

2. Nina

The car is in the driveway; the blue glow of three screens lights up the interior. I open the car door, sink into the passenger seat and place the bag containing this evening's dessert between my legs to make sure the bowl inside doesn't tip.

'Ugh.' I look at my husband. 'I almost want to change my mind.'

Fredrik hits the ignition button and the car starts.

'About what?'

'The party. Their party. How crazy *are* we, to let twenty teenagers celebrate New Year's Eve in our house?'

Fredrik sighs. 'It'll be fine. Smilla and Jennifer can handle this.'

We turn on to Agnesfridsvägen and pass the school and Videdals Square. Beyond the roundabout I can see Vita Höja, a complex of nine-storey apartment buildings. Their glowing windows create a yellow mosaic behind the bright green Coop grocery sign.

My stomach aches. I truly don't want to ruin the evening by worrying about the girls, but my anxiety is only getting worse the more distance we put between ourselves and our home.

Just moments ago, I came to a standstill at the front door. There was so much I suddenly wanted to say to my daughter. About how deceptive hard liquor can be, about never going along with something that doesn't feel right,

7

about how she is so wonderful and how everyone – in a perfect world – should be able to dress however they please but that a see-through top can send unintended signals. For starters.

By then it was too late for a bunch of admonitions. And the girls know the score: twenty people max, no drugs (absolutely no drugs), hard cider or beer only. The bar cabinet is locked, and the key is in my wallet.

I turn to Fredrik. 'Maybe Smilla and Jennifer can handle this. But we don't even know half the kids who are coming. Smilla claims they invited only classmates, but they could be anyone.'

'We have to let ourselves trust her.'

'I'm sure we can trust Smilla, but Jennifer . . .' I try to find the right words. 'Jennifer has . . . never cared about boundaries. You know what a handful she was when she was little, all the stuff she got up to. And Smilla always just went along with her.'

'They're seventeen now,' Fredrik points out. 'Not eleven.'

I feel myself deflate. There is no point in having this discussion, especially since all the decisions have already been made.

There are plenty of reasons not to let underage teenagers have unsupervised parties. But my scepticism about the girls' party is primarily based on uncomfortable facts: I don't like Jennifer. I don't trust her, and I don't like her.

It pains me to admit it. I work with children, and I'm usually able to find the key to any little heart. Or at least worm my way in gradually, if nothing else.

But Jennifer's heart has always been a locked mystery to me. As a little girl she was wild and loud and demanded to be the centre of attention. When Jennifer and Smilla played, I was always worried something would happen. Later on – when they became teenagers – I was terrified; I laid out clear rules for Smilla and made sure she was aware of the consequences should they be broken.

The girls' friendship has always been a difficult balancing act. I never wanted my feelings to spill over on to Smilla. Jennifer is like a sister to her. And Fredrik takes Jennifer's side every time.

Personally, I think it's a relief that the girls don't spend as much time together these days. This idea about throwing a new year's party together came as a bit of a surprise. An unpleasant one.

'It's all about learning that with freedom comes responsibility,' my husband says, as if he's reading my mind.

With freedom comes responsibility. Fredrik is repeating our mantra from the last few weeks' worth of discussions, and I have to bite my tongue to keep from repeating my own objections from those same discussions.

It's not that he hasn't voiced any concerns about the party. But all the while he's maintained that it's much better for them to celebrate at home in our neighbourhood than to 'be running all over town'.

I do buy that argument, but the problem is that we won't have any way to check up on them. We'll be at a different party in a different part of town. And currently I can think of a thousand ways a new year's party with Jennifer Wiksell might go wrong, even in a safe residential neighbourhood.

I turn to look over my shoulder. Two pairs of eyes are staring with great concentration at glowing screens; two pairs of ears are stuffed with white plastic. I give up on my attempt to make contact and face forward again.

Traffic is heavy on Inre Ringvägen; I suppose lots of people are on their way to celebrate the new year. I try not to think about the girls' party and force myself to shift focus to our own celebration and the party we're about to attend.

I hope the mousse will suffice. It'll be served with passionfruit-and-oatmeal lace cookies. Originally I had planned, in a childish act of protest, to purchase ready-made cookies from the store. But at the last moment I changed my mind and baked my own. Showing up at Lollo and Max's house with store-bought cookies for new year's dinner would be social suicide.

I glance at my husband. It wasn't so long ago that I would have shared my thoughts with him. We would have joked about our friends' perfect, curated home and the chaos of our own, and Fredrik would have consoled me. He would have said that, for one thing, Lollo and Max have only Jennifer to take care of, and, for another, interior decorating and preparing food have always been Lollo's greatest interests.

We used to love discussing our friends' strengths and flaws, and I realize that in a lot of ways it was about reminding ourselves of our own superiority. Because we always arrived at the conclusion that our way of life was the best one.

Recently, those conversations have fallen away. We never talk about our friends, about ourselves or about anything at all, really. All we discuss are family logistics, things that have to do with the kids. I miss *us*.

I could blame all the years of having little children to care for. But Vilgot started school last fall and he's pretty independent. Anton is in seventh grade and Smilla's almost eighteen.

'Are we there yet?'

A small finger scratches at my coat and I turn around.

'Almost. Don't you know where we are?'

'Nope.' Vilgot's golden curls bounce when he shakes his head. 'It's totally dark out.'

'See where it's a little brighter over there?' I point. 'That's Klagshamn.'

Vilgot seems satisfied with this and goes back to his iPad.

I look out the window at the flat landscape whizzing by. The fields are edged with rows of bare willows bending towards the sea. Veils of mist hang above the muddy ground; it's hard to tell where the sky starts and ends. Winter in Skåne.

'Nasty weather.' Fredrik turns on the fog lights but flips them off again when they don't make any difference. 'Guess we won't be able to see any fireworks tonight.'

'Do you have to be such a downer?' I ask.

'A downer? I'm just telling it like it is.'

'Didn't they ban rockets?' asks a cracking voice from the back seat.

'The kind with a stick are illegal,' Fredrik says as he turns towards the village. 'But cake fireworks aren't.' He looks at me. 'I imagine Max has stocked up with the biggest cake he could get his hands on.'

Max likes to show off, and Fredrik has never taken it in his stride. My husband believes that the main reason Max does anything is to show the world that he can afford it. And maybe that's partly true. But I think Max just likes doing crazy things. He wants to be the life of the party, the guy who's always up to something fun.

Max runs a successful real-estate agency in downtown

Malmö that was founded by his father. Max Wiksell has probably never read a book in his life, but he's got a nose for business and is extremely goal-oriented. According to Lollo, he works nonstop, and it seems to pay off.

Max drives new cars, drinks old whisky and wears expensive watches. And, although Fredrik claims he doesn't care about those kinds of status symbols, it's clear that he feels the pressure to assert himself alongside Max – most often by doing the exact opposite of what Max does, and sometimes by showing off his competence in arenas where Max *wishes* he were well informed (whisky) but, in fact, doesn't have much to offer.

For my part, I – unlike Fredrik – can laugh at Max when he edges into boasting or turns into Mr Know-it-all. And, since Fredrik – unlike me – can laugh about Lollo's home-made sourdough, I guess we're even. I've never been able to avoid comparing myself to my attractive, thin, domestic friend. Even though I know it always puts me in a bad mood.

We park a short way down the road; the Wiksells' fleet of cars takes up all the space in their generous driveway. A sea of patio candles burns outside of the huge white house, and through the panorama window in the living room I can see people with champagne coupes in their hands. I spot Malena tossing her head back in one of her famous peals of laughter, and for the first time in forever I feel festive.

Maybe this evening won't be so bad after all. We're going to ring in the new year with good friends. The boys are with us, and Smilla, well, she's almost an adult, after all. It's time to cut that umbilical cord.

'I'm sorry.'

I place a hand on Fredrik's thigh.

He looks at me.

'For what?'

'Oh, it wasn't fair to call you a downer. You're right. This weather is nasty.'

He smiles, but it doesn't quite reach his eyes.

'I'd already forgotten.'

3. Fredrik

In six hours, it will all be over. Or, no, hold on, in seven hours. I'm sure we won't head home right after the clock strikes midnight. But in seven hours, max, I will be walking back down this path – in the opposite direction. And, when I think about it, seven hours do go by pretty quickly. It's not even a full day of work. I'm going to make it.

In seven hours, all these patio candles will have burned out. I will be carrying a sleeping Vilgot in my arms, and the taxi will be waiting out on the street.

Hold on a sec. I walk faster.

'Did you book a taxi?'

Nina stops and turns around. Her hair is done up for the party; there's glitter on her eyelids.

'*You* were supposed to do that.'

Damnit! How could I forget, when all I want is to get out of here?

She stares at me. 'You don't mean to tell me that you *forgot* to book a cab?'

'It'll be fine. I'll work it out.'

'Exactly how do you plan to work it out?' Nina raises her eyebrows. 'You usually have to make the booking a week ahead of time. At the latest.'

'I told you, I'll work it out.'

There must be something seriously wrong with my brain. I've been forgetting things. Important things. It's not like me, and it scares the shit out of me. Am I getting Alzheimer's?

Nina sighs. 'Well, I'm not about to drag two dead-tired kids on to some bus in the middle of the night. Just so you know.'

She purses her lips, and Anton looks at us.

'Are we staying over now or what?'

'No,' Nina says firmly. 'We're going home.' She gives me a pointed look. 'Dad will work it out.'

The front door flies open and a beaming Lollo appears. She's holding Chanel, the family's poodle, who has a huge, sparkly bow securing a tuft of fur on her head in honour of the evening.

'Welcome!' Lollo's dress, like Jennifer's, is tiny and black. 'Come in, come in.' Our hostess backs away and we follow. 'Wow, boys, you've grown so much. Anton, you're almost as tall as your father. And Vilgot! What a little cutie.'

Lollo puts Chanel down and gives each of us a hug. Nina, who first hands her a fancy bouquet wrapped in cellophane, gets an extra-long embrace.

'Here you are, finally.' Lollo lets go but keeps one hand on Nina's shoulder. 'It's ridiculous how time flies. When did we last see each other? Was it really Midsummer?'

I know it was, but I don't feel like speaking up. Nina quickly objects, saying that we *must* have gotten together since, and while they exchange banter I hang up Vilgot's coat. He's still standing by the shoe rack, suddenly shy in front of all these new and forgotten faces.

I wipe my shoes on the hall rug.

'Is it okay if I keep my shoes on?'

'Of course.' Lollo smiles. 'Shoes are a must or the party's a bust!'

I wonder if she just came up with this or if it's an actual saying. Either way, it's stupid.

Nina swaps her boots for high heels and herds Vilgot and Anton into the living room.

'Come on,' she wheedles when Vilgot hesitates. 'I'm sure Lollo put out some nuts and soda for you.'

That works. Our youngest son's snack radar has been activated.

I admire my wife for her ability to handle little kids. Her patience with them is out of this world. She was born to be a preschool teacher; she loves her job, and I know she is appreciated not only by her kids but by their parents and her colleagues.

'Fredde!' Max thumps me hard on the back. ''Sup?'

No one but Max calls me Fredde.

'Not much. You?'

'Shit, man. Life is good. Did you get a drink? Bubbly's over here.' Max extends one long arm and grabs a glass of champagne. 'Here.'

Dom Pérignon, naturally. It wouldn't do to skimp on quality; people might start to suspect business is bad.

'Thanks.' I raise my glass. 'So, another New Year's Eve.'

'And we're only getting younger.' Max leans towards me and lowers his voice. 'Did you see Malena's new friend?'

I glance around the room, but I don't see Malena or anyone who might be her escort for the evening. Nina is helping Vilgot pour Coke into a small glass, and in front of them are two couples who were at last year's party too. Both couples are Max and Lollo's neighbours, and I recall that I was seated next to one of the women last time, but unfortunately I don't remember which one it was. They

16

look nearly identical this year as well: cascades of blonde hair, black dresses, black pumps.

Their husbands, though, I can tell apart. Jens Stenman is almost as broad as he is tall; Magnus Göransson is on the verge of skeletal. Together they remind me of Laurel and Hardy.

'Malena's boyfriend is a Muslim,' Max whispers, looking at me expectantly.

I know Max Wiksell; I know exactly the reaction he's after. And, to be honest, I am actually a little extra curious about Malena's boyfriend now. But airing those thoughts would only give Max fodder for his already black-and-white view of the world.

'So?' I say. 'Half my students are Muslim.'

'Yeah, yeah. But with *Malena*, here in our house. I mean, who would ever have thought you'd be ringing in the new year with a –'

'Is he religious?' I interrupt.

Max frowns. 'What do you mean? He's a Muslim.'

'Yeah, but is he a *practising* Muslim? Does he go to mosque? Does he pray every day? Does he drink alcohol?'

'No idea,' Max says with a shrug. 'Guess you'll have to ask him.'

Just then Malena enters the living room in the company of a dark-haired man. I don't know what I was expecting, but he looks like a perfectly average middle-aged guy at a new year's party. Suit, dress shirt and tie.

'Fredrik!' Malena steers him in our direction. 'Good to see you.' She gives me a long hug and turns to her new love interest. 'This is Adem.'

We shake hands, and Max takes the opportunity to mingle elsewhere.

'Malena keeps insisting on introducing me as Adem,' the dark-haired guy says in a strong Malmö drawl. 'But please call me Adde. Everyone else does.'

'Fredrik,' I say. 'Nice to meet you. I'm married to Nina over there, in the green dress.' My wife has advanced from the array of snacks to the two neighbour couples. She laughs and clinks her glass with theirs in a toast.

As we turn towards that small group, it's as if I see things through the eyes of our newcomer. I have a sense of seeing Nina for the first time, and it strikes me how beautiful she is. Her amber eyes, her naturally accentuated eyebrows, her brown curls. I love her – the realization is almost a surprise – and I love that ringing laugh. When did I hear it last?

'Nina and Lollo are my old friends from high school,' Malena explains to Adde.

He smiles. 'Your partners in crime, from what I understand.'

'Exactly.' Malena looks at him adoringly. 'We were dangerous as teenagers.' She turns to me. 'And I hear Jennifer and Smilla have taken the baton. You locked up the alcohol, right?'

'How old are they?' Adde asks.

'Seventeen,' I reply. 'Smilla will be eighteen in February.'

'Best years of anyone's life,' Adde says with a smile.

'What?' Malena pretends to be offended. 'I thought the best time was *now*, now that you've met me.'

Adde kisses her on the cheek. 'Of course. The best time is right now.'

4. Lollo

Nina is standing in the entrance to the kitchen. She's holding a champagne coupe in one hand and a few greasy peanuts in the other. Her pea-green dress suits her; she looks unusually chic tonight. Chic but too fat. Nina has always suffered from a lack of willpower. I find it so strange that she can't control herself. She would have looked so darn good without those ten extra kilos on her.

'Do you need any help?'

'Thanks, I'm fine,' I say. 'Malena was in charge of the appetiser, and it's already on the table. The situation is under control.'

Nina pops a nut into her mouth, comes a step closer and lowers her voice. 'Have you talked to our new star? Adde, right?'

'I only said hi. But he seems pleasant enough.'

'And handsome,' Nina says with a smile.

I turn on the tap and drench the dishcloth with hot water.

'They usually are. Handsome, I mean.'

'Let's hope it sticks this time.' My friend lets out a little sigh. 'For Theo's sake, at least.'

'Yeah, seriously.' I wring out the cloth and start rubbing it on two brown spots that have already begun to stain the white marble countertop. 'Hey, are Theo and Anton upstairs? They're looking after Vilgot, right?'

'I was just up there.' Nina glances at the ceiling. 'Theo

and Anton are playing video games and Vilgot is watching. So far he seems perfectly happy with that.' She sips her champagne and looks around the kitchen. 'That patterned tile turned out so well. It really freshens everything up.'

'I know, I love it! It's hand-made, imported straight from Morocco.'

Nina traces the scrolling pattern with her index finger. 'Sounds expensive.'

'We bought it through the agency, so no tax,' I say, annoyed with myself even as I say it.

Why am I trying to defend myself? I don't want to talk money. We always end up there, and I don't know if it's down to curiosity or jealousy on Nina's part. Things must be tight for her family, with two teachers' salaries and three kids. But that's their own choice. No one forced them to choose careers that don't pay well. Fredrik went so far as to quit his engineering job when Smilla was little, because he wanted to do something more 'meaningful'. Hand to God, it's absolutely mind-boggling. How could you just give up half your salary? Nina should have put her foot down.

I look at her and add, 'Max thought the whole project was a waste. The old tile had been there for only three years. But I managed to convince him.'

Nina smiles. 'You're usually pretty good at that.'

'We all have our special talents.'

I rinse a plate and put it in the dishrack; I'm not about to reveal that I had to cry my way to those tiles. Not because of the cost – Max hardly ever cares about the money. It was more that he didn't understand *why* I wanted them. But it was easier to squeeze out a few tears than to try to explain that our old tile was hopelessly outdated, and that I, as an interior designer, really need to stay at the cutting edge.

'And you have lots of them.' Nina takes another sip of champagne and leans against the counter. 'How's the blog doing?'

No one seems to understand how much work it is to come up with topics, take pictures, upload them, write content and put it all together. I bet I spend fifteen hours a week on that damn blog – and so far it has hardly any readers. But I know my blog will eventually be a fantastic window into my bricks-and-mortar shop, and the online store as well – I just have to do a better job of promoting it.

Nina doesn't wait for an answer. 'Your photos look professional,' she continues. 'I've checked out the blog a time or two.'

'Feel free to share my posts on Facebook,' I say. 'My customers are mostly women our age and up, and we still hang around there sometimes. Unlike the kids.'

'Speaking of kids . . .' A crease appears between Nina's eyebrows. 'Have you heard from Jennifer?'

'Nope. But that's probably a good sign.'

Nina nods, but she looks unconvinced and starts pacing back and forth by the kitchen table.

'We weren't quite on the same page, Fredrik and I.'

'About what?'

I dry my hands and hang up the towel.

'About whether we should let twenty teenagers into the house or not. Among other things.'

It's a bit late to bring that up now. We've gone over and over the girls' party on the phone probably three times over the past month, but our concerns have only ever been about alcohol and drugs. Nina never said a word to suggest the venue might be an issue.

'Well, I mean . . .' She smiles and throws up her arms. 'I agreed to it all, so it is what it is . . . But, you know, I'm still a little worried.'

I try not to sigh aloud. Nina is an expert worrier. She sees problems everywhere she looks, often before they've even appeared. It's almost always Smilla she's worried about. Smilla this and Smilla that. Poor kid, it can't be easy to live with a mother hen like Nina. You have to be able to trust your children, especially once they're the girls' age. Furthermore, they need to be allowed to make their own mistakes. If you remove every obstacle that appears in their way, how are your kids supposed to handle the hard stuff later in life?

'Oh, here you are, gossiping in the kitchen.'

Malena comes dancing over to ABBA's 'Happy New Year', which is blaring in the background. Her sequinned dress might be overkill, but it looks good on her.

'Don't I get to be included?' she asks.

'Of course.' I nod in Nina's direction. 'You can start by getting your friend here to stop being a wuss.'

Malena cups her chin in one hand and pretends to be studying Nina head to toe. 'Let me see . . .' She lets go of her chin and raises her index finger. 'My thorough analysis tells me you've been standing around fretting about all the fun Smilla and Jennifer are getting up to tonight. Am I right or am I right?'

I can't hold back my laughter. We've always been alike on this front, Malena and me. Our joint opinion is that there's no point in worrying ahead of time. It's so unnecessary. And boring. Without us, Nina probably would have worried herself to death by this point. Or at least she would have led a much duller life.

'What?' Nina gives me a forlorn look. 'There's nothing unusual about being a little anxious. Sure, Smilla's been to parties before, but this is the first time it's been at our place, and –'

'Come on.' Malena touches Nina's arm. 'It's going to be just fine. They're practically adults. And besides – think about us at that age, all the things we did back then.'

Nina makes a face. 'Exactly.'

Malena cracks up, and I follow suit. Even Nina has to laugh. But then she grows serious again. 'By the way, how is Theo doing?'

Malena looks confused. 'Theo? With what?'

'Well . . .' Nina blushes. 'I mean, Anton mentioned that Theo was having a rough time. I wasn't quite sure what it was all about, but –'

'Oh, that.' Malena waves a dismissive hand. 'This past fall was a little tough on him, with the move and everything. A new class and a whole lot of new people. You know Theo.' She gives a huge smile. 'But we can't just stand here moping around. Let's go have a toast with everyone else.'

Nina's bubbly sloshes over the rim as Malena links arms with us and pulls us into the living room.

'You have to stop worrying about the girls, Nina!' Malena has to shout to be heard over the music and the rising hum of voices. 'Trust them. No news is good news.'

5. Fredrik

'And you know what I said?' Stenman bleats. 'Hell, I said, "For that price you can't even get a fucking dinghy!"'

This fellow has long since passed the realm of tipsiness. His face is flushed, and he's laughing so hard his shirt gapes over his bobbing belly. It's been at least ten minutes since he started recounting the time he tried to sell his sailboat two summers ago, and the muscles of my jaw are cramping up.

I have nothing against boats; Dad had an old motorsailer that he kept in Gottskär, and we frequently took it out in the summertime. The problem is one Jens Stenman. Like most of Max's acquaintances, he is a conceited braggart. I *know* the only reason Jens is prattling on about his boat is because he wants to tell us how much he sold it for. And I could not care less.

'Damn straight,' says Magnus Göransson. 'People haven't got a clue these days. Think they can haggle about anything.'

Stenman nods. 'When I'm selling something . . .' He wobbles but grabs the edge of the table. 'If the caller can't speak Swedish, I hang up on the spot. I mean, they come from more primitive cultures. Places where you can walk around markets haggling all the time.'

'Exactly.' Magnus is eager to chime in and leans forward. 'Here's a tip. When I sold my Arcona 465, I hired a broker. It was a damn relief not to have to deal with all that. Serious brokers have contacts all over Europe, plus they can really drive up the price, so it's worth the cost in the end.'

I raise my glass. 'Just going to get a refill.'

My feet navigate across black-painted oak parquet and plush rugs, away from the Mutual Admiration Society. There's something about men in groups that makes my skin crawl. Nine times out of ten, you haven't even said hello before the peacocking sets in. Then it's all about jobs, cars, boats and money.

I spot Nina, Malena and the blondes who are married to Jens and Magnus gathered in one corner. It's one peal of laughter after the next over there, and I give the group a wide berth, sensing that my presence would ruin their cheerful atmosphere.

Lollo hurries back and forth between rooms.

'Do you need any help?'

'Definitely not.' She smiles but doesn't stop moving. 'Have some more champagne and relax, Fredrik.'

I can't relax. My collar is scratchy; there must be a tag still in it. I go out to the front hall, open the door and stand on the steps. The cool December air reminds me that we'll be leaving soon, that it's going to be only a few hours.

Breathe, Fredrik. Breathe.

I go back inside, put my glass on the bureau by the mirror and sneak upstairs.

Theo and Anton are in the den, on the sofa. Each is wielding a controller with able hands. Vilgot is only inches from the screen, experiencing each turn on the winding racetrack up close. In the centre of the oval glass table sits an untouched bowl of nuts.

'Hi, guys.' I sit down next to Anton. 'Going okay?'

'Awesome.' Anton's focus doesn't slip for a second. 'I'm about to win.'

'In your dreams,' Theo mutters.

As the hubbub on the ground floor increases, I lean back and watch the race cars, wishing I could stay up here all night. But when I glance up, I'm looking straight into Jennifer's room, and I immediately change my mind.

Theo swears tersely as his car flies off a cliff. Black-and-white-checked flags wave for Anton.

'Sick!' he cries.

I turn to Theo. 'Make sure you beat him next round, or else he'll get too cocky.'

Theo flashes me a smile while Vilgot makes a grab for Anton's controller. Anton holds on, but Theo hands his over immediately.

'One lap,' Anton growls at his little brother. 'Just one, got it?'

Theo has always been kind to Vilgot; he lets him join in despite Anton's protests. It must be at least partially because Theo doesn't have any siblings of his own to squabble with. But he's also just a good kid. Apparently he's had a tough time making friends, and maybe that's why he's spending New Year's Eve with two young kids. Sure, Anton is only two years Theo's junior, but the difference between thirteen and fifteen can be huge.

Theo shows Vilgot what to do. His voice is soft, his eyes partially hidden by his brown fringe.

And suddenly it's not Theo sitting there. It's Simon. I blink a few times to get Theo back, and in doing so I realize that he's exactly the same age Simon was when he died.

My little brother was a shy and quiet boy too.

'So how are things?' It's a struggle to keep my voice from trembling.

'Things?'

Theo reaches across the table for the nuts.

'You changed schools, right? Do you like Tygelsjö?'

He shrugs.

'Come on, Dad.' Anton elbows me in the side. 'It's New Year's Eve. We're gaming. Do you have to be here?'

'Take it easy.' I stand up. 'I'm leaving.'

The open door is like a magnet; my eyes are drawn to it. I can't stop them.

A white lace bra is draped over the headboard. It looks like it was tossed there in a hurry, on the way to the shower. But it could also be a very purposeful arrangement.

I hurry down the stairs.

6. Nina

'Well, I think it's about time for a toast!'

Ivanka stands up and waves a wine glass in the air.

I'm not entirely sober myself, but Ivanka Stenman is way ahead of me. Her eyelids are at half-staff, and her bright red lipstick has rubbed off on her front teeth.

'Good plan.' Max stands up too. 'Hey, shouldn't we have a song first?'

'Of course!' Magnus Göransson shouts so loudly my right ear is deafened. 'Come on, duckie. Give us the dirtiest one you've got.'

Ivanka giggles and smooths her short dress. '*I* don't know any dirty songs.'

'Duckie! Duckie! Duckie!' Magnus chants.

Jens Stenman joins in the cheer as he pounds the table.

'Excuse me.' A tense voice rises above the racket. 'Please remember there are children present.'

For a moment, the room falls silent and everyone turns towards the voice.

It belongs to my husband. I try to catch his eye, but Fredrik is staring straight at Max and Ivanka; he looks like he wants to murder them. What's his problem?

'Just a suggestion.' My table escort breaks the silence. 'I could give you a *really* dirty song. In Arabic.'

'Oh, no way.' I poke Adde in the side. 'That's cheating. How are we supposed to be sure it's actually dirty?'

He grins and rises from his chair. 'You'll just have to trust me.'

With his wine glass in one hand, and using the other as a baton, Adde begins to sing. I clap my hands, Lisen joins in, and Ivanka makes a spectacle of herself in what I can only assume is supposed to be a belly dance. It's not long before everyone is on their feet, dancing a homespun belly dance or clapping in rhythm. Everyone but Anton, Theo and Vilgot, who have torn themselves away from their video games to eat dinner. Naturally, Fredrik isn't participating either.

'I mean, these pictures are going to go down in history!' Lollo cries, brandishing her phone.

Ivanka, who is eager to pose for the camera, dances so violently that she falls over.

'Cheers, damnit!' Max says, hauling her to her feet.

I sit down, wipe away tears of laughter with my napkin and take a sip of white wine. It tastes heavenly. Not too sour and not too sweet, and, what's more, it's perfectly chilled.

'Mama.' Vilgot squeezes between me and Magnus. 'May I be excused now?'

When I turn my head to say yes, the world sways. Oops. How many glasses of bubbly did I actually have before dinner? I've lost count. Better eat more.

'Of course you may.'

I try to pat Vilgot on the cheek, but he slips away and I turn back to Adde.

'Delicious wine. Good appetiser too.' I devour a small pierogi and move my chair closer to my fellow guest. 'So what was it about? That song you sang.'

'I can't tell you.' Adde's dark eyes sparkle. 'It's not suitable for your innocent ears.'

'Innocent?' I hiccup. 'Excuse me. This always happens when I drink.'

'It was a lullaby,' he says.

'What?' Laughter bubbles out of me. 'Really?'

Adde nods and picks up a few olives from his plate. 'But now you should tell me something about Malena.' He pops an olive in his mouth and leans back. 'Give me something truly embarrassing.'

'There's certainly a lot to choose from.' I turn towards the end of the table. 'Malena! Your boyfriend here wants me to reveal all your youthful sins.'

She interrupts her conversation with Lisen.

'What do you mean? My past is perfectly spotless.'

Everyone laughs, even as the room fills with Jens Stenman's rumbling voice. 'Cheers!' Stenman is standing again, and it takes him a few swipes to grab his wine glass. 'Cheers to our lovely hostesh and a new year's party for the ages.'

7. Fredrik

It's fascinating that people can sit in one spot for so long, talking about nothing at all, and apparently still enjoy themselves. I look around the massive dining table and cannot find a single person, besides myself, who appears to be suffering from boredom.

With a newcomer in the group, Max has leaped at the opportunity to tell all the old anecdotes from his youth. These stories grow more and more dramatic each time they're repeated, and, given that I've been spending time with Max Wiksell for over twenty years, they're starting to approach the level of classic hero legends.

No one at the table reveals that these stories are rehashed. Instead they play along, laughing aloud in all the right places. Adde too laughs dutifully. Or else he actually thinks this is fun.

Malena's new love interest is Nina's table companion, and they seem to be having a good time together. Whenever Max takes a break between stories, they bring their heads close together for what must be, as far as I can tell, intimate conversation. It's clear that Nina has had quite a bit to drink, with those broad gestures and that silly giggle.

I feel left out. And I'm very well aware of the reason: everyone is drinking. Everyone but me.

The decision was made after the pre-dinner drinks. I realized Nina was right: it would be downright impossible to get a taxi. Sleeping over is out of the question; seven hours is more than enough time here, and I'm the one who forgot to book the car. So, instead of spending the evening downloading apps from every taxi company in town, I decided to take it easy on the drinks: a small glass of champagne before the meal, a glass of wine with dinner and a mouthful of bubbly at midnight. It shouldn't be an issue to drive home after that.

'You're a teacher, right?'

My table companion has turned towards me. We've exchanged a few pleasantries during the evening, and I still haven't been able to determine whether she's the same neighbour with whom I shared a table two years ago. But it sounds as if it could be.

'That's right. Gym and math. In high school.'

'Do you like it?' She cocks her head. 'Most of what you hear about school these days is just miserable. Kids who can't behave, teachers who have too much to do . . . our youngest graduated five years ago, so I've sort of lost touch with the world of education. Is it as bad as it sounds?'

'Personally, I think it's fine. Of course, how much you like it has a lot to do with where you work, but at my school we have a good principal who actually deals with any problems that arise. It's impossible for there to be zero issues when two hundred teenagers exist under the same roof. And I like my colleagues.'

'So has it changed? Does it seem like the kids don't have any respect for you teachers?'

I shrug. 'We have to earn that respect too. But, sure, compared to a decade ago, there's a difference.'

I rack my brains for a way to change the subject. I no longer enjoy talking about my job. I'm a good teacher, and I've always thought it was fun and stimulating to spend time with young people. But now that it's all up in the air, I don't want to think about it.

Besides, this conversation is a painful reminder that there's a party under way in our house at this very moment. I sneak a look at Nina and find that the alcohol seems to have had a calming effect on her. For my part, I would very much like to throw myself into the car, drive straight home and call the whole thing off. Anyone who has ever been seventeen knows that the kind of parties you had at that age were the absolute worst. Or the best. Depending on how you look at it.

My table companion opens her mouth to say something else, but Lollo rescues me from further interrogation.

'Everyone! Hello!'

She stands up at her place and taps her wine glass hard with her dessert spoon.

'You're gonna give a speech?' Max slurs. 'What a fuckin' bore. Well, make it quick!'

Everyone laughs – maybe to smooth over his declaration. I look around again. Do we usually get this drunk at our parties? Am I extra annoyed with everyone because I'm sober, or have people been unusually generous with their pours?

'Well, you know, it's almost . . .' Lollo glances at her watch and grins. 'In one hour it'll be a *new year*!' At this point a lot of cheering breaks out, and our hostess has to pause until it's reasonably quiet again. 'And I thought we should each say something about the year we've had. Maybe the best thing that happened? And then we can say something about our hopes for the coming year. Wouldn't that be fun? Just something quick, I mean.' She turns to her husband. 'Did you hear that, Max? Short and sweet, can you manage that?'

Everyone laughs again.

My entire being protests this suggestion. My head is pounding, my palms are sweaty, and my vision seems to flicker. I want to run away, but it's like I am frozen to the fluffy seat cushion.

'What a lovely idea!' my table partner cries. 'I'll start.'

'Perfect.' Lollo smiles. 'Go ahead, Lisen.'

Lisen. That was it.

And Lisen starts talking. She launches into a long-winded oration about a new job and one or more grandchildren. Then come her expectations about various travels and so on and so forth for all eternity.

I pour myself more water from the carafe in front of me and pray to the higher powers that turns will pass to the right and we'll never make it all the way around.

But when Lisen is finished, Lollo points at me.

'Your turn, Fredrik.'

My heart is pounding; I try to smile, but I can tell that my lips are actively resisting, and all I produce is a stiff grimace.

'Come on, Teacher,' Max's voice booms from across the table. 'Skeletons in your closet or something?'

'Excuse me.' I rise from my chair. 'I'm just going to check on the boys. I thought I heard Vilgot calling. Why don't you go in the other direction?'

'Don't think you're going to get out of this!' Max bellows.

I want to strangle him slowly, but I say something about being back soon and hurry out of the room.

8. Nina

'Your turn, then, darling.' Lollo looks at me. 'We want to know – what was the best part about this year? What are your hopes for next year?'

I take a sip of the dessert wine to buy time. When this round of sharing began, it seemed like a fun thing, a typical Lollo thing, but suddenly it feels important to say something admirable.

In a few minutes it will be a new year, the perfect opportunity to toss out old Christmas decorations and bring in fresh tulips. But that doesn't sound like much. Why am I thinking of flowers? I've had way too much to drink; I still feel a little woozy.

Adde nudges me in the side. 'Yoohoo, dinner companion of mine. Have you got stage fright?'

I don't want to giggle, but a giggle sneaks out anyway, an extension of this evening's earlier fits of laughter. It's been a long time since I've had so much fun at a party. Adde really is both pleasant and funny. I hope Malena can hold on to him – he seems perfect for her. A stable guy who still has that gleam in his eye.

'Well, let's see . . .' I smile at Lollo and try to gather my thoughts. 'It's been a good year, but I don't know if I can come up with any particular highlights.'

Lollo cocks her head. 'Surely you can think of *one* good thing?'

The more I think about it, the harder it is. Upon closer

examination, the past year has been a bit of a stinker. Fredrik and I have mostly been out of sync, either not talking much or arguing. Vilgot has had four ear infections, Smilla and I have fought about basically everything we could possibly fight about, and we had to cut our vacation short due to a water leak in the kitchen.

'Okay,' I say at last. 'The best part was that everyone in our family is doing fine and that we have such wonderful friends.' There's a wolf-whistle, probably from Max, who embraced the compliment straight away. 'As for next year, I hope . . .' My eyes wander around the table and stop at Fredrik's empty chair. 'I hope we'll continue to do fine.'

Jeez. On a scale of one to ten, how boring am I? Is my family's wellbeing the only wish I have for the future? That's pathetic. Everyone else has mentioned new challenges at work, exciting travels and running marathons.

Have I become a stodgy old lady? Presumably. Is that why Fredrik doesn't want to talk to me any more? Because he thinks I'm old and boring? And ugly?

We never have sex now. I've hardly even thought about our non-existent sex life before, but suddenly it hits me: we don't have one.

There have been children in the house for so long that desire has more or less been pushed aside. And, to be perfectly honest, I haven't exactly missed the sex. There's so much else revolving through my head: work, family logistics and God knows what else. In that state, relaxing and indulging in pleasure most often seems like an impossible equation.

But when was the last time we made love? Could it have been six months ago? If so, that has to be a record – not even after each child was born were we celibate for so long.

My husband is still in good shape; the touches of grey in his hair are charming, and he has a sporty, youthful sort of style. For my part, I've put on a few kilos since we met, and my grey hairs aren't nearly as charming as his.

A thought comes to me out of nowhere: is Fredrik having an affair? Is he seeing another woman? Someone younger, thinner and more fun?

I pick up one of my half-empty glasses and take a big sip. The wine still tastes good. My gaze moves down and I adjust my dress, which has bunched up at my waist. I note that at least there's nothing wrong with my breasts. And I'm not *that* fat.

'Okay!' Lollo shouts. 'Fredrik is off hiding somewhere, so Max will finish us off.' She looks at her husband. 'And you have three minutes, not a second more. We need to make it outside before midnight.'

No one else stood up to deliver their little speech, but Max does, of course, and he begins with a theatrical throat-clearing.

'Dear friends.' He looks out across the table as if he were a priest and we his pious congregation. 'It has been a tremendous year. Business as usual, lots of balls in the air. Which is right up my alley, as you know.' He finds his wine glass, takes a sip and puts it back on the table. 'And it was a good golf year too. Down to a 6-handicap now.' Someone applauds and Max continues. 'For next year, I hope our embarrassment of a government closes the borders completely. You can hardly walk down the fucking street —'

Lollo pokes him in the side. 'Let's not get into boring politics, darling.'

Max ignores her comment. 'And you don't need a

goddamn doctorate to realize that Sweden's got problems. The streets are full of beggars and other trash who don't pull their weight.'

'That's enough.'

Lollo sounds a bit firmer this time, and Max throws up his hands, eyeing her with a bleary gaze.

'But it's true.'

This is *so* awkward.

'Don't pay any attention to him,' I whisper in Adde's ear. 'Max has had a lot to drink. He doesn't usually –'

'My father saw this coming twenty years ago.' Max is on a roll now; he's waving his arms around. 'He saw that Sweden was on the road straight to hell. And it's not like it's become any better. Shit, it won't be long before we're celebrating the Muslim new year instead.'

Malena stands up. 'Excuse me, but it so happens we have a Muslim guest here tonight. Why don't you just aim all your hate straight at him?'

Max looks pained for a moment but quickly recovers.

'What the hell, Malena?' He turns to Adde and beams a big smile his way. 'Obviously I'm not talking about *you*. You speak Swedish, and work, and pay taxes. I'm talking about those *other* people, the ones who live on welfare and –'

'That's enough!' Fredrik is standing in the doorway. 'You're drunk, Max. And you're talking a lot of rubbish. We don't want to hear any more of that bullshit.'

'Come on, Fredde.' Max grins. 'Don't be so fucking woke. Open your eyes and admit that Sweden's got problems. Big problems.'

Fredrik takes a step towards the table, fixing his gaze on Max.

'The biggest problem in this country is that people like you –'

'Excuse me!' Lollo desperately bangs her spoon against her wine glass. 'There are only ten minutes left in this year, and I suggest we move to the balcony. Champagne will be served in a moment.'

We quickly break up; everyone practically runs away from the table. A quiet but intense conversation has arisen between Adde and Malena.

Fredrik approaches me with brisk steps.

'Come on,' he says. 'We're leaving.'

'Now?'

'Yes.' He is seething with rage. 'Now. It is not fucking possible to stay even a minute more.'

I rest one hand on his arm, partly because the ground is swaying beneath my feet.

'Calm down, honey. We can't just rush out of here. Lollo has prepared a whole bunch of things for the stroke of midnight, and it's not her fault that Max turns into an idiot when he drinks too much.'

'He's always an idiot,' Fredrik mutters. 'But for the most part he manages to keep his nasty thoughts to himself.'

'Let's do the toast first. Then we'll go home.'

I kiss my husband on the cheek and pull him into the hall. Anton and Theo are standing by the door, coats on in anticipation of the upcoming fireworks show.

'Is Vilgot asleep?' Fredrik asks, and Anton nods.

A few minutes later, we're out on the balcony, which Lollo has transformed into something straight out of a fairytale with the help of string lights and lanterns. The lanterns are placed in groups, tastefully arranged alongside winter plants in burlap-wrapped pots. Lollo, who's wearing something fur-like, is busily pouring champagne into flutes. I notice a fantastic ice lantern with ivory roses frozen inside melting on the table next to the glasses. How does she have the energy?

The neighbours have gathered in couples before the balcony door; Adde and Malena are off to the side a bit, on their own. Malena is making wild gestures as Adde puts a hand on her arm, apparently trying to calm her down. Max is out on the lawn along with his fireworks. I can see him bending down beyond the pool roof.

'Don't get too close!' Fredrik tries to catch the boys' attention, and then he turns to me. 'He shouldn't be messing with those in his condition.'

I look at Max. A few strands have escaped the rest of his slicked-back hair, and are hanging over one ear. He's fiddling with a box of matches and letting out long strings of profanities; apparently it's hard to get them to light in this damp air.

'I think it'll be okay,' I say, handing my husband a glass. 'Good thing the worst rockets are banned.'

The chill has sobered me up a little. From now on, every second drink has to be water.

Just then, Lollo cries 'Happy New Year!' and controlled chaos breaks out. Fredrik and I mingle with the rest of the partygoers. We exchange toasts and hugs and wish each other a good start to the new year.

At last, Max manages to get a match lit, and shooting stars in a variety of colours rise into the grey-black sky. We clap and give exaggerated shouts of enthusiasm each time a fresh glittering cascade of sparks shoots up over our heads.

I hold Lollo's designer glass in my stiff, frozen fingers,

lean back towards Fredrik and nestle my way into his warm embrace. In silence we study the results of the neighbours' significantly less-grand fireworks, which sparkle above the hedge.

I twist my body and try to meet Fredrik's gaze. 'Happy New Year.'

He smiles. 'Happy New Year, Nina.'

We clink our glasses. I'm about to say something about how this has been a year from hell, but at the last second I change my mind. Ringing in the first, trembling minutes of the new year with a bitter comment seems fateful, as if that bitterness might take root and set the tone for all the minutes to follow. Maybe it is now, in this very moment, that we have the chance to put the past behind us and start anew.

I know the calendar is a human construct, and that this new day is no different from the one we left behind. But maybe the symbolism – new year, new possibilities – could be a help for once. Maybe we can use it to find our way back to one another.

I stand on tiptoe and give Fredrik a kiss. We clink our glasses again and a voice inside me says that everything is going to be okay, that things can only get better.

9. Fredrik

I leave the balcony under the pretence of using the bathroom. In reality, I can't stand Nina's loving gazes. I am not worthy of them.

Behind the locked door I land on the toilet seat, where I bend over to rest my head in my hands. How did I end up here? In this situation. If only I hadn't . . . I heave a deep sigh. How many times have I returned to this thought? *If only I hadn't* –

My train of thought is cut short as my phone, in the pocket of my blazer, starts to play my favourite song. A flutter in my stomach. Has something happened at the party back home?

I fish out my phone, see an unfamiliar number on the screen and exhale. But my relief vanishes as quickly as it came. An unfamiliar number could mean that a friend of Smilla's is calling – because Smilla has drunk herself half unconscious. Or maybe it's a neighbour, calling to say that they've reported the party to the police because of loud music or gunshots.

Def Leppard plays on. I stare at the series of numbers as if it were a code. A secret message that I, as a math teacher, should be able to decipher. But the numbers don't tell me anything, and in the end I bring the phone to my ear.

All I hear at first is a rhythmic scraping sound. Footsteps, maybe. Then comes the rustling sound it makes when a gust of wind blows over the microphone.

'Hello?'

My voice is drowned out by crackling on the other end.

'Hi, Fredrik.'

I freeze.

'Jennifer?'

She giggles.

'The one and only.'

'Is something wrong? Where are you?'

'Almost home.'

'Home?' I try to figure out what she means. 'You're on your way *here*? To your house?'

It sounds as if she trips and falls under the radar for a moment. Soon enough I hear her breath in my ear again.

'Yup.'

'But why aren't you at the party?' I swallow. 'With Smilla?'

'Aw, the party sucked . . . and I thought we could talk a little.'

'T . . . talk?'

My lips don't want to behave.

'Exactly. Talk.'

Shit! I look around the spacious bathroom. As if I might find a hidden door that would lead to someplace where I could hide indefinitely. But there isn't one, of course. I have to take the bull by the horns.

'Jennifer, where exactly are you right now?'

'At the bus stop.'

'Which one?'

Jennifer sighs. 'I told you –'

'Are you in Klagshamn?' I pace between the door and the jacuzzi. 'At the end of the line?'

'Yeah, but why –'

Shit!

'Jennifer, now listen carefully.' I try to sound firm. 'Stay where you are, and I'll come to you.'

'What? But –'

'Stay there,' I hiss between my teeth. 'Do you hear me? Do not move a muscle. I'll be there in a few minutes.'

Everyone else is still out on the balcony, so I'm able to grab my coat unnoticed and sneak out through the front door. The only one who sees me is Chanel. She's lying in her basket, trembling, her eyes wide. Someone should have stayed inside with that poor dog through the worst of the fireworks.

Outside, the street is deserted. I can see the occasional fireworks in the distance, but the thick fog limits visibility. The next-door neighbours seem to have gone back inside after the stroke of midnight. As I jog along the sidewalk, the voices from the party grow more and more distant, eventually disappearing entirely.

Deep down, I knew this day would come. All autumn I have been waiting for her to drop the bomb. And I can't imagine why I didn't defuse it right away.

I should have talked to her, explained things and cleared the air. Instead I buried my head in the sand and imagined that time would heal any potential wounds. Or at least make them fade a bit.

Apparently that wasn't the case.

I haven't gone very far before I spot her. She comes reeling out of the woods on high heels; of course she didn't remain at the bus stop.

'I told you to stay put.'

She smiles. Her eyelids are half closed, but I can just see enormous pupils. Is she high?

'You seem nervous, Fred . . . rik.' Her voice is sluggish.

'I'm not nervous. I just think you picked a silly time to have a talk. And it seems unnecessary for you to come home and make a scene while your family has guests over. If that's what you were planning to do.'

'I'm not gonna make a scene.' Jennifer giggles as if she's just said something really funny. 'I want to talk. Just. Talk.'

'If this is about what happened last summer –'

'Exactly.' She stops giggling, takes a step in my direction. 'You toyed with me, Fredrik. You stepped *all over* me.'

'Please, Jennifer.'

Jesus fuck. She is drunk, and maybe high on something too. What should I say? How do I make her understand?

'Jennifer,' I start again. 'I understand if you were disappointed. And I've already told you the deal: I like you. I always have. But we're talking apples and oranges here.'

She glares at me.

'What?'

'Forget it. What I'm trying to say is that just because a person is friendly, that doesn't mean they're out after physical love. Shit, Jennifer, I should have talked about this with you right away.'

'Physical love?' Jennifer gives a joyless smile. 'You talk like a professor sometimes. But you can't get out of this. Because the way I remember it, you were pretty damn physical.'

'*You* were the one who . . .' I start over again. 'We had been drinking. We smoked up. It was a mistake, and I have never regretted something so much in my entire life.'

She shoves past me and starts to walk in the direction

45

of her house. I reach out a hand; I don't want us to get even a metre closer to the Wiksells' home, but I only manage to catch hold of her unbuttoned coat.

'Let go.'

She yanks herself loose and keeps walking.

'Stop!'

This time I grab hold of her upper arm. Jennifer tries to resist, but I manage to drag her back in among the trees.

We're standing across from each other on one of the many well-trodden paths through the woods. A nearby streetlight casts a faint glow over her face. Her mascara has run; she's swaying back and forth and looks like she might fall over any second.

'Jennifer.' I struggle to sound calm, lowering my voice. 'I'd be happy to talk about it, if you like. And you need to sober up. We could take a walk and then I'll drive you back to Smilla. Does she know you took off?'

Jennifer doesn't seem to be listening. She tries to pry my hand away, and her sharp nails scratch my wrist.

'Let me go!' Jennifer is shouting now. Roaring. 'You disgusting old creep! Don't touch me! Do you hear me?'

'Jennifer, stop it.' I want to trap her arms, but it's impossible – she's windmilling them. 'Do you want all your neighbours to come outside and see you in this condition? Is that what you want?'

She snorts. 'I don't give a shit about them.'

Jennifer jerks away so suddenly that I lose my grip. And, because I'm no longer providing resistance, she falls helplessly backwards into the scrubby foliage. It takes only a few seconds, but I see the whole thing happen in slow motion: the shock in her blue eyes, her black coat like a flapping sail around her body.

46

Suddenly there is perfect silence as the whole world seems to hold its breath. In reality, it's just that I have stopped breathing, and, when Jennifer's voice breaks the silence, my relief is enormous.

'Fuck, that hurt.'

She sits up, holding her head.

'Are you okay?' I crouch down. 'Let me see.'

Jennifer bats away my hand. 'I said don't touch me!'

'Come on.' I hold out my hand to help her to her feet. 'Don't be childish. You can't just sit here all night.'

She slowly turns to look up at me. Her gaze is dark. And full of scorn.

'Go away, Fredrik. Leave me alone.'

'For Christ's sake, Jennifer.' I'm about to stand up, but my coat catches on something and I lose my balance; I nearly end up right on top of her. 'Sorry.'

'You fucking sicko! I'm calling the police!'

Jennifer's voice slices through the deserted neighbourhood.

I rip my coat loose and scramble to my feet. My heart is hammering at my ribs, and for a moment I have the feeling that someone is watching us; I think I see shadows slipping away among the trees.

'Come on,' I say. 'It wasn't —'

'You won't get away with this, Fredrik.' I'm surprised when Jennifer manages to leap to her feet. She takes a step in my direction and leans towards me, so close that I can smell the alcohol on her breath. 'You know that, right?'

10. Lollo

'Can I get a refill?'

Lisen holds out her glass as if I were some sort of servant.

'Of course.' I pour more for each of us and lower my voice. 'I apologize about Max, he –'

'Oh, don't even worry about it.' Lisen gives me a conspiratorial smile. 'Actually, I think all of us share his sentiments, but so few of us are brave enough to speak our minds. You can't even breathe a word about the integration issue in this city without being called a racist.'

She sails on and I look around. Where did Malena and her boyfriend go? Not home, surely?

Max is still out on the lawn, cleaning up the remains of the fireworks. It's beyond me why he had to air his views *tonight*, in front of Malena's new fling. Malena looked like she was ready to murder someone. And Fredrik probably would have loved to help. Sometimes that man is so softhearted it's exhausting. Hell, he can hardly listen to a Norway joke without saying, 'But not all Norwegians!' Jesus. We all need to joke around now and then.

I do agree that Max crossed a line. What he said was so overblown – he's *always* exaggerating, especially when he's drunk. Besides, Malena's boyfriend seems quite normal – he had wine with dinner and was perfectly pleasant; he didn't stand out at all.

'Lollo, thank you, sweetie, for a fantastic evening.'

Nina is standing in front of me, her cheeks rosy. The drizzle has made her hair curl at the ends; the look in her eyes reveals that she's had a fair amount to drink.

'Thank *you*, honey,' I say. 'The dessert was delicious.'

It wasn't, but why would I say anything different? Upsetting people with the truth has never been my thing.

Nina's eyes search the balcony. 'Where are Adde and Malena?'

I shake my head and she giggles.

'Not so brilliant of Max to –'

'I know,' I say. 'It's really stupid to start talking politics when you've had too much to drink.'

'In my opinion, it's stupid all of the time.' Nina leans forward and puts her lips to my ear. 'Have I mentioned that I think politics is *boring as shit*?'

Nina is a hoot when she's drunk.

'No, you haven't actually – I thought you and Fredrik talked about world issues around the clock.'

She suddenly looks serious. 'We're not talking much these days.'

'What do you mean? Is something wrong? Did you have a fight?'

'No. No, nothing like that. We've just been married a long time and, like, with three kids . . . Oh, you know, same old story.' Nina's face cracks into a smile. 'But I shouldn't complain. A new year means a fresh start, right?'

I fill our glasses and take a selfie as we toast, careful to make sure the ice lantern is visible in the background. The red badge on my messaging app shows that I have two new texts. They are from Agneta and Jennifer, both of whom sent something just before the stroke of midnight. Hope you're well! my stepmother writes, adding that Dad sends his greetings. Jennifer has sent a red heart and the words Happy New Year! I include several hearts in my reply.

'You can stop worrying.' I hold the phone up in front of Nina. 'Jennifer just texted. Things are just fine at your place.'

Nina looks so relieved that I am struck by a guilty conscience. Jennifer didn't say a word about how things were going. But, even so, I'm not lying. After all, if she composed a text with all the words spelled correctly, she can't be blackout drunk.

We move indoors, where it's warm. Max has taken it upon himself to act as DJ; Lisen and Ivanka are bopping around the living room; Jens is conked out on the sofa, looking generally like a wreck.

I quickly post the selfie to Instagram and Facebook with a brief message: Happy New Year, you wonderful people! I make sure to add #lollosdesign and #designonline, but also #happynewyear, #friends and #love. Personal posts typically get lots of likes. People like to see *me*, the face behind the brand; they want to see more than just pictures of picture frames and throw pillows.

'We look so good.' Nina hangs over my shoulder. 'You'd never guess we'll be turning fifty in a few years.'

'Right?' I give her a gentle shove. 'And please don't remind me.'

'Aw.' Nina grins. 'Age is just a number. It's how you feel in here' – she points at her head – 'that counts.'

I can only agree. Nina's smile is contagious, and I am struck by a sudden wave of gratitude for everything I have: my family, my friends, my beautiful home.

'Come on, let's go find Malena.'

11. Fredrik

It's raining, a gentle drizzle that I can hardly feel but is visible in the glow of the streetlights. The party must have moved inside again, yet I can hear the music from Max's enormous sound system from far off. The very thought of going back to the drunk partygoers exhausts me.

The door closes with a click. Chanel watches me as I move from the hooks under the hat rack to the bathroom. As soon as I lock the door, my legs give out. I sink to the floor, tilt my head back and close my eyes, feeling the cool tiles through my shirt. Contradictory voices bicker in my mind. I take a deep breath and try to make them stop.

It doesn't work.

Go back, whispers one voice. *Show you're a man, take control of the situation.*

Go home, the other voice roars. *Go home and hope for the best.*

I have no idea how long I sit on the floor, but eventually I manage to get up again.

My legs shaky, I approach the sink, turn on the tap and let the hot water run until it's steaming. The soap is the colour of lavender and smells like it too; the rough bristles of the nail brush restore life to my frozen fingers. I watch as the dirt slowly disappears down the drain. I'm startled when something pinkish-red suddenly trickles down along the white porcelain.

My heart pounding, I stare into the basin. The water is

running clear now, but I'm sure it wasn't my imagination. A cold chill runs up my spine.

I had blood on my hands.

More soap. I must squeeze a handful from Lollo's ridiculous pump, drench the nail brush with it and rub my hands until my skin stings. Around the same time, it becomes clear to me what I have to do.

The music blares from the living room, and I have no trouble leaving the house unnoticed once again. Chanel doesn't even lift her head as I take my coat from the hook and sneak to the front door.

12. Nina

'Hello, Nina. May I tempt you with a delicious drink, milady?'

Max hands me a stemmed glass. A slice of lemon is perched on the rim.

'What is it?' I take the glass and try a sip. 'God, that's good. You are a mixology genius.'

'I know.' He smiles. 'Many years of practice.'

'Mmm.' I drink some more. 'Fantastic. What's it called, did you say?'

'A Gin Sour.'

Whitney Houston's 'I Wanna Dance with Somebody' is blaring from the speakers. I take a step on to the living-room floor, close my eyes and let the music wash over my body. My head fills with the singer's voice; the bass vibrates in my belly. The old rhythm is still there. I've always been a good dancer.

We should go to parties more often. If all you do is sit at home like a couch potato every single night, it's easy to forget how lovely life can be.

I open my eyes, see Lollo and Ivanka over by the window and join them.

'Do you know where my husband has gotten to?' I shout into Lollo's ear.

She shakes her head. 'Haven't seen him in a while.'

'It doesn't matter,' I say. 'Fredrik's mood is as sour as this drink. He's such a downer.'

Lollo laughs and looks around. 'He must be here some-where,' she says. 'But Malena and Adde aren't; they took Theo and left a while ago. I guess they had prebooked a taxi.'

'It looked like they were arguing,' I say.

'Adde and Malena?' Lollo raises one eyebrow. 'When?'

I have to think for a moment.

'Out on the balcony. But I'm sure it was nothing ser-ious. She should take good care of him. Hell of a nice guy, that Adde.'

'Definitely.' Lollo smiles. 'One of the nicest ones yet.'

I take a sip of my drink, then set my glass on the table and float across the room to the tune of 'Moonlight Shadow'.

Why did all the good music come out when we were young?

13. Fredrik

By the time I get back, Max has started a playlist of eighties hits and everyone is going wild. And, by 'everyone', I mean Lollo, half the neighbours and Nina. Adde and Malena seem to have abandoned this sinking ship just in time.

I tap Nina on the shoulder. 'We have to go now.'

'There you are!' My wife's face lights up. 'Come dance.'

She throws herself around my neck and gives me a wet kiss on the cheek.

'It's almost one thirty.' I twist out of her grasp. 'Time to put the boys to bed.'

'Come on, Fredrik.' She pouts like a grumpy three-year-old. 'Don't be such a drag. Just one more song. Please.'

I have to steel myself to keep from shouting or yanking her off the dance floor with force; I say, with a hard-won calm, that I'm going to get the boys ready and after that she'll have to join us.

At that moment I hear the intro to Madonna's 'La Isla Bonita', and Nina quivers with joy. She gives a happy little cry and bounces over to Lollo, thrusting out her hip to bump her friend in the side. They hug, laugh hysterically and start dancing.

I leave the disco and go upstairs.

It's dark in the den; the TV seems to be stuck on a loop of credits. I find a light switch and turn on the ceiling light above the coffee table.

There's no sign of Theo, but my sons are lying side by

side on the sofa. Vilgot's soft little hand is in Anton's half-grown, sinewy one. Their faces are relaxed, and without warning I feel a stabbing pain in my chest, as if my heart had suddenly tied itself into a knot.

I wake Anton. He nods sleepily when I ask him to gather his phone, Vilgot's iPad and whatever chargers they brought.

Getting Nina to leave the living room is quite the undertaking; she has to hug and say her goodbyes twice over. I linger in the doorway, feeling the knot in my chest pulling tighter. Lisen nearly knocks me over with her dancing. Max grins, raises his glass and gestures pointedly at Jens Stenman, who is sprawled on the sofa with his mouth half open.

By the time I finally manage to lead Nina to the car, the drizzle has turned to rain. My wife is giggly and loose-limbed and plops heavily into the passenger seat. The icy precipitation whips at my cheeks.

Five minutes later, Vilgot is buckled in. Nina is already sound asleep, with a string of saliva glistening at the corner of her mouth. Anton's head is propped against the car window. He's snoring evenly. I drive down to the turn-around and then head east. I'm beyond grateful that I don't have to talk to anyone.

The car sails along the quiet residential street like a ghost ship. Most neighbours seem to have crawled into bed a long time ago. The occasional Christmas lights brighten a window.

At the intersection I glance to the left and am startled when I think I see a familiar figure on the narrow road. An instant later there's not a soul to be seen – only the fog whirling just over the ground.

There's no other traffic, and we're soon on the highway.

In the vicinity of Inre Ringvägen I see the occasional taxi ploughing through the rain. My fingers cling to the steering wheel as if it were a life preserver, something I must hold on to tightly to keep from going to pieces.

I stare out the windshield, trying not to think of anything but what I see. The dark asphalt, the white lines, the streetlights, the illuminated lamps on the taxis.

You didn't do anything, Fredrik.

You just talked to Jennifer.

And then you drove home.

New Year's Day, 2019

Tuesday

14. Nina

Kneeling before the toilet, I curse myself. I will never drink again. Not a single drop. It's not worth it. The memory of all the champagne I tossed down my throat last night makes my stomach turn inside out and I heave once more.

After a long time spent with my back against the tiles, I decide to get up. I splash my face with icy water, brush my teeth, swallow an ibuprofen and leave the bathroom on shaky legs.

Only when I reach the bedroom door do I realize that the bed is empty. I stare at the half of the double bed where Fredrik should be, blinking a few times just to make sure it's not an illusion. But, no, he's not there. What time is it? Have I slept half the day away?

I don't have the energy to investigate more thoroughly. As I wait for the painkillers to kick in, I lie still and listen for sounds that might tell me what time it is and what the rest of my family is up to. I seem to have drunkenly misplaced my phone; in any case, it's not in its usual spot on the nightstand. Fredrik's phone isn't in here either. We really should invest in a good old-fashioned alarm clock.

I prick my ears, but all I hear is the faint popping of the radiators. There are only two possible explanations for this silence. Either Vilgot is still asleep, or Fredrik has gone out somewhere with him. I cross my fingers for the latter. And I hope they stay out for a long time.

In that same instant my mind goes to Smilla. Did I talk

to her and Jennifer when we got home? I don't remember. Which prompts more questions. How did we even get home? And when did we leave Lollo's? Now that I think about it, I don't remember much of *anything* that happened after midnight. All I can recall are vague images of dancing in the living room and a table full of gin drinks.

Oh my God. My cheeks go hot. I just hope I didn't do or say anything stupid.

The notion of going up to peek into Smilla's room remains just that: a notion. I'll go check on her soon; I just need to rest a little longer.

The next time I wake up, it's because of a familiar dinging sound. My phone. I turn my sleep-heavy body, stick my head over the edge of the mattress and discover that my purse is under the bed.

The ding turns out to be one of the very irritating notifications I haven't managed to turn off, and the phone says it's just after ten o'clock. That must mean it couldn't have been much past eight or eight thirty when I was in the bathroom. No wonder the house was quiet at that point. But it also makes it odd that Fredrik was up. Maybe he's being sick in the upstairs bathroom.

I slowly sit up, stick my feet into my well-worn sheepskin slippers and leave the bedroom. My headache has eased; all that's left of it is a vague reminder that I should try to avoid any sudden movement. I walk past the kitchen and find that the counter is covered in glasses and bottles, but I'm grateful that at least they're all gathered in one spot. A whiff of sour wine reaches my nostrils, and I have to swallow a few times when a similar taste rises in the back of my throat.

So the girls drank wine after all. I glance around the

living room. It looks reasonably clean, and nothing seems broken. Maybe we can forgive them.

When I finally reach the bathroom door on the first floor, my heart is pounding hard and fast. I don't know if it's down to all the stairs I just climbed and my general health, or whether I'm actually worried about what I might find in there. Maybe it's both.

I prod the door, which swings open without a sound. No Fredrik. If he is throwing up, he's not doing it here. And why would he be anywhere else if he's not feeling well?

A rush of heat washes through my body. Did we come home together? Or did I come home without Fredrik and the kids? Are they still at Lollo and Max's place? Fragmented images flicker through my mind's eye. I see Anton sleeping in the back seat and Fredrik carrying Vilgot up the stairs, but I'm not sure if these pictures have anything to do with yesterday.

The door to Vilgot's room is ajar, and I enter the dim space. Thank goodness. His hair surrounds his head like a halo; I can see the bedspread rising and falling. It must have been an awfully late night – Vilgot hardly ever sleeps in like this. I back out, grateful for every minute of peace and quiet I can get.

My thoughts are like molasses. If Vilgot is home, where's Fredrik? He didn't go to the gas station for breakfast rolls, did he? I think it's been a decade since he did that. But maybe he wants to surprise me. Maybe breakfast rolls are Fredrik's way of signalling a fresh start.

Before I go back downstairs, I check to make sure that Anton and Smilla are in their beds too. Anton is startled when I open the door, but he doesn't wake up. Smilla is sleeping like a log.

Just as I'm about to close her door, I remember Jennifer. Wasn't she supposed to sleep over? I crack open the door again and glance around at the floor, but I see no Jennifer among the piles of laundry. She's not in the bed either, so I can only assume she decided to go home instead. Maybe we even saw each other before we left the Wiksells'. It's so terribly embarrassing to have blackouts like this.

Once I've checked the guest room and the garage without finding any sign of Fredrik, a nagging fear begins to eat away at me. What if something happened? What if he did go out to buy rolls after all, but had a heart attack and is lying unconscious somewhere along the way? The gas station isn't that far. If that is where he went, he should be home by now.

I go back to our bedroom to get my phone, but the screen is black, no new messages. My fear merges with anger. We usually tell each other whenever we're going to leave the house. What the hell kind of hide-and-seek game is he playing? Is he upset because I had too much of the good stuff last night?

After a quick shower I toss my nightgown in the hamper and put on a sweatsuit. My phone remains dead silent on the kitchen counter as I put on coffee and clean up the remains of Smilla's party: I unload the dishwasher, load it with the sticky glasses and close the door so I won't smell them. The wine bottles go in a paper bag that makes it only as far as the front door.

I'm just about to go back to the kitchen when something gives me pause. Fredrik's shoes. Both his dress shoes and his sneakers are neatly lined up on the shoe rack. I shift my gaze to the coat hooks and find that his coat is in its usual spot as well. A long thread dangles from the fabric; one side seam appears to have split.

The thought that came to me last night is back, the one I only touched upon and let pass. Now it comes flying in at high speed, setting my heart to racing again. Is Fredrik cheating on me?

With bare feet. And no coat.

Of course not. I'm ashamed of my suspicions. There must be another explanation. Calm down, Nina, I exhort myself. Have a cup of coffee, get some food in your belly, breathe.

I sit down at the kitchen table with my coffee and a slice of bread with marmalade, browsing aimlessly on my phone. My fingers automatically open Facebook, and the first thing I see is a photo from last night. Lollo and I are standing on the balcony, clinking our glasses and smiling at the camera. Well done, Lollo, for managing to make even Nina Andersson look decently attractive. Must be some filter.

I jump when the phone alerts me to a new text. Happy New Year! See you Saturday! XOXO C

My sister has attached a picture of herself, her Belgian wife and their four-year-old daughter. All three are wearing beautiful dresses. It doesn't take a filter for Claudia to look like she stepped straight out of a fashion magazine. She's three years younger than me and got Dad's black hair and Mom's blue eyes. She's slim and willowy and looks like she never breaks a sweat. Pauline, her daughter, is a miniature copy of Claudia. At least in appearance.

Monique, whom Claudia met through her EU position in Brussels, looks pretty boring, but, if Claudia is to be believed, she's the best wife and mother in the world. I can't really weigh in on that claim; we hardly ever see each other, and it's hard to get to know each other well when you don't speak the same language. At least, that's what I always say when someone asks what she's like, my sister-in-law. Maybe the truth is that I never really have the energy to put in the effort. I'm just not all that interested in her.

> Thanks, same to you. Safe flight and hi to the fam.
> Can't WAIT to see you! XOXO

I leave the text app and bring up Facebook again, going back to the photo of me and Lollo.

To think that we've known each other for almost thirty years. And yet we're like strangers to one another these days. Drifting apart from your high-school friends is probably more the rule than the exception. But, for some reason, possibly the hangover, it feels so incredibly sad.

The first time I saw Lollo was on a warm August day in the late eighties. It was orientation day at Borgarskolan, where we were starting high school. None of us knew anyone in our new class, and by chance we ended up sitting next to each other. Malena was sitting on Lollo's other side. She too felt lost at the big school and came to the cafeteria with us when it was time for lunch.

After a few lunch breaks it was clear that all three of us loved Madonna, which was all it took to form an inseparable trio for the rest of our high-school days.

We knew all of each other's secrets back then. Lollo and Malena knew me better than my own parents did.

I study Lollo's dyed-blonde hair and heavily made-up face. Do we spend time together because we like each other? Or so we can tag each other on Facebook? Do we just do it out of habit?

We continued to get together after high school, but not nearly as often. Our evenings of intimate girl talk were replaced with couples' dinners and parties with our plus-ones. It was probably around that time that the glue that held us together began to disintegrate.

Maybe the fact that our partners are so different had something to do with it. Malena's men have come and gone. Despite their differences, Max and Fredrik have come along for the ride, have found their own way to hang out together. Maybe they've even managed to appreciate one another every now and then.

As recently as last night, Fredrik was ready to end his friendship with Max, but I suspect that, as usual, Max's blunder will be swept under the carpet. We've always been aware of Max's opinions and just let them go. Max is one of those people who can get away with just about anything. He's generous and has the gift of being able to entertain his guests. No one wants to be the one to ruin a pleasant dinner.

I guess I've tolerated Max for Lollo's sake, figuring that Lollo is the one who's my friend. Max now comes with her as a package deal, and I've tried to keep him at a reasonable distance. It's been harder for Fredrik to do that.

Lollo, Malena and I don't see each other very often these days. When Smilla, Jennifer and Theo were little, we had a brief period of pretty frequent contact, mostly for the children's sake.

Now it's a Midsummer and New Year's Eve thing. 'The old gang', we call ourselves.

I can't separate tradition from what I actually want. Do I really want to spend time with these people? Do they make me happy? Do they lift me up?

There's a jingle of keys at the front door.

15. Lollo

Chanel is whining from the far end of the bed. I grab my phone. Ten thirty. It's fine.

'Good girl.'

I get up and open the glass door that leads to the garden. Chanel launches herself into the rumpled January grass, clearly desperate to go. She does her business, then lowers her nose to the ground and vanishes under the bushes by the shed.

It's so nice to have a fenced-in garden. It's also nice to have a dog that doesn't need hours of exercise each day. I'll let Chanel work off some energy for a few more minutes before her breakfast of dry kibble is served in the kitchen.

On my way back to bed, I slip into the bathroom. For once I'm pleased with what I see in the mirror. My face isn't showing any obvious signs of last night's party. My eyes are clear and alert, my skin smooth. Refraining from alcohol after midnight is an old but underrated trick. I don't have time to be hung over. Still, today I plan to give myself a few extra minutes under the cosy comforter.

I cuddle up close to Max. He's snoring lightly, lying on his back with his arms sticking straight out from his body. Even in this unflattering position, he's obviously attractive: that straight nose and thick hair; those broad shoulders. I chose well when I married Max. He's given me the life I always wanted.

I shove the pillows behind my back, grab my phone

and recline. First I open Instagram, then Facebook. The post I put up yesterday has received lots of likes, and several people have admired the ice lantern. Good. I make sure I thank everyone with a heart or a personal greeting. Thanks, that's so sweet! Have a lovely New Year's Day. I'd love to see you at the store – open regular hours tomorrow!

Lisen has posted a blurry photo from the dance floor, with the message: Party with the best neighbours! Thanks, Lollo and Max, for a wonderful evening! I reply: The guests make the fest! and add a few hearts.

A thumbs-up emoji and Nina's profile pic rises on the screen. Apparently she's also awake and out on FB. I wonder how she's feeling. Adorable little Nina. It's too bad she has to drink copious amounts of alcohol to be able to let go of her anxiety, which only seems to be getting worse with age.

Nina has certainly always been the conscientious one in our group. The mom friend. In our high-school years, Malena and I manned the gas pedal, while Nina preferred to hit the brakes. And maybe that was a good thing – who knows what might have happened otherwise.

Early morning on the Amiralsgatan Bridge. We'd been at a party in Lund, hopped off the bus on Drottninggatan, and were walking along in bare feet with our high heels dangling from our fingers. The sun was coming up; we were giggly and silly. I can still remember that feeling of total freedom. We were about to graduate, and our whole lives lay before us. As we reached the midpoint of the bridge, Malena and I had a sudden urge to take a swim in the canal. We were halfway over the railing, when Nina broke into desperate sobs.

'You'll kill yourselves! Or at least end up disabled for life! Do you want to go to the ball or not?'

That last bit hit home, so we stopped and resumed

walking as if nothing had happened. The memory comes back to me now and then, and each time it does I beam thanks to my practical friend. She was right. It would have been a terrible idea to jump in the canal. Then as now.

I close Facebook and stretch out in the bed. My body creaks in several places; must have been all the dancing. Not used to that.

Max's snoring escalates but stops abruptly when he flips over. A vague memory washes over me. A memory of waking in the middle of the night and reaching for his hand, only to find that he wasn't there. It could have been a dream, of course.

Time to get up. On my way to the kitchen I check to see if there are any messages from Jennifer. There aren't. I expect they're sound asleep right now, she and Smilla both. There's probably no point in trying to reach her before three. Teenagers have no trouble snoozing the day away.

On weekends, when Jennifer sleeps until lunch or even longer, I often feel like rousing her. I want to take firm hold of her shoulders and inform her that life is too short to be spent in bed. But I suppose I slept an awful lot too, at that age. And I know exactly what her reaction would be. She would look at me like I was an idiot, turn to face the wall and go back to sleep.

That look, the one that conveys that I'm totally stupid and don't understand a thing, drives me mad. After all, I'm more than twice her age and could tell her a thing or two about life – if only she wanted to listen. But, for the most part, a conversation with Jennifer is like talking to a wall.

When I stop to think about it, we don't have any conversations at all. I usually just call out to her closed door that dinner is ready. She calls back that she's coming, and then she doesn't say a word as she sits at the table, chewing without taking her eyes off her plate; she hardly speaks even when addressed. Sometimes I wonder if it's worth the trouble.

If Mom were still alive, I'd ask her. Because I assume that she would have tolerated me, against all the odds, if she had managed to live that long.

After Mom died, I often lay awake at night having long conversations with her. I asked questions and imagined replies that fit whatever I wanted to hear. There, in the darkness under my soft blanket, she was always on my side.

I load a cappuccino pod into the coffee-machine, then take a few croissants from the freezer and place them in the oven. While I'm at it, I get out the juicer. Max likes fresh-squeezed orange juice.

The sky outside the kitchen window is a depressing shade of grey. The air is heavy with rain, and the wind is shaking the bare treetops. Three young girls in trendy hats are coming down the sidewalk. They walk close together, the fur pom-poms on their hats bouncing in time with their steps. The girl in the middle is holding a cell phone, and the other two lean in to see the screen.

One of the girls reminds me of Jennifer when she was little. She's taller than the other two, and I can see honey-coloured hair beneath her hat.

Time flies. And I know it's not easy to be a teenager. But it sure as hell isn't any easier to be the mother of a teenager. Every word you say is wrong.

Good thing a few hearts come flying in by text once in a while. Surely that must mean something, right?

16. Fredrik

I cautiously close the door and bend over, propping my hands on my knees. Tiny drops of sweat land on the floor.

'*Where* have you been?'

Nina is standing on the half-flight of stairs down to the entryway, and I curse inwardly; I'd been hoping she was still in bed.

'What does it look like?'

My wife eyes me from head to toe, and her expression goes from accusation to astonishment.

'Were you out running?'

I bend down to untie my shoes. 'Yes.'

'On New Year's Day?'

'Yes.'

'Are you crazy?' Nina's voice rises an octave. 'That could have been *dangerous*!'

'Dangerous?' I stand up again and start to peel off my workout clothes. 'What do you mean, dangerous?'

'Don't play dumb. You're a gym teacher, you ought to know it's dangerous to put a strain on your heart when your system is full of alcohol.'

'But I'm not full of alcohol.'

I take my clothes from the floor, squeeze by her on the stairs and head for the bathroom.

'What do you mean, you're not . . .' Nina follows me. 'Hey, could you not walk away when I'm talking to you?'

I turn around. 'I hardly drank at all last night. And I'm

the one who drove you home. But I suppose you might not remember much about that trip?'

The question knocks her off balance, and her next question is less aggressive. 'You *drove* home?'

'It was my fault we didn't have a taxi.' It's a struggle to keep the irritation out of my voice. 'And I realized there would be no point in trying to get a cab, so I decided to drive instead.'

'Oh –'

'Is it okay if I shower now?' My hand is on the door handle. 'I'm freezing.'

The door closes with a bang, and the silence that follows is unbearable. The adrenalin and the loud music kept my thoughts in check while I was running, but now they're back in full force.

Blood in the sink.

I lift the lid of the hamper, and as I do I catch a glimpse of my face in the mirror, and recoil. It's the face of a total wreck.

Last night was horrible. I tossed and turned between the sheets, first sweaty, then freezing. It was impossible to settle down. Absolutely impossible. I don't know how many times I was on the verge of waking Nina up and telling her everything. Or at least select parts.

But how can I do any of that now without digging myself even deeper into this hole?

17. Nina

Ivanhoe has been on TV for a while by the time Smilla comes downstairs. She's as white as a ghost.

'Morning, sweetie.' I'm reclining on the sofa with a blanket over my legs. 'Or good afternoon, maybe.'

'Afternoon.' She yawns. 'I don't know if it's good, exactly.'

'Did you have fun last night?'

I pat the spot beside me, inviting her to sit, but Smilla shakes her head. 'Need a shower,' she says, shuffling towards the bathroom.

I wonder why I'm so disappointed each time it happens. Because I know being inquisitive isn't the right way to go about it. Smilla never shares anything on demand; she wants to be in control and choose the time and place to give us parents some rare insight into her life. But I'm very curious about how the party went last night. And I don't think it's too much to ask for her to tell us. Considering that we offered our home as the venue.

I sink back into the pillows and watch as the TV zooms in on Anthony Andrews's boyish face. It's weird how I stare at this boring movie year after year, just because it's always broadcast on New Year's Day. Then again, I guess it's about as much as anyone can handle after a wild night of partying. A film where every line is etched into your grey matter allows your attention to drift now and then.

Vilgot is sitting in a corner of the sofa, playing a Bamse the Bear game on his iPad. Anton's upstairs, in all likelihood

wearing his big headset and fully immersed in a totally different sort of game. Today is the kind of day that comes with
no screen-time limits whatsoever.

What Fredrik is up to, I have no idea. He seems to have
gotten up on the wrong side of the bed, saying he didn't
sleep well and brushing me off with monosyllabic
responses when I try to talk to him. I circle back around
to assuming he must be huffy because I had a good time
at the party last night while he had to stick to Coke and
water. But it's not my fault he forgot to book a taxi.

Even when I tried to bring up one of Fredrik's favourite topics, Max and his predictions about Sweden's
imminent systemic collapse, all I got were curt responses.
Usually that's a sure thing if you want to get my husband
all riled up. And, after last night, there is a heck of a lot
more fuel to toss on that long-burning fire.

The movie is extra boring this year. I get out my phone
and lazily browse Facebook instead. Pretty soon I can
sense a pattern. Just about everyone seems to have been at
an *amazing party* with *the greatest friends* where they ate *fantastic food*. Now they're all hung over, watching *Ivanhoe* and
craving pizza.

I could have posted the exact same thing, but I'm not
interested in splashing myself all over social media. Not
like Lollo. She styles her whole life to make it look good
on Instagram and honestly seems to believe that people's
status updates reflect real life. Lollo doesn't seem to get
that people avoid talking about family fights, alcohol
problems, mental health issues and general world-
weariness on social media.

For my part, I've come up with some pretty elaborate
plans to start an anti-account where I post only the rough

stuff. But I dropped the idea out of fear that no one would get the irony.

The phone dings and a message pops up on screen. Speak of the devil. Hi, Nina! Thanks for coming yesterday! How are you feeling? Possibly not so great ;-) Are the girls up yet? I tried to text Jennifer but she isn't answering. Will you ask her to call? XOXO Lollo

A current of uneasiness starts in my belly and washes through my body. I get up and go to the kitchen, where Smilla is eating breakfast.

'Hey . . . Lollo's asking about Jennifer. Wasn't she going to sleep here?'

Smilla doesn't look up from her phone. 'She went home.'

The anxiety returns.

'But' – I look at the screen again – 'she's not home. Lollo thinks she's still over here.'

Smilla shrugs, apparently indifferent. 'I don't know where she is. She said she was going home.'

I find her indifference galling.

'Smilla, look at me when I'm speaking to you.' She aims a black look my way, but I press on. 'Exactly when did Jennifer leave?'

Smilla sighs and throws up her hands. 'I don't know, I told you!'

Incredible. I try not to roll my eyes.

'But you must have some idea.'

'Eleven thirty, maybe?'

'That early? Are you sure she was going home?'

Another sigh. 'She *said* she was going home. But maybe she went to Ali's instead – what do I know?'

I truly do not want to act like an interrogator, but, since my daughter never gives me more than an inch at a time, I have to keep questioning her.

'And who is Ali?'

'A guy in her class,' Smilla mutters.

She looks at her phone again and her damp hair falls over her eyes.

'Is he Jennifer's boyfriend?'

'Maybe. I don't know.'

'Come on, Smilla.' I approach the table. 'What do you know? Were you at the same party? Are you friends?'

Smilla pointedly gives her phone a shove so it flies across the table. She looks at me. 'My response to Question A is "Not much", to Question B, "Yes", and to Question C, "I don't know."'

Now I *have* to roll my eyes.

'You don't know if you're friends?'

'I don't wanna talk about it.' Smilla pulls her phone back and hastily stands up. 'Jennifer was going home – that's all I know.'

Her empty juice glass lands in the sink, and an instant later Smilla's on her way back upstairs.

I am left standing in the kitchen, and my eyes land upon a wilted amaryllis. Its blossoms, once so magnificent, are now drooping sadly, and what's more they've dropped their bright yellow pollen all over the windowsill. It's high time to take down the Christmas decorations. Is there anything in the world as passé as Christmas gnomes after new year's?

'Fredrik?'

All I can hear are the trumpets of a jousting match in progress from the TV. I peer into our bedroom. No Fredrik. He's not in the guest room, and not in the bathroom. Did he go out again? My worry about Jennifer mixes with annoyance at my husband's odd behaviour.

'Fredrik!'

I hear a faint voice over the sound of the television. I go out through the utility room and open the garage door.

He's sitting on the old office chair by the tool bench, but he doesn't actually seem to be doing anything. He looks absolutely wrecked, and I stop short in the doorway.

'What's wrong? Did something happen?'

He runs his fingers through his hair, making it stick out every which way.

'No.' His eyes are bloodshot. 'No, nothing happened. I'm . . . just really tired.'

'But why are you sitting out here?'

There's something about Fredrik's expression that scares me, and the uneasy feeling in my belly intensifies. Is he going to leave me? Is he sitting here planning his escape? I can't bring myself to ask, and I realize I'm terrified of the answer.

'I'm coming,' he says without looking my way. 'I'll be right in.'

I turn around to go back inside, but then I stop.

'Hey, listen. Lollo just messaged me looking for Jennifer. You know, since she was supposed to sleep over here. But, according to Smilla, Jennifer was headed home by eleven thirty. It doesn't feel right. I mean . . . what if something happened?'

Fredrik gives me a quick glance.

'Oh, you know teenage girls. She probably just went home with some guy instead.'

'She said she was going home. To her place.'

'Maybe she didn't want to tell Smilla about him.'

I let my gaze wander from the pegboard above the tool

bench to the shelf of banana boxes, old flowerpots, skis and helmets of all sizes. And bing bang boom: a strange thought takes hold. This is my whole life, right here before my eyes. Like objects in a museum, organized chronologically into different eras. Childhood, teenage years, college days, having babies . . .

A sound from Fredrik brings me back to the present.

'From what Smilla said, it sounded like they had a fight,' I say. 'Smilla and Jennifer, that is.'

'There you go.' Fredrik stands. 'Yet another reason Jennifer didn't want to say where she was going. I'm sure she'll turn up tonight.'

There's a certain logic to Fredrik's words. And it's so very *me* to always imagine the worst. Might as well not worry Lollo too much.

I go to the living room and sink back on to the sofa.

Hi, Lollo! Thank you! What a great party! I wasn't feeling so hot this morning but I'm doing better now. Jennifer didn't sleep here – maybe her plans changed ;-) I'm sure you'll hear from her soon. Hope you enjoy the rest of your new year's! XOXO Nina (F says hi too of course)

18. Lollo

I read Nina's message but can't make sense of it. The words seem to jump around and slip away until I have to start over from the beginning. It's as if my brain is purposefully mixing them up, like it's trying to shield me from this information. But when I finally arrange the words into a coherent sentence, they become crystal clear.

Jennifer didn't sleep here.

I stare at the screen. What does she mean? If Jennifer didn't sleep there . . . I rise from the kitchen chair and hurry up the stairs to the den.

'Jennifer didn't sleep over at Smilla's last night!'

Max is sprawled on the sofa. The final scene of *Ivanhoe* is on the TV and a glass of Coke is on the table.

'Huh?' His eyes look small and tired. 'Who didn't sleep where?'

'Jennifer is *missing*!' I brandish my phone. 'She didn't stay over at Smilla's like we'd planned.'

'Calm down, Lollo.' Max sits up. 'Shit, my head.' He rubs his temples, looks at me. 'What do you mean, missing? Have you tried to call her?'

I glare at him.

'Obviously. I've been texting and calling for hours.'

Max reaches for his own phone, which is on the table.

'Maybe she sent something to me.'

I *know* Jennifer hasn't sent anything to Max. I'm our family's communications hub, and Jennifer always comes to me first, probably because Max is so hopeless at responding. I don't understand why it's so damned hard for him to shoot you back a response when you've asked a simple question. He usually blames it on a house showing or bad reception on the golf course.

Max shakes his head. 'Nope, nothing.'

'But . . .' I try to stave off panic. 'What should we do?'

Max takes a sip of Coke and sets the glass back on the table.

'Just wait, I suppose.'

'Wait?' I stare at him. 'But something might have happened. It's not like Jennifer to ignore my texts.'

'You're exaggerating, Lollo. You're always complaining about how she never responds.'

'Yeah, but . . .' I wave my phone at him again. 'This isn't the same. There's a huge difference between not checking in before dinner and not letting someone know you've decided not to sleep where you said you were going to. Anyway, she usually gets back to me after a while. But this time it's been radio silence since just before midnight.'

'Call Smilla,' Max suggests. 'Jennifer must have told Smilla where she was going.'

I go back down to the kitchen and start to search through my contacts list. Smilla isn't saved in my phone, so I have to call Nina. The nails of my left hand tap at the kitchen counter as it rings on the other end.

'Hi, Lollo.' Nina's voice sounds close by. 'Did you get hold of Jennifer?'

'No, that's why I'm calling, and I . . . is she home? Smilla?'

My voice is shrill, the words are all coming out in the wrong order, and I suddenly feel ridiculous. It's not like me to get so worked up. Worrying is Nina's thing. And which one of us was trying to convince Nina, hardly twenty-four hours ago, that the girls are old enough to take care of themselves?

I take a deep breath and start over from the beginning.

'I was just hoping to have a quick talk with Smilla. I mean, you know, maybe she overheard something about Jennifer's plans.'

Nina doesn't respond right away. And when she does open her mouth, her voice sounds forced, overly breezy.

'For sure! Of course you can talk to Smilla. Just hold on one sec.'

I hear rustling as Nina moves around the house. Then I hear Smilla's voice. It's impossible to make out what they're saying, but it's perfectly clear that mother and daughter are annoyed with one another.

After what feels like an eternity, there's a crackle on the line.

'Hi, Smilla. How are you?'

'Fine.'

I wait for her to go on, but apparently her responses are just as elaborate as those Jennifer typically provides.

'Look, I just thought I'd check . . . Jennifer was supposed to sleep over with you, but, from what I hear, that's not what happened. Did she say where she was going?'

There's silence for a moment, and then she replies. 'She said she was going home.'

'Home?' Panic explodes inside me. It's pumping into every vein, flowing into every last blood vessel, spreading throughout my body. 'She was going *home*?'

'Yeah,' Smilla continues. 'That's what she said, but she

could have changed her mind. As I already pointed out to Mom.'

I close my eyes and breathe through my nose, trying to keep from snapping at this kid. What a goddamn farce this conversation is.

'So when did she leave?' I manage to ask at last. 'Jennifer, that is.'

'At eleven thirty.' There's a faint sigh on the other end. 'I think. Could have been quarter to.'

'And she was going to take the bus?'

'I assume so.'

'Okay.' My patience is wearing thin. How can Smilla act so blasé when her best friend is missing? 'Thanks, Smilla. Now I know. Have a good day.'

'You too . . .'

There's something hesitant about her tone, so I don't hang up right away – and, sure enough, there's more to come.

'I tried to get hold of Jennifer too,' Smilla says. 'But . . . well, she didn't get back to me either.'

I sit down, trying to ground myself. For the umpteenth time I unlock my screen and search for any sign of life from Jennifer. Her most recent message is the new year's greeting she sent just before midnight. There are no more texts, nothing on WhatsApp and no new messages on Instagram.

Why did she leave the party and all her friends so early? Before midnight!

Something must have happened. And Smilla *must* know what it was. She was there. Didn't she seem a little on edge?

Could Jennifer have headed to a party at some club in

town and convinced Smilla to cover for her? If Smilla's lying to protect Jennifer . . . if those young ladies have cooked up some tall tale to hide the truth, they're in hot water. It's unacceptable! It's just not okay.

I look again at the time of the text: 11.56 p.m. That's so far in the past now. It's hours ago. Jennifer might have fallen into the hands of a rapist. Or *several* rapists. She might have been abducted, locked up, drugged . . .

My heart is racing. Horrifying images flash through my mind. I don't know where they're coming from, but this flood cannot be stopped; the images well forth as though they've always been somewhere in my mind, just waiting to be set loose. Mangled body parts, blood, tears. A feeble voice in my head calls for 'Mama'.

I swallow hard and have to grab the edge of the table to keep from falling. And, for the first time ever, I understand why Nina keeps Smilla on such a short leash.

19. Fredrik

'We'll call your number when your order's ready.'

I nod and take a seat along the wall, rubbing the little yellow ticket between my sweaty fingers. Back and forth. Back and forth.

Recently our local pizzeria came up with a practical way to deal with the New Year's Day rush. There are only three kinds of pizza to choose from, and ordering ahead isn't an option – it all has to be ordered on site.

This system works out well for me this year. I needed to get out of the house; I was having trouble breathing in there. And, since no one can say exactly how long it might take to make our pizzas, I took the scenic route on the way here, strolling aimlessly through the neighbourhood.

Ever since Lollo called Nina earlier this afternoon, I've been expecting a call from the police, my pulse ever rising. Or at least I've been prepared to see a news item on my phone about a missing seventeen-year-old girl.

I reach for a gossip magazine and sink deep into the chair, feigning great interest in two reality-show stars I've never heard of and their upcoming wedding. The magazine is meant to ward off any human contact, eliminate the risk of conversing with chatty neighbours.

Hollow-eyed denizens of the Husie neighbourhood, wearing tracksuit pants and puffy jackets, form a constant stream at the cash register. They buy pizzas and two-litre bottles of Coke, then venture back out into the raw, chilly evening. I watch them go from behind my gossip mag and almost start to feel at home where I sit. This hard chair in the pizzeria feels like a safe zone.

I can picture staying here forever, reading celebrity gossip and avoiding communication with the world outside. I wouldn't have to go home to Nina's worry and irritation. I wouldn't have to be a cheerful, creative dad. I'm a bad person.

'Fifty-three!'

I reluctantly stand up to get my pizzas and pay. On the way out I run into Jonas, one of our most talkative neighbours. I manage to avoid striking up a conversation by smiling, pointing at the pizza boxes and muttering something about all the hungry mouths at home.

'Bon appétit,' Jonas says cheerfully. 'And Happy New Year!'

The first thing I see is the car. Max's black SUV is parked in the driveway, making our own decently sized station wagon look like a toy car in comparison.

My heart is pounding like it wants to escape my chest. I wish I could drop the pizzas on the sidewalk and run as fast as I can. But that wouldn't be a good look. I have to try to act normally. It's crucial that I do – otherwise I might as well go directly to the nearest police station.

I take a few deep breaths, try to make the muscles in my face relax and open the front door.

'That took forever.'

Nina looks at me through the balustrade between the entryway and kitchen. I kick off my shoes, walk up the half-stairs with my jacket on and put the pizza boxes on the table. My gaze sweeps across the three faces.

'If I'd known you were coming, I would have bought more pizzas.'

'No worries.' Max waves me off. 'We'll be leaving soon.'

'Thanks for last night, by the way,' I say.

My thanks are aimed at Lollo. She looks all torn up behind her well-spackled façade; her eyes are blank.

Being confronted with Lollo's fear makes me feel ill. I wriggle out of my jacket and hurry back down to the entryway. Facing the coat hooks, I say what has to be said.

'I heard about Jennifer. You still haven't managed to get hold of her?'

'No,' Max replies from the other side of the balustrade. 'Lollo is worried; she wanted to come over and talk to Smilla. For my part, I don't want to suspect the worst. You know how teenagers are. Maybe Jennifer's phone is dead. Maybe she went to some friend's house, and . . . well, don't ask me.'

I come back up to the kitchen, avoiding Lollo's glassy eyes, and turn to Max.

'I'm with you. It's silly to get worked up for no reason. Maybe Jennifer's been asleep half the day and then she just forgot to check in.'

Max gives me a grateful smile and pats Lollo's arm. 'Hear that, honey?'

Lollo doesn't smile. 'I'd still like to talk to Smilla again,' she says.

'Of course.' Nina looks at me, but I have a hard time guessing what she's trying to convey. 'I'll go get her.'

While my wife disappears upstairs, I spend more time than is necessary getting out plates and glasses. Meanwhile, my brain is frantically trying to think of something to say. Something ordinary, something that has nothing to do with Jennifer.

'Are you sure you don't want a bite?' I point at the pizza boxes.

'It's fine.' Max tugs at his hair, apparently not quite as calm as he says he is. 'We'll grab something at home.'

Nina's back, with Smilla in tow. Our daughter stops hesitantly at the kitchen doorway.

'As I'm sure you understand, I'm worried about Jennifer,' Lollo says, wasting no time on pleasantries. 'I just thought . . . how was she when she took off?'

Smilla's eyebrows go up. 'What do you mean?'

I can see it's a struggle for Lollo to keep her irritation in check.

'I mean exactly what I said. How was she? Happy? Sad? Angry?'

'She . . . uh . . .' Smilla looks down at the floor. 'I guess she was . . . the same as usual.'

'As usual?'

Smilla nods.

'Now you listen to me.' Lollo's tone is sharp. 'This is serious. Nina mentioned that you had a fight, you and Jennifer. Is that true?'

Smilla is suddenly breathless. She covers her eyes and starts to sniffle. An instant later, she's howling with sobs.

My legs aren't working, but Nina rushes over.

'What is it, sweetie? Did something happen last night? If it did, you have to tell us, don't you see? We're all worried about Jennifer.'

Smilla pulls her hands away from her face and looks at Lollo, then collapses into her mother's arms. 'I'm sorry!' Her shoulders shake. 'It's my fault! It's all my fault.'

'Sweetheart.' Nina smooths Smilla's hair. 'What's your fault?'

Lollo is as white as a sheet but doesn't say a word; she just stares at Smilla.

'*What's* your fault?' Nina asks again, shooting me a look that's clearly meant to telegraph that I ought to come to her rescue, take charge and do something about this situation.

I take one step towards my daughter but can't bring myself to touch her; I have the feeling that I will somehow ruin anything I touch.

'Smilla, you know you can tell us anything,' says a voice that belongs to me but doesn't sound like me. 'Whatever you tell us, it doesn't matter, as long as it's the truth. The truth will always come out in the end.'

The world around me goes fuzzy. All I can hear is my own heartbeat thundering in my ears, and I quickly turn to Nina. 'Should I go get the boys before the pizza gets cold?'

My wife stares at me. 'Maybe you could hold off on that for a few minutes?'

I force myself to stay put, rubbing my moist palms on my jeans.

Lollo pounds the table with her fist. She stands up and strides over to Smilla.

'Just tell me what happened! Jennifer is missing, and you need to tell me everything you know. Everything! Do you hear me?'

Max places a hand on Lollo's arm. 'Take it easy.'

'Take it easy?' She shakes off his hand. 'How am I supposed to "take it easy" when my daughter is missing?' Her voice breaks. 'Please, tell me how I could possibly take it easy!'

Max throws his arms around his wife. To my eyes, it

looks more like a straitjacket than an embrace, but it's effective.

'I'm sorry,' she whispers, her head against Max's chest. 'I'm sorry. I'm just so –'

'It's fine, Lollo. We understand,' Nina says. She leads Smilla to a chair, crouches down beside her and strokes her hair again. 'Sweetie, just tell us anything you know. I'm sure you'll feel better once it's out.'

Smilla dries her tears with her sleeve and looks at us, her eyes full of despair. My stomach sinks. How much does she know?

Smilla doesn't know a thing, I try to convince myself. *Not a thing*.

'I told her off,' Smilla says at last. 'I was angry because she'd had too much to drink and she didn't want to help me clean up.'

My shoulders slump and Smilla launches into a description of a chaotic night full of party-crashers and excessive drinking.

'I'm sorry, Dad.' Her tongue catches a bit of snot that has trickled on to her upper lip. 'They cracked the lock on the bar cabinet and drank up most of it. I promise I'll pay for it.'

'Don't worry about it.' I try to smile, but my lips feel numb and impossible to control. 'We'll work it out.'

Nina has stood up and has one hand on Smilla's shoulder, but it's me she's looking at.

'What did I tell you? I *knew* this would happen.'

'You agreed to it,' I say.

'Yeah, because I felt like I had no choice!' Nina practically spits out the words. 'Smilla was plaguing me like a gnat, and you were a fan of the idea from the start. I never had a chance with you two. "With freedom comes respon-sibility" indeed. That turned out just great, didn't it?'

'Excuse me.' Lollo's tone is sharp again. 'Could you two have this argument some other time, maybe?'

Nina blushes. 'I'm sorry, Lollo. Of course –'

'C'mon, everyone.' Max lets go of Lollo. 'Let's just get to the bottom of this once and for all.' He glances around and his gaze lands on Smilla. 'You say you had a fight. And it was because you wanted help cleaning up?'

Smilla nods.

'But that was before midnight.' Lollo barges into the conversation. 'Why would you be cleaning then?'

'I was the one who . . .' Smilla falls silent and starts over. 'It looked like a war zone, people vomiting, and I just wanted everyone to go home. Jennifer didn't care; she thought we should keep partying.'

Max runs his fingers through his hair, which immedi-ately flops into his face again. He must have forgotten to use that oily goo that normally keeps his curly hair slicked back, flat and shiny.

'Did Jennifer leave right after you fought?' he asks.

Smilla nods again. 'She just ran off. Said she was going home.'

'And you didn't try to stop her?' There's a hint of accus-ation in Lollo's question.

'No, I did. I said I was sorry. I begged her to stay. But I didn't run after her. There was so much to do here.' Smilla lets out a sob, looking at her mother. 'I . . . I was afraid I wouldn't have time to get it all cleaned up, I had promised –'

Nina's hand squeezes Smilla's shoulder. 'I know you worked really hard, sweetie. The house looked great this morning.'

I can't help but notice the way Lollo is pursing her lips.

Max clears his throat and turns to Smilla. 'You said you thought Jennifer had had too much to drink. Does that mean she was drunk when she left here?'

At first Smilla gazes down at the table, but then she looks up. 'She'd had quite a bit to drink, but I don't know how drunk she was when she left.'

'Did she have her phone with her?' Lollo asks.

'I assume so.'

'But if she wasn't sober . . .' Lollo looks at Max. 'Oh, God! She could be lying in a ditch. Someone might have lured her off somewhere . . .' She grabs Max's arm. 'We have to call the police! This minute.'

'Hold on.' A wrinkle has appeared on Nina's forehead. 'Smilla, that guy you mentioned . . . could Jennifer have gone over to his house?'

Lollo stares at Nina, then at Smilla. 'What guy?'

'Uh.' Smilla's eyes shift here and there. 'Someone from Jennifer's class, is all. I don't know if they're together or anything, but . . . I saw them . . . I did see them kissing.'

'Oh my God!' Lollo exclaims. 'And you're only mentioning this *now*?'

'I . . . I didn't think –'

Nina's eyes flash. 'Exactly how is Smilla supposed to know in what order you prefer to hear things? She's answering your –'

'What's his name?' Max interrupts, pulling his phone from his pocket.

'Ali,' Smilla mutters.

'Ali?' Something in Max's gaze changes; his jaw works beneath his tanned skin. 'What's his last name?'

'No idea,' Smilla responds hastily. 'But he's in Jennifer's class. If you have a class list or whatever –'

'Okay, great. We'll look it up at home.' The veins on Max's forehead look like they're about to burst, and blotches of red are spreading above his collar. 'Come on, Lollo. Let's go.'

He more or less yanks his wife out of the kitchen.

Lollo turns back as they go and looks at Smilla. 'I'm sorry. I had no idea she was seeing anyone, and –'

'It's fine.'

'And thank you for telling us,' Lollo continues. 'It's too bad you had a fight, but . . . but I'm sure you'll make up soon, right?'

Smilla doesn't look convinced.

20. Nina

'Why is Lollo calling the police?'

Anton looks at me as he folds a big piece of pizza in half and shoves it whole into his mouth.

'Who told you that? That she was calling the police, I mean.'

'Vilgot.' Anton chews and swallows. 'So is it true?'

I nod, not quite sure what to say. How much should we tell the boys? I'm sure Jennifer will be home again soon, and it feels like there's no reason to make a mountain out of a molehill.

'Is she?'

Anton won't give up, and I turn to Fredrik, hoping he'll have a nice, vague response ready to go. But it seems Fredrik hasn't even heard the question. He's sitting in his place, staring vacantly ahead, apparently off in a world of his own.

What is going on with him? He spent the whole new year's party grumpy as a badger, and his mood sure as heck doesn't seem to have improved today. Is it our marriage he's brooding about?

I've known Fredrik half my life, and I can read him like an open book. If he thinks I won't notice anything, he's got another thing coming. It's impossible to keep secrets from someone you've lived with for over twenty years. I'll have to just ask him what's up, straight to his face. But not in front of the kids.

'Hello – is she?'

'Maybe,' I respond diplomatically. 'Lollo is a little worried because she hasn't heard from Jennifer. But I'm sure it will all be fine. Did *you* have fun last night? With Theo?'

Anton shrugs.

'Is he doing better these days?'

Yes, I am fishing for some sensitive information here. And, yes, perhaps it is wrong to use your children for such purposes. But I try to tell myself it's all out of concern on my part, that I care about Theo.

Malena has never wanted to discuss his mental health, and I imagine she views her son's problems as a personal failure. Still, it's no secret that Theo has been left out of things at school and even bullied at times.

Malena's usual solution has been to move him to a different class or a different school. That might have worked when he was younger, but changing classes now really isn't an option for a kid like Theo. You can only hope he was involved in the decision-making, and that there was a good reason for it.

I have a pet psychological theory that Malena's constant stream of boyfriends is one of the reasons behind Theo's instability. It must do something to a child's capacity to trust others when someone they've started to bond with suddenly disappears from their life. Especially when it happens again and again. And I also get the sense that Theo feels a little forgotten now and then. Malena's focus is most often on her own love life, not on motherhood.

'What do you mean "doing better"?' Anton asks.

'You said he was having a tough time at school, or something . . .' I pick up a half-eaten pizza crust that's landed on the table and put it back on Vilgot's plate. 'But that was a while ago, so I'm sure it's better now.'

'No idea,' says Anton. 'We were playing video games, not talking.'

Smilla stands up. 'May I be excused?'

'Are you done already?' I look at her. 'Don't you want more to eat?'

'No.' She pushes in her chair and walks over to open the dishwasher. 'That's why I want to be excused.'

'Can't you stay and talk to us for a while? Tell us about the party last night.'

Smilla slams the dishwasher closed and leaves the kitchen without a word.

Vilgot turns around and watches his sister go. 'Why is Smilla so grumpy?'

'Smilla's always grumpy,' Anton says, reaching for one of the pizza boxes.

I glance out the window: the streetlights along the walking path outside form a string of pearls, blurry yellow points in the darkness. A deep sigh escapes me. Apparently Fredrik wasn't the only one who woke up on the wrong side of the bed today. And, in Smilla's case, it's clearly because of Jennifer.

I truly hope she's telling the truth when she says she doesn't know where Jennifer is. Teenagers are *supposed* to keep secrets from their parents – it's part of the separation process. But to look Max and Lollo right in the face and lie to them? That's a bit much. She could see how worried they were.

That goddamn party. The more I think about it, the more furious I am. Did any good come of that gathering? Not the way I see it.

Smilla had camouflaged the plundering of the bar cabinet well; she'd closed it properly. Apparently a simple lock is no match for thirsty teenagers.

Anton and Vilgot leave the table, and Fredrik and I remain. There are two large pieces of pizza on his plate. He's hardly touched them.

'You're not eating.'

'I'm not very hungry.'

Fredrik is always hungry. I examine his pale face.

'And you're sure you're not hung over?'

'One hundred per cent.' Fredrik stands up. 'Are you finished?'

Without waiting for my response, he takes both our plates and carries them to the sink. I watch my husband as he goes. His quick, confident movements and his drawn-up shoulders make me think of Leif, Fredrik's dad. The similarity makes me uneasy. Are we turning into Leif and Pirjo?

My in-laws have never exactly been fountains of cheer, but ever since what happened with Simon they've been shuffling around their huge house like the living dead. Grief and bitterness have etched themselves into their faces, carving out deep furrows in the wrong spots. They probably would have benefited from a divorce, both of them.

'Are you seeing someone else?'

I direct the question to Fredrik's back, and he slowly turns around. 'What did you say?'

My face goes hot. I suddenly feel like I've set something in motion, something big, something that might end in disaster. Am I really ready for that?

Maybe not. But Fredrik heard me; he's only buying time, and there's no turning back now. There will never be a *good* time to court disaster.

'I asked if you're seeing someone else.'

'Come on, Nina.' Fredrik leaves the dishwasher and approaches me. 'How . . . why? Where on earth did you get that idea?'

'*Are* you?'

I'm not about to drop this.

'Of course I'm not.' He pulls out the chair beside mine, takes my hands. 'How could you think such a thing? I love you.'

When our gazes meet, I see a candour in Fredrik's eyes, a candour I haven't seen in him for a long time. And, once again, I'm ashamed of my suspicions.

'I'm sorry.' Totally out of the blue, I start to sob. 'Oh my God, I'm sorry. I don't know what got into me, but . . . well, I feel like you've been a little . . . out of it, recently and . . . you've been acting so weirdly today, and –'

'Shh.' Fredrik leans over and kisses the tears from my cheeks. 'I'm the one who should apologize,' he murmurs. 'I've been . . . work has been stressing me out . . . it's just been a lot, and yesterday . . .' His voice breaks. 'Yesterday I realized how much I love you and the kids, and how much of a pain I must have been recently.' His eyes are shiny. 'I'm sorry.'

My big, strong husband looks so fragile. My darling Fredrik.

An instant later, we collapse into each other's arms, shaking with sobs. The embrace is a clumsy one; Fredrik's stubble scratches my cheek, and his breath tickles my ear.

'Can you forgive me?' he asks.

'Of course.' I lean back to look him in the eyes again. 'But why didn't you say anything? About being stressed at work? There's always some way to deal with that, isn't there?'

He nods and sniffles, and we cry a little more. It feels strange, but I'm also relieved. Fredrik loves me. He's not lying. I know him well enough to be sure of that.

Once we've calmed down, we dry our tears and adjust our clothes. Although we don't speak as we clear the rest of dinner away, I feel a togetherness, as if we're closer than we have been for a long time.

I watch Fredrik as he folds the empty pizza boxes and feel a sudden rush of something that resembles lust. It's an unfamiliar sensation.

'I love you,' I whisper, slipping up behind him and pressing myself to his back.

Midsummer's Eve, 2007

Fredrik

I'm on my way out to the deck with a basket of bread but stop when I hear Max's irritated voice.

'Let go, Jennifer.'

He's carrying a large tray of aquavit glasses and has to step sideways to avoid his daughter's onslaught.

'But I want you to come right now!'

Jennifer yanks at Max's sleeve; he lets out a curse but manages to set the tray on the table without the glasses tipping over. Then he whips around.

'I can't come right now. You need to learn to *wait*.'

'NOW!' Jennifer bellows, slamming her fist on the table. The glasses jump. 'Now, now, now!'

'Do you have to stand right in the way, honey?' Nina is suddenly behind me with a platter of herring in each hand. She lowers her voice. 'Why can't we just serve the herring straight from the jars? This is so Lollo. We're all starving and on the brink of a nervous breakdown, but the table still has to look like something out of some fancy magazine.'

'NOW!'

Jennifer's worked herself up until her freckled face is bright red.

'I'm on vacation,' Nina whispers in my ear. 'Don't feel like being a preschool teacher today.'

A second later, Lollo is crowding her way past us. Her high-heeled sandals clip-clop on the wooden decking, and her mouth is a thin line. She grabs Jennifer by one arm and pulls her close.

'That's enough,' Lollo hisses. 'If you don't behave, there will be no candy and no dancing around the Midsummer pole for you tonight. Is that understood?'

'Ow!' Tears spring to Jennifer's eyes. 'That hurts.'

Lollo lets go and turns to us with a stiff smile on her lips. 'She's always exaggerating. That didn't hurt.'

Jennifer stamps her feet as tears spurt from her eyes. 'It did too hurt.' She kicks the leg of the table.

'Jennifer!' Lollo's voice is shrill. 'Didn't you hear what I just said?'

I walk over to the table, put down the bread basket and squat in front of the little girl.

'Did you need help with something?'

Jennifer immediately shifts focus and takes my hand.

'We want to play croquet, but we don't know where to put the white hoops.' She tugs me towards the steps. 'Smilla says they should be like a cross, but I don't think so! There aren't enough of them.'

'Only the hoops in the middle have to make a cross,' I say. 'Come on, I'll show you.'

Jennifer looks pleased. She drops my hand, wipes her eyes and dashes ahead of me around the side of the house.

In the garden I find both Smilla and Theo. Theo's gotten hold of a croquet mallet and is fully immersed in some sharpshooting practice. He howls with delight each time a ball hits one of the windswept pines on the property line.

Malena and her new boyfriend, whose name I've forgotten, are thoroughly entwined on the lounge furniture up on the deck. They've only got eyes for each other and appear to have missed the croquet drama entirely.

Jennifer rushes right up to Smilla, who's standing in the centre of the lawn with a wrinkle of concern between her eyebrows.

'You were wrong.' Jennifer's legs are planted wide and her hands are on her hips. 'I *knew* you were wrong.'

Smilla glares at her friend. 'I *know* there has to be a cross!'

'Yeah, but your dad says –'

'I've seen it,' Smilla interrupts. 'We had a cross last time.'

'Come on, girls.' I move between them to prevent a scuffle. 'No need to argue. You were both right.'

I gather up the wickets and divide them evenly between the girls. Then, together, we set up a child-friendly course.

'Perfect,' I say. 'You did a great job.'

Jennifer beams with happiness.

21. Lollo

'Ali.' Max slaps the steering wheel. 'Wouldn't you fucking know it.'

'But it's a good thing if she's with him,' I say. 'I mean, I'd rather find out she's at some guy's house than that something has happened.'

The news about Ali has given me a sliver of hope. Jennifer's silence might be related to some sort of plan to keep her new boyfriend a secret. She knows her father and realized that he wouldn't approve of Ali.

Max scoffs. 'So you don't think something could have happened at this Ali's house?'

'Well . . . sure, of course it could, but if he's her boyfriend –'

'I'll tell you one thing.' Max turns to me. 'If this bastard hurt Jennifer, if he so much as touched a hair on her head . . . I swear to God he'll wish he was never born.'

Max has been going on like this since we left the Anderssons'. I close my ears and gaze through the windshield, looking at the expanses of muddy fields on either side of the road. I feel a stab of pain in my chest when I understand Jennifer could be somewhere out there in the dark. Alone, cold, maybe injured . . .

Although hopefully she's not hurt at all. Just being thoughtless and crushing on a new boy.

That must be it.

I cling to hope. Deep down, I'm aware the very opposite

could be true, but I have to hang on, have to keep my head above water.

We're going to call the police. Just to be on the safe side. I'm sure they can help us track her phone, or . . . I don't know. There has to be something they can do, right?

It's possible they'll say we're worried for no reason. The Malmö police have a lot on their plate, to put it mildly. And no one wants to seem hysterical. At the same time, it would be terrible if we waited too long – in case it turned out we should have called right away.

We're just going to see if we can find Ali in the school directory first. It would be embarrassing if we couldn't give them the full name of the boy who might be Jennifer's boyfriend, should they ask.

Just before we left, Nina asked if I had contacted any of Jennifer's other friends. And it struck me then that I don't know who they are. She never brings any friends home from school these days; she always says no one wants to come all the way out to our place. And she seldom heads back into town once she's home for the day.

I thought it was because of school, that she doesn't have time to see people now that she's in high school. But, when I think about it, she's been spending most of her time in her room – even on the weekends. Does she *have* any friends? Is she being bullied? Why haven't I asked?

Max turns into our driveway, and the engine goes quiet. I look at him. 'Do you have any idea who Jennifer is friends with?'

He seems confused, as if he's forgotten who I am.

'Uh, no . . . What do you mean?'

I'm about to repeat what I so recently said to Smilla – that

I mean exactly what I said – but I realize it's best not to upset him. We have to stick together right now.

'Oh, I was just thinking . . . I don't know who she hangs out with. It feels . . . kind of bad.'

Max shrugs. 'No idea. It's probably . . .' He doesn't say anything for a moment. 'Isn't there an Emma?'

'I think there is an Emma in Jennifer's class.' I open the car door and swing my legs out. 'But I don't know if they hang out after school.'

'If we find Emma in the directory, we can call her,' Max says, stepping out on to the driveway.

I nod, squeezing my phone in my hand.

On our way to the front door, Max takes out his phone but quickly sticks it back in his pocket. It's not hard to see the disappointment and frustration in his movements.

I feel like an intruder in Jennifer's room. Max doesn't seem to feel the same. He's going through it like a tornado. Yanking open desk drawers, rifling the closet, digging through bags and baskets. His hair is tousled; his eyes burn. Whether they're burning with rage, fear or determination is hard to say.

'What the hell did she do with that directory?'

My gaze falls upon the bookshelf and the few books there. One of the spines reads MALMÖ HIGH SCHOOLS in white capital letters. The Malmö high-school directory isn't a slim volume – it's as thick as a Bible and bound in hardcover.

'There.' I point. 'It's on the shelf.'

Max pulls it out, and a few minutes later thirty young faces are staring up at us from the desk. All I see is Jennifer; she seems to lift off the paper and become real. Her long hair, in that same style all girls her age wear. Her straight nose, the summer freckles that hadn't yet faded when the photo was taken at the end of August, her smile. The smell of her perfume suddenly wafts by, and I bite my lip to keep from bursting into tears.

I have to keep it together. Jennifer hasn't even been missing for a day. Sudden whims are just par for the course, when you're a teenager. Why am I catastrophizing?

Max's index finger glides across the shiny page, moving from name to name, eventually landing on *Ali Hassan*. He's the only Ali in the class, and Max's phone comes out right away. He fiddles with it for a moment, then groans.

'This is fucking ridiculous! There are a hundred and forty-five Ali Hassans in this city.'

'Check by age,' I suggest.

Max clicks a few more times before muttering that it looks like you have to be over eighteen for your number to be listed online. He asks me to ask Smilla.

'I don't have her number,' I say. 'And I don't feel like talking to Nina again. I'm sure the police can look Ali up if it turns out to be necessary.'

After a few minutes of arguing, I happen to flip over a piece of paper on Jennifer's desk. It turns out to be a handwritten guest list with the heading 'New Year's Eve, 18/19'. Underneath are about a dozen names, divided into two categories: 'From class' and 'Other', The first name on the 'From class' list is Emma Lundberg, and two lines down we find Ali Hassan. Ali is one of three guests whose phone number is scribbled in the margins.

Max brings the phone to his ear.

'Are you calling him?' I gape at my husband. 'Shouldn't we leave that to the police?'

Max gestures at me to be quiet, and, when someone picks up on the other end, he goes out to the den. I don't want to follow him all the way, but I stand in the doorway so I can hear what he's saying.

The conversation sounds awfully muddled from the start. At first, this Ali – who is apparently the one we're after – doesn't seem to understand who Max is. Once he figures it out, I can tell that Ali is flatly denying everything Max is trying to get him to admit.

'We will be going to the police with this,' Max keeps saying. 'So if you know anything, you might as well tell me now.'

The other voice rises in volume but I can't make out any words.

'I know where you live,' Max concludes. He hangs up and kicks at the sofa. 'What a fucking clown.' Max looks at me and imitates broken Swedish: '"I swear, man. I swear on my mother." How the hell can anyone talk like that? Huh? "I swear on my mother." What a load of shit. We live in Sweden.'

'Okay, but what did he say? Did he know anything about Jennifer?'

'Not a thing.' Max sighs. 'Little Ali Baba was at the party, but he says Jennifer left before he did. And that she left alone. Anyway, I don't trust that kid for a second. I intend to make sure the police head out to Lindängen and scare the shit out of him.'

'I can call Emma,' I say, hoping to avoid any more phone calls of a similar nature.

Max paces back and forth as I text Nina to ask for Smilla's help.

It's not long before Emma Lundberg's number pops up

on my screen. I type in the digits, and my heart beats faster with every ring on the other end.

Let Jennifer be there. Please, let her be there.

But, just like Ali and Smilla, Emma says Jennifer left the party at some point not long before midnight and that she hasn't seen her since.

'She hasn't texted you?' I ask. 'Or sent a Snap or anything?'

I'm a little clueless about Snapchat – I've got the app installed, but I never use it. Jennifer, though, is a frequent user. A few years ago she was crazy about all the different filters. Maybe she still is.

'Nope,' Emma says. 'Do you think something might have happened?'

A few minutes later, when Max calls the police, I am overcome by a strong sense of surrealness. I can't believe this is happening. My husband is calling the police to report our daughter missing.

22. Fredrik

Vilgot's breathing has become heavier, and I could leave without waking him now. But I don't want to – I can't handle being near Nina and Smilla. They remind me too much of things I would strongly prefer not to be reminded of.

I feel like I'm dissolving from the inside, as if everything I'm made of has begun to disintegrate. It's probably only a matter of time before my whole body gives in. Which organ will kick the bucket first? My heart? My brain? My lungs?

Vilgot turns over restlessly in his sleep. I stroke his tangled hair, feel the heat of his breath on my neck. My body gets heavy, and suddenly I'm back in the darkness. I feel the damp air and hear the thud on the cold ground. My heart beats faster.

Oh, dear God, help me.

My prayer is idiotic. Before 2001, I believed in God. Or, rather, I hoped there was something bigger, something we humans could turn to in times of trouble. But that hope vanished in the moment Simon took his own life. Trying to find my way back to any faith now would be only piteous and pathetic.

No one can help me now. Especially a god.

I want to start crying again. I could cry forever. It was nice to have that moment with Nina in the kitchen. We were crying for different reasons, but for a second it lessened the pressure inside. Nina seemed relieved afterwards, and it was nice to be able to answer a question honestly for once: she's the only one for me.

I start when I hear voices downstairs. My heart shifts gears again, starting to beat frantically. Are Lollo and Max back? Is it Smilla's friends? The police?

I hold my breath and listen. It's a man and a woman. They don't sound like teenagers, must not be Smilla's age. It must be the police.

Shit.

Part of me wants to dash down the stairs and tell them everything, just pour out the story from beginning to end, unload my burden on to them. The other part of me wants to hide in Vilgot's closet, invisible to the outside world.

I lie in bed, completely immobile. It's not an active decision; I'm more or less paralysed. Lying still is probably my best option. No one can blame me for staying with my son.

My pulse sings in my ears. Even so, I hear footsteps on the stairs – quick ones – and the door glides open.

'Fredrik?' Nina whispers. 'Are you asleep?'

I close my eyes.

'Fredrik.' She nudges me. 'The police are here.'

I try to look like I just woke up.

'There are two police officers standing in our front hall.' Nina's voice sounds forced. 'They want to ask Smilla some questions. I want you to be there.'

I glance at Vilgot.

'But Vilgot –'

'He's asleep.' She shoots me a look of irritation. 'Come on. They're waiting.'

I can't stand eye to eye with two police officers. It's impossible.

But I have no choice.

As I walk down the stairs, my fear is replaced with rage. Fucking Jennifer! I squeeze my right hand into a fist and feel the urge to punch the wall. Goddamn fucking Jennifer. It's *your* fault this is happening!

A voice in my head reminds me:

You didn't do anything, Fredrik.

You just talked to Jennifer.

And then you drove home.

The words form a protective shell, a shield to hide behind.

By the time I get downstairs, my wife, my daughter and two plain-clothes officers have taken seats around the kitchen table. The air in the room feels heavy and thin, as though the anxiety and gravity of the situation are causing the molecules to move more slowly.

Smilla is slouched on her chair, looking miserable. Nina, wearing tracksuit pants, with her hair in a sloppy bun, has an arm around Smilla's shoulders.

I offer my hand to the nearest officer, trying for a firm handshake.

'Fredrik. I mean . . . I'm Smilla's dad. I apologize, I just woke up . . . I drifted off putting our youngest to bed.'

'Marko Stojković,' says the policeman.

His brown eyes meet mine, and I get the sense that he can see right through me. My stomach drops and the dizziness, which has been coming and going all day, is back. Somehow I still manage to get to the other side of the table to greet the other officer.

'Helena Svärdh.' She wears her blonde hair in a ponytail and has bright blue eyes; she points at the empty stool beside Nina's. 'Have a seat.'

I plop on to the stool, grateful not to be standing on these shaky legs.

'Our visit is in regard to Jennifer Wiksell,' Helena Svärdh continues. 'We just came from talking to her parents, and, from what we understand, Jennifer was last seen here, at your house.'

I nod, unable to make a sound.

Marko Stojković directs his attention to Smilla.

'Is it still okay if we ask you a few questions?'

Smilla agrees in a voice so soft it's hardly audible.

'I'm sorry, but . . .' Nina looks at the two officers. 'Is this an interrogation?'

Helena Svärdh smiles and holds up a notepad.

'Yes,' she says. 'But that just means that we're documenting the conversation. And Smilla isn't under any sort of suspicion. We just want to question her for information.'

Nina seems satisfied with that response.

'Okay, then, Smilla.' Marko Stojković starts over. 'So you and Jennifer Wiksell had a party here last night. Can you tell us about it?'

Smilla squirms in her seat. 'What do you want to know?'

'Who was here, for instance,' says the officer. 'Whether anything out of the ordinary happened during the evening. What time Jennifer left, why she left, things like that.'

Smilla starts to talk. This time she offers a few more details than last time, when it was Lollo sitting across the table.

I want to listen, but I'm having trouble focusing. I have to devote all my energy to staying on my seat and trying to look concerned but not panicked. I can't see Nina's expression, but I can tell by the mood in this room that she's getting more and more upset.

I guess my wife has been proved right about the girls'
new year's party, and I know I'm going to have to pay for
encouraging it. In more ways than one.

Nina has always been an opinionated person. It's one
of the things that made me fall for her. We used to spend
hours having discussions, endlessly examining issues from
every angle. In recent years, raising children has been our
most frequent topic. When you get right down to it, we
have similar ideas, so our discussions have mostly been
about smaller details like screen time and how much the
kids should help out around the house. Still, our conversations sometimes get a little heated and end in loud
arguments. In the light of what's going on right now,
those arguments seem absolutely pointless. But everything is relative.

I feel an elbow in my side and become aware that all
eyes are on me.

'Fredrik, are you listening?'

Nina looks shaken.

'I'm sorry.' My face flushes. 'My mind must have been
elsewhere . . . what –'

'I was just asking what time you came home yesterday.'
Marko Stojković is gazing curiously at me. 'Your wife
couldn't quite say, so –'

'Uh . . .' I try to smile but feel an uncontrollable twitch
at the corner of my lips. 'Well, I know I started packing up
around two, but I don't think we got on our way until two
thirty. Which means we should have been home just
before three.' I look at Nina. 'That sounds about right,
doesn't it?'

'Exactly.' She avoids eye contact with me. 'It must have
been around three.'

'So you were driving?'

Officer Stojković doesn't quite seem to believe that I stayed sober and drove the family home in my own car on New Year's Eve of all nights.

'Yes, I forgot to book a taxi so it fell to me to be the designated driver.'

'I see.'

'We don't usually stay out so late, but it was a nice party, and ... well, new year's only comes once a year.' I don't know why I'm still babbling, but my mouth is running of its own accord. 'The boys had fallen asleep. Vilgot conked out before midnight. There is a city bus that would take us most of the way home, but it didn't seem fair to the kids to wake them up and make them sit on a bumpy bus for over an –'

'Was there anything else?' Nina interrupts, turning to the two officers.

'Just one more thing.' Marko Stojković looks at Smilla. 'How was Jennifer feeling?'

'Well, like I said, she was drinking.' Smilla sounds annoyed. 'I don't know how she was feeling when she took off, but I assume she was pretty drunk.'

'I'm sorry.' The officer smiles. 'I didn't make myself clear. I was thinking more of Jennifer's mental health. Whether she was acting like her usual self. You know each other pretty well, right?'

'We've known each other since we were little,' Smilla says. Her eyes get shiny, and she looks down at the table. 'But we haven't spent that much time together since we started high school.'

'You don't go to the same school?'

Smilla shakes her head, her eyes still on the table. 'She goes to Petri. I go to Latin.'

'Do you think she was acting like her usual self?'

'I've never seen her drink that much before . . .' Smilla looks up. 'But, like I said, we haven't spent that much time together lately.'

'Is there any particular reason for that?' Stojković leans forward slightly. 'Not seeing each other as much?'

'No. I don't know . . .' She shifts in her seat. 'I've tried, but I guess Jennifer's had a lot going on with school and stuff.'

The policeman nods.

'Thanks, Smilla. You've been a big help.' He stands up and pushes in his chair. 'We may be in touch again.'

Helena Svärdh closes her notebook and follows her colleague's example.

Smilla looks at them, and suddenly tears are running down her cheeks.

'Do you think . . .' She snuffles. 'You're going to find her, right?'

Marko Stojković looks determined. 'We're going to do our very best.'

2 January 2019

Wednesday

23. Nina

Dawn finds its way into the bedroom; dust motes swirl in the light filtering through the blinds. Fredrik appears to be dead asleep. He's facing the window, and all I can see is his tousled brown hair against the pillow, the contours of his body under the covers.

I haven't slept a wink. For a while, in the middle of the night, I considered getting up and taking one of those sleeping pills the doctor prescribed for me early last autumn. But then I got worried that I might end up too out of it and be unable to wake up if one of the kids needed me.

Everyone is torn up about Jennifer. Vilgot fell asleep before the police arrived, thank God, but he asked a lot of questions before that; he was upset and wondered if Smilla was going to disappear too.

Anton hasn't said a word about the whole thing, but I can tell it's getting to him. Jennifer isn't exactly close to the boys, but she's always been part of their lives, thanks to our friendship with the Wiksells.

Smilla cried herself to sleep while I stroked her hair and told her over and over that she absolutely must not blame herself. I let her know she was right to tell Jennifer off, that anyone would have done the same. Smilla feels like Lollo and Max and the police all blame her for Jennifer's disappearance.

'Lollo hates me, Mom,' she sobbed.

I'm inclined to agree that Lollo's tone was a little too

harsh, but I know it came from a place of anxiety. It can't be easy to control your emotions in the situation she and Max suddenly find themselves in. I explained as much to Smilla, and I also said the police are just doing their job, that they have to ask questions of everyone who saw Jennifer on New Year's Eve.

Fredrik doesn't seem to want to talk about Jennifer at all, and I don't want to push him since he's not feeling so well right now. He needs to focus on himself.

It was a strange experience, crying together yesterday, but I'm glad he finally got some things off his chest. Because what he told me really does explain all the stuff I've been concerned about recently: why he's seemed withdrawn, why he's been so irritable and short with me.

It's just too bad that his confession had to coincide with Jennifer's vanishing into thin air. I wish we could be pouring all our efforts into Fredrik's problem right now, before the new school semester begins. It's always possible to find a solution when you're overwhelmed at work.

The Jennifer situation is less straightforward.

I'm having trouble shaking off the sense that everything is our fault, that our family is a big part of whatever it is that happened to her. And that's what kept me up all night. Obviously I didn't say so to Smilla, but, no matter which way I look at the story, I come to the conclusion that we're to blame. At least partly.

Because if we hadn't allowed the girls to have a party at our house, it never would have happened. Something else could have happened, but not precisely this. And not only did the party take place at our house, but Smilla had a fight with Jennifer. Whether or not she was right to tell Jennifer off, our daughter is involved. *We* are involved.

I'm not superstitious by nature, but more than once during the night I found myself wondering if *I* might have something to do with Jennifer's disappearance, thinking that this is my punishment for giving voice to my feelings for her, that this is a test, that I have to reconsider.

But it doesn't help that Jennifer is missing. It doesn't mean I like her any better. Still, I hope she'll be found safe and sound. I mean, I hope she's already *been* found safe and sound. I don't wish her any harm.

In the darkest hours, Vilgot's questions came back to me.

Is Smilla going to disappear too?

I tried to imagine it was Smilla who had staggered out the door at eleven thirty on New Year's Eve and hadn't been seen since. It was impossible. I couldn't hold on to the thought – it hurt too much.

I have to call Lollo. She's annoying in a lot of ways, but yet she's one of my oldest friends. If she needs my support, then that's what she'll get.

My phone starts to blink on the nightstand. I pick it up, hoping for a message saying that everything is okay, that Jennifer is home and the whole thing was nothing but teenage rebellion gone too far. Instead a news alert flashes across the screen.

Seventeen-year-old girl missing after new year's party.

24. Lollo

It's not until I'm standing with my car key in hand, my purse dangling from my elbow and Chanel under my other arm, that I realize I can't do this. I cannot go in to the shop today. I cannot stand behind the counter and smile at the customers, discuss the colour palette of throws and price flowerpots.

I thought it would be a good idea to act like everything is normal. I told myself these ingrained routines would help to distract me. That they would keep me from going crazy. So, after a sleepless night, I got up, showered and dressed. I drank my coffee and let Chanel out. I brushed my teeth. Just as I always do on weekday mornings.

But I can't do it any more. My head is pounding, and there's a cold sweat trickling down my spine.

I sink on to the chaise longue in the front hall. Chanel wiggles out of my grip and bounds away. Halfway into the living room, she turns around and looks at me, still bouncing. *Come on, Mama!* she seems to be saying. *Catch me if you can.*

I lean back against the wall, and a sour liquid that tastes like coffee rises in my throat; I stare at my dog without really seeing her. My purse slides down my arm, landing upside down. I hear coins and lipsticks rolling across the floor, but why should I care?

Nothing matters if Jennifer doesn't come home.

We haven't spoken in years. I don't know my daughter; I'm no longer acquainted with who she is. Ten- or twelve-year-old Jennifer, I knew well. But seventeen-year-old Jennifer is in many ways a stranger. I have no idea who she spends time with or what plans she has for the future – I don't even know how she's feeling.

It was embarrassing, sitting across from those two police officers, hardly able to answer half of their questions. 'Is she doing well in school? Who does she spend her free time with? Has she seemed down or depressed recently?'

They must have wondered why we bothered to have children at all.

Jennifer's been hard to reach lately. She mostly walks around like a storm cloud, slamming doors. We've let her be, figuring that it was just a passing phase. And I'm sure we're not the only parents who do so. Because, let's be honest, how many parents have the strength, after a long day of work, to spend evenings trying to cheer up a surly teenager?

I'm sure it'll get better if we can just make it through this rough patch. Sometimes I fantasize about a sweet mother–daughter relationship, the kind you see in the movies. On the big screen, the young-adult daughter and her mother go on spa weekends and trips abroad together. They drink champagne, giggle and share everything with each other, like best friends.

For my part, I wasn't particularly chatty as a teen either. Poor Agneta. I was twelve when she moved in, and I thought she was taking my dad away from me. Which in some respects she was. But Agneta was smart in that regard. She never forced our relationship; she gave me space and understood that a teenager needs plenty of time alone, time for their own thoughts.

But maybe Jennifer's unfortunate attitude isn't just about teenage stubbornness and hormones. Maybe something happened to her along the way. Maybe her mental health has suffered. Lots of teenagers have mental-health issues these days, so who's to say Jennifer couldn't be one of them?

I throw my arms around myself and realize that my cheeks are damp.

'Jennifer, where are you?' I whisper, clasping my hands together as if this will help me to reach her.

If you just come home, I'll show you how much you mean to me.

Max has been out searching for her half the night. I wanted to go along, but he ordered me to stay behind.

'Someone needs to be here in case Jennifer comes home,' he said, vanishing into the darkness.

He came home in the early morning, telling me how he had inched the car along the bus route between Husie and Klagshamn – not just once but several times. He had searched the city centre, driven around the outer suburbs and at last combed Klagshamn. With no results.

Beyond this, Max seems to be putting all his energy into that Ali. Ali this and Ali that. I don't want to hear another word about Muslims and whether or not they can be trusted. For my part, I'm not at all certain that Ali is involved. Besides, I think it's up to the police to figure that out.

Chanel lays herself down at my feet. She must be wondering why her mama is stuck in the front hall. I pat her head and wonder if I'll ever have the strength to stand up again.

Jennifer is *reported missing.*

This is not a nightmare.

Jennifer is gone.

The police who were here last night seem competent. But everything is moving awfully slowly. I got the sense that they believe Jennifer is staying away of her own free will. Maybe we shouldn't have mentioned her argument with Smilla; it seems the girls' fight was nothing but more fuel for that theory.

I don't buy that explanation, though. Jennifer had a falling-out with Smilla, not with us. I understand why Jennifer left the party, but I don't understand why she hasn't come home.

Just before we went to bed, a detective called – her name was Lina Torres or something like that. She gave us an update on the situation, saying they had tried to track Jennifer's phone but either it was turned off or the battery was dead. Which means it can't be traced. To my ears, that seems patently absurd. We can do heart and kidney transplants, but we can't trace a goddamn phone if it's switched off? That's fucking ridiculous!

They'd also questioned Smilla, Ali Hassan and Emma Lundberg. According to Max, who took the call, none of the kids had changed their stories: Jennifer left the Anderssons' house around eleven thirty and they hadn't seen or heard from her since. Apparently Ali was sticking to his claim that he and Jennifer weren't a couple, that the kiss Smilla had seen was a one-time thing. Max doesn't seem fully satisfied with that, though; he keeps complaining that the police should come down harder on Ali.

The officers who came by asked for a recent photo of Jennifer. Given the rush I was in, I couldn't find anything but last year's school picture, the one that's been in my wallet ever since it was taken.

For a year and a half I've been greeted by that same smile. Each time I open my wallet it's there: that year-one smile, full of expectation and optimism for the future.

Now that little plastic sleeve is empty.

Chanel noses my leg, whining and looking at me with her big dark eyes. Just then, the doorbell rings.

Jennifer?

Jennifer.

'Dear God,' I mutter, standing up. 'Dear God, let it be Jennifer.'

I trip over my purse and nearly crash headlong into the door, but I manage to catch myself and stay on my feet.

Just as I'm about to open the door, it hits me that this is how the police typically give death notices. They tend to deliver that sort of news in person, not over the phone. My insides go cold and I let go of the door handle as though it has suddenly become electrified.

Another ding-dong echoes through the front hall. It's clear that whoever's on the other side isn't about to give up. I consider locking myself in the bathroom and covering my ears until the house is quiet again. But then I remind myself that it could be good news.

Jennifer.

I take a deep breath and open the door. I'm full of relief that I'm not standing eye to eye with a police officer, and also disappointment that it's not my daughter.

It's Nina.

Shit, I really can't handle Nina today. Perfect, self-righteous Nina, whose perfect, self-righteous daughter naturally knows exactly how much alcohol she's drinking at any given moment and never acts irresponsibly.

Nina clearly felt that Jennifer had only herself to blame. How could you expect anything but nasty consequences when you drink too much and ditch your friend, leaving her to deal with the aftermath of a party? Nina seemed more worried about Smilla having to clean up without any help than about Jennifer, who . . . who isn't here.

My friend throws herself into my arms. She squeezes me so tightly I almost can't breathe.

'Oh, Lollo. I saw something about Jennifer online.' She lets go, takes a step backwards and looks at me. 'So she hasn't come home?'

She launches onward before I can reply.

'It's . . . it's so horrible . . .' Her voice breaks; Nina seems close to tears. 'I'm sure I can't entirely imagine how you're feeling right now, but I just thought . . . I thought maybe you could use some help . . . or company, or –'

'Thanks, but that's okay.' I have to put a stop to this torrent of words. Nina obviously doesn't know what she's talking about; she's only here because she felt obliged to come. 'I've heard from Dad too. He's been texting all morning, saying he wants to come here. But I'd rather be alone right now. And I've always got Max, of course.'

Nina cranes her neck to peer down the hall. 'How is he doing? I mean . . .' She lowers her voice. 'How is he taking it?'

'He left for work before I got up, so –'

Nina's eyes go wide. 'He went to *work*? Today?'

I realize it doesn't sound great, but then again I was on my way to the shop too just now.

'I guess it's a way to help pass the time. And why should we sit here at home, just staring at each other? It won't make Jennifer come home any faster.'

'No, that's true . . .' Nina adjusts her scarf and clears her throat. 'Are you sure you don't want me to stay for a while?' she asks. 'I mean, I'm off work and we don't have any plans.'

I nod, trying to make my lips stretch into a smile.

'I'm sorry, but I really don't have the energy for company today. I'm beyond exhausted.'

'No worries, Lollo. I should have called first, but . . .' Nina's eyes are suddenly full of tears. 'You haven't heard any more from the police?'

Why does it feel like she's fishing for information rather than asking out of genuine concern?

'Because, I mean,' she continues, 'they came to our place late last night, but they couldn't say much at the time. And I saw police dogs down the street just now as I was driving here.'

'No, nothing new,' I reply. 'Unfortunately.'

I don't want to wallow in my anxiety; somehow it feels like a failure to admit to Nina that I'm worried. To Nina in particular. Instead I repeat the male officer's reassurance that they receive reports of missing teenagers every day, and that most cases have a happy ending.

'Right, I've definitely heard that.' Nina's voice is brighter now. 'It's easy to forget in the midst of it all. I'm sure Jennifer has a good explanation. These kids don't understand how much we worry. It's probably a question of maturity, the ability to put yourself in someone else's shoes.'

My only response is to nod; I can't think of anything more to say.

'Well, then . . .' Nina hesitates for a moment before hugging me again. 'We'll talk later, Lollo. Take care of yourself now. And promise you'll let me know if you need anything.'

Halfway down the steps, she turns around. 'I *really* hope Jennifer comes home soon. We're thinking of you.'

I quickly pull the door closed and collapse into a heap on the hall rug.

25. Fredrik

She's sitting at the kitchen table, using a teaspoon to stir one of our big blue ceramic mugs. Her hair falls over her shoulders, gleaming in the pale sunlight. Each time the spoon strikes the inside of the mug, it makes a clink.

Clink, clink. Clink, clink.

A shiver runs down my spine. Why is Jennifer here?

A second later, Smilla glances up and meets my eyes.

'Are you sick or something? You look wrecked.'

I let out my breath. 'I just have a little headache, that's all.'

That's a lie. I have a terrible headache, bordering on a migraine. Clearly I'm also hallucinating.

Smilla returns to her phone, which is in front of her on the kitchen table. I turn towards the cupboards and try to get hold of myself. Then, as casually as I can, I go to the coffee-maker and start fiddling with filters and the coffee scoop.

'How are *you* doing?' I turn around. 'Did you get any sleep last night?'

My voice sounds weird again. But maybe it's just the sound inside my skull that's different.

Smilla sighs, pushing her phone away. 'Not much.' Her eyes glisten. 'Shit, Dad, this is the worst thing that's ever happened to me.' She snuffles. 'Like, seriously. I don't know what to do. As soon as I close my eyes, there she is in front of me. And when I go online I get bombarded with pictures of her and all this bullshit gossip. There's already a thread on Flashback, and –'

'Flashback?' Sweden's answer to Reddit. I switch on the coffee-maker and sit down at the table, where I take a slice of bread from the basket. 'What are they saying there?'

As if I haven't already taken a fine-tooth comb to the internet, searching for every word that's been written about Jennifer Wiksell and her disappearance.

'All sorts of things. That she's a whore, that she's ugly, that they hope she was raped, that . . .' Tears are pouring down Smilla's cheeks by now. 'How the hell can people be so horrible? They don't know a thing about Jennifer. Not a *thing*!'

'Don't read that stuff, Smilla. Like you said, it's all just a load of crap.'

'But I want to *know*.' She looks at me. 'I was thinking that there has to be someone out there who knows where she is, and . . .'

I tear a paper towel from the holder on the table. My hand is shaking so hard that my whole arm sways. As soon as Smilla has taken the piece of paper towel, I rush to withdraw my hand and sit on it.

'Skip the internet for today,' I say. 'Watch a good movie instead. Call a friend. Distract yourself. I'm sure Jennifer will turn up. She probably just got up to something and is afraid of getting in trouble for it.'

Smilla dries her eyes and smiles faintly through her tears. 'Yeah. Shit, am I ever going to let her have it once this is over.'

There's a racket from the front door. Nina hangs up her coat, takes the stairs two at a time and enters the kitchen.

Smilla looks up. 'Where have you been?'

'At Lollo's,' Nina says, sweeping past the kitchen table.
'And?'

There's a gleam of hope in Smilla's red-rimmed eyes.

'I'm sorry.' Nina takes a mug from the cupboard, pours some coffee and leans against the counter. 'There hasn't been a word from Jennifer.'

'But what were you doing there?'

My gaze jumps back and forth between Smilla and Nina. Each time I move my eyes, there's a jolt of pain that makes me want to squeeze them shut.

Nina comes over to the table and pours a splash of milk into her coffee before returning to her spot by the counter.

'I just stopped by to see if she needed help with anything. Or some company. But she didn't seem all that interested –'

'What were *you* supposed to help Lollo with?' Smilla looks sceptical. 'Jennifer is missing.'

Nina shrugs. 'I don't know.' She takes a sip of her coffee, slurping it. 'I just thought she might . . . that Lollo might need support. Someone to keep her company, make coffee, fix some food. It must be awfully hard, I remember how hard it was for Grandma and Grandpa when –'

Smilla bolts up from her chair. 'You're talking like Jennifer is dead!'

She stomps out of the kitchen, leaving the blue mug on the table.

'Well.' Nina watches Smilla go, then turns to me and throws up her hands. 'I obviously said the wrong thing again.'

'Maybe it wasn't the best idea to bring up Simon,' I say.

Nina glares at me. 'Now *you're* getting on my case? I was

just going to explain . . .' She sighs. 'Best to say nothing at all, I guess.'

'Smilla's worried,' I say, realizing as I do that my slice of bread is still lying untouched on the table in front of me.

'We're all worried.' Nina sinks on to a chair. 'I just don't understand . . .'

The sentence remains unfinished. I extricate my right hand. Even though it's half asleep, I manage to cut a few slices of cheese, which eventually end up on my bread.

Nina looks at my sandwich and then at me.

'Don't you want any butter?' She frowns. 'You're not on a diet, are you?'

'Of course not.'

We sit in silence. I chew, but I can't taste anything.

'I just don't understand why they can't trace Jennifer's phone,' Nina says after a while.

The bread expands in my mouth, and I have to wash it down with coffee before I can respond.

'Did Lollo say they couldn't trace the phone?'

'No, but if they could . . .' Nina sets her mug on the table. 'If they could trace it, they ought to have found Jennifer by this point.'

'Her battery probably died,' I say. 'Or else the phone was off. I don't think they can trace it then. It has to be broadcasting a signal in order to be found.'

I try to sound like I've never thought about this before. But I *know* a cell phone can't be traced without a signal.

'Sure.' Nina nods. 'But shouldn't the police be able to figure out where she was before the phone died?'

I clear my throat. 'Yes, I suppose they can do that.'

And, if they do, they might discover that Jennifer was in Klagshamn after midnight. And eventually they'll probably be aware that one of her last calls went to me. But that won't tell them a thing about what happened. It just reinforces what Smilla told the police: that Jennifer was going to take the bus home. I can provide a plausible explanation for the call to my phone. If anyone asks.

'I'm sure Jennifer has a copy of her phone on some server too,' Nina continues thoughtfully. 'Like iCloud. The police should be able to go in there and read her messages and stuff . . .'

She's suddenly eager, talking faster. 'If Jennifer has a Mac and an iPhone, they can, like, communicate with each other. I see my texts on my computer sometimes. Don't ask me how it works, but that's how it is. In that case Lollo should check Jennifer's computer. It must still be at their house. Maybe I should call Lollo. In case she hasn't thought of that.'

My wife is no dummy. And I've never claimed she is, but her hopelessness with technology is practically a point of pride with her. I don't own any Apple gadgets, and I find Nina's information disturbing. A computer in Jennifer's room that might have captured her last text messages . . .

To be sure, we never sent each other any texts. She called me. But who knows what Jennifer got up to on the bus out to Klagshamn. She was furious, high as a fucking kite, and had a whole hour to kill besides. She might have texted people to say she was about to meet someone. Who knows what she might have plastered all over social media.

'I'm sure Lollo has already thought of that,' I say.

'Do you think . . .' As Nina looks at me, a shadow of worry causes her pale brown eyes to darken.

'Do you think Jennifer ran away from home, on purpose?'

I shrug. 'She hasn't been gone very long. Teenagers go missing all the time. And most of them come back.'

'Lollo said more or less the same thing.'

My head is about to explode. I stand up.

'You didn't finish your breakfast.' Nina looks at me in concern. 'Are you feeling okay, Fredrik? Is it the stress —'

'Oh my God, just relax.' My voice is harsh and I try to move back towards an easy-going tone. 'I just need to check on something, be right back.'

Mauritius, Winter 2013

Lollo

'Can I have ice cream?'

This is fucking unbelievable. I look up from my magazine and regard Jennifer through my brown-tinted sunglasses.

'You had ice cream after lunch. Ice cream once a day is plenty.'

'Once a day?' Jennifer kicks her legs over the edge of her sun lounger and stares at me indignantly. 'We're on *vacation*! And you guys have had at least three drinks today. I should get as many ice creams as you get drinks.'

'It's not good for you to eat a lot of sugar.' I flip back to the first page of my article. 'Have a slice of melon instead.'

Max, who's stretched out to my right, looks up from his phone. 'Listen to your mother, Jennifer. You'll turn into a fatty if you eat ice cream all the time.'

Jennifer pouts.

'Alcohol isn't good for you either,' she mutters.

'That's enough, Jennifer.' I look at her again. 'We're grown-ups, and you're a child. We know what's best for us, and we know what's best for you. This is not up for discussion.'

Jennifer throws herself dramatically back into her lounger. 'There's nothing to do.'

Her arms are crossed and the corners of her mouth are downturned. I bite my tongue. There can't be a child in the world who's more of an ingrate than ours. Here we are, on vacation for two whole weeks, staying at a luxury hotel with a fantastic pool, and this kid has the nerve to complain. The fact is, she's done nothing but complain since we got here.

It's been only four days. How are we supposed to survive? I count to ten, find my gentlest voice and suggest a dip in the pool.

Jennifer stands up and plants her hands on her hips. 'But there are only babies here. I don't want to swim with babies!'

It's true that the hotel is full of families with small children, and that most of the kids here are younger than Jennifer, but sometimes you have to make your own entertainment. Besides, Max has been in for a swim with her.

I put my magazine down on my knees. 'Sit down, Jennifer.'

'I'll stand if I want to!'

'Sit down,' I hiss. 'You are acting like a baby, and if you don't tone it down, everyone will hear what you're saying.'

Jennifer shrugs. 'Don't care.'

I turn to my husband. 'Say something. Help me out here.'

Max looks up from the stock-exchange numbers, dazed, and I roll my eyes.

'Tell your daughter to behave herself. I can't deal with this any more.'

He fishes a bill from his wallet and holds it up in the air. 'You can have some ice cream. If you promise to stop whining.'

Jennifer darts around my lounger and yanks the bill from her father's hand. Without a word, she slips into her flip-flops and heads over to the combination bar-and-kiosk under the palm-thatch roof.

I look at Max. 'What are we going to do?'

He shrugs.

'How did we manage in Thailand?' I ask.

'The Kiddie Klub,' Max replies, staring out at the turquoise sea beyond the infinity pool.

26. Nina

It's not very cold – it might even be a few degrees above freezing – but the wind is strong enough to force the damp air through every layer of my clothing. I tug my hat further down over my ears and zigzag around the piles of dog poo on the gravel pedestrian path. Scraps of paper and cigarette butts are scattered under the bushes that line the walk. Here and there a plastic bag is caught, fluttering anxiously in the breeze.

January is not Malmö's best month, but all this trash makes the city twice as ugly. How can people view their surroundings as public landfill? I'd like to visit the homes of people who litter and dump my garbage on their living-room floors.

At the start of our relationship, Fredrik often said he loved my high level of civic engagement. I would discuss anything from public littering to tax evasion with the same enthusiasm.

Those days feel long gone. My engagement has faded, and the rare discussions we do have now are almost exclusively about the kids. We squabble about how to raise them, which rules to implement, and how much allowance they should get each month. But it was just yesterday that Fredrik said he still loves me.

Do I love Fredrik? I suppose I do. At least when he's the person he was before he stopped talking to me. He spent most of this past fall just sighing. No matter what I said, he responded with an irritated sigh or raised eyebrows. Sometimes I get the feeling that we don't agree on anything, that Fredrik *elects* to have opinions that are the opposite of my own, just to be contrary.

At the moment I feel like I don't know him at all, and his moodiness is driving me crazy. One second we're close, sharing confidences; the next, we're adrift at sea on separate rafts, bobbing ever further from one another.

And, instead of feeling sympathy for him, I find this sad-sack act nothing but irritating. It's as if, in the last twenty-four hours, he's given up and is now just wallowing in his own misery.

At the same time, I'm not quite sure how long Fredrik has been feeling this way. Chronic stress is no laughing matter; I've seen it time and again. Cecilia at work was on disability leave for years, and she still can't work full time, even though she'd really like to. I have to keep in mind that Fredrik's mood has nothing to do with me personally.

We met in a basement club in Lund. Fredrik was dressed up as a glam-rocker, with a long-haired black wig, tight gold pants and a shiny floral shirt that bared his chest. I was supposed to be some sort of hippie. I'd found my costume at the thrift store and felt cool in my bell-bottoms and batik tunic.

Malena was the one who'd convinced me to ditch studying for exams that night. 'You can't spend every moment studying,' she'd said. 'Your brain needs to rest between-times. Trust me. I'm almost a nurse.'

Vicky, one of Malena's classmates, was throwing a seventies-themed birthday party, and most of the guests were nursing students. To compensate for the excess of women, she'd also invited a whole bunch of students from LTH, Lund Technical College. Fredrik was one of them.

We ended up next to each other for dinner, and we clicked right away. It was disarming to be wearing costumes, and we spent the first few hours really getting into our roles as rock star and hippie chick, joking around and making up extensive backstories for our imagined characters.

It wasn't until the end of the evening that the wig came off. And I wasn't disappointed. Fredrik Andersson wasn't just funny. He was attractive and fit, and he seemed to have a very different sort of depth from the other guys I'd met. Fredrik was the kind of person who could see beyond his own nose.

On the day of our wedding, I felt like I'd won the lottery. I couldn't believe my amazing luck. But in her speech, just before we sank the knife into the three-tiered cake, Malena reminded me that luck had nothing to do with it. 'Don't ever forget who you have to thank,' she said, bringing down the house.

I sincerely hope these past six months are just a difficult parenthetical in our relationship. I hope it's not long before we can look back on this time with a smile and say something about how tough and unnecessary it was. Then we'll pat ourselves on the back for having tackled Fredrik's problems and fixed them so brilliantly.

As I pass Videdal School, I get a sudden whim and fish out my phone. With my right mitten between my lips, I dial a number and then stick the mitten in my pocket. Ring after ring chimes in my ear, and I'm just about to hang up when I hear a faint voice on the other end.

'Is that you, Malena? Did I wake you up?'

'It's me.' She clears her throat. 'And you didn't wake me up. I'm just a little hoarse.'

I ask if she's heard that Jennifer is missing. She has, and we agree it's terrible. I tell her about our visit from the police last night, about the girls' party and their fight. Malena asks a thousand questions and I answer them as best I can. It feels good to talk to someone who reacts normally, with neither rage nor apathy.

'I mean, it's all just horrible,' Malena says, cutting me off mid-sentence. 'I've been putting off calling Lollo, because I don't know what to say. What are you supposed to say?'

I give her a rundown of my failed attempts to help.

'Don't take it personally, Nina. Lollo must be beside herself with worry. It can be hard to have company when you're feeling so awful.'

'I know.' I'm almost to Amiralsgatan, and I decide to cross to the opposite sidewalk. 'But when you're at your worst, it's hard even to know what you really need. Maybe she would feel better if she talked to someone.'

'I suppose I should call,' Malena says. 'It definitely feels weird not to show sympathy somehow. But I also don't really feel like it, after all that stuff with Max.' She sighs. 'I mean, you heard what he said about Muslims, right? And that Sweden is on the fast track to hell, or however he put it.'

'Hard to miss.' I have to stop in the middle of the road to keep from being run over. 'How long did you stay?'

'We left around two. Adde wasn't quite as angry as I was – I guess he's used to hearing that sort of crap. But I was so ashamed to have brought him there. To think that one of my closest friends would say something like that –'

'I get it.' I turn on to the path by the clinic. 'Fredrik wanted to head home right after dinner, but I felt sorry for Lollo. I didn't want her to have to celebrate alone at midnight.'

'I felt *exactly* the same way.' Malena coughs. 'I could have left on the spot. But Adde convinced me to stay for the toast and, well . . . I lost track of time. It's not like Max's opinions are news to anyone. And up to this point he's managed to keep a lid on it, but fuck if the gasket didn't blow completely this time. He spewed shit everywhere.'

'He was plastered,' I say. 'Not that that's any excuse, it definitely isn't . . . Honestly, I was pretty drunk myself. I'm sure I would have been angrier if I'd been sober. Someone should really call him on his behaviour, not just look past it.'

'Although . . .' Malena sighs again. 'Right now, none of that seems quite so important. With Jennifer and all.'

I walk on as I listen to Malena taking a drink and swallowing several times. Coffee, I'd guess. Malena has always been into her coffee.

'What do you think happened?' she asks.

'I don't know, I have no idea. You don't want to imagine the worst, and at the same time . . .'

I hesitate for a moment, unsure of how honest I should be.

'At the same time what?'

My friend sounds like she's egging me on.

'I mean, you know Jennifer.'

'Mmm, I know what you mean.' Malena slurps on the other end. 'Jennifer's not exactly the dependable type. And, to be totally honest, I think she can be kind of a pain.'

My shoulders relax. '*God*, I'm so glad to hear you say that. I've always thought I was the only one who felt that way. I always feel like an evil person for never warming to her. After all, she's Lollo's daughter.'

Malena coughs; I think she's holding her hand over the microphone, but she's soon back.

'Darn cough.'

She clears her throat again.

'You know,' I say, on a roll now, 'sometimes I think there must be something wrong with Jennifer, like something diagnosable. But you don't want to criticize other people's kids. It's like, the worst thing you can do.'

I pass the sporting fields at Husiegård. Two little boys, neither of whom is dressed for the weather, are playing ball on the gravel pitch closest to the parking lot. The whitewashed church tower gazes down at me from its rise.

'It's like swearing in church,' I add, and suddenly I'm reminded of the time Jennifer forced Anton to eat berries he knew were poisonous. Anton was distraught, and I know that in the heat of the moment I told Lollo they should consider getting their child examined. I suppose she's never quite forgiven me for that.

'That stuff is so damn hard.' I'm really gathering steam now. My right hand is stiff with the cold, and I try to wriggle it back into my mitten, but no such luck. 'And we've got such different views on raising kids. According to Lollo, Jennifer can do no wrong. She's just being creative, spontaneous or forgetful –'

'Creative my ass,' Malena scoffs.

'Lollo has always come down hard on me . . .' I have to pause to pull away a few strands of hair that have blown

143

into my mouth. 'She's always on my case for being too strict with Smilla. But maybe she won't be quite as bad after all this.'

'Probably not,' Malena mutters over the clatter of dishes.

'I suppose I shouldn't say "I told you so."' I laugh. 'Then again, I just did. I mean, I don't wish Jennifer any harm. I really don't. But Lollo and Max are so inconsistent in their parenting. One second they're shouting at Jennifer about some really minor shit, and the next they're defending her tooth and nail – when what they should actually be doing is calling her out on her bad behaviour.'

It's so nice to have your opinions affirmed. Still, there's a bitter taste on my tongue. Not every difficult child is diagnosable. And for children who do get a diagnosis, stern correction is no help; it takes a different set of tools. Besides, we're talking about a missing person. What if it's not a matter of thoughtlessness or teenage rebellion? What if something really has happened?

'Anyway,' Malena says. 'I'm sure Jennifer will turn up soon. She's got street smarts; she doesn't take any crap.'

As we end the call, the streetlights on Ellenborgsvägen come on. I put my phone away and find a sticky Mentos at the bottom of my coat pocket. After a few seconds of hesitation, I pop it in my mouth and put on my mitten.

The sidewalk is deserted. On this whole walk, I've run into only three people, not counting the boys on the soccer field. A total of five people and two dogs. I guess folks just don't want to be outside in this wind; they would rather sit at home feeling cosy in front of the TV.

I have no desire to go home. Both Smilla and Fredrik will be like two walking powder kegs, ready to explode at any moment. It's impossible not to be affected by their moods.

I'm going to have a serious talk with Fredrik this very night. We have to be able to talk to each other without one of us fleeing to a different room. We're not Leif and Pirjo. Not yet.

And I'm convinced that if Fredrik can just calm down and name the things that are stressing him out, put them into words, we'll come up with a solution. I could help him to write a proposal, a plan of action, something concrete to bring to the headmaster on the very first day of the semester.

We'll simply have to try to put this Jennifer stuff aside for a few hours and focus on our own concerns.

Family first.

27. Lollo

I glance at the wall clock. Quarter to four. That means at least two hours before Max comes home. Two more long hours to while away. I have no idea how I'm supposed to manage.

So far I've been pacing back and forth from room to room. I go to the kitchen and immediately forget what I'm doing there; I sit on the sofa but stand up just as quickly. I tried to eat lunch but just opening the fridge made me feel nauseous. The new year's eve leftovers are still untouched in their big bowls, smelling like sour old garlic.

The shop is closed. My intended opening hours for the Christmas and new year's holidays are posted on the door, but I can't imagine there's been much of a rush to visit Lollo's Design today. Maybe someone was hoping to exchange a Christmas present. Maybe someone else wanted to buy a hostess gift ahead of Epiphany and had to turn right back around as soon as they got there. I don't care.

My body is restless. And I'm sure it's partially because I didn't sleep last night. Typically, sleepless nights make my legs feel antsy; today I'm antsy and itchy all over. I wish I could turn my skin inside out and scratch and claw at it.

All the while I keep seeing Jennifer's face. It's as though she's etched herself on to the backs of my eyelids to remind me of her absence.

I have to do something. I can't just wander around in

here like a lost soul. But what are you supposed to do when your child is missing? What *can* I do?

Maybe I should go out and look for her. The only problem is, *where?* Her friends say Jennifer was headed home, but Max has already looked around here. It's like she walked out the Anderssons' door and was swallowed up by the darkness.

What if something else happened at the party? Something Smilla isn't telling us. Maybe that argument turned into an actual fight. Someone – Smilla? – could have whacked Jennifer on the head with a bottle. The bottle might have hit just right, and Smilla might have convinced some of the boys to hide the body.

I gasp for air as if I've swallowed a mouthful of water, and my hand flies to my lips. What is wrong with me? How could I even think something like that? Smilla and Jennifer have known each other since they were born. Smilla would never hurt Jennifer. Never.

All the kids must be telling the truth: Jennifer left the party before midnight. And that means she could be absolutely anywhere. She could have taken the train over to Copenhagen. She could be sitting in an apartment in Lindängen; she could have hopped on a bus to Stockholm or even Haparanda. Heading out to find her would be as pointless as looking for a needle in the proverbial haystack.

What are the police doing? Anything? Do they believe Jennifer is hiding out somewhere of her own volition? Do they still think she doesn't want to come home because she had a fight with Smilla?

Something is eating me up from the inside. Nibbling and gnawing. I grab my phone to Google the Malmö police and find a number that leads me to an automatic menu. A few keypad selections later, I land in a queue. I keep wandering through the house as I listen to the droning voice counting down the calls ahead of me, one by one, excruciatingly slowly.

'Malmö Police.'

'My daughter. She's missing. You have to do something!'

'Pardon me, but –'

Although the person on the other end has tried to interrupt, there's no stopping me now.

'You have to talk to every single bus driver who was working on New Year's Eve!' I shout. 'You have to question every last person at the party! Every last one! You have to act now. Do you hear me? She could die before you get your asses off your comfy chairs! Jennifer could die!'

Sobbing, I collapse on the kitchen floor, exhausted after this release.

'Please,' I whisper. 'You have to find her.'

'What was your name?' the man at the switchboard asks gently. 'I didn't catch your name.'

'Lollo,' I say, but then I correct myself. 'Louise. Louise Wiksell.'

'You said your daughter is missing. Has a report been filed?'

I close my eyes, trying to gain control of myself and my voice. 'Yes. We filed a report yesterday. I'd like to talk to Lina Torres.'

'Lina Torrero.' I hear fingers typing at a keyboard before the man returns. 'I'll try to transfer you.'

The phone rings three times before a voicemail picks up. 'Extension 754 is not available. Leave a message after the tone or wait –'

148

I hang up on the recorded woman's voice and lean against the refrigerator door. My heart is racing. I close my eyes but quickly open them again; I don't want to be in the dark.

I can't give up hope.

I must not give up hope.

My fingers trembling, I bring up my recent contacts and press 'Max'. Here too I am greeted by a mechanical voice that informs me the subscriber is temporarily unavailable.

Damnit! How can he not pick up on a day like today? How can he be at work?

A glance at the phone in my hand causes me to do a double take. The red badge at the top-right corner of the Facebook icon reveals an enormous amount of activity – I have a record number of notifications. And I might have guessed as much. Jennifer's picture was in the paper this morning, and now the hordes are descending. I can just picture how my Facebook wall is strewn with hearts and crying emojis.

But I don't want the fake sympathy of my superficial acquaintances. *I want to find Jennifer.*

An instant later it hits me that I could post a picture of her to Facebook, a better picture than was in the paper. I could actually make use of my clients and old classmates, ask them to keep their eyes peeled and share my post. People are usually very helpful when it comes to kids and animals.

I just don't know if I can bring myself to look at those crying emojis. I don't know if I can bear to read what people are writing. I don't want to be the mother everyone assumes is an idiot because she can't keep track of her own child.

Then again, maybe I am an idiot and a failure as a mother. Besides, I want Jennifer to come home. That's all I want. And someone on Facebook might be sitting on valuable information. I *have* to look, there's no avoiding it.

My index finger taps the blue-and-white icon, and it feels as if time stands still while the new content loads. My eyes dart, rushing to see what comes up. As if what is written there will hurt less if I read it quickly.

Just as I suspected, my feed is flooded with recent posts from friends, acquaintances and friends of friends. But I don't see any accusations. No one has written that I have only myself to blame. Most of them seem genuinely worried, and all this concern makes the surreal situation more concrete; it makes me as weak as jelly.

The tears I've been holding in throb in my body as I scroll through hearts and hugs of support. On WhatsApp, Instagram and Messenger I find kind words and sincere comments. But nowhere do I see any sign of life from Jennifer. And no one has anything to say about her whereabouts.

The red badge on Messenger shows a white number seven. It's Dad, trying to contact me. He's called too, four times. But I can't handle talking to Dad right now; I can't handle layering his worry on top of my own.

I go back to Facebook. Someone has mentioned Missing People. Should we contact them? I get my laptop from the front hall, sit on the sofa in the living room and Google my way to their website. It's too much text. I skim through it, jumping from paragraph to paragraph.

For Missing People to help, there must be a police report on file. And there is. I quickly move on, click on 'Report a Missing Person' and start to fill in all the information. But, after a while, I realize maybe I should check with Max first. And maybe we should talk to the police too. So they know.

Instead I start looking through the pictures on my phone. If I'm going to post something on Facebook, I need to find a recent picture of Jennifer. Preferably one where she's not trying to look seductive.

That will be difficult. Recently Jennifer hasn't wanted me to take many pictures of her. In the few photos my camera has managed to capture, her chest is pushed out and she's pouting in that particular way almost all the young girls do when they're getting their picture taken.

To be honest, I myself have tried on those duck lips a time or two. Plump lips are attractive. But, unlike the kids, I just look ridiculous. One hundred per cent ridiculous.

After going through all the pictures, I have settled on two options. One photo is from Midsummer's Eve, during our lunch down in Falsterbo. Jennifer wasn't expecting to be photographed and looks a little surprised. At the same time, she looks natural and is staring straight at the camera. She's tan, with just enough make-up, and there's a flower tucked in her hair.

Lovely Jennifer. She looks so much like my mother. For years after Mom's death, Dad kept a framed photo of his first wife on his nightstand. A close-up, her blonde hair ruffled by the breeze, her eyes merry. I think Dad snapped that picture on their first or second date.

Sometimes, when I was home alone, I would pad into Dad's bedroom and sit down on the edge of the bed. I would hold that frame in my lap as I studied every milli-metre of Mom's young face, trying to find similarities to my own. But no matter the angle, I always looked more like Dad. And I imagine the photo ended up in the attic once Agneta crept under the covers in that double bed.

I take a few deep breaths, swallowing my despair. It sits there ticking in my chest, on the verge of exploding. But I have to keep it together. If I fall apart, I won't be of any use. Breaking down now would be a betrayal of Jennifer.

Tears spring to my eyes and I blink to refocus. One hand captures the salty liquid running down my cheeks, and I study option number two.

The picture was taken sometime last fall, possibly on my birthday. Jennifer looks more serious in this one; her blue eyes are dark, almost black. She's paler. But still just as beautiful.

Where are you, Jennifer? My darling child, why won't you come home?

28. Fredrik

Should I spill it all to Nina? Just give her the whole story from start to finish? Maybe I would feel better afterwards. It seems like getting stuff off your chest is what all the psychologists recommend.

But my wife is so punctilious. An upstanding person. Law-abiding. A good citizen. Some people cut in line or send their children through more than once when there are freebies to be had. Nina is not one of those people. She's the sort of woman who will cycle right back to the store if she finds a pepper she didn't pay for in her grocery bag.

The front door slams. Nina is puttering around in the hall. I hear the familiar sound of her footsteps as she moves to the kitchen; I hear her blow her nose, toss the tissue in the garbage, close the cupboard door. More footsteps. They're approaching the bedroom, and I sit up properly in my office chair and prick up my ears.

After over twenty years under the same roof, I can judge Nina's mood solely by listening to how her heels hit the floor. Today her heels say she's determined. Not angry but determined.

'What are you doing?'

She's standing in the doorway. Hat hair and rosy cheeks.

'Nothing much. Just looking some stuff up online.'

She enters the room, places her hands on my shoulders and massages them gently.

'Are you looking at computers?'

She leans over to study the screen more minutely. Her breath reveals traces of coffee and mint.

'Uh, yeah. I'm . . . thinking of getting a Mac.'

She stops rubbing my shoulders, grabs the back of the chair and spins me around. Then she brings a hand to my forehead.

'There must be something seriously wrong with you, Fredrik.' She takes her hand away as a smile tugs at one corner of her lips. 'Do you have a fever?'

My eyes are level with Nina's breasts. She's standing way too close and I'm having trouble breathing, but I manage to say something about certain old dogs being able to learn new tricks after all.

She laughs.

'Never mind,' I say, closing the browser. 'I didn't say I'm *going* to buy something. I was just looking around a little.'

'Listen . . .' Nina sits down on the end of the double bed. She gives me a beseeching look. 'We have to talk.'

'Talk?' I start to spin the chair with my foot, but I stop it and turn back the other way. Left, right. Left, right. 'About what?'

'About us,' Nina says. 'Or maybe mostly about you. Can you sit still?'

I let my foot rest. 'What about me?' I ask, and immediately I want to bite my tongue.

Nina sighs. 'You told me yesterday that your mental health is suffering because you're stressed at work.'

'It's fine. I'll try to get a handle on it when school starts again. Have a talk with Inga-Lill.'

'Can't you tell me?' She crosses her legs and leans forward.

'Tell you what?'

'Why you're so stressed out, obviously.' Nina throws up her hands. 'Is it the paperwork? Or is it the students? Some particular project, maybe? You're still on that anti-bullying committee, right? You could drop out if it gets to be too much, couldn't you?'

Why is my wife so fucking stubborn? There's nothing to tell. Not about my work situation, at least. Everything is fine at work. Not great, but fine.

I stand up. 'Seriously, there's nothing to talk about. I've just got too much on my plate. But it will all work out.'

'Are you walking away from me again?' Nina looks up at me from her spot on the edge of the bed. 'We've hardly started talking here.'

'I'm not walking away, I'm standing right here.'

She gets to her feet and takes a step in my direction. 'It looks like you're on your way out of here.'

My turn to sigh. 'I'm standing right in front of you.'

'It's just . . .' Nina puts her hands on her hips. 'Suddenly it's totally impossible to have a normal conversation with you. How are we supposed to find solutions to your problems if you can't even *talk* about them?'

I throw my arms around her. Not because I want a hug, but to make her be quiet, to make her stop analysing me.

'Nina, *you* don't need to solve any problems. *I* will figure this out.'

At that moment, Nina's phone starts to ring somewhere in the house. She pelts out of the bedroom, but I hardly have time to take a breath before she's back in the doorway.

'We have to clean.'

'What?'

Nina goes to the bed and yanks at the duvet cover.

'You heard me.' She straightens it out, tucks it in and fluffs it. 'Claudia and Monique are on their way over.'

Shit. Not them. Not now. Preferably never.

'Here? Why?'

Nina picks up a magazine from the floor and places it on the shelf beneath the nightstand.

'They're on their way from Kastrup Airport. Wanted to stop by and say hi.'

'You could have told them we're not home . . . or anything, but –'

My wife shoots me a sharp look. 'Claudia is my sister.'

'But you don't like her.'

'I do too! And they won't stay long. Now get moving – help me out here.' She's already halfway to the kitchen. 'Should we do mulled wine? Or coffee? What do you think?'

29. Nina

'Hello, hello!'

My sister beams with as much cheer as the string of lights that's draped over the bush behind her. She's wearing a fitted ivory coat, and her long dark hair is partly covered by a hat from GANT. The brand tag is clearly visible even though it's discreetly sewn into the seam.

Next to Claudia is Monique, who is smiling with her whole face. Her striped scarf hangs nonchalantly over her dark wool coat. Pauline's hand holds Monique's tightly. The four-year-old observes me with big brown eyes.

'*Bonjour*, Nina.'

Monique leans forward and smacks her lips under my ear. It takes a lot of willpower not to recoil. That Continental cheek-kissing is not my style. I've never grasped how many kisses it's supposed to be, or how many times you switch sides before you're finished.

Claudia hugs me tightly and my blouse sticks to my back. I'm still sweaty from the vacuuming and have just barely had time to change from sweats to jeans before the doorbell rang.

'It's so great that you could stop by. Come on in.' I squat down. 'Hi, Pauline. Remember me? Aunt Nina.'

The girl turns her head and buries her face in Monique's coat.

'Hardly.' Claudia laughs. 'She was only two and a half the last time we saw each other.'

Monique pushes Pauline ahead of her, and soon everyone has come into the warm. The front hall seems unusually cramped, almost claustrophobic. I suddenly notice how worn our front door is. Entire shards of wood have come loose at the bottom edge, and the brown stain looks all wrong next to the light grey walls I painted during the Easter break.

'You'll have to excuse the mess,' I say with a sweeping gesture, and as I do I happen to catch sight of myself in the mirror. My hair is going every which way. It must be thanks to my hat, which is made of synthetic material. 'We weren't quite prepared to receive such special company today.'

Claudia seems to be looking for a hanger but doesn't say anything. In the end she hangs her coat on a hook next to Vilgot's grubby snowsuit. I can't help but hope it leaves a stain, gets a little brown Skåne mud on that ivory fabric.

We leave the hall. Pauline needs to use the bathroom and Monique takes her. I set course for the kitchen.

Claudia follows me and stops in front of the fridge door, where schedules, reminder notes and old photos are hung all askew with a variety of creative magnets. Someone should do something about that mess.

'So how are things with you all?'

Claudia goes over to the table, picks up the newspaper and flips through it idly.

'Super.' I toss a dozen frozen Lucia buns into the microwave. 'How about you?' I look at my sister. 'Are you still liking Brussels?'

'It's great.' Claudia drops the paper. 'Work is busy. As usual.' She smiles and fingers the diamond in her wedding ring. 'But we just got an au pair. A really great girl. From

Spain. Ana is studying French in Brussels, and we're just thrilled with her.'

I bite my lip and count to ten.

'The two of you haven't considered cutting back your hours?'

'Wouldn't work,' Claudia says. 'No one in my unit works part time. Same for Monique.'

She notices Fredrik and lights up.

'My favourite brother-in-law!' Claudia throws herself at my husband. 'It's been ages.'

Fredrik is looking a little more alert now. When the hug-fest is over, he heads for the living room and greets the other two.

The microwave dings. I open the door, take out the Lucia buns and place them on a platter.

Claudia comes over to me and lowers her voice.

'Is he all right?'

'Who?'

'Fredrik. He's pale as a ghost.'

I stand on tiptoe to reach the napkins in the cupboard. Claudia flings up an arm and takes them down without effort. She's the one who got Mom's long legs. I had to settle for Dad's considerably more compact build.

'He's a little stressed at work, that's all,' I say.

'May I be excused?'

Anton has been fidgety for a while, and I know he hates sitting down with adults he doesn't know. Being forced to answer questions about school and soccer. And in English this time, besides.

Since Fredrik doesn't react, I nod and Anton wriggles his way out of his chair. Smilla slips away in his wake.

Vilgot sneaked off as soon as he had finished the last gingersnap, but Pauline is still sitting on the sofa between her parents. I can tell from Claudia's expression that she thinks our kids have bad manners.

'What time are you coming on Saturday?' she asks.

My sister has given up trying to talk to Fredrik and has turned all her attention on me.

'Not sure. Around lunchtime, maybe. Or else we'll eat lunch at home first. I guess we'll have to check with Mom, see what she thinks is best.'

I don't envy Mom and Dad having Claudia's family to stay with them for five days. Mom says they enjoy having them for a visit, but I have my doubts. Dad told me Mom usually spends weeks being hysterical before Claudia and company arrive. 'You'd think it's a visit from the royal family themselves. Hell, Inger runs herself ragged.'

Monique finally checks her watch. She mumbles something to my sister, who gets up and begins to clear away the mugs.

'It's about time for us to be heading out now,' she says. 'We told them we'd be there around six.'

'Already? That's too bad. But we'll see each other soon.'

Claudia smiles. 'It'll be fun for the kids to spend some time together. We want Pauline to get to know her cousins.'

As if Anton and Smilla are interested in spending time with a little girl over a decade their junior who prefers to speak French.

'Fredrik,' I say a little more loudly than I mean to. 'Will you clear the table?'

He starts, as if I've just woken him from a deep sleep, and immediately leaps from the sofa. His movements sluggish, he begins to place napkins and glasses sloppily

160

on the tray. To keep from exploding with irritation, I pick up the coffeepot and hurry to the kitchen.

'Thanks for the coffee and treats, sis.' Claudia sets a few mugs in the sink and is on her way back to the living room when she stops by the kitchen table. 'Ugh.' She nods at the open newspaper. 'Have you seen this?'

'What's that?'

I put the cookie tin in the cupboard and close the door.

'This.' My sister points. 'I saw the headline before we sat down. About the missing girl.'

Claudia leans over the table. I hold my breath and send up hope.

'Wiksell?' She looks at me, her eyes wide. 'Jennifer *Wiksell*! Isn't that Lollo's daughter?'

I let out my breath. 'Yeah.'

'Oh my God, Nina! Why didn't you say something? This is awful! What do you think happened?'

Fredrik enters the kitchen. He sets the tray on the counter and turns around. 'To what?'

My sister points at the paper again. 'To her.'

He goes over to Claudia and peers over her shoulder.

An instant later, Fredrik grabs the back of a chair with both hands. He seems to be frozen solid at the end of the table; all the colour has drained from his face, and his breathing comes in fits and starts.

'Fredrik?' I hurry over and place a hand on his arm. 'Are you okay?'

Fredrik doesn't respond. He just stands there with his eyes closed. His lips are pressed together in a firm line. He swallows several times, then suddenly lets go of the chair and rushes to the bathroom.

30. Lollo

I look around, lost, as if I've never been here before. White walls, white furniture, white sheets. White and lilac pillows. All according to Jennifer's wishes.

Even last night it felt wrong to rummage around in here. I kept having the feeling that she might come tromping in at any second and demand to know what the hell I was up to.

My stomach ties itself in knots as I look at the tangled bedsheet and the bra hanging over the headboard. The fluffy slippers next to her dresser make me want to cry. And that is precisely why I have been avoiding Jennifer's room today.

But, now, here I am. Because the more I think about it, the more convinced I become: if there are any answers to our questions, they must be in here, in the room where Jennifer spends the better part of her waking hours.

The police seem to be slacking, but not me. Each second throbs through my body, reminding me that time is passing.

Something has to happen.

I go over to the desk, pull out the top drawer of the filing cabinet and rifle around in the mess I find there. Pens are scattered among erasers, paperclips and rubber bands. The next drawer contains some notebooks and lots of loose-leaf paper. School stuff, apparently. I pick up one sheet of paper on which Jennifer has written answers to questions about World War Two.

History was never my favourite subject in school. Well, maybe it was in middle school, when we read about the Viking Age and built a Viking village out of papier-mâché. That was fun. But then my interest waned. Why wallow in the past when you can look to the future?

I put the paper back in the drawer and browse through the other sheets but don't find anything of interest. Assignments in Swedish, math and English are mixed in with information from the guidance counsellor, an invitation to a student-council party and a brochure from a company that sells graduation caps. Already? That seems premature. I close the drawer and just stand there. What am I looking for?

I assume what I'm hoping to find are clues about Jennifer's life. But where could they be? And what do I mean by clues?

Both Nina and Malena kept diaries when we were in high school. I personally felt it was kind of naff. At the same time, I would have given my right hand to know what they wrote.

Nina was always careful to hide her diary when someone came into the room, made a big deal of it. Only once did she leave it open on her desk. It seemed like it was just asking to be read. I remember thinking maybe she left it there on purpose. Because she *wanted* me to see it.

The pages were full of her scribbles and made my heart gallop in excitement, but as usual it was Nina herself who saved me from a major overstep. I heard her footsteps outside the door and hardly caught more than a few words before I threw myself back on the bed. Still, my guilty conscience plagued me for weeks.

Does Jennifer keep a diary? Embarrassingly, I have no idea. I've certainly never seen her write in anything that looks like a diary. She's always staring at a screen, no matter the time of day. She's either staring at her phone or her computer or both of them at the same time. Maybe she writes on her laptop?

My stomach does a flip. The computer! How the hell could I have forgotten her computer? It must be the lack of sleep that's turning my mind into molasses.

I spin around, surveying the room. Jennifer's laptop is usually on her desk, but now the surface is neat and empty. Did she bring her computer to the new year's party? That might suggest a planned escape. You don't bring your computer to a party if you're planning to come home the next day.

Hope rises in me, but then I catch sight of something silver under a magazine on the nightstand. My hope is extinguished.

I pull out the computer, sit down on the bed, open the lid and watch the screen slowly come to life. Under a round picture of a yellow, one-eyed figure there is a grey field that contains the words 'Enter password'. I heave a deep sigh. Of course it's password-protected.

I close my eyes and try to think. If I were Jennifer, what would my password be?

Chanel

Doesn't work.

Jennifer

Doesn't work.

Jenni

Doesn't work.

123456

Doesn't work.

I try all the same names but with a lower-case letter to start. I add a full stop at the end, and then I try adding Jennifer's birth year. But the computer refuses to let me in.

Then I have a sudden inspiration and type in a different name.

Jussi

I'm in.

31. Nina

'It's probably stress rather than the stomach flu. Like I said, Fredrik's been really overextended at work for some time now. Please, don't mention anything to Mom.' I fix my gaze on Claudia. 'She'll only worry. And don't mention this business with Jennifer –'

'They probably still subscribe to *Sydsvenskan*,' my sister interrupts.

She's standing just outside the door with all her winter gear on, having managed to evacuate her whole family within the space of a few minutes.

'They do,' I say. 'But I bet Mom hasn't had time to read the paper today. I suspect she's been otherwise occupied since you're coming.'

'Okay.' Claudia shrugs. 'Tell Fredrik to feel better.'

My sister looks at me as though we've purposefully tried to infect her with the stomach flu during one of her rare visits to her homeland.

'See you on Saturday,' I say, waving to Monique, who's already getting into the white rental car.

Claudia turns on her heel; I pull the door closed and hurry back to the bedroom.

Fredrik is lying on the bed, on top of the covers. His eyes are closed, and he isn't moving a muscle. For a split second I think he's dead, and my whole body goes cold. But when I sit on the edge of the bed, he gives a start, opens his eyes and gives me a weak smile. I take his hand; it's trembling.

'Fredrik, your hand –'

'I know,' he mutters. 'But it's no big deal, it'll pass.'

I pat the top of his hand and discover three red stripes, three parallel scratches. They look as if they might be infected.

'What's this?'

'Nothing.' Fredrik makes a face. 'I scratched myself on a branch the other day.'

'Were you working in the garden?' I turn his hand over. 'When was this?'

'I don't know exactly when.' He shoots me a tired look. 'And I wasn't working in the garden. I probably just picked up a stick on my way to the car or something.'

'Maybe that's when your coat got ripped.'

'My coat got ripped?' Fredrik goes stiff and looks perplexed. 'What?'

'On the side seam,' I say. 'It came apart and the threads are just hanging from it.'

'Oh, that . . . it's been that way for a long time.'

He closes his eyes again and I sigh.

'Fredrik, I'm starting to feel worried about you. Really concerned. What if you've got some serious illness? Something that affects your energy levels. What if it's not stress after all? You might need actual medical care.'

Fredrik opens his eyes. 'Would you quit your nagging?' He sounds annoyed now. 'There is nothing seriously wrong with me. I just felt a little nauseous, is all.'

I drop his hand and stand up. 'I'm not nagging. And how can you be upset with me for being concerned? Don't you get that I want to know what's going on?' Tears sting behind my eyelids. 'I hardly recognize you!'

'Nothing's going on,' he says tonelessly. 'Just leave me alone.'

Our rafts are drifting ever further apart; the sea foams and crashes around us.

Smilla is flipping through the newspaper. She's wearing leggings, thick socks and a big hoodie that used to belong to Fredrik. The hood is tugged down low to hide her face, but when I enter the kitchen she pulls it back and looks up.

'It's about Jennifer.'

She nods at the open paper on the table.

I try to shake off my frustration, reminding myself that Fredrik isn't feeling well, that he can't help his behaviour. With one arm around Smilla's shoulders, I lean over and skim the brief article.

It's the same bulletin that they posted online this morning. The photo must be a few years old: Jennifer looks younger than she does in real life. In the last sentence the police ask for any help the public can provide.

Smilla turns around, pressing herself to my chest without a word. I squeeze her firmly, and the warmth from her body seeps into my own. Thank God my daughter is here with me in this moment.

'I love you, Smilla,' I mumble, inhaling the scent of her tousled hair. A heavenly mixture of shampoo, conditioner and hairspray.

'I know,' she says, adding, 'I love you too.'

A door upstairs opens, and Anton's voice finds its way down the stairs. 'When's dinner?'

'In a little while.' I raise my voice. 'Don't start any new games.'

Anton's door slams, and Smilla wriggles out of my embrace. 'What are we having?' she asks.

'No idea,' I reply. 'But we'll figure it out.'

Smilla lingers in the kitchen. She stands for a while in front of the December page of last year's calendar. The picture is a family photo from two Christmases ago, an exception to all the Vilgot pages that are standard in our family calendars these days. I like that picture. We all look happy. And it's because we were having a good time. Anton was the one who, after many failed attempts, managed to get the old selfie stick to work.

We should spend more time together. The whole family. When was the last time all five of us did something together? I rack my brain but I can't think of a single family activity since last summer, when we were on Gotland and – to the delight of some – ended up having to return home early. Dinners at home don't count. And Christmas Eve is mandatory.

Maybe we could make Smilla and Anton come along on little trips sometimes, take the opportunity while they're still so young. Because when we do manage to do things together, we typically have a really nice time.

It's just a matter of getting through those first few hours of heavy sighs and headphones in ears. No, that's not all – first and foremost it's about having the energy to plan things to do. We've become worse at that recently. But this weekend we're going to Mom and Dad's, at least. That trip counts.

Smilla leaves the calendar and goes over to the window,

turning her back to me. 'What do you think the police are doing now?'

I turn on the tap and fill a big pot with water. Pasta and tomato sauce it is tonight.

'You mean, are they looking for Jennifer?'

Smilla mutters something inaudible and I turn my head, studying the delicate figure that almost vanishes inside that huge hoodie.

'No idea, sweetie. I don't know how long a person has to be missing before they launch an honest-to-goodness search.'

'Well, they didn't seem to be in much of a hurry last night, anyway.'

'I expect the police like to wait and see,' I say, salting the water. 'It's not unusual for teenagers to go missing without really being missing. They forget to say where they're going, they run away from home because they had a fight with their parents . . .'

Smilla turns around and looks at me with shiny eyes. 'But Jennifer would never go anywhere without telling someone.'

'Are you sure about that?' I open the fridge and look down into the salad compartment. 'You haven't been as close recently.'

On the bottom of the drawer are two yellow onions and a wilted head of lettuce. I pick up one onion, which immediately slips from my hand and rolls on to the floor. Smilla catches it and places it on the chopping board with a bang.

'I've known Jennifer all my life.'

'I know. But people change. And you might not have noticed if you don't see her as often.'

My thoughts happen to turn to Lollo and Malena, our friendship, and how it's changed over the years. From a feeling of 'us against the world' to two festive family gatherings per year and almost non-existent contact between-times.

'It's just . . .' Smilla lets out a sob. 'I thought the new year's party would fix everything and make it good again.'

I put the knife down on the chopping board and approach her.

'What do you mean, good again? Have things been bad?'

'Not bad, but . . .' Smilla rubs her eyes. 'We hadn't seen each other since last summer, hardly even on Snap. I thought it was because of school, that she was too busy. But now . . . it all just went to picccs.'

'Oh, honey.' I put my arms around Smilla. 'I'm sure that was a really sweet gesture on your part. You can't help that it turned out the way it did.'

'Where's Dad?'

She slips out of my grasp and looks around, unaware of the drama that took place in this kitchen just an hour ago.

'Dad is resting.'

'Is he sick?'

I devote all my attention to chopping the onion, putting off my response. Smilla's nearly an adult. I could share my concerns with her; she might understand. But I don't want Smilla to spend time worrying about her father on top of everything else. She's got enough on her plate.

'No,' I say. 'He's just been really busy at work and needs time to rest up.'

She looks at me but doesn't say anything.

'Sometimes it's just what happens,' I continue. 'That

exhaustion doesn't hit you until you take a break from work and have time to relax.'

'Okay.' Smilla shrugs. 'But is he going to eat? Should I set a place for him?'

Tears spring to my eyes. Must be the onions.

32. Lollo

Jussi was Jennifer's first teddy bear. Or *is*; he still exists. A classic brown teddy that Dad and Agneta brought when they visited their grandchild in the hospital. Jussi got his name when Jennifer started to talk, and he's made every move with us. From the apartment in Slottsstaden to the row house in Bunkeflostrand to our current home. Hour after hour he has sat on Jennifer's ever larger beds, staring at us with his sad little face.

But when we redecorated her room last winter, he was banished.

'He doesn't match,' Jennifer said, placing him in a box that was destined for the attic. 'He's too brown.'

My daughter has never been the nostalgic type, so I'm really quite surprised that she would use 'Jussi' as a password. He must have been staring at her when she set up this computer at the start of her first year of high school. Back then he was still part of the decor.

I look at the screen and see that the browser is open. Jennifer seems to have stopped in the middle of a YouTube video, and I click on the left-hand arrow to go back into the history. A different clip comes up. Both are about applying foundation.

For a brief moment I wonder if it's wrong of me to look at Jennifer's computer before the police do. What if I destroy some important clues? But what kind of clues would those be? And what might they lead to? Besides, no one has asked about the computer.

My neck itches, and I scratch my skin until it stings. Why the hell hasn't anyone asked to look at Jennifer's computer? Isn't that one of the first things the police usually do when someone is reported missing?

I open her email program and quickly skim the long list of senders. Almost everything seems to be related to school. Teachers have sent assignments; Emma Lundberg sent an email about preparations for some group project. The name 'Samira' attracts my attention, so I open her email. Who is she? It turns out that Samira, just like Emma, is in Jennifer's class, and they worked on a report in English class together.

All these reports and group projects – why hasn't she mentioned them? My cheeks go hot, because I know the answer to that question, and it makes me feel guilty. We weren't interested. We didn't care. Largely because we've never *had* to care.

Jennifer has always been self-motivated when it comes to school – in every subject but math it's been smooth sailing. She's smart, and the greatest challenge for Jennifer's teachers has always been keeping her engaged. School has only ever been an issue when she feels bored.

In elementary school there were some teachers who claimed Jennifer had discipline problems and led her friends into mischief. But those teachers shut up when it turned out it was their lessons that were lacking, that they had failed to give her sufficiently stimulating tasks.

I have spent many parent–teacher meetings explaining the situation to whiny teachers. It's so typical of today's schools that only the rotten eggs get attention and support, while those who are advanced are hindered in their development.

Since Jennifer started high school, we haven't had any complaints. I expect the instruction finally matches her level – and perhaps even provides a challenge.

Among the school emails are ads from a few online retailers where Jennifer likes to order clothes. When she turned sixteen, we arranged things so she could manage her own purchases online, without our involvement. We always ended up fighting when Max or I tried to help her, mostly because Max usually questioned whatever she wanted to buy. My husband enjoys luxury items and gadgets, but, at the same time, he's cost-conscious.

No one would ever accuse Jennifer of being cost-conscious, though. That first year, she spent over her maximum every single week, but Max's many lectures must have helped because it's been a long time since we had to pitch in and bail her out.

I freeze as Chanel comes padding into the room and realize that I'm on tenterhooks. As if what I'm doing is wrong. And I know Jennifer would lose her mind if she knew I was looking through her emails.

'I'm sorry, darling,' I whisper, just as I discover a lone Word document that's sitting in the right margin of the computer desktop.

The document is named 'Random' but something tells me that name has nothing to do with its actual contents. I double-click and realize right away that my gut feeling has been a helpful guide. The hairs on the back of my neck stand up as I see the heading on the screen: *For You*.

It's certainly not any sort of diary, at least not the way I imagine a diary to be. Each section of text is dated, but they have nothing to do with what Jennifer did during the day in question. They're more like poems. Very unexpected.

> 5 July 2018
> The air was electric.
> Did you notice?
> You must have.
> Your hands.
> I want to feel them on my body.
> Again.

The words on the screen make me feel embarrassed. And ashamed. This isn't meant for my eyes. But I force myself to keep reading, so I scroll down to the last page.

> 28 December 2018
> I love you.
> I hate you.
> But I hate me more.

The most recent entry leaves a heavy lump in my stomach. Was she writing about Ali after all? Does Jennifer have an unrequited crush on him? Maybe this is just a matter of classic teenage angst after all, longing for true love.

It doesn't matter. The poems don't give me anything to go on; they say nothing about where she might be. I close the document and study the open tabs in her browser.

Jennifer has been watching a Netflix series and stopped right in the middle. And she's watched other YouTube videos. Cute kittens.

Facebook is open in the final tab. Jennifer uses Facebook? I remember helping her to open an account there years ago. This was before she was thirteen, but I gave her a fake age and found a profile picture on the condition that she friend me so I could keep an eye on her activity.

Thank goodness Jennifer never did much on Facebook. She only seemed interested in reading what other people posted. A few years later Instagram got popular and she dropped Facebook entirely, saying that it was for old people.

But apparently she's come back to it. When I select the tab, I'm startled.

The profile picture shows a young woman in half-length. Her breasts are pressed up and together, almost leaping from her tiny top. Her lips are blood-red and half open, her eyes smoky and half closed. This woman looks like a porn star. And a B-list one at that.

But there can be no mistaking who it is. It's my daughter. It's Jennifer. The background image is a collage of black lace and red roses.

Jennifer Wicked.

What's this? My head buzzes as I scroll down through her posts. There aren't many of them. I can see that the profile picture was added sometime in September. The background image was changed by Jennifer Wicked in early October, and a price list was published at the same time.

I read the top entry on the page and swallow hard.

My heart starts to beat faster as my eyes dart from the profile picture to the entry and back again. I'm no dummy. Obviously I understand exactly what I'm looking at, but I can't take it in. My brain refuses to assimilate this information; it tries to find some other explanation.

Jennifer couldn't have posted this voluntarily. Someone must have tricked her! I read the entry again.

Breasts 250 kronor
Full length 500 kronor
Video 1000 kronor

A powerful wave of nausea overtakes me. I look around, feeling a sudden need to hide what's on the screen. Who has seen this? Is this page public?

I check the settings and quickly find that, no, thank God, this page is private. Jennifer Wicked has only about forty friends, and I hurry to bring them up, glancing frantically through the whole list. All her friends are men, and I don't know a single one of them. That they're there must mean that Jennifer accepted their friend requests, but there doesn't seem to have been any activity on the page. There are no likes, neither of her profile picture nor of the cover photo. And no one has left any comments.

Weird.

My head spins as I try to make sense of it. Could it be a joke? Is she just messing around with her friends?

I calm myself. It must be. This isn't for real. When I think about it, it would be such a Jennifer move to toss out some random comment about posing for nude pics online and then pretend to go all the way with it. She would certainly be capable of setting up a Facebook profile with a price list just to make waves.

Our daughter has always been a challenge because of her curiosity, stubbornness and desire to test boundaries – her own and those of others. I think these are positive traits. You can go far in life with curiosity, stubbornness and a little dash of hellraiser in you.

For my part, I'm more bothered by people who don't dare to stick their necks out. There are so many people walking around feeling bitter about their boring lives even as they're too cowardly to try anything new. You have no right to complain if you haven't even tried to make a change.

Throughout the years, people have occasionally thought Jennifer went too far. We've often been told she's tactless. One parent of a girl on her soccer team even maintained that Jennifer was inconsiderate, that she lacks empathy. Both Nina and Malena have, at times, suggested that she might be diagnosable somehow, hinted that we should get her checked out.

To think that adults could just casually spout such things about a child. What unfair accusations! Jennifer knows how to look out for number one and dares to forge her own path. She always has. And isn't that how we want to raise our girls? Even the schools try to teach them to have ambition, sharp elbows and self-confidence, don't they?

People talk about girl power, but there's clearly a double standard in Swedish society – that goddamned Jante law. You should be direct but not too direct – that's being too pushy. You should have sharp elbows but not too sharp, because that means you're rude. People who show self-confidence are so often labelled as braggarts.

Jennifer has never been one to do things in moderation, and I think Nina's and Malena's criticisms stem from a place of envy. While Jennifer has a tough skin and can handle herself, their kids are so over-protected that they can hardly wipe their own asses without help. In my opinion, Theo, that poor thing, is pathologically shy. I've wondered on occasion if he's autistic or something, if *he's* the one who needs professional help.

I redirect my attention to the Facebook page again, and when Jennifer Wicked's seductive eyes meet my own, I have to look away. I can't handle seeing my daughter like this. Sure, it's a good thing to be curious, but this time Jennifer has crossed a line.

'Why are you doing this to us?' I mutter. 'And to yourself?'

Once again, I tell myself that the page must be meant as a joke. The empty comment fields support my conclusion. But it isn't funny. And if the police decide to take away her computer, it's not going to look so good. They might get the idea that this is something Jennifer does for real. And they wouldn't understand if I explain that this is just classic Jennifer, just an example of her sense of humour.

The burst of adrenalin increases again, and my nausea is back. I close my eyes, sit perfectly still and try to think clearly. Eventually, the obvious realization comes to me: I have to delete this page.

I quickly click my way to the settings. Since I'm logged in as Jennifer Wicked, it should be easy to shut down. The little arrow darts across the screen and under 'Manage account' I find the option to 'request that your account be deleted'. But an instant later I realize this has to do with what should happen when the account holder has died. My fingers lift off the keyboard.

Died.

I close my eyes again, and get the feeling that if I read the words once more they'll become reality.

No one has died. No one has died.

I repeat that sentence like a mantra.

After a few deep breaths I force myself to open my

eyes; I skim through the tiny text and find a spot where a living account holder can deactivate their account. But apparently some information will remain – friends and messages, for instance.

That's utter bullshit. So it's totally fucking impossible to vanish from Facebook? Are we signing a lifetime contract by uploading our mugs there?

I hastily weigh my options and in the end decide to deactivate. It seems to be the least terrible alternative. And hopefully it will minimize the risk that the police will discover this page if they ever go through the computer. If I deactivate the account and then delete the browser's history, it should at least make it harder for them. No one will be searching for a Facebook account under the name Jennifer Wicked. They'll look for Jennifer Wiksell. And I can't imagine there will be much to find on the old account.

I guide the cursor over the screen and am just about to click the right box when my phone starts ringing. It's sitting next to me on the bed and I answer as if in a trance, without looking to see who it is.

'Hello, Lina Torrero here, detective with the Malmö police.'

All the blood rushes out of my head and the bed sways. There is only one question I want to ask, but there seems to be a circuit loose somewhere. The words get stuck in my throat.

'Unfortunately, we have no news about Jennifer,' the woman says, as if she has read my mind. 'Your husband was informed as much earlier today, but he's not answering the phone right now. I just wanted to see if either of you was home. We'd like to borrow Jennifer's computer.'

'Computer?'

My voice is faint and trembling.

'She has one, right?' Lina Torrero asks.

'Yes.' I swallow. 'Yes, definitely. She has one.'

'Great. One of my colleagues will swing by and pick it up this evening.'

And with that, the call is over.

I put down the phone and stare at the screen before me. It's 6.28 p.m. Six thirty. The past hour has flown by. But where is Max? He should be home by now. And why didn't he pick up when the police called?

Maybe he's in the car. Max has never cared about the cell-phone laws, but it also wouldn't be out of character for him to ignore a call.

I look at the numbers again, just to make sure I'm not mistaken about the time. As I do, I catch sight of a small red symbol up in the right-hand corner of Facebook.

Jennifer Wicked has three unread messages.

33. Fredrik

Two gentle knocks and the door glides open. Padded footsteps approach.

The mattress creaks as Smilla sits on the edge of the bed. I open my eyes and see my daughter's profile as a silhouette in the sharp backlighting from the hall fixture. Her little nose – which is bigger than when she was born, of course, but has always been very small – and her round cheeks. Sometimes I can see baby Smilla so clearly in the young woman she is today. On this particular day, it makes me want to cry.

'We're going to have dinner,' she says. 'Want some?'

'Not right now. I'll eat in a bit.'

The fact is, I'm starting to get pretty hungry, but sitting at the table with the rest of the family for a whole meal sounds like utter agony.

'How are you feeling?' Smilla asks. She looks concerned.

'I'm just a little off. It'll pass.'

'You're coming to Grandma and Grandpa's, though, right?'

'Grandma and Grandpa's?'

'Yeah.' Smilla rolls her eyes. 'You know, Mom's parents?'

I frantically search my memory for any clue.

'Um . . . when . . .'

Smilla stares at me. 'Honestly, Dad. We're going there on Saturday.'

'Oh, the dinner.'

We always eat dinner at Nina's parents' place for Epiphany. They live in Höör, not far from Malmö, but we usually stay the night and take a trip to Skåne Zoo before we head home. It's a tradition that began when Smilla was little and was rekindled when Vilgot arrived. This year, Pauline will be the youngest.

The thought of spending an entire day with my parents-in-law and Claudia's family makes my nausea return in full force.

It's nothing against my in-laws. They're regular, friendly folks. Rodrigo came to Sweden from Chile in the seventies, got a job at a car mechanic's in Höör and stayed there until retirement. I like him. He's easy to talk to and has a good sense of humour. Inger is an anxious woman, always eager to please everyone. But at the root of that anxiety is a kind heart. Inger always helps out and seldom complains; she's an amazing grandmother.

It's just that I can't look them in the eye right now.

Nina's little sister isn't a bad person either. But she's certainly in a class all her own. Claudia is smart and almost exceptionally beautiful. At the same time, she's spoiled, superficial and basically obsessed with money and what you can buy with it. She can be awfully funny, but Nina has a tendency to be annoyed with everything Claudia says and does. Being under the same roof as the Gonzales sisters is like picking your way through a minefield.

This is the year the Epiphany tradition will be broken. At least on my part.

'We'll see how I'm feeling on Saturday,' I say.

Smilla nods and is about to get up when she seems to think of something else and looks at me again.

'Mom was just talking to the police. They want me to come in for questioning tomorrow.'

Something squeezes my chest.

'Questioning?' I try to keep my voice steady and sit up to get air. 'Why?'

Smilla shrugs. 'I don't know. All they said was that they wanted me to come in.'

It's all over. Bringing in Smilla is nothing but a way for the police to get at me. They want to make me nervous, make me lose my cool.

'We'll . . . go with you. One of us, anyway.'

'It's fine,' Smilla says. 'I can handle it.'

'Are you two coming?'

Nina's voice slices through the house; it's noticeably irritated. Smilla leaps to her feet.

'I'll say you're going to eat later,' she mumbles, leaving the bedroom.

I lean back and sink into my pillow again. For a long time I lie on my back in the half-dark, unable to think a single clear thought. Words and images tumble through my mind. I see Jennifer, hear her voice. In an attempt to shut out the sound of it, I press my palms to my ears. Instead, my rushing pulse becomes more and more obvious. It gets louder and louder, faster and faster.

I let go and press my fingertips to my eyelids until my eyes ache.

Still, Jennifer's face doesn't go away.

I see her fall, see her lying on the cold, damp ground.

Could I have left something behind? Something that's still hidden among the leaves? A receipt, a shopping list. Anything at all.

I have to go back.

34. Lollo

My middle finger moves across the touchpad. My hand is shaking so hard that I have trouble hitting the mark, and the little black arrow jumps around the screen like a disoriented fly.

'For Christ's sake, Lollo.'

I try again, a little slower this time. It works. Yet when the arrow is finally hovering over the message symbol, I stop, suddenly hesitant. Do I really want to know? Do I want to see what conversations are taking place?

No, I don't want to know. I want to keep living life in the belief that the whole Jennifer Wicked idea is a bad joke. I want to deactivate this account and pretend it never existed.

But, in order to help Jennifer, I have to turn over every stone. I have to be brave enough to look under the dirty ones too. What if something bad happened to her as a result of this Facebook page? What if she arranged to meet one of the men on the friends list and has been kidnapped or raped or . . .

I rein in my runaway thoughts by double-clicking the chat bubble and turning my attention to the text that comes up on the screen. The first of the three unread messages is written by someone who calls himself Willie Winkie.

> money all sent
> already hard

The next message is a blurry photo of an erect cock. I'm nearly sick all over the keyboard, but I manage to control myself and read the third message.

> hey what gives??
> we had a deal
> you won't get away with this! nasty little whore!

I want to flee. I want to run all the way to the harbour and toss the laptop into the sea, throw it way out in the waves and let it sink to the bottom. Jennifer Wicked is apparently no joke. This page is active, and when I read the last message once more I realize the inevitable: I can't shut down this account. I have to hand this computer over to the police just as it is, and I have to tell them what I found so they don't have to waste time searching for it.

But I also realize this information is going to ruin Jennifer's life. Destroy us as a family. As soon as the police catch wind of the Jennifer Wicked page, the news will be leaked to some bloodsucking journalist. And it won't be long before the public is fully aware of the missing Jennifer's special 'hobby'.

People will be ruthless. Jennifer will no longer be an innocent teenage girl but a maladjusted pervert who sells nude photos online. Max and I will no longer be the poor parents who miss their daughter but two horrible monsters who lost control of their child. Some people will think that we're the ones responsible.

Darling Jennifer, what are you doing?

My mind whirls faster and faster, and my vision flickers.

'Louise Wiksell.' My voice sounds strange. 'You are a bright woman. You are efficient and smart. So *be* that woman now, for Christ's sake. If there was ever a time you needed your skills, it's now.'

I turn to look at the screen again, reading and scrolling further up the conversation.

> Okay. I'll send the video when the money is in my account.
> Swish: 07023838762

Jennifer's last message to Willie Winkie was sent at 4.03 p.m. on Monday. This must have been right before Max drove her to Smilla's. She could have sent the message from the car, on her phone, but it doesn't really matter. The important thing is that we know Jennifer hasn't been active as Jennifer Wicked since the afternoon of New Year's Eve. And I suspect it will be simple for the police to trace Willie Winkie.

Jesus, what a creep. How can anyone have the nerve to use a screenname so closely linked to a nursery rhyme? When I was little, I loved that rhyme, and the idea of a sweet man in his nightgown making sure all the children were safe at home.

My fingers suddenly move across the keyboard. They're flying fast, and I see them forming words. Warning bells go off in my head, but I ignore them and press 'enter'.

> Sorry. Something came up.
> Can we meet up?

I stare at the screen, waiting for the three rolling dots that mean someone is typing.

I come to my senses and take a breath. What are the odds Willie Winkie is online at this very moment? Why would he want to meet up with a girl he's annoyed at? And what have I *done*?

The police are going to pick up the computer this evening. What if they take this message as a sign Jennifer is unharmed, and close the entire investigation?

I throw myself over the keyboard, move the arrow to my message and am just about to click 'delete' when three small dots show up.

New Year's Eve, 2015

Fredrik

'Come on in.' I put Vilgot down and wave the Wiksells into the house. 'Nina's in the shower and the kitchen is in total chaos, just as tradition dictates.'

Lollo glances at the mirror to make sure her hairdo survived the walk from the car to our front door.

'No problem,' she chirps. 'We'll lend a hand.'

The door is hardly closed before we hear more voices outside. Max opens it to greet Malena and Theo, who are shivering in the dark.

Apparently Malena is single again. The guy she brought last year didn't last long.

'Damn, it's cold.' Malena stamps snow off on the doormat and throws her arms around Max. 'All good?'

She squeezes further into the hall to hug Lollo. Nina comes dashing down the stairs. Damp hair and the distinct scent of Acqua di Giò. She joins in the hugging and then provides each guest with a coat hanger. Malena and Lollo change shoes; Theo steals upstairs to find Anton. Vilgot whines and tugs at his mom's dress.

'Where are you hiding Smilla?' Malena asks. She looks around.

'Last I saw her, she was trying on clothes,' Nina replies, scooping Vilgot into her arms.

I herd Malena, Lollo and Max towards the pre-dinner drinks that are waiting in the living room, and then turn to Jennifer.

'Run on up to find Smilla, she's –'

The words catch in my throat as I discover that Jennifer is still just inside the front door, still with all her outer-wear on.

'Well, hello.' I walk over to her. 'Just standing here?'

Jennifer gazes down at her black sneakers.

'Is everything okay?' I ask tentatively. 'Did something happen?'

She looks up at me with tears in her eyes. 'I hate Dad.'

'Oh, my. That sounds serious. What did he do now?'

I hope she doesn't take my comment as sarcasm. It seems completely understandable for Jennifer to be angry at Max. There's always a reason to be annoyed with that man.

'Dad said that my new year's resolution has to be to get a better grade in math.' Jennifer's eyes flash. 'Why does he always have to complain? And how can you even think about math on New Year's Eve?'

I throw up my hands. 'Seems like poor timing. Even for me.'

Jennifer shoots me a blank look. 'Even for you?'

'I'm a math teacher.'

She giggles and catches a tear with her index finger.

I meet her gaze.

'Are you having a hard time with math?'

Jennifer shrugs.

'I got a D. But it was close to an F.'

'Lucky it wasn't an F, then.'

Jennifer nods and sighs. 'But Dad thinks I should do better.'

Rage boils inside me. How can Max focus on the nega-tives when Jennifer has brilliant grades in every other subject? Why would a parent use such bad psychological judgement?

'You can't be the best at everything,' I say. 'And I'm sure your dad had good intentions with that new year's resolution. He probably thought it would encourage you, that you could tackle math together.'

Jennifer doesn't respond.

'If you want, I can help you,' I continue. 'Not today, I mean. But another day.'

'Would you?' Jennifer is eager. 'Dad and I always practically murder each other when he tries to help me. All his math is, like, from the Stone Age, and he refuses to learn the new way. I think Mom actually knows more, but she's useless at explaining it.'

'Of course I'll help you.' I reach out and take her coat. 'Now go up and see Smilla. She's waiting for you.'

Jennifer wipes away more tears, carefully, to avoid smearing her mascara. Then she toes out of her shoes and leaves the hall, heading upstairs.

Halfway up, she turns around. 'Fredrik . . .'

I stop short.

'Yes?'

Jennifer smiles. 'Thanks.'

'No problem. I love math.'

35. Lollo

I stare at the two little words in the grey window. I read them over and over again. I don't understand, I don't want to understand.

Too late.

What does he mean? What the hell does Willie Winkie mean that it's 'too late'? Surely he isn't saying that –

I feel feverish. Dizzy. What am I going to do? Is there anything I can do? Should I call the police again?

Then I take a deep breath and try to think logically. The police are on their way. Lina Torrero said they were going to pick up the computer. This isn't my job.

I take my phone from the bed and snap a photo of my message and the response that just arrived. Then I erase today's messages, close the chat with Willie Winkie and click on the speech bubble on the toolbar.

The most recent messages on the Jennifer Wicked page return to the screen. There aren't many of them, and I jump between them at random. One user, someone called Sound Judgement, has written something incomprehensible about 'tram'; another seems to want only to spew a lot of basic misogyny; and a third, who goes by the name Mama's Boy, supposedly got a photo sent to his phone.

My attention is drawn by the chat just below the Willie Winkie one. This man's name is Petter Silvén, and he must be pretty fucking stupid. Who visits sites like this without creating a fake account?

I lean closer to the screen and study Petter Silvén's face, then click on his photo to bring up his page. The cover photo shows a motorcycle parked in front of a brick façade. The photo itself is poor quality, greyish and blurry. Petter Silvén has no eye for aesthetics, that much is clear.

How old could he be? Twenty-five? Thirty-five? His eyes are blue and his brown hair is worn in a boring style. His sparse beard might be there to hide a double chin, but it's not working. The uneven patches only make him look grubby and unkempt.

I click to bring up the five messages Jennifer and Petter Silvén have exchanged. They were all sent on the same night, a few days before Christmas Eve.

> PETTER SILVÉN:
> You're hot. Meet irl?
> JENNIFER WICKED:
> It'll cost you
> PETTER SILVÉN:
> How much?
> JENNIFER WICKED:
> 3,000
> PETTER SILVÉN:
> 1,500?

Jennifer didn't even dignify that with an answer. She must have been insulted by the offer. In some sick way, I'm glad to see that Jennifer doesn't sell herself for just any bargain price, that she puts a high value on what she has to offer.

At that moment, I hear the sound of a car door closing. Are the police here already? I photograph all the names in Messenger, do the same with the friends list and email myself the document with the little poems. Chanel, sleeping beside me, jumps when I slam the lid of the laptop.

Max storms in the front door just as I'm coming down the stairs, and we almost collide.

'Where have you been? Why didn't you pick up when I called? Don't you know I worry about you?'

Three questions in a row are two too many for my husband. Without making eye contact, Max heads straight for the hooks under the hat rack.

'I had to work late.'

'Today?'

I clench my jaw and breathe through my nose.

Max hangs up his coat, then turns around to look at me with an expression that suggests I am an idiot.

'Yes. Today. I am in the middle of a sale, and neither the seller nor the buyer cares about my personal life. They want things to move quickly.'

I stare at Max and suddenly feel that for the first time I'm seeing him for who he really is. It's like he's standing there naked in front of me, without his expensive clothes and without the shiny Rolex around his wrist.

I don't like what I see. How the hell can he think about real estate when our daughter is missing? How can he care about his goddamn clients when Jennifer needs us more than ever before?

'Jesus Christ, you're insane! Our daughter is missing, and you have to *work late*!'

I stomp out of the kitchen, afraid of what might come out of my mouth next. My heart is pounding. I expect

Max to rush after me, to lecture me about how things work in the real world, that *business as usual* is the order of the day, if you want to survive as an entrepreneur 'in this goddamn communist state'.

But Max doesn't follow me. Instead he goes to the bathroom and runs the tap for an eternity. What is he doing?

I set Jennifer's laptop on the kitchen table and glance at the wall clock. It's almost quarter to eight. Lina Torrero said they would come get the computer this evening, and I'd been planning to tell Max about Jennifer Wicked before they did. But I don't feel like it any more.

A normal father in Max's situation would have left work early today. He wouldn't have stayed at the office longer than usual. No, hold on. A normal father in Max's situation wouldn't have fucking gone to work in the first place. He would have called in at the Malmö police and demanded that every resource be devoted to searching for his missing daughter. He wouldn't sit around talking on the phone to completely unimportant people who want to buy or sell a goddamn house.

'I'm sorry, Lollo.'

Max is standing in the kitchen entryway. And he really does look sorry. His greying curls hang in clumps; his eyes look tired.

I don't say anything, just wait for him to go on.

'It . . .' He takes a step towards me. 'I'm sorry I came home late. But there was something I just had to do.'

My fury is rekindled.

'How can *anything* be more important than Jennifer? What the hell is *wrong* with you?'

Max opens his mouth to say something but is interrupted by the harsh ring of the doorbell.

'That must be the police,' I say, picking up the laptop.

Max doesn't move a muscle.

'The police?'

'Yes.' I bite the inside of my cheek to keep from screaming at him again. '*The police* are looking for our daughter. As you may recall.'

Max doesn't say anything, so I go on: 'They're here to pick up Jennifer's computer. Unlike you, I'm trying to do something about this situation. Furthermore, *I* picked up the phone when the police tried to reach me.'

I pull open the door and icy air sweeps into the hall. On the steps is a young man in uniform who looks like he stepped straight out of the police academy. For some reason, I'm disappointed. I'd been hoping to see one of the officers who was here yesterday.

'Markus Svensson, Malmö Police,' he says, holding up his badge. 'I'm supposed to pick up a computer.'

'Here.' I hand it over. 'Do you need the charger too?'

'No, we'll manage.'

Markus Svensson must be a beat cop, and as such I'm sure he knows no more than we do about what's going on with the investigation. So it would be completely useless to mention what I've just found on Jennifer's laptop.

'Do you have Lina Torrero's direct line?' I ask.

As I recall, no number popped up on the screen when she called me earlier this afternoon.

'Call the operator and they'll transfer you,' he replies. 'Is there anything else I can help you with?'

I shake my head.

Markus Svensson turns on his heel and goes back to the patrol car in the street.

I wonder what the neighbours must be thinking. They

know what happened – they have the internet and read the paper – but this is like a reality show. A patrol car on their very own street, main characters they know personally. Can't get more exciting than that.

Just as I'm about to close the door, I think I see a flash from the bushes closest to the road. What on . . . I stretch to get a better look and, sure enough, behind the evergreens is a figure in black with a huge zoom lens aimed at our front door.

Shit.

I turn around to tell Max, but I don't see him.

'Max.'

I stay at the door; I don't want the crouching figure to vanish from sight.

'Max!'

The second time I shout, the figure gets up. An enormous camera hangs from a strap around his neck. I expect him to run away, but instead he takes a step on to the path and into the glow of the streetlight.

'Are you Louise?'

I purse my lips.

'Nisse Nylén, *Kvällsposten*.' The man takes another step in my direction, and now I can make out a bloated face under his black hood. 'Can I get a statement about Jennifer's disappearance? Do you know anything further?'

How does he have the nerve? I slam the door so hard that the doorframe rattles, and, when I turn around, Max is right behind me.

'What's going on?'

'I just found someone from *Kvällsposten* in the bushes. Those fucking parasites.'

198

Max shrugs. 'Sure, but it's to be expected, right? Missing teenagers are always a hot item in the media. People like reading about that stuff.'

'I know.' I glare at him. 'But this time it's *us*. And our *daughter*.'

Max approaches me and places a hand on my shoulder. 'You didn't say anything, did you?'

'Of course not.'

Max smiles.

And I am befuddled. A nasty journalist is sneaking around in our bushes and my husband seems relieved. Pleased and relieved.

Suddenly my head is burning. Red and orange spots dance in my vision and I throw myself at him blindly.

'How the hell can you just stand there looking happy?' My fists hammer his chest. 'How can you be happy when Jennifer is missing? Why don't you care?'

'Lollo, that's enough. Of course I care, but it's just –'

Max tries to fend me off, but I've found a strength I wasn't aware of and can't stop hitting him.

'I've been roaming around the house by myself all day.' My face is full of tears and snot. 'You didn't even call to check on me. What kind of person are you? What kind of father are you? How can work come before your own child? Are you completely devoid of feelings, or –'

'Lollo!' Max roars. 'Calm down.'

I've stopped hitting him, but instead I grab the lamp on the bureau in the hall and throw it full force on to the tiled floor. The sound of the glass shattering is wonderful.

'Lollo, get a hold of yourself!' Max takes a step in my direction. 'You're acting hysterical, goddamnit!'

A sudden calm washes over me. I stand my ground, fixing my gaze on my husband and staring into his wide eyes.

'Our daughter has been missing without a trace for almost two days. What would you say is more normal? Being hysterical? Or being indifferent?'

36. Nina

I've just come down from upstairs after an unusually protracted bedtime for Vilgot, when Fredrik appears in the
kitchen. He's wearing the same jeans as before, but has put
on a fresh t-shirt, and his hair is damp, so he must have
showered.

I turn on the tap brusquely and grab the dishcloth.

'The leftovers are in the fridge.'

My voice is cold and I really don't want to be an ice
queen, but I'm having trouble getting past our last conversation. I just can't forget how he snapped at me, how he
brushed off my fears.

And, besides, the kitchen is in exactly the same shape
that it was when I went upstairs with Vilgot a few
hours ago.

'Thanks.' Fredrik comes to me. 'I think I'll just have a
cup of tea.'

I turn off the tap, wring out the dishcloth and start rubbing dried tomato sauce off the counter. Fredrik needs to
get something in his stomach. Despite the attempt at
freshening up, he looks incredibly worn out.

I cast a glance over my shoulder. 'Don't you want something to eat?'

He shakes his head. 'I guess my stomach needs a break.'

I go back to the counter and find it's as clean as a
scratched-up old wooden countertop from IKEA can be.

The dishcloth gets another rinse before I drape it over the tap and look at Fredrik again.

'But surely some toast couldn't hurt.'

He doesn't seem to hear me. Instead he fills the kettle, turns it on and puts an arm around my waist.

'You'll keep me company, right?'

'What?'

'Don't look so shocked.' He smiles and lets his hand slide down over my bottom. 'I asked if you wanted a cup of tea.'

Without thinking, I take a step to the side, realizing a moment too late that I've just pulled away from my own husband. I feel silly.

'I don't know.' The digital clock above the oven says it's almost nine thirty. 'It's been a long day . . .'

Fredrik opens the middle cabinet and takes out two mugs, the blue ones we bought from that delightful potter on Gotland last summer.

'Come on, Nina.' He opens the pantry, and takes stock of the tea stash, selects two kinds and puts the boxes on the counter. 'You said you wanted to talk.'

'I did. Earlier this afternoon.' I start for the hall. 'Can't we do this tomorrow instead?'

Maybe I'm being a hypocrite. Deep down, I want nothing more than to talk to Fredrik. I want to know more about his problems at work, and I want to help him solve them.

At the same time, though, I really want to give him a taste of his own medicine.

'Hold on.'

Fredrik comes after me and puts a hand on my arm. It's not a mild gesture; he grabs me hard enough to make me stop. I turn around and am startled when I see his face. There's something about his expression, a shift in his blue eyes that I can't interpret.

A split second later, he lets go and returns to the counter.

'Here's what we'll do,' he says. 'You get ready for bed, put on your pyjamas and stuff.' He fishes two teaspoons from the silverware drawer and turns around, waving the spoons in my direction. 'Meanwhile, I'll fix the tea. Chamomile with milk and honey, right?'

The question is posed with a smile, and my animosity fades.

It is rather sweet of him, after all, to be so concerned that we get a moment together. My persistence must have paid off – he has finally realized we need to talk.

'That sounds nice,' I say, feigning nonchalance.

37. Fredrik

Just after one in the morning, I dare to assume the whole family is asleep – or at least that they are in their rooms, busy playing video games or watching a movie. Smilla and Anton have totally flipped night and day now that it's Christmas vacation.

I fold back the covers and slip out of bed. Nina turns over and sighs, and for a moment I think she's about to wake up.

She shouldn't be able to. I dissolved a sleeping pill in her tea before we went to bed, and she drank it all as I sat beside her on the sofa. To be sure, the effects are strongest for the first few hours. Maybe the pill has stopped working already.

I stand stock still in the dark, listening to my wife's easy, regular inhalations and trying to calm my own. As soon as her breathing gets heavier, I take my phone in one hand, my clothes in the other, and sneak out the bedroom door.

A few minutes later I'm leaving the house and stepping into the starry night.

We have a modern Japanese car. It's quiet; it makes a purring sound that reminds me of a stand mixer. Still, when the engine starts, I feel like I've just turned over a rumbling V8. I fear that the whole neighbourhood is suddenly sitting straight up in bed, and I expect to see Nina's face in the bedroom window any second now.

But nothing happens. No lights come on, no doors open.

With my lights off, I back out of the driveway and crawl slowly through our row-house neighbourhood. When I reach Agnesfridvägen, I turn on the lights, press the gas pedal harder and drive down towards Inre Ringvägen.

Traffic is light. Of course it is. Who is out on the road at this hour besides professional drivers, emergency services and shady types?

This whole situation is absurd. As recently as two days ago, I was a perfectly ordinary middle-aged father, a popular teacher with good references, a man with a broad social network. I was far from perfect; we all make mistakes. But now I don't know who I am any more. I'm a different Fredrik, an unfamiliar man.

When I reach Badvägen my heart begins to pound uncontrollably, and I consider pulling a U-turn. If there's anywhere I should not be seen, this is it. Especially not in the middle of the night. An intense wave of nausea comes over me, and the cold sweat makes my hands slip on the wheel. It's not too late to turn around, but I force myself to go on.

The school parking lot is empty and a lone car sticks out, but it would be beyond stupid to stop too close to the grove, so I decide to park outside the school building after all.

With my hood up over my hat and my eyes on the asphalt, I hurry along the deserted sidewalk. On the footpath, protected by the surrounding houses and trees, it feels a little easier to breathe.

A few minutes later I reach the grove. The moonlight and the streetlamps help me scan the area. I'm systematic about it, leaving nothing to chance. All I can hear is my own breathing and the frozen leaves crunching beneath my feet.

The police might have been here to look around. If I left anything behind, it might already be tucked into one of those transparent evidence bags they use – at least in the movies.

But if they haven't been here yet – or if they were here but were a little sloppy – there's a chance some object that could lead back to me is littering the area. Nina mentioned some loose threads on my coat. Could a thread count as evidence?

I broaden my search area, looking further out towards the road and approaching the widest path that crosses through the grove. My feet kick at tufts of grass; my hands bend back thickets. I see a flash of something among the leaves and crouch down. It turns out to be a frozen puddle.

I didn't leave anything behind here. And the rain from New Year's Day will have washed away any flecks of blood.

I get the sudden sense that someone's watching me and jog back towards Badvägen. Just as I turn right to head for the car, I spot two bicycle lights. They're near the school and approaching fast. Two voices echo through the silence.

It's not a well-considered action. On pure instinct I twist my body a quarter-turn and cross the street. Instead of following the path, I keep going into the trees, tripping over rocks, stumps and fallen branches. A thorn, maybe from a blackberry bush, scratches my cheek and a deep rabbit hole nearly fells me.

The undergrowth is thick here, not suitable for night-time walks. But right now the lack of accessibility can only be an advantage – no bicycle lights or curious eyes can reach me here.

A moment later I'm standing at the edge of the limestone quarry and gazing out at the black water. The treetops are reflected in the shiny surface, which shimmers with moonlight. It's beautiful and eerie at the same time; it reminds me of all the ghost stories I read as a kid. Stories about people who died a painful, unjust death and later came back to get revenge on their killers.

The cyclists pass. I can't see them, but I hear their lively chatter from a distance. An icy wind sweeps in from the quarry, dissolving their voices. I shudder and am just about to step into the road when something makes me glance at the water again.

I see something way down there. A bundle.

My pulse hammers at my throat as I lean out over the steep slope. At first all I can see is my own breath, and I wonder if it was an illusion. But, a moment later, the bundle is back.

It's some sort of fabric. It's caught on a branch and part of it seems to be below the surface of the water.

With one hand I grab a rough tree trunk so I can lean even further over the edge, and I gasp.

A small detail, a narrow belt, has worked its way out of the fabric and is following the motions of the water like seaweed.

That information is more than enough. It's all I need.

That soaking wet piece of fabric is a lightweight black coat.

3 January 2019
Thursday

38. Lollo

Who can sleep when their child hasn't come home? When there are no shoes in the hall and the bed stands empty? Who can relax with a mind full of ruminating thoughts?

It's almost four thirty, and I haven't slept a wink. My heart is pitter-pattering just beneath my skin, and I'm freezing despite the comforter and an extra blanket. I can't seem to close my eyes. I stare into the dark, looking at all the normal, familiar things around me without seeing them.

All I want is to hear the sound of a key in the lock, the rustle of a coat and the padding of socked feet. I want the door of the microwave to be closed – bam! – too hard. I want to hear the clatter of a spoon stirring cocoa powder into warm milk. I want the light to be on when I walk into the kitchen for my morning coffee. And I want to find the half-empty milk carton forgotten on the counter.

But the house is quiet. So quiet that I sporadically hear Chanel's tiny sighs from her basket in the hall during the night. There's nothing from upstairs. Max seems to be sleeping soundly.

This is the first time in our twenty-plus years of marriage that I've *chosen* not to sleep in the same room as Max. We've had to sleep separately for various reasons before, but not even when Jennifer was little did we do so voluntarily. If she woke up at night, I would go to her room and sit beside her crib until she fell back asleep. Then I would return to our room and crawl in beside Max.

I didn't want to have Jennifer in our bed. I was afraid she would suck all our energy and ruin our relationship, which has always been pretty dependent on sex. I thought it would be preferable if Jennifer just sucked all the energy out of me, so Max was well rested when he left for work. I would only be at home anyway.

Now, seventeen years later, I can see that this was a bad decision. Staying home with a baby is at least as demanding as hawking houses and apartments. Especially when you've got a fussy baby. If I'd brought Jennifer into our bed, Max probably wouldn't have slept quite as well. But *I* would have had twice as much sleep. It seems likely I would have been a better mother, a mother with patience and energy.

When I look back on Jennifer's new-born days, it's nothing but a fog. But I never complained. I didn't dare to complain, since I was the one who compelled Max to give me a child. To be perfectly honest, I had to shed a few tears to convince him to contribute his sperm. He was completely uninterested in creating a family. Then, as now, his job came first. But I know Max loves Jennifer in his own special way.

At least, that's what I believed up until yesterday.

We went to bed angry. Against all recommendations. But I simply couldn't apologize. I meant every word I said, and I stand by them. There must be something wrong with Max.

After I'd swept up the shards of glass from the hall floor, I called the police and successfully convinced them – despite the late hour – to transfer me to Lina Torrero. I was surprised when she actually picked up.

'I almost expected to get your voicemail,' I said. 'Do you work around the clock?'

She replied that 'There's a certain amount of overtime involved when you're in the middle of an investigation.' Being in the middle of an investigation makes it sound, to my ears, as if they've got tons to go on. But, in fact, Lina Torrero had no new information to share. 'We're plugging away.'

Without mentioning my little transgression, I told her what I'd found on Jennifer's computer. And, the fact is, it was a relief to share my discovery with someone. Even though that someone was a police officer. Lina Torrero didn't pass judgement, or at least she didn't seem to. She listened without interrupting me and asked a few questions when I was done.

I expect Max's reaction will be the polar opposite. And that's one of the reasons I haven't said anything to him yet.

'My colleague just arrived with the computer,' Lina Torrero said during our conversation. 'The technicians will look through it tonight.'

I asked if she thought Willie Winkie could be involved somehow.

'He certainly could be,' Torrero replied. 'But we'll continue to investigate multiple possibilities simultaneously.'

What those possibilities might be, she couldn't tell me 'due to the ongoing nature of the investigation'. I was, however, informed that the police were planning to bring a search-and-rescue dog to Klagshamn. She couldn't say whether it would be happening immediately or in the morning.

In addition, Missing People had been in touch to say they're planning to organize folks to comb our area this afternoon. The push had come from a few of Jennifer's classmates, and, according to the police contact at Missing People, the general public has shown great interest in participating in the search.

My first reaction was panic. Then I felt guilty. *We* should have contacted Missing People, us, Jennifer's parents. I shouldn't have hesitated; I should have reported her disappearance on their website right away. What will people think, to know that her classmates got in there before her own family did?

Lina Torrero put my mind at ease, saying she was grateful I had managed to get into Jennifer's laptop. She assured me that no one is going to think about who organized the search. And she made it clear that everyone completely understands when next of kin don't have the strength to participate.

But of course we'll participate. Well, I intend to, at least. I have no idea what Max is planning to do.

I hear a car engine revving down the street. I pick up my phone and see that it's 4.35 now. Apparently one of the neighbours must leave for work at this hour. Poor soul.

Instead of putting my phone down again, I check for recent messages. Nothing has happened since I last checked around two o'clock. People are asleep. People whose children are safe in their beds are asleep at this hour.

I open my email and find five unread messages there. One of them is the email I sent to myself, the one with Jennifer's poems. My index finger stops above the blue-and-white icon. Something tells me to hold back. Maybe I'm afraid of getting too close to an uncomfortable truth.

But what could be worse than what I've already learned? Not much.

I open the document and start to read, ploughing through one poem after the next.

> 23 June 2018
> Only you
> No one else understands me.
> You see my soul.

> 15 July 2018
> I admit that it's crazy
> But I want you.

> And I know you want me.
> Deep down, you do.
> So why won't you say it?

I close the document. The poems still aren't any help. There are no names, no places. Nothing.

A sudden whim makes me open the web browser and Google my way to an address finder. I want to find some personal information. I type 'Petter Silvén' into the search field and discover, as it loads, that my hands are shaking. Must be the lack of sleep.

When the results pop up on the screen, I get goose-bumps all over. The man in question lives just a few hundred metres away from us – in one of those linked houses over by the shop. That can't be a coincidence. Jennifer told people she was going home. But, in reality, she must have planned to meet this Silvén guy. Their conversation on Messenger ended abruptly, but it could have continued by text or on Snap.

I click on the name and learn that Petter Silvén will turn thirty-two on 3 April. If I like, I can send him flowers via Interflora. Apparently he shares an address with someone called Sandra Larsson, but that makes no difference to me. Just because a person lives with a partner doesn't mean they're any less likely to commit crimes.

Fifteen minutes later, I'm standing on the sidewalk outside Petter Silvén's home and trying to see right through the peach-coloured brick walls. My heart is pounding. Is my Jennifer inside? Is this where she's being held prisoner? I want to run up and bang on the door, scream at the top of my lungs, wake that bastard up and drag him into the street.

But I stay put, staring at the black windows, which seem to be staring right back. There's no light on anywhere, no sign of life. Maybe it's no wonder, given the time of day.

A classic family car, some model of station wagon, is parked in front of the garage. Someone has placed a big grey pot next to the front door and stuck an undersized decorative fir tree in it. The space in front of the linked house is divided into three narrow rectangles: lawn, flagstone and asphalt. Neat but unimaginative.

When a light comes on inside the house, I take a quick step to the side, trying to find a spot behind the hedge where I won't be spotted. A woman dressed in a long black quilted coat with a hood might seem a little suspicious. Especially if she's standing stock still and staring at a stranger's house at five in the morning. I should get out of here before one of the neighbours calls the police.

After a brief trip up and down the quiet street, I'm

back in the same spot. At that very moment, an advent star lights up in one of Silvén's windows and I try without much success to hide. My phone will have to be my alibi. I pretend to look at it even as I sneak glances at the window.

The whole room is lit up now. The kitchen is done all in white: white paint on the walls, white cabinets. It hurts my eyes. A blonde woman with a little baby on her arm is moving around inside. Apparently Sandra Larsson and Petter Silvén are new parents.

What a fucking cliché. New dad can't get any and searches for sex online.

Jesus Christ. I'd like to knock on the window and tell Sandra Larsson what her despicable partner is getting up to while she's feeding the baby and changing diapers.

A light comes on upstairs, and I turn on my heel and rush off.

39. Nina

'You don't have to come.'

Smilla and I are walking along Östra Tullgatan. It's just past nine in the morning, and the pale winter sun is only just making its way between the tall buildings.

'But I *want* to come,' I say. 'I at least want to make sure you know where to go.'

My daughter sighs. 'I'm not five any more. I can ask someone if I can't find my way.'

A thin layer of ice has formed on the canal. We cross the bridge and follow the water along Exercisgatan. A lone gull sails over our heads and lands on the ice. The grass on the slope is stiff with hoarfrost and looks like it's been dipped in sugar.

'Come on.' I pull Smilla across the street, where the massive complex towers loom over us. 'We have to hurry.'

The gable wall to our right is decorated with coats of arms. I can only identify the topmost one, which is for the police, but symbols like keys and axes give a certain amount of insight into the general goings-on here. At least in my imagination.

Shiny metal letters inform us that we have arrived at the judicial centre. I pull the door open and we walk in. Smilla is no longer protesting. Maybe she finds it comforting to have her mother nearby after all.

'Smilla Andersson, is it?' asks the woman behind the glass.

A visitor's badge is slipped through the narrow opening. 'Please take a seat while you wait.'

The woman points at the benches behind us.

I'm just about to ask if I can be present while Smilla is interviewed when my phone starts ringing in my bag. With an apologetic smile for the woman in the booth, I step aside and take out my phone.

It's Mom. And I notice that she's also just sent a text full of capital letters and exclamation marks. My guess is she missed yesterday's notice in *Sydsvenskan* and has only just now seen today's front page.

Thank you, Claudia.

Smilla sits down on a bench as I move a few more steps away from the glass booth.

'Hi, Mom. Sorry I didn't answer your text, I didn't see it –'

'I just read about Jennifer,' she interrupts. 'Oh my God, Nina, we just about choked on our coffee here at breakfast. Why didn't you say anything? It's dreadful. *Dreadful.*'

'I know. It's awful. I –'

'What could have happened?' Mom cuts me off again. 'Surely she can't have . . . how is Smilla holding up?'

'Smilla's okay,' I say. 'She's right here. We're at the police station.'

'The police station!' Mom cries. 'But why? I hope she isn't a suspect in –'

'Mom, please, calm down. If you'll be quiet for two seconds, I'll tell you what's going on.'

'I'm sorry, Nina, I –'

'I know this comes as a shock. I was on the verge of calling you more than once yesterday, but it just didn't happen – everything has been such a blur.' I pause, trying to remember what Mom actually asked, and then I go on:

'No one is any sort of suspect. The police just want to talk to Smilla because she's one of the last people who saw Jennifer before she went missing.'

'Did something happen at the party?' Mom asks. 'Is there some reason she took off and never came back?'

I turn around and look at the bench where Smilla was just sitting. It's empty.

'Nina?' Mom sounds worried. 'Are you still there?'

I scan the lobby, examining every bench and following the row of windows to the glass wall that faces the entrance. No Smilla.

'I'll call you back in a bit.'

Holding tightly to my phone, I hurry over to the booth. 'Excuse me.'

The woman behind the glass looks up from her computer screen.

'Did you see whether someone came to get my daughter Smilla just now? I was on the phone and I must have missed –'

The woman smiles. 'The detective was here thirty seconds ago. Your daughter is in good hands.'

A wave of heat washes over me. I'm sweating rivers under my down coat and I open the zipper.

'But I thought that I could maybe . . .' I yank off my scarf. 'That I could be there during the interview. Isn't there supposed to be a guardian present if you're under eighteen?'

'Not necessarily,' the woman says. 'Would you like me to call someone?'

I shake my head, thank her for her help and head for the exit.

A steady stream of visitors passes through the glass doors in both directions, and I leave the building in the wake of a younger couple. They appear to be a few years older than Smilla and Jennifer, but their faces are much more harrowed. Why are they here?

In a flash, my brain has painted a biased picture of difficult family circumstances, substance abuse and criminality. As soon as the couple get outside, the girl pulls a crumpled pack of cigarettes from her coat pocket, which, in some peculiar way, confirms my bias. The girl lights a cigarette and pulls in the smoke as though it's a life-sustaining substance.

I find a spot to stand not far from the main entrance. My coat is still open and the cold air feels wonderful as it finds its way under my shirt. Is it normal to have hot flashes before fifty? Maybe I should get these sweats checked out. And, even if they are normal, they're a huge pain.

The tall, dark building reaches for the winter sky. I study the façade. Is Smilla behind one of those many windows? It irks me that she's being questioned without me, but, on the other hand, maybe it's for the best. Hopefully she can give a more honest version of what happened on New Year's Eve without me in the room. After all, she's well aware of my views on that blasted party.

In fact, it seems to me that Fredrik could have dragged himself out of bed and come with Smilla today. He was the one who convinced me to let the girls party at our place. He should have to deal with the consequences. But Fredrik refused to get out of bed this morning, claiming that he hadn't had a moment's sleep all night. I don't think he's lying, but he sure could try a little harder. For Smilla's sake.

To be perfectly honest, I'm almost more worried about Fredrik's health than Jennifer's disappearance. I would never say so out loud, but it's the truth. I can't help how I feel. Jennifer is our friends' daughter, someone I've always had trouble getting my head around. Fredrik is my husband. He's the father of my three children, and, although I'm finding him hard to love at the moment, I do love him and have for years.

That talk we were supposed to have last night was a total fiasco. In my naivety, I believed that Fredrik would open up to me, but as soon as we sat down on the sofa he seemed to have other ideas. We didn't say anything new, just bolted down our tea and sniped at each other for a while. It all came to a miserable end when I was suddenly bone-tired and had to go to bed.

Before Smilla and I drove into town, I suggested Fredrik call the clinic and try to get a doctor's appointment, preferably for today or at least later this week. Just so they can run some tests and check his blood pressure and listen to his heart. Because something is off. Fredrik hasn't been himself since New Year's Day, and yesterday's sudden attack doesn't exactly make me less anxious. Sure, the nausea could be stress-related, but it's always best to rule out physical causes before you decide the issue is down to your mental health.

The lack of sleep can't be helping. Maybe he can get a prescription for a mild sleeping tablet. If not, he could try one of mine. They work pretty well.

An older woman passes on the sidewalk. She looks like Mom and I fish out my phone.

'How's it going?' she asks. 'Is the interrogation over?'

The below-freezing temperatures start to get to me and I pull my scarf out of my purse, wrapping it around my neck as best I can with one hand.

'No, she's in there now.'

'Without you!' Mom's voice is shrill. 'They're interrogating a minor without a guardian present?'

I sigh.

'Smilla's almost eighteen, and she didn't want me to come along.'

'But can that be legal?'

'I guess it must be.' A fresh hot flash goes through my body and I loosen the scarf. 'It's the Swedish police questioning her, not a terrorist organization.'

If Mom is annoyed by my remark, she hides it well.

'You're still coming on Saturday, right?'

'Yes, that's the plan, anyway. But I'm not quite sure about Fredrik –'

'Why? Is he sick?'

Thank you again, Claudia.

I don't relate the whole story, but it doesn't help – Mom is still worried. I came by my paranoid tendencies honestly. We decide to talk again soon.

I put my phone back in my pocket and see Smilla coming through the doors. A young woman, nearly grown and well on her way to an independent life. I gasp for breath and feel, for an instant, how the ground sways beneath my feet.

Jennifer is missing. Truly missing. And it could just as easily have been Smilla.

40. Lollo

My heart is racing; a scream echoes in my mind. I open my eyes wide and look around. The coffee table, the rug and the artwork on the opposite wall – it's all familiar, all specifically selected by me. My pulse slowly returns to normal, and I'm back in reality. A reality that's much worse than the dream I just awoke from.

I was dreaming about Jennifer. She was on the sofa in our summer cottage in Falsterbo. I tried to talk to her, but she wouldn't respond; it was as if there were a glass wall between us. Jennifer was just as clear as a high-resolution photograph with perfect focus. Yet she couldn't hear me.

My dreams are usually vague and incoherent, so maybe last night's images are a sign. Could my subconscious be trying to tell me something important?

Typically I don't believe in interpreting dreams, tarot cards and all that hocus-pocus. I believe in facts. Full stop. But my daughter is missing, and I'm prepared to turn to fortune-tellers, mediums – anyone at all. If someone were to call and tell me Jennifer went to the moon, I'd do anything to get myself there.

Chanel comes prancing across the floor and stops in front of the sofa. I lift her up and bury my face in her soft fur. Is Jennifer in Falsterbo? Could it be that simple?

The officers who were here on New Year's Day asked if there's anywhere Jennifer might have run off to for unknown reasons. We mentioned the summer cottage, and maybe they went down to check it out on Tuesday evening. But I'm sure they haven't been back since, and she could have arrived later.

I kick off the blanket and sit up on the sofa, reaching for my phone. Why haven't the police called? Haven't they brought the search-and-rescue dogs to Klagshamn yet? Or maybe they were here, but didn't find anything. I gulp. Didn't find any*one*.

Then again, this should be a good sign. If there's no trace of Jennifer nearby, that can only mean one thing: she's somewhere else.

It's almost ten o'clock. Strangely enough, after my outing to Petter Silvén's house, I managed to fall asleep. I woke up again when Max got up, but I pretended to be sound asleep until the front door opened and closed. I must have dropped off again once he was gone.

How the hell can he go to work? Does he just not give a damn that Jennifer is missing? Or is he trying to avoid *me* by staying away? We should be supporting each other at a time like this.

A vague thought slips into my mind. My heart beats faster and my mouth goes dry. I fumble for the glass of water on the table in front of me, trying to shake off the thought before it takes hold. But it's burrowed in under my skin, irritating and bothering me like a poisonous thorn.

How can I really be so certain Max is at work? My husband has sure as hell been acting strange ever since Jennifer went missing. He's hardly shown his face here at home. And, when he is here, he's pretty distant. Emotionless.

But if Max isn't at work – where is he?

The poison spreads. I lift my nose from Chanel's fur

and take another sip of water. I put the glass down and gaze at the room, arguing with myself.

No, says a powerful voice inside me. Max has many faults and shortfalls, but he would never – never, ever – be capable of hurting Jennifer.

On the other hand, Max has never taken more than a lukewarm interest in his daughter. I'm the one who's had to go to all the parent–teacher and progress meetings. I can count on the fingers of one hand all the times my husband went to a soccer match, even though Jennifer played for almost nine years. And, while I'll never win a Nobel prize for patience myself, Max has basically zero patience for Jennifer. She often drives him mad.

For most people, there's a huge step between being angry with someone and physically lashing out at them. I've never seen Max resort to violence. No, wait, that's not true. He did once beat the shit out of some guy who accidentally spilled beer on me. But that was years ago, just after we met. Max was younger back then, and more of a hothead.

He might have *accidentally* hurt Jennifer. By mistake. Jennifer might have annoyed him, said something stupid. But when would that have been? We were having a party here, and Max was practically glued to the computer, choosing songs and pouring drinks all night.

My body quakes as if it wants to help me dispel these thoughts. They're absurd and completely beyond reason. Am I cracking up?

I need to hear his voice, hear him promise me that Jennifer will come back, that everything will be fine.

My phone has slipped out of my hand. I pick it up, unlock the screen and find 'Max'.

One ring.

I don't even understand where this anxiety is coming from. For heaven's sake, this is my own husband I'm calling.

Two rings.

My heart is beating so hard it hurts.

Three rings.

It goes to voicemail.

That settles it.

I stand up. Chanel, who was still in my lap, rolls down my legs and lands on the rug with a shrill yelp. I mutter an apology and run down to the bedroom.

The bed is unmade and the blinds are down; my cosy sweatsuit is tossed on the wicker chair. I pull the pants on over my nightgown, ignoring the fact that it gets all bunched up at the waist. The zipper of the hoodie won't cooperate, so I leave it open. There's a hair band on the vanity. I pull my greasy hair into a low ponytail but don't dare to look in the mirror. When was the last time I showered?

My purse is still where I left it on my way to the shop yesterday morning. The thought of Lollo's Design stops me in my tracks. Should I put a note on the door?

It's simple: no. All I should do is look for Jennifer.

Chanel, who seems to have recovered from being dumped on the floor, comes bounding over when she hears me at the front door. She thinks I'm going to the shop, and wants to come along. Her disappointed eyes follow me out.

As I jog towards the driveway I dig my car key out of my purse. I unlock the car and hop in. My red Mini Cooper is the apple of my eye, but today it's nothing but a mode of transportation. A machine that will carry me from Point A to Point B.

From Klagshamn to Falsterbo.

41. Fredrik

A crack runs diagonally across the bedroom ceiling. It was there when we moved in but has become longer with each passing year. During the first few years we lived here, Nina complained daily that we should hire a builder to put up drywall instead. But we haven't managed to get around to it. There's always something else that needs fixing, in some other part of the house, something more urgent.

I observe the irregular black line above my head and concentrate on thinking only about it.

The crack. Think about the crack, Fredrik.

If we had more money, I wouldn't hesitate to bring in loads of builders to fix everything at once: the upstairs bathroom, the kitchen, the whole shebang. But builders are always wanting to be paid, and kitchens and bathrooms aren't exactly cheap rooms to renovate. And, unfortunately, I'm not a do-it-yourself type. If there's any trait I would have liked to inherit from my dad, it would have been his handiness. But he kept that gene to himself.

When I told Dad I'd quit engineering and started studying to become a teacher, I'd never seen him so disappointed. It was like the last spark of light left him.

But, for me, it was a huge relief. Sitting cooped up in an office and calculating material stresses all day was soul-crushing; it wasn't a good fit for me at all. The chance to educate young people, supporting them and watching them develop, felt a thousand times more meaningful.

With emphasis on *felt*.

My gaze wanders along the crack and stops at the light fixture, where a fine spiderweb is taking shape. A pale spider with a small body and long, skinny legs is working on a web that most closely resembles fuzz.

I happen to think of Max Wiksell. That man certainly never needs to pinch a penny. And his house is in no need of renovations. Instead of staying put in the row house they purchased when the kids arrived, like we did, he had quite the pool mansion slapped together just a few kilometres from the sea. I'm not envious of the house in the least – it's way too gaudy for my taste – but it would be nice to have a little more money left over at the end of each month.

It strikes me that, if I'd kept working as an engineer, I could be earning more than twice as much as I do today. But it wouldn't have been worth it.

I close my eyes. How the hell can I be thinking about renovations when I'll probably never get to see the results? Will Nina even be able to stay in this house on only one salary? Is there any sort of insurance that pays out when a family member ends up behind bars?

And how will those around us react when the truth comes out?

The shame I feel when facing my family is the worst. That I've betrayed my children feels worse than my betrayal of Nina. She's an adult and will, with any luck, be able to move on without lasting effects. But children are so sensitive. The things you experience in childhood can leave deep scars.

Like for Jennifer.

Think about the crack.

It's not helping. I open my eyes, stare at the spider

above my head and ask myself for the thousandth time how everything could have gone so thoroughly to hell.

My right hand strikes the comforter, pounding hard and frantically. That doesn't help either. The mattress gives way under the blows of my fist, providing no resistance. I want to hit something until my knuckles bleed.

The crack!

Simon slit his wrists in the bathtub. Mom was the one who found him, when she came home from work, and I often wonder how long he lay there before he died; I wonder what he was thinking about. How much time do you have to think? How long does it take for your life to drain away?

Sometimes I have this dream in which Simon changes his mind and calls for help. In it, I usually see myself running like a madman without ever getting anywhere.

Tears spring to my eyes. I try to make my mind a blank, but I can't do it. The coat is on the bottom of a dumpster in Elisedal now. Yet there it hangs in my consciousness like a black storm cloud.

I don't know what I was thinking. Why did I pick it up? Why didn't I just leave it there? If someone finds the coat now, it's all over.

Shit. Shit, shit, shit!

I wipe my tears on the comforter and hear a familiar voice droning in my head.

You didn't do anything, Fredrik.

You just talked to Jennifer.

And then you drove home.

I hear the front door close, and the sound yanks me back into the real world. The world where people ask questions, demand answers and want you to get out of bed.

I've spent the whole morning wrapped up in my covers like a pupa in a protective cocoon. I've slipped in and out of sleep, trying to pass the time and keep my thoughts under control. The boys haven't bothered me even once. It's surprising how quiet and calm a six-year-old can be if you give him unlimited screen time.

Determined heels approach the bedroom.

The crack, Fredrik. The crack.

'How are you feeling?'

Nina sits on the edge of the bed, bringing with her the scent of fresh air. She strokes my hair, and I resist a powerful urge to shove her hand away. Her touch makes me feel uneasy.

'So-so,' I say. 'How'd things go for Smilla?'

Nina shrugs. 'Fine, I guess. She said they asked more or less the same questions as they asked here, the day before yesterday.'

'We should fix this ceiling,' I say.

'I think we should work on fixing you first.'

Nina smiles and I try to smile back, but I'm not sure if it works.

'Are you coming up to Mom and Dad's with us this weekend?' she continues.

'I don't think so.' My eyes go back to the crack. 'I think I need a few more days' rest.'

'So it's that bad, then?' She sighs. 'Sounds to me like you need to take sick leave. Have you called the clinic yet?'

'I've been sleeping.'

Nina sighs again. 'Please, Fredrik,' she says at last. 'Call the clinic. For my sake, if nothing else. I'm *worried* about you. What if you get worse?'

Nina falls silent, running the fingers of one hand back

and forth across the comforter, smoothing invisible wrinkles in the floral duvet cover.

'Sounds like the police asked some questions about us too.' She looks at me. 'I didn't quite understand it, but, the way Smilla put it, they asked about our relationship with Jennifer.'

'What kind of nonsense is that?' I sit up. 'Is that how they think they're going to find her? By asking about *us*?'

Nina's eyes are shiny and wet. 'Oh, Fredrik!' She buries her face in her hands and sobs. 'I feel so guilty.'

'Guilty?'

'Yeah.' Nina rubs her eyes and lets her hands fall to her lap. 'For one thing: that *goddamn* party.' She glares at me. 'Jennifer got drunk *here*. She was *here* when she argued with Smilla, and she disappeared from *here*.'

I make a feeble attempt to protest, but Nina goes on. 'For another thing – and this is the part that's really getting to me – I've always treated her badly.'

Can't she just shut up?

'What do you mean, "treated"?'

'Come on, you *know* I've never been a huge fan of Jennifer. I thought it was such a pain when she and Smilla were so intensely close for a while. All these things are always happening around Jennifer. Bad things. But I never took the time to ask how she was doing, I never cared. I just got annoyed because I thought she was a handful.' Nina snuffles. 'And now . . . what if something terrible happened to her just because no one bothered to care?'

'She has parents,' I say. 'If Jennifer was having problems, it wasn't up to you to fix them.'

Nina's eyes are full of reproach. 'Any adult who notices

that a child is faring poorly is duty-bound to help. It's called being a decent human being, Fredrik.'

I bite the inside of my cheek hard and taste blood.

'Come off it, Nina. You don't know anything about Jennifer's feelings. Maybe she just wants to push boundaries.'

'But what if it isn't . . . what if she . . .' Nina gives another sob. 'What if she's dead?'

I pat her arm. 'Jennifer will turn up again.'

Nina shakes her head and looks at me mistrustfully. 'I thought so at first, but it's been days. Where on earth could she be?'

'Anywhere.' I try to keep my voice steady. 'With a guy, with a friend . . . she could be absolutely anywhere.'

'I think something happened.' Nina stands up. 'Not even Jennifer is cruel enough to let Max and Lollo suffer like this. One day, fine. That would be like her. For attention. But this . . .'

She wipes her face on her sleeve and heads for the door, but turns around before she's out of the room.

'Do you want lunch or anything?'

The thought of food makes me gag, but I have to eat. My body needs sustenance to function. I've already had one hallucination, and if it happens again Nina will call an ambulance. Or drive me straight to the psych ward.

'I'll have to have a little breakfast first.'

She stares at me.

'You haven't had breakfast yet?'

'No, I . . . I just woke up.'

Nina whips around without a word. Her heels click against the floor as she hurries upstairs.

42. Nina

I *may not* be angry with Fredrik. He's sick. Suffering from stress. Possibly burned out. I have to have patience; I can't demand that he bounce right out of bed after a few days' rest.

Still, I stomp my feet a little extra as I go. It's childish, but I *am* angry. Just because you aren't feeling well and need some rest doesn't mean you can completely ignore your children. What if Vilgot had decided to go outside? Fredrik could have at least plonked himself on the living-room sofa, with a view of the front door.

I stomp all the way up the stairs too. To make a point. Or maybe to vent some anger. I don't want my bad mood to affect the children. They haven't done anything wrong; they're totally innocent this time.

Anger or worry? I have a hard time telling them apart; they feed on each other. At the moment I guess I'm mostly disappointed. And guilty as sin. Because, at its core, that disappointment comes from egoism, pure and simple.

I'm disappointed that this Christmas break hasn't been the cosy time off we planned. And I'm disappointed that the beginning of the year hasn't been the fresh start I was hoping for on New Year's Eve.

Because I remember that much, despite the champagne fog. I remember standing on Lollo's balcony feeling hopeful that Fredrik and I would find our way back to each other. That we would start to talk again, to share our innermost thoughts, to make love.

Instead, the exact opposite has happened. And Fredrik can't help it. No one gets sick on purpose. But it annoys me that he won't call the clinic, that he just lies around doing nothing.

It's possible that this is all part of his illness, that someone who has a stress-related breakdown actually isn't *able* to act and sees their whole existence through a dark filter. But then why won't he allow me to help him? Is it really going to make him feel better just lying there in the bedroom staring at nothing all day?

Leif refused to seek any outside help after Simon's death. My father-in-law claims that all psychologists and therapists are left-wing hippies. He thought Simon's suicide was a family matter, not the sort of thing other people should interfere with. But Fredrik doesn't share that opinion, does he? As I recall it, he encouraged his dad to talk to a therapist.

I think Pirjo saw a psychologist for a few years, but those conversations don't seem to have led to much of anything. My in-laws have stopped communicating. And I have a feeling they blame each other for what happened.

I knock on Anton's door and open it without waiting for a response. The room is stuffy and smells like bad breath with a hint of Dillchips.

'Anton.' I poke my sleeping son. 'It's almost eleven thirty. Time to get up.'

One eye opens.

I open the blinds with a purposeful clatter and crack open the window. How can anyone sleep in this stench?

Anton whines from under the covers.

'Up and at 'em,' I say in a feigned chipper tone, promising in the same breath that pancakes will be served in the kitchen in half an hour.

In the next room, my six-year-old is sitting in bed with his iPad in his lap. His eyes are wide open; his body is shaped like a cheese curl. I sit on the edge of the bed and run my fingers through his hair. Vilgot stares intently at the screen, hardly seeming to notice I'm there.

'Hey,' I say, moving a bit closer to him. 'What do you say we turn off that screen and you come down and help me make pancakes?'

'Have to clear this level first,' he says.

'Is there a lot left?'

'Can you be quiet? I'm *contentrating*.'

'Sorry.' I do my best to keep a straight face. 'But turn it off after that, okay?'

I get up, bend down and pick up three odd socks that are scattered across the cityscape rug.

Strange times we live in. The city on this rug has long since become a ghost town. No one drives Matchbox cars along its grey roads any more; no one parks outside the store or dispatches police cars with lights and sirens. Kids don't *play* any more. They game.

My usual surge of guilt washes over me. We *have* to get better at regulating his screen time. It's already too late for Smilla. And we might not be able to do anything about Anton's habits at this point either. But we can still save Vilgot.

On my way down the stairs, I decide, for the umpteenth time since Vilgot was born, that starting now there is going to be a change. Starting now, we will play, read books, play board games, go to the playground – we'll even just suffer through it when our kid is bored. After all, creative play often starts after a period of tedium and the whining that follows.

When Smilla was an only child, we were exemplary parents. I had just received my preschool-teaching licence and was bursting with everything I'd just learned about pedagogy and child development. Fredrik was an enthusiastic father who liked to play around and have fun.

Simon's suicide was fresh in our memories too. We'd just seen what could happen to someone who closes themselves off and stops spending time with real live people. Not that every computer geek develops a case of depression or becomes antisocial, but we wanted our daughter to play with friends her own age and spend time out in the fresh air.

When Anton was born, we were more tired than the first time around, but we kept up our high standards. We went on outings, went ice-skating in the park, did crafts and read stories.

Then Vilgot arrived and all our principles went right out the window. There were only two of us to offer comfort, help with homework, drive to soccer practice and prepare food. There were three kids. Each time I gave in to their whining about playing computer games I thought it was an exception, because we were stressed out and overworked at *that particular moment*. But it just kept happening. The computer and the iPad have become a third parent.

'Can you come here?'

Suddenly Smilla is behind me, signalling at me to follow her into her room. I imagine she wants to show me something on a screen, something she wants me to pay for. But instead she pulls her door closed behind us and just stands there in the middle of the room. I can't quite interpret the expression on her face.

'Is something wrong?'

'You could say that.'

A thousand thoughts whizz through my mind. About drugs, about Jennifer, about what else might have gone wrong during that ill-fated party. Was someone raped? Smilla?

'Can you be a little more specific?'

I try to hide the fear that courses through my body – just because my daughter wants to tell me something for once doesn't mean it's catastrophic news.

'Max beat up Ali last night,' Smilla says calmly. 'And said he was going to kill him.'

I try to make sense of that information. Max. Ali. Kill.

'You mean the guy who might be Jennifer's boyfriend? Her classmate?'

She nods.

'And you're saying Max *hit* him?'

'Yep.'

'Where did you hear this? How do you know it's not just a rumour?'

I can well imagine that Max would *like* to punch that guy. But I just can't believe he'd actually do it.

'I heard it from *Ali*.' Smilla points at her phone. 'He posted on Snap. One eye is totally swollen shut and it looks totally nasty, and Ali's dad filed a police report. Max said a bunch of racist shit too.' She gives me a pointed look. 'Not exactly the first time either.'

So Smilla has picked up on that too?

Well, of course she has. Smilla has grown up on the east

side of Malmö. Her friends have roots in all corners of the world, and she's extremely attuned to remarks that imply some sorts of people might be worth less than others.

'That sounds totally crazy,' I say, despite my great relief that Smilla herself is fine. 'But it's still probably best to take it with a grain of salt. Until we know more. Maybe Max has a different version of what happened.'

'I trust Ali.' Smilla looks very serious. 'He would *never* exaggerate or make up something like this. He's really broken up over it, Mom. Max accused him of, like, kidnapping Jennifer. He said he would kill Ali if he didn't tell him where she was. Max is fucking deranged. We have to stop hanging out with them.'

I don't know what to believe. Rumours spread so quickly these days, sometimes way too quickly. And I remember the telephone game our elementary-school teacher let us play when we had a little extra time in class. There was usually nothing left of the original sentence once it had passed through twenty-five little mouths and just as many ears.

'Smilla,' I say. 'Hold off on adding to the mess until I've talked to Lollo.'

'What do you mean?'

'You know . . . don't spread this any further.'

'Are you kidding me?' Smilla scoffs. 'The whole internet is boiling over.'

I throw up my hands. 'Okay, I get it. But I'm still going to call Lollo. You always have to try to see both sides of the story.'

'Whatever.' Smilla takes her phone from the desk. 'Anyway, Missing People is going to look for Jennifer out in Klagshamn today. I think I'll go.'

No! is my first thought.

'Can you handle it?' I say instead.

'Why not?' She shrugs. 'Feels good to help out.'

'I understand that. But what if –'

What I want to say is, *What if* you *find Jennifer? You don't want to find her there. Because if you find her in Klagshamn it's not likely that she'll be alive.*

But I can't say that.

'What if what?'

Smilla gives me a searching look.

'Oh, nothing . . . It . . .' I'm sweating, trying in vain to find the right words. 'Why are they looking in Klagshamn?'

'Because Jennifer said she was heading home, I assume.'

The door opens, and Vilgot sticks his head into the room.

'You were going to make pancakes,' he says, fixing his gaze on me.

I take his hand. 'I am. Come on, let's do it.' On my way out the door, I turn to Smilla. 'Do whatever you want to do, sweetie. But if you go, be sure to dress warmly. It's freezing cold. Do you want Dad or me to come?'

Smilla shakes her head. 'Some of Jennifer's friends are going. I'll go with them.'

Vilgot bounces down the stairs, talking about strawberry jam and ice cream to go with his pancakes. I think about Max and what Smilla just told me.

It can't be true. It *must not* be true. I can just picture the headlines: SUCCESSFUL REAL-ESTATE AGENT ACCUSED OF ASSAULT. Or MALMÖ REALTOR ATTACKS CHILD. And the Islamophobia on top of it all.

Oh my God. I have to call Lollo.

As we crack eggs, measure flour and whisk it all together,

my thoughts turn to the upcoming search and Missing People. Personally, I have mixed feelings about that organization. I don't doubt there are people who are driven by a genuine desire to help, who want to do something positive for society. But I'm just as certain that lots of participants in a search just do it for an excuse to snoop, to get the latest gossip, to revel in other people's misfortune.

At the same time, I understand that, when someone close to you is missing, you'll grasp at every last straw, that you'll take all the help you can get.

I probably would have welcomed Missing People with open arms, if I were in Lollo's shoes.

43. Lollo

The car zooms down the highway. I'm driving too fast, sticking to the left lane like glue all the way to the Näset exit and continuing at speed along Highway 100. Someone honks at me on the roundabout by ICA Toppen, but I don't care – I just keep going.

The open countryside spreads out before me. A bundled-up woman is defying the cold and walking her dog by the water; otherwise the footpath is deserted. I speed up even more but have to hit the brakes when a light turns red just before the Falsterbo Canal.

My fingers drum against the wheel. I glare angrily at the traffic light as though that will make it change faster. When I finally get a green light, I put the pedal to the metal and fly, tyres squealing, towards the bridge.

On the other side of the canal, the sea view is replaced by houses and trees; bare branches flicker in the corner of my eye like a blurry grey film. I stare at the road ahead. The asphalt vanishes beneath the car metre by metre.

Not until I reach Ljungen do I start to worry about what I might find at our summer cottage. Deep down, I don't believe Max has anything to do with Jennifer's disappearance. But since the thought occurred to me, I have to see with my own eyes. I have to be one hundred per cent sure.

My heart beats faster as I turn off towards the little

village. Is the speed limit forty here? If it is, I don't care. It feels like death is on my heels.

And I have to beat it there.

As the car bumps along the grassy, overgrown dead-end lane that leads to our summer paradise, I feel a tight band of pressure across my chest. As soon as the engine falls silent, I fling open the door and take a few deep breaths. I draw the faint scent of seaweed into my nose, waiting for the pressure to abate.

My eyes seek out the cottage. It looks so gloomy without the flowerpots and patio furniture that's always on the deck in the summertime. The pine branches move in fits and starts thanks to the gusty wind.

My car is the only one around. That should mean that Max isn't here, and my shoulders relax a bit.

Jennifer, though, might very well be hiding in the house. It's possible to take a bus here. The buses run as often now as they do in the summer; lots of people who live year-round on the peninsula commute to Malmö and Lund.

I suddenly feel like I'm getting warm, like I'm on the right track. If Jennifer's been having problems and wants to be by herself, naturally she would have come here.

She's always loved our house in Falsterbo. Since she was born, we've spent every summer here; we've celebrated every Midsummer and birthday here. Jennifer was born in September, which is usually a lovely time to visit. Clear, brisk air but still warm and sunny. We often eat her birthday cake outside. Last year we even went for a swim.

Why didn't I come here earlier? It's like I've been

walking around at home in some sort of torpor, without thinking rationally. But now that my brain is finally working again, it's obvious: she's here. This is where she's been all along.

I glance at the picture window and think I spot her on the sofa: her head bent over her phone, her shiny hair like a curtain hiding her face.

Jennifer.

I stumble across the grass, dash up the stairs and yank at the door handle. To my great surprise, the door is locked. I take a few steps to the left and peer through the window, pressing my nose to the glass.

There's no Jennifer on the sofa. It's empty. But I could swear I just saw her there a moment ago.

Back to the door. I bang hard on it.

'Jennifer?'

Silence.

'Jennifer.'

Not a peep.

'Are you there?'

My chest aches with disappointment.

'Jennifer.' My voice is weaker now. Whispering, pleading. 'Sweetie, Mama is here. Please open the door and we'll figure this all out.'

At last I give up and dash around the corner of the house, over to the woodpile. I cautiously run my hand along the downspout and fish out the spare key. That it's still there doesn't necessarily mean Jennifer isn't here. She might have used the main key, the one that's usually hanging in the key cabinet back home. Why didn't we check if it was still there? Or did we?

I fumble with the key, then get it into the lock and turn

it. I open the door and find myself standing on the navy-blue rag rug.

Time seems to have stopped inside the cottage. Next to the stack of cushions for the patio furniture is the striped canvas bag. The string from one of Jennifer's bikinis hangs over the edge – as if she's on her way to the beach for a dip and has just set the bag down for a second while she fills her water bottle.

'Jennifer?' I dart from room to room but find no sign that the house is occupied. Everything looks just as it did when we closed it up for the winter early last October. The bedspreads are taut; the pillows on the sofa are in a neat row, and the refrigerator is empty aside from a few jars of olives.

Once I've checked the last room, I sink on to the hall floor, absolutely exhausted.

'Jennifer!'

Tears stream down my face as I call her name.

I don't know how long I sit there, but at last I take my phone from my pocket and call the only number that feels logical to call right now.

'Lollo! How are you? I've been trying to call. Did Jennifer come home?'

'Dad,' I sob. 'I need you to come.'

44. Fredrik

I've showered and dressed. Jeans and a sweater. Shower-
ing and putting on clothes are the kind of thing most
people are expected to do every day. A normal activity.
I'm playing normal.

'Want a cup?'

Nina holds up the coffeepot as I enter the kitchen.

'Please.'

I rummage around among jars and bags. That's normal
too. Looking for a cookie to go with your coffee is the sort
of thing normal people spend time doing, now and then.
Normal people don't think about how it works when a
dumpster full of construction scrap is collected. They
don't wonder how much of the contents becomes visible
in that instance. Or whether a black coat will stick out
among the other items. Whether anyone would react.

An empty packet of Ballerina cookies reveals that once
upon a time there were cookies in the cabinet. The box of
Aladdin chocolates is almost empty too, but at least the
kids have left three for their parents. The 'disgusting' ones,
with liqueur – Nina's favourite.

I sit down at the kitchen table and look out the window,
noting that the neighbours across the street must be having a party, or at least some sort of gathering. Three
unfamiliar cars are parked on the street in front of their
house.

'It's Lykke's birthday today,' Nina says, glancing at the

246

neighbours' house. 'Maybe we should go over with some flowers.'

'Is it a big birthday?'

'She's sixty.' Nina turns back to the coffee-maker as she whistles the chorus of the Beatles' 'When I'm Sixty-four'. It sounds horrible.

Presumably this is the sort of stuff I'll miss the most when I'm in prison. Nina fixing me coffee as I listen to her off-key whistling, the fact that the kids have eaten all the cookies in the house.

My wife sets two mugs on the table. She takes a carton of milk from the fridge and sits down across from me. She stuffs a dark truffle into her face and I pour a splash of milk into my coffee.

'Did you have any breakfast?' she asks.

I nod.

'Brunch. A couple of eggs and some toast.'

A modified version of the truth. Or, rather, a lie – I couldn't get down more than half a slice of toast before I had to stop.

'At least you don't seem to have a stomach bug,' Nina says. 'Because you probably wouldn't have wanted to eat this soon.'

'What are the kids up to?' I ask to change the subject.

'Anton and Vilgot are upstairs. Anton's playing video games, I imagine.' Nina rolls her eyes. 'I had this plan to limit the kids' screen time and Vilgot reluctantly agreed to put down his iPad. But Anton totally lost his mind when I told him he couldn't play more after lunch. And I don't have it in me to fight that fight today. Not now, when everything is so . . . difficult.'

'Difficult?'

Nina throws up her hands. 'Yeah, with all this Jennifer stuff . . . I can't let it go, can't put it out of my mind. And then there's you . . .' She gives me a crooked smile. 'You're not okay, and I can't face an argument with Anton right now. Not on my own. It would be nice if we could be a united front.'

My stomach lurches when I realize that Nina is probably going to be on her own for every fight from now on.

She looks at me. 'What do you think?'

'About what?'

'About the gaming.' Nina sighs. 'Are you even listening to me?'

'Yes, I'm listening. I just happened to think of something, is all.'

She leans over the box of chocolates. 'Mmm. How can you not like rum raisin? It's *so* good!'

Watching my wife eat chocolates is definitely something I will miss. In all likelihood I will miss everything about my regular old everyday life. Lying beside Vilgot at night, listening to him breathe as he sleeps, driving Anton to soccer practice with seconds to spare. I imagine that I'll even miss Smilla's withering comments.

'Is Smilla home?'

Nina shakes her head. 'No, she just got the bus out to Klagshamn.'

I go cold.

'Klagshamn?'

'Yeah, it seems Missing People is organizing a search this afternoon. Smilla said she wanted to help. To be perfectly honest, I don't know if it's such a good idea. I mean, what if *Smilla* were to find Jennifer, or something? I don't think she . . .'

I zone out, unwilling to hear more. Sour bile fills my mouth, a mix of coffee and stomach acid. I swallow. And swallow again.

'Fredrik?' Nina looks concerned. 'Is everything okay?'

The whole kitchen is spinning.

Breathe, Fredrik. Take a deep breath.

'You're white as a sheet.'

Nina's voice sounds tinny, distant.

'I . . .'

Breathe, for God's sake.

'It must be the coffee or something. Maybe coffee isn't such a good idea right now, my stomach is —'

I fly from my chair and hurry to the bathroom, where I only just manage to raise the lid of the toilet before my body expels what little was in my stomach.

A little coffee. A little bile.

'Fredrik!' Nina is standing outside the bathroom; her voice is shrill. 'Do you need help? Should I come in?'

'No.' I lie down, resting my cheek against the dusty bath mat. 'I'm fine now.'

45. Lollo

'Hello?' Dad stops short, apparently shocked to find me on the floor of the front hall. 'Oh, sweetie.' He hurries over, crouches down and places a hand on my shoulder. 'What's going on? Has . . . Is Jennifer . . . Did she come home?'

I shake my head.

'Okay, what are you doing here?'

'I . . .' A sob wells up from my chest, and the words catch in my throat. 'I don't know.'

The tears blur out rugs, walls and furniture.

'Come on.'

With some effort, Dad gets up and then puts out his hands. Those big, warm hands that have carried me and comforted me. There are more wrinkles now, and age spots. But their warmth is just the same.

I get to my feet and discover that Agneta is standing just inside the door. She hurries over to give me a firm squeeze.

'It's just so awful.' My stepmother takes a step back and looks me in the eyes. 'Come sit down on the sofa, Lollo, and we'll see if we can't find a little coffee around here somewhere.'

Dad hasn't moved and is shifting his weight from foot to foot.

'Lennart,' his wife says sharply. 'Will you get the coffee?'

He nods and Agneta nudges him gently towards the kitchen.

'He's always been so besotted with Jennifer,' she whispers when Dad is out of earshot. 'He's taking all of this pretty hard.'

I look at her through my tears.

'Don't talk like that. Jennifer isn't dead!'

'No, of course not.' Agneta gives my arm an extra squeeze and leads me to the sofa. 'I only mean he's worried about what might have happened.' She adds, 'We all are.'

A moment later, when Agneta joins Dad, who's pottering around the kitchen, I sink deeper into my New England-style throw pillows. I remember how much work I put into creating this theme, which is mirrored in the interior design and in our outdoor spaces. White walls and pale grey floors. Blue and red details. Knots and anchors. Brass and white wooden furniture. The big dining table made of driftwood. How the hell did I have the energy?

My fingers dig down between the sofa cushions. I drag my nails along the rough canvas, pressing so hard it hurts. Suddenly I feel something that isn't fabric. A piece of paper? I use two fingers as pincers and bring up a crumpled scrap of paper. It's a receipt from Burger King at the Mobilia shopping centre in town. And, for some reason, I read the date.

2 JANUARY 2019. 1.25.43.

I gulp. Who on earth ate *two* hamburgers here the night before last? Max? Max and Jennifer? Someone else?

Max claimed he was out looking for Jennifer at that time. But who else would have been here? It's not as though the key is hidden all *that* well, but . . .

'Here. A little coffee will do you good.'

Agneta places a tray on the table. It's the white wooden tray with a big blue star in the middle. Shabby chic. She hands me a mug and I obediently take it, even as I shove the receipt into the front pocket of my sweatpants with my other hand.

We don't say anything for a while as we sip our coffee. It's as though we're all gathering the strength to go on. Dad stares out the picture window, his eyes sad.

'Do you want to talk about it?' Agneta asks at last. 'All we know is what's been in the paper.'

I set my mug on the table and take a deep breath. Then I tell them all about the girls' party, the fight, what the police have said and today's search effort. I don't mention what I found on Jennifer's computer. 'Jennifer Wicked' would only upset and disappoint them. And maybe they would blame me for Jennifer's ending up there. The useless, clueless mother.

I end by telling them about my dream, how I saw Jennifer sitting here on this very sofa. That the dream led me to wonder about Max will remain my secret. The receipt is burning a hole in my pocket.

'I was manic. Or . . . in a trance. Yes, that's exactly how it felt. It was like someone else was steering me around. Like someone told me to come here. And when I couldn't find Jennifer . . . well, it was like the spell was broken.' I try to determine from their expressions whether they're about to drive me to the psych ward. 'Maybe it sounds weird, but . . . that's what happened.'

Dad doesn't say anything, just clears his throat. Agneta leans towards me and places her hand on mine. 'We've been so worried. Lennart's been trying to call you. And text you, but –'

'I know,' I interrupt her. 'I saw, but . . . I just couldn't respond.'

'We understand, Lollo. We know.' Agneta lets go of my hand. 'And thank God you're not alone. You've got Max. If it weren't for him, we would have been knocking on your door ages ago.'

Dad looks up from his cup of coffee. 'Where is he today? Max?'

'Um . . . he's at work.'

'At work?' Dad looks astonished. 'When –'

'There was just some minor thing he had to deal with,' I rush to say. 'I'm sure he's home by now.'

'That's good.' Agneta smiles. 'Do you want a ride home? I don't think you should drive today. You can ride with me, and Lennart can drive the Mini Cooper back.' She turns to Dad. 'That's okay with you, isn't it?'

'Sure. Of course it is.'

Agneta has always held a lot of sway over my father.

'And you could get some groceries on the way,' she continues. 'That way I can make dinner for us all later.' Agneta looks at me. 'You have to eat something. And I really don't think you should join in the search, Lollo. It would be too much.'

We've had our dust-ups over the years. When I was a teenager. Back then we argued every day about all the usual teenage stuff: money, curfews, behaviour. It could get pretty heated at times.

We also bumped heads a number of times when Jennifer was little. I thought Dad and Agneta devoted too much of their time to networking and golf and told them so; I complained that they didn't spend nearly enough time with their granddaughter.

But, at the heart of the matter, it was probably just that I needed a break from Jennifer now and then. And I suspect that they, like me, thought it was too much to spend a whole day with her.

Now I see genuine concern in my stepmother's eyes. Agneta truly wants to help. And, for the first time in a long time, I let someone else take the wheel.

46. Nina

I sit on the edge of the bed and place a hand on Fredrik's arm. He jumps, as if my touch is painful.

'Look . . .' I begin. 'I'm really not sure I should leave you alone.'

Fredrik turns his head to look at me. 'Why not?'

'Well, because . . .' My eyes fill with tears. 'I . . . I'm just so worried about you, Fredrik. You're not okay. What if you throw up in your sleep and suffocate on –'

'Come off it, Nina.' His voice is surprisingly sharp. 'I'm not a new-born. And I'm not some blackout drunk. There's nothing to worry about, I'm telling you. If you just leave me alone for a while I'll get better.'

'That's what you said yesterday.'

'And I got better.'

His gaze is stern. Cold.

I stand up, move a few steps away from the bed and end up just standing there, fumbling for words. Who is this man in our bed? Should I call the mental-health clinic? Will he go back to being himself, or is he going to be like this from now on?

I have no words. Instead I go to the kitchen, pour out my cold coffee and refill my mug with fresh. Fredrik's cup goes into the sink with a bang.

I sit back down at the table. Same mug, fresh coffee. No company. *Same, same, but different.*

I don't know what to do about Fredrik any more. Cecilia

from work once said that stress-related illnesses are almost as hard on close family as they are on the patient. I didn't quite agree at the time, but now I'm starting to see what she meant. It's hard, not being able to count on your partner, not knowing how much you can demand of them.

The thought that Fredrik's current state might persist for months terrifies me. And yet we've only been dealing with this for a few days.

My theory about cheating is sneaking around the peripheries of my mind, but I don't think it would explain Fredrik's behaviour. He seemed to answer honestly when I asked. Fredrik has never been much of an actor, and that's why it's chafing at me. There's something else he's hiding. Something unrelated to being overworked. But what is it?

Could it have to do with money? Is he afraid we're heading into financial trouble?

Our finances have always been tight, and it's extra tough now that we have two teenagers in the house. Maybe Fredrik discovered I borrowed from our savings to buy the down jacket Smilla asked for at Christmas. Maybe he's thinking about how the internet bill needs to be paid before the first of February. But why wouldn't he just say so?

It strikes me that Fredrik started to go downhill right around the time Jennifer disappeared. A little shiver goes through my body. Could there be a connection?

I quickly push that thought out of my mind. The only reasonable connection is that he's worried about her.

Darkness has fallen over Malmö, and the party across the street is still going full swing. My guess is that it'll go on for a while yet. Lykke's Danish relatives really fit the stereotype when it comes to celebrations.

I send a text to Smilla. How's it going? XO

She doesn't respond right away so I reach for the paper. A headline about an assault conviction makes me think of Max. I'd like to call Lollo, but I decide to wait until the search is over. Is she taking part? Would I have?

I reach the conclusion that I probably would have helped out, despite the risk of facing my worst nightmare. As soon as I've formulated that thought, I want to take it back. How could I even *think* something like that? Why am I so negative?

There *has* to be a happy ending. There just has to be.

Vilgot comes into the kitchen. He examines the table, looking for hints of treats. I extend an arm and pull him into a hug. He wriggles loose and points at the box of chocolates.

'You were eating candy.'

'Chocolate you don't like,' I say. 'Have some fruit instead. There are clementines.'

Vilgot goes to the fruit bowl and selects a clementine, which he plunks on the table in front of me.

'Peel.'

'Mom, can you please peel this for me?' I correct him.

He smiles, showing the gap in his top teeth, and my heart swells. I'm struck by how truly lucky I am, despite everything. My three kids are healthy and here with me. We have a good house, jobs to go to and food on the table every day. Fredrik doesn't quite fit the pattern at the moment, but I'm sure we'll get him back in shape again. It's a temporary problem, I tell myself, handing the peeled clementine to my son.

'What did you say?' Vilgot asks.

A little wrinkle between his eyebrows.

'Did I say something?'

He nods and I pat him on the head. 'Then I was just thinking out loud.'

At that moment, my phone starts to ring and Vilgot dashes upstairs.

I pick up the phone and see Smilla's name on the screen. My stomach lurches. Why is she calling? Smilla hardly ever calls me; she prefers written communication.

I accept the call and bring the phone to my ear. 'Hi, are you on your way home?'

It's not a question, it's a hope.

'Mama!'

Smilla is howling with tears. I hear a clamour of voices in the background.

'Sweetie, what's going on? Where are you?'

'In Klags . . . in Klagshamn. Mama, you have to come here!'

Smilla is crying hysterically, and I hear rushing and scraping sounds on the line. She doesn't need to say more. I can already guess what's happened, and I don't know if I can handle this.

But I have to. For Smilla.

'Can you walk to the bus stop?' I ask with as much calm as I can muster. 'Can you walk there and stay put? I'll be there in . . . in about twenty minutes. Okay?'

No response, only noise.

'Can you hear me, Smilla? Are you walking to the bus stop?'

'I . . . I'm walking now,' she sobs.

I run back and forth between the hall and the kitchen, grabbing my car key, phone and outerwear. At the last second, I realize I should probably alert Fredrik.

'Are you awake?'

I push open the bedroom door and take a step into the dim light. Fredrik mutters a yes. He's facing the window and doesn't make any effort to turn in my direction.

'I'm going to pick up Smilla. Will you keep an eye on Vilgot for the time being?'

Fredrik flips over and sits up in bed.

'Did something happen?'

'I'm not sure. But Smilla was totally beside herself, so I'm guessing . . . well, it didn't seem like good news.'

'Oh my God!' My husband looks at me, his eyes full of pure terror. 'Oh my God.'

47. Fredrik

As soon as the front door closes, I crawl out of bed and look for my computer. It turns out to be on the desk. My legs shaking, I stagger to the chair and land heavily on its seat.

When the screen doesn't immediately unlock, I wonder if I've forgotten my password. There's pressure at my temples. Is memory loss the first sign of going crazy? Or is it actually something that happens at a later stage? Maybe I lost my mind a long time ago.

I start over from the beginning, spelling slowly, using my right index finger, and – there. On my third attempt, the screen unlocks, and I bring up Google and weigh, for the first time ever, the two options under the logo: *Google Search* and *I'm Feeling Lucky*. The latter would certainly be a welcome change.

Then I come to my senses and type 'Jennifer Wiksell'. A logical thing to search. But that turns up only rehashed news. Despite some intense searching, all I find are articles and items that have been online for days now. I try various combinations of terms: 'missing girl', 'seventeen-year-old found', 'missing girl found', 'discovered in Klagshamn' – but there are no new hits; everything I see is marked previously read.

Fuck! The words on the screen flicker in my vision and, my fingers trembling, I try two new words: 'Missing

People'. Although it's only a matter of seconds, I find the wait for the results nearly unbearable.

A photo of Jennifer is the first hit, but there is only a paragraph about the search, which seems to be over now. They probably haven't had time to update the site yet.

Jennifer smiles at me from the screen. I close my eyes.

'Dad?'

My reaction is so violent that I nearly fall off the chair. I turn towards the sound to find Vilgot standing in the doorway.

'Want to play UNO?' He approaches me. 'Look!' A small finger points at the screen. 'There's Jennifer!'

I turn to the computer and shut its lid. Vilgot is startled by the bang it makes and looks at me, puzzled. 'Why'd you do that?'

My mind is a blank; everything is spinning. I want to throw up.

'Daddy.' Vilgot tugs at my sleeve. 'Why did you take Jennifer away? I want to see her!'

'Vilgot,' I say in a voice that's unfamiliar but seems to have become permanent, 'I'm too tired to play UNO right now. Maybe later. I just need to get some rest.'

My son pouts. 'You've been resting all day,' he mutters.

'I know. But I'm tired. Mom and Smilla will be back soon.'

'Is Jennifer coming too?'

My head is buzzing; sweat is trickling down my back.

'No,' I whisper. 'I don't think so.'

Vilgot puts both hands on his hips and fixes his eyes on me.

'So when can we play? In how many minutes?'

I slowly rise from the chair and teeter back to the bed.

'I don't know, Vilgot. But, if you let me rest, I'll be there soon, okay?'

He looks sceptical.

'Can't you play on your iPad in the meantime?'

'Can I? Mom said –'

'Go ahead,' I say, waving him out. 'I'll talk to Mom.'

Vilgot whirls around and, an instant later, he's running up the stairs on eager feet.

I lean back and stretch out on the bed.

My body is shaking so hard it scares me. It feels like someone is tightening an iron band around my head, harder and harder.

Am I having a stroke? A heart attack? Am I about to die?

48. Nina

It's snowing. The temperature has been creeping towards freezing, and strong gusts of wind buffet the car as I enter the highway. My eyes are aimed straight ahead, but I hardly see where I'm going; my focus is elsewhere.

What if Jennifer is dead?

No!

No, no, no.

With both hands clamped on the wheel, I send up a silent prayer: *Dear God, let Jennifer be alive.*

I search for a sign in the black sky, something that will show me my prayer has been heard. But all I can see, besides darkness, is the swirling snow striking the windshield.

Something tells me that the worst has happened. Smilla seemed awfully torn up. If Jennifer is alive, Smilla would be relieved, not hysterical.

How, as a parent, can anyone make it through the news that your child is no longer living? If Jennifer is dead, how will Lollo and Max go on?

And Smilla. Jennifer and Smilla have known each other since they were born, and they've been incredibly close at times. Like sisters. Smilla *must* understand that what happened is in no way her fault. Jennifer left the party voluntarily; no one chased her off.

If Jennifer is dead, I'm going to need someone to talk to, someone to lean on. Sure, Fredrik is still around, but it's like I've become a single mother to four children. He's impossible to talk to right now. And his reaction when I told him about Smilla's call was . . . surprisingly emotional. It was almost unsettling to see him so beside himself, so despondent.

Maybe his general mental state is part of it. For the time being, Fredrik seems to be one big, exposed nerve. Besides that, he's one of the few adults who has stood beside Jennifer come hell or high water. He does deserve credit for that, I suppose. Fredrik has never nagged at Jennifer or raised his voice to her. He has always taken the time to listen and explain. For a while he even spent afternoons at the Wiksells', plugging away at equations.

I suspect that's the very reason why my husband is such a popular teacher. Fredrik really sees each pupil and treats them with respect; he always manages to find the person behind all the other things the rest of us so often get caught up in. At least, that's how he usually is. I hope that part of him is still around when this is all over, and he comes out on the other side.

It came as a bit of a shock to me when Fredrik told me out of the blue one evening that he wanted to take leave from work and start studying to become a teacher. In my world, the timing was all wrong. Smilla was a baby and we were planning to have more children. We'd also talked about moving to a bigger house. But I supported him. Fredrik wasn't happy at his job back then, and said that Leif had more or less forced him to become an engineer.

There's no doubt my father-in-law is a dominant sort of person, a man of strong opinions, but I never quite understood how he could have forced Fredrik into an engineering degree. Fredrik was over eighteen when he began the programme, and he could have made his own decision. I think it's more likely that Simon's fate might have been a factor when Fredrik changed tracks – the realization that life is short, that it's important to follow your heart, and all of that.

I nearly miss the exit for Västra Klagstorp. I hit the brakes almost dangerously hard and make it off the highway after all, then continue driving south-west. The snow whirls across fields; it comes rolling in billowing sheets, but at least it melts when it hits the road, thank goodness. The wipers are struggling to keep the windshield clear.

What will happen if Jennifer is dead?

There will be a funeral. I swallow hard. So far in my life I haven't been to many funerals, and I thank my lucky stars for that. The few funerals I have attended involved saying farewell to elderly people, older relatives who lived long, full lives. Jennifer has – or had – her whole future ahead of her.

I give a start. What a macabre imagination! How can I be thinking about funerals when I don't even know what's happened? How can I let my thoughts run away with me like this?

It's four on the dot and I turn on the radio. The local news isn't reporting anything that could have to do with Jennifer. I change the station and find a news report in progress, covering national news, but there's nothing about a missing seventeen-year-old there either.

A Chinese space probe has landed on the far side of the moon, credit card fraud is increasing in Sweden, and after the weather report there will be a programme discussing the best way to get in shape after the gluttony of Christmas and New Year's Eve.

I turn off the radio as I take a right at the roundabout at Nygårdsvägen.

Smilla is standing beneath a streetlight, but her face is hidden in the shadow of her hood. She's not alone; there are two other teenagers at the bus stop. They're huddled close together, united in some sort of disorganized group hug. The snow is really coming down, and in the glow of the streetlight the flakes look larger and more plentiful than in the darkness nearby.

I park the car, hop out and call to Smilla.

She turns around and starts running towards me.

'Oh, Mama!' She throws herself into my arms. 'They found Jennifer. She's d-e-e-e-ad!'

Smilla's tall, thin body is racked with sobs, and in the face of her panic I have to suppress my own. I wrap her in my arms, stroking the back of her coat with one hand, mumbling, 'Shh' and 'Oh, sweetheart' into her ear.

When her tears have run dry, she pulls out of my embrace and turns around. The two teens are standing a few steps away, but I can see they've been crying – their eyes are red and puffy.

'Tindra and Ali are in Jennifer's class . . . can they ride back to town with us?'

'Sure. Of course.' It feels good to have something concrete to do, to focus on something I know I can handle. 'Hop on in. The car is warm.'

Why did I say that? Their classmate is dead. What does it matter to them if the car is warm or cold?

Tindra and Ali get into the back seat; Smilla curls up on

the passenger seat beside me. Before I turn around in the cul-de-sac, I glance to the right and discover a group of people further down the short road. They look like they've gathered at the intersection where you'd turn to get to the Wiksells'. Many of them are wearing yellow vests; some are hugging. Past the vests, through bare branches, I catch a glimpse of flashing blue lights. There must be at least one patrol car out on Badvägen.

I don't understand how this could have happened. Was Jennifer really so drunk that she got off the bus at the last stop, fell asleep just a few hundred metres from her house and froze to death?

A chill runs down my spine. Surely she wasn't murdered, was she? Who would want to kill Jennifer? It's not as though she's involved with the Malmö underworld. Or was she? A boyfriend on the periphery of a criminal gang? Maybe she happened to get caught in gunfire?

Could it be a robbery gone wrong? Or was she raped, maybe? Could the killer have followed her, raped her and then killed her so she couldn't talk?

My macabre fantasies are back, and I can't stop them. A thousand questions roil inside my head. Where was she found? Who found her? Have the police made a statement on the cause of death yet? But I don't want to press the kids for answers, so I keep my questions to myself and concentrate instead on getting us back through the snowstorm in one piece.

When we reach Borrebackevägen, I glance in the rearview mirror, trying to get a glimpse of the passengers in the back seat. They're sitting on either side, staring blankly into the darkness.

Quiet tears are trickling down the boy's cheeks. Ali. Is

this the Ali Max supposedly beat up yesterday? Yes, the evidence is plain to see. One of Ali's eyes is black and blue.

The sight of the crying boy with the black eye is heart-breaking. If Max is responsible, I dearly hope he goes down for it. I wouldn't mind giving him a taste of his own medicine myself.

'She was in Kalkan,' Smilla says suddenly.

I squeeze the wheel tighter. 'In the quarry?'

'Oh, Mom, it's horrible!' Smilla sobs. 'What if she was there all along? If only I'd gone with her, if only I'd . . .'

She doesn't finish her sentence; she can't. Her sobs take over. I place a hand on her thigh, but quickly move it back to the wheel. It's no good steering with one hand in this weather.

'Smilla, listen to me. None of what happened is your fault. Jennifer left the party of her own free will. And you asked her to stay, didn't you? You tried.'

Smilla is sobbing helplessly now. I've never heard her cry like this before. The sounds she's making are new and almost unbearable to listen to.

'I could have gone with her too,' comes Ali's voice from the back seat. 'I heard her saying she was going to leave. But I . . . I didn't try to make her stay.'

Smilla's breathing has calmed a little bit.

'Now listen here,' I say, trying to include all three of them in my exhortation. 'You have to stop blaming your-selves. I know it might feel like you played a part in all this, but, from what I've heard, Jennifer's decision to leave the party was all her own. And it's not unusual for someone to duck out of a party early. It happens all the time. There was no way you could have known what would happen to her.'

None of them says anything, but they appear to be absorbing my words. I try to make eye contact in the rear-view mirror.

'Will there be an adult there when you two get home?'

Both Ali and Tindra nod.

49. Lollo

'Dinner is ready!'

Dad is calling from the bottom of the stairs.

I am freshly showered, wearing clean clothes and sitting on the sofa in the den. I can hear Agneta rummaging among pots and pans and dishes in the kitchen. I stare at the TV without seeing it. No one has been in touch after the search, and that should be a good sign. But my gut feeling is telling me otherwise.

To distract myself I'm putting together a puzzle in my mind, trying to produce a clear image of my daughter with the help of the pieces I have. Age, appearance, shoe size, year in school and favourite subjects are easy. They form one stable corner. But what does she want to be when she grows up? How is her mental health? Who does she spend time with? And why did she put that awful page up on Facebook?

It's impossible to keep going; I'm missing more puzzle pieces than I have. We've lived under the same roof for over seventeen years, yet I know almost nothing about her. My own daughter.

The tears start flowing again.

'Lollo?'

I jump at the sound of my name, then turn my head and see the man who's now halfway up the stairs.

My dad. I'm surprised to see how old he's become. His formerly thick grey hair looks thin now; his shirt hangs loosely over his belly where it used to be tight. Perhaps, like me, the past few days of worry have aged him.

It must have been tough for him to be left on his own with an eight-year-old daughter when he'd just turned thirty-five. I could be a hell of a terror when I was little. I was stubborn and demanding and tried every method of seeking Dad's undivided attention. And I wasn't any less demanding as a teenager.

Our relationship improved as soon as I moved out. My relationship with Agneta got better too. Only then, with some distance, did I realize she was good for Dad. He'd actually become a happier person once Agneta came into the picture.

Sometimes it annoys me that Dad is such a doormat, that he lets Agneta have her way with absolutely every-thing. But Dad seems to like her bossy style. I guess he likes not having to make any decisions. She's got the ideas; he's got the means. Convenient.

In any case, my father has always been there for me. He's always done his best, been there in the background, ready to spring to my aid if necessary.

And he loves Jennifer.

'We're eating now.' Dad's voice is gentle. 'You'll join us, right?'

For obvious reasons, the mood around the kitchen table isn't a cheerful one. Max showed up just as the rest of us arrived home from Falsterbo. He didn't ask where we'd been, and I didn't ask why he was home so early. Maybe one of his colleagues had advised him that 'business as usual' doesn't send the right message when your daughter is missing.

If he even was at work. The Burger King receipt is in my purse now, and I'm going to confront Max – but not in front of Dad and Agneta.

The silence is palpable. The only sound is our silverware scraping our plates, and the clock ticking on the wall. Tick-tock. In the end, time still passes.

Chanel comes trotting in to see if there's anything yummy on the floor. Dad can never resist sneaking her a bite, and today is no exception. Normally I would scold Dad, but I let it go this time. Chanel's eating habits don't matter.

Nothing matters.

Except Jennifer.

A gust of wind rattles the kitchen fan. We launched right into a typical, chaotic Skåne snowstorm on our drive back from Falsterbo, and the wind has only gained strength since. A sparse white blanket has formed on the ground, but it will probably melt within a day.

'How long was this supposed to last?' Agneta looks out the window.

'The wind was supposed to die down by morning,' Max says. 'And it was supposed to stop snowing around midnight. I checked before I started home from work.'

So that was why he came home early. To avoid being snowed in at work – or wherever he was. I glance at my husband. He has put his knife aside and is shovelling down his rice. My eyes follow his hand, which moves mechanically between his plate and his mouth. Up and down. Up and down. His knuckles are covered by a large bandage.

'What happened there?' I ask, pointing.

'Oh, nothing.' Max waves his fork. 'Got my hand caught when I was fixing something on the car.' He turns to Dad and Agneta. 'Why don't you sleep in the guest room? It would be reckless to drive in this weather.'

Dad looks hesitant. I know he prefers to sleep in his own bed. But Agneta nods.

'That sounds good,' she says. 'Better than spending half the night stuck in a snowbank.'

Dad is just about to say something more when the doorbell rings.

An icy chill spreads through my chest. I hold my breath. Dad and Agneta exchange glances. They're thinking the same thought I am. None of us has mentioned the search since we left Falsterbo, but apparently we've all been battling the very same fears all afternoon.

Max gets up and goes to the front hall. Chanel scampers back and forth between the kitchen and the front door, yipping and wagging her tail.

It must be plain to see that I'm having trouble breathing, because Agneta stands up and places both hands on my shoulders, massaging them.

'Breathe,' she whispers. 'Let's not expect the worst.'

I hear voices in the hall. Max's voice, of course. And another two besides. I recognize one as belonging to Lina Torrero.

No.

Oh, no.

I don't want to be here.

'It's the police.'

Max is standing in the doorway to the kitchen, but he's become a different person. His face belongs to someone else. The man in the doorway looks like someone I know very well, but I can't quite place him.

No, wait. It's Dad. He is thirty-five and standing on the

pink rug in my room, his eyes teary and red. I know what he's about to tell me, and I don't want to hear it.

'Shall we have a seat on the sofa?'

Max's voice is weak and unsteady.

I'm not here any more. My body is only a shell, and a shell can't talk. Lollo isn't here. She's someplace where she doesn't have to listen, think or feel.

'Lollo?' Max repeats.

'That's a good idea,' Agneta says, somehow managing to get my body to move towards the living room.

'Lina Torrero.' Someone who doesn't match the image in my head at all puts out her hand. 'We spoke on the phone the other day,' she adds.

I was picturing a middle-aged woman. Lina Torrero appears to be under thirty. She's short, with jet-black hair in a tight ponytail, and looks like she has roots in South America. I take her hand and am surprised at its warmth. My own hands are cold.

'Marko Stojković,' says a tall man with a neatly trimmed beard, extending a big paw.

I recognize him. He was here on New Year's Day.

We sit down around the coffee table. I take deep breaths, trying to prepare myself for the horrific news I know is coming.

But I can't prepare myself.

I don't want to.

Agneta drapes an arm around my shoulders; time stands still and rushes on all at once.

Lina Torrero looks at Max and then at me, and opens her mouth.

'Unfortunately, I have to tell you that Jennifer is dead.'

A scream builds inside me but gets stuck on the way

out. My tongue is thick and it feels like a thousand needles are piercing my lips.

Max lets out a muffled sound. It's a plaintive, whimpering sound that seems to come from deep inside. He buries his face in his hands and his body shakes.

Lina Torrero doesn't say anything for a moment and only attempts to speak again once Max lifts his head.

'As you know, Missing People performed a human-chain search here in Klagshamn this afternoon. There was also a search-and-rescue dog.'

She pauses. No one says anything. My gaze drifts to the window, and in the mild glow of the outdoor lights I see the snowflakes hurtling to the ground.

'We got a call around three thirty,' Torrero continues. 'The dog had made a discovery in the limestone quarry back there.'

'But why didn't you look there earlier?' Agneta asks. 'Jennifer has been missing since New Year's Eve, and, from what I heard, she told everyone she was heading home.'

Torrero nods. 'We began by searching the area where the party was held. Without getting into technical details, we couldn't see any indication that Jennifer had, in fact, gone home. Nor had she been captured on any of the security cameras on public transport, and we had no luck with the taxi companies either. Yesterday evening we got hold of the bus driver who was driving the late-night routes on New Year's Eve, and he recognized her. Unfortunately, we had no dogs available at the time, but early this morning one of our K9 units searched the area – with no result. Even dogs can make mistakes.'

Her voice is grave but gentle and melodic. I only catch

fragments of her continued explanation; I hear words like 'forensics' and 'preliminary investigation' but don't react. Only when she says 'autopsy' does my scream tear loose and make its way out.

My head fills with a deafening sound. My throat burns. Agneta whispers, 'Shh, shh' as her fingers press into my shoulder. I thought she was the one holding me up, but maybe we're helping each other now.

Dad rocks back and forth in his seat. His eyes are open but glassy. Seeing Dad is like catching a glimpse of my own pain. My chest aches; my head is pounding.

The scream ebbs out.

'I want to see her,' I whisper. 'I want to see my daughter.'

'Of course,' Torrero says. 'It would be best for the medical examiners to complete their examination first.' She looks at her colleague. 'Can you call them and find out where they are with that?'

He stands up and walks to the kitchen. Torrero goes on: 'The investigation is entering a new phase now, and we'd like to talk with each of you a little more.' She looks at me, then at Max. 'I understand if you don't have the strength for that today, but it would be great if we could do it tomorrow.'

Max wipes away his tears, rubs his eyes with both hands and clears his throat. 'We might as well do it right away,' he says. 'Can you manage, Lollo?'

I nod without having the foggiest idea of what I'm agreeing to. A single sentence plays on repeat in my head, and, no matter how hard I try, I can't make it stop.

Jennifer is dead.

50. Fredrik

The bedroom walls are closing in, pressing in on me even as the air in the room slowly vanishes. My breathing is laboured, and each attempt to draw in oxygen is torture.

I have to get out. And fast. Preferably before Nina and Smilla get back.

There can only be one reason for Smilla to call, and I don't want to be confronted with her despair. How can I face my daughter's grief? What can I say? How can I ever look Smilla in the eye again? How the hell can I ever look *anyone* in the eye after this?

When Simon died, I was the one who had to deal with the practical details. I'm the one who talked to the police, contacted the funeral home and informed our relatives. It was like Mom and Dad were paralysed. As soon as I walked in the door, they let go of all responsibility and piled it on to me.

Maybe those tasks were the only reason I made it through the first few weeks. I wrote a list and checked off item after item. Blue ink on lined paper. Mom has always kept a little pad of spiral-bound paper on a shelf in the kitchen. She likes to use it for her shopping lists, and I so clearly remember having to flip past the start of a list to find an empty page. At the top of the page, in Mom's handwriting, it said COKE. The elixir of a late-in-life child. My parents never drank soda, so it was all for him that the basement pantry was stocked with Coke ahead of each weekend.

We only lived together for five years, Simon and me. We didn't know each other very well. But I liked him. And he was my little brother. Whenever I visited my parents, I tried to take the time to sit down and have a talk with him, man to man. He was a quiet kid, and it was easy to lose track of him in all the hubbub around Christmas and Easter. But I should have called him on the phone too, asked how he was doing, checked in.

Shit. Why was I so fucking self-involved back then? Always striving, moving forward, upwards. And I didn't even like what I was doing. If I'd continued along that track I expect I would have hit a wall for real.

It's clear that Nina is starting to doubt my made-up diagnosis of burnout. She's not just worried now; she's angry.

I have to pull myself together. The problem is that I've lost control of my body. It's no longer doing what I want it to. What an eerie feeling. Eerie and unfamiliar. My body has always been my best friend. It's always been healthy and strong and up for a challenge, and it's an important part of my work identity. As a gym teacher, you want to set a good example.

Who will replace me? Maybe it will be some young, fresh-out-of-college type. I'm sure that will make an impression with the students.

I get out of bed, go to the front hall and put on my coat. I realize that my phone is in the bedroom, so I go to get it.

It's been on silent and there are several missed messages on the screen. The top one is from Dennis, my colleague and tennis partner. Damn. What day is it? Wednesday? Thursday? We usually play tennis on Thursday evenings and had decided on a match before Epiphany weekend. I compose a quick text and stick my phone in my pocket.

At that moment, a bright light pierces the frosted glass next to the front door. The dull sound of an engine increases in volume and then stops suddenly. Car doors slam.

My brain short circuits and I just stand where I am. When Nina and Smilla come through the door, I'm still there in the middle of the hall, with my coat and hat on but no shoes on my feet.

Smilla hurries straight up the stairs with all her winter gear on. For a moment Nina seems to consider going after her, but then she throws herself into my arms instead.

'Oh, Fredrik!' She rests her head against my chest and gives a sob. 'It's just terrible! Jennifer is dead. They found her in the quarry.'

'No.' I hide a sudden wave of dizziness by clinging to my crying wife. 'How . . . do they know what happened?'

Nina leans back and gazes at me with glistening eyes. 'No idea. All I know is it was a search-and-rescue dog that found her. That's what Smilla heard.'

I'm about to say something about how Jennifer must have been awfully drunk to end up in the water there, but I change my mind.

Anything you say can and will be used against you in a court of law.

'How is Smilla?' I ask instead.

'It's so hard to know.' Nina pulls out of my embrace,

wiping her eyes with a mitten. 'She's in shock, I think. Swinging between different emotions. I hope . . . I hope we can give her the comfort she needs. She might end up needing professional help.'

A fresh wave of dizziness comes over me and I swallow hard. Nina studies me from head to toe with a frown.

'Where are you going?'

I automatically bring both hands to my hat, tugging it a little further down over my ears.

'I was going to take a walk.'

'There's a hell of a snowstorm. And Smilla . . .' Nina nods towards the stairs. 'I mean . . . I could maybe use a little help.'

'I won't be gone long. Just going to take a lap around the neighbourhood.'

'So you're feeling better, then?' There's a trace of irritation in her voice.

'A little.' I find my winter boots, which have been on the rack, untouched, all season. I step into them and tie them snugly. 'And a little fresh air can never hurt.'

Nina sighs and bends down to pick up her purse from the floor.

'Hey, listen . . .' She opens her purse and rummages through it. 'Someone called from the police earlier.'

My heart skips a beat, then runs amok. The coat. Shit. Someone must have found it.

'It was you she wanted, and said she'd called a few times.' Nina looks at me. 'Did you have your phone off?'

My heart is pounding so loudly that I have trouble hearing what she's saying.

Nina reads from a wrinkled scrap of paper. 'Her name is Lina Torrero.'

'*I'm* supposed to call the police? Why?'

'I don't know.' Nina has started up the stairs and now turns around. 'I didn't ask. But I imagine it has to do with Jennifer. And I promised you would be in touch.'

51. Nina

The living room is restful and dark. The only light comes from the Advent candelabra on the table in front of me. My eyes are drawn to the flames: the flickering glow reflects off my glass, giving the red wine a warmer tone.

I lift the glass, bring it to my lips and take a big sip. My throat feels warm, and soon the warmth spreads through my whole body. My shoulders relax a bit. After a few more sips, my thoughts stop competing for attention; they kindly line themselves up and wait their turn. It's not hard to understand why alcohol is addictive.

Anton has said goodnight but, when I think about it, he could very well still be awake. If no one tells him not to, he can easily stay up playing video games until sunrise. I'll have to go up and check on him in a bit.

Smilla and Vilgot are sleeping in our double bed. Smilla's tears were contagious, so I ended up with two hysterical children on my hands. My solution was to put them both in the same spot and let them each hold one of my hands until they fell asleep.

Smilla can't stop blaming herself. She thinks Jennifer killed herself because of their fight. I have a hard time imagining that it was suicide. Jennifer has always seemed so strong and confident, at least on the surface. But a strong-arm robbery or rape seems just as unlikely.

In any case, the better part of the evening was spent trying to convince Smilla that their fight, all by itself, couldn't have led to suicide. I don't know how many times I said, 'If Jennifer took her own life, there must have been other reasons, reasons we don't know about.' But Smilla wouldn't listen to that explanation. She wailed and screamed and for a few moments was beyond reach.

I got my phone and dialled the triage nurse, but as I was being connected I suddenly felt hesitant, unsure of how to explain what was going on, so I hung up. A moment later, Smilla was back. Still agitated but responsive.

As I'd expected, Fredrik hasn't been any help. He's in Smilla's bed now, and didn't seem to have anything against getting a room to himself. As soon as he came home from his walk, he said goodnight and went upstairs. My husband is acting more and more strangely. He's been knocked out in bed for days, and suddenly he just has to go out for a walk – in a snowstorm?

I set the glass on the table and lean back on the sofa with a big yawn. This day feels like a whole life; I can't believe it was just this morning that Smilla was interviewed by the police. And, speaking of the police, why did that Lina Torrero want to talk to Fredrik? I didn't get a chance to ask if he ever called her back.

She probably just wanted to ask him about Jennifer's mental health. Fredrik and Jennifer were close. I almost wonder if Fredrik didn't know her better than Lollo and Max did. It might sound unfair, but sometimes I got the sense that they weren't all that interested in their daughter, that she was only around for decoration, or like an accessory for Lollo's perfect Instagram life.

Then the day's events catch up with me and I struggle to catch my breath.

Jennifer is dead.

A few days ago, she was standing in our kitchen, all dressed up, giving me grey hair. Now she doesn't exist any more, and we'll never see her again.

It's inconceivable. Surreal.

The new year began with a raging hangover and it's only grown worse since. Yet my troubles are nothing compared to what Lollo is going through.

I try to imagine the scene at the Wiksells' right now. I'm sure they're having trouble sleeping too. Is there outside help to be had when something like this happens to you? Do you have to track down assistance on your own, or is there some system that's automatically set into motion when someone is notified of a death in the family?

I wonder how Max is taking it. Macho Max. Mr Wiksell, who can never take anything seriously, who always has to make a joke out of everything. There's no way he can laugh this off, is there?

And Lollo. Poor, poor Lollo. Max deserves just as much sympathy, but I feel for my friend more than I do for her husband. Lollo lost her mother when she was little. She doesn't talk about it very often, but obviously it must have been traumatic.

Life is so fucking unfair.

I pick up my glass and take a sip of wine. Should I get in touch with Lollo? Call or text or maybe send flowers? I don't know what you're supposed to do when someone loses their child. It seems ludicrous to have a bouquet delivered. Who cares about flowers when their life has just come crashing down?

I'm sure Lollo's Facebook timeline is full of condolences, hearts and crying emojis. But I have no need to make a show of my emotions there. Besides, Lollo and I have known each other over half our lives, and at that point comfort shouldn't come via social media. But calling her . . . no, that would be like marching in on the Wiksells' special-order tiled floor in dirty clogs. At least, so soon after they learned of Jennifer's death.

I put my glass down and pick up my phone, bring up 'Lollo' from among my contacts and open a new message.

Dear Lollo,

That's as far as I get. What on earth am I supposed to say? What would I want to hear if I were in her shoes? I don't even want to think about it.

I heard what happened and I'm so sorry, we're all devastated. We loved Jennifer

No.

We have so many lovely memories of

No.

I toss the phone on the sofa beside me, drink more wine and stare out the window. It's still snowing but not as hard. I feel a sudden wave of melancholy. Why don't I have anyone to talk to? Do I have to go through this on my own?

My fingers fumble for my phone and soon I've brought up Malena on Messenger.

Awake? I write. Time to talk?

A green dot under her profile picture shows that she's online. I stare at the chat as though it will speed up her response time. And maybe it does, because soon enough a single word appears on the screen:

Definitely

'You heard, didn't you?' is the first thing I say.

'Yeah, I read about it online a little while ago.'

Malena's voice makes the surreal more real, and I suddenly feel short of breath.

'Smilla . . . Smilla helped out with the search,' I manage to say at last.

Malena gasps. 'What? She did?'

'She wanted to. I didn't think I could stop her. But she wasn't the one who found Jennifer, thank God. It was a search-and-rescue dog.'

There's a brief silence before Malena says anything.

'It's so crazy,' she says. 'You always think this sort of thing doesn't happen in real life, and then it happens to *Jennifer*.'

'I was thinking the same thing,' I say. 'And here we were, talking crap about her the other day. It feels so –'

'So what?' my friend asks. 'You're not thinking it's your fault, are you?'

I can't help but smile. 'I spent a few hours trying to get Smilla to understand that none of this is her fault . . . and here I am, feeling guilty.'

'Oh, please, Nina. Why?'

Malena almost sounds angry.

'Well, you know . . . the party and all that. How we let them have it here, and it got out of hand.'

'Forget the party,' Malena says firmly. 'Jennifer could have committed suicide, or –'

'Do you really believe that?' I interrupt.

'I don't know.' Malena sighs. 'What else would it be?'

'Not a clue,' I say. 'But suicide and Jennifer don't really seem to go together. She wasn't the type.'

'There's no special type when it comes to suicide,' Malena objects.

'No, of course not . . .' I lose my train of thought for a moment but keep talking: 'It's just that Lollo never mentioned anything about Jennifer's being depressed.'

'Maybe she didn't know. Lots of people just carry their problems around without talking about them. It's pretty common for people to keep stuff like that to themselves. Believe me, I've seen it a lot.'

A couple of candles have burned down to the decorative moss and, just to be safe, I bend forward to blow them all out.

'Maybe that's exactly why we should have been supportive instead of waiting for her to come to us.'

An image of Fredrik's pale face pops into my mind, and I blink a few times to make it go away; instead I fix my gaze on the half-empty wine glass before me.

'I'm sitting here draining a glass of wine by myself,' I confess. 'I needed to relax somehow.'

'As well you should,' Malena says. 'I could use something calming myself.'

Her approval prompts me to pick up my glass and take a massive gulp.

'Have you talked to Lollo?' I ask.

'No.' Malena sighs again. 'I really should have been in touch earlier this week, and now I'm even more leery. I mean . . . what can you say?'

'I don't know. I just tried to write her a text, but everything sounds wrong.' An idea suddenly comes to me. 'You wouldn't want to have coffee tomorrow, would you? It would feel good to talk.'

'Tomorrow?' I hear Malena moving around her apartment. 'I just have to check on something. Hold on.' For a long time all I can hear is a rustling sound on the line. 'Sure, that should work,' she says at last. 'Are you free in the afternoon?'

Thank God for Malena. She knew Jennifer, and she knows Lollo. But above all she is acting normally in the midst of the current chaos.

'That'll be perfect,' I say, just as I remember the situation at home. 'Assuming Smilla feels better. I don't know if I want to leave her alone.'

'Isn't Fredrik around?'

'Yes, but . . .' Something swells in my throat. I try to swallow it down, but it doesn't work. 'We'll . . . I'll tell you tomorrow.'

'Sure.' Malena seems to hesitate. 'Is everything okay, Nina?'

'No.' My throat throbs. 'No, it's not okay at all, but . . .' I take a deep breath. 'I'm sorry.'

'You don't have to apologize,' Malena says gently. 'I can imagine you're having a really rough time right now.'

'But it's not just that. It's Fredrik too. He . . .' It feels like the spot below my ears and way back in my throat is going to burst; my eyes are about to overflow. 'He's acting so weird. He says he's stressed out because of work. But I don't know . . . At first I thought there was someone else . . .'

I'm overcome with tears, and it's impossible to keep talking. It's like I've been collecting these tears and caching them inside me, and now there's no room for any more. They gush out and some of them find their way down the hand that's holding my phone; the cuff of my sweater gets damp.

Malena waits patiently until I'm done sobbing.

'Do you want to talk about it?' she asks.

'If I start talking now you'll never get me to stop, and you'll have to sit up half the night.' I heave another sob and laugh at the same time, which makes a snorting sound. 'It's probably better if we wait until tomorrow instead.'

We arrange to meet at Espresso House at Hansa at three o'clock, and hang up.

I grab my phone and compose a text.

> Darling Lollo, I heard about Jennifer. It's just terrible and
> we're all so sorry about what happened. I don't know
> what to say that won't seem pathetic and silly.
> But I want you to know that we're thinking of you,
> and our hearts are with you.
>
> I hope you have someone there for support. Promise
> me you'll get in touch if there's anything we can do.
>
> Big hugs from Nina, Fredrik and the kids

4 January 2019

Friday

52. Lollo

I meet Jennifer in the strange margins between dreaming and waking. She's a new-born, lying on my chest with a thin white cotton hat on her little head. She's so tiny that even the smallest hat is too big. I take in the sight of this wrinkled bundle with equal parts of terror and love. A new life. My responsibility.

Suddenly she's a one-year-old, toddling along with her chubby fingers gripping the handle of her baby-walker, her diaper serving as a cushion when she falls.

Then she's five, sporting crooked pigtails. She's going to a party, and I've dressed her up in a skirt and a blouse with puffed sleeves. We're hardly out the door before her tights come off. I scold her, grab her arm roughly. The waistband snaps across her belly.

An instant later, she's eleven. A tall, skinny soccer girl with red cheeks, sweat on her forehead and a big smile. She's just scored a goal. Or maybe an amazing sliding tackle.

Teenage Jennifer is more nebulous. First she's standing in the front hall, on her way to school in a low-cut shirt and too much make-up. Then she's on her bed, her face bare, wearing a sweatsuit. She's got her computer in her lap, studying for a test. History. Or maybe social studies.

Jennifer fades away and I squeeze my eyes shut, trying to stay in that place. My hands fumble at the air. I cry out, begging and pleading.

I don't want to leave my darling girl.

When I open my eyes, there is daylight beyond the blinds. My face is wet. Was I crying in my sleep? I must have been. But how can it be possible? How can I sleep when Jennifer is dead?

Jennifer is dead.

Each time the words run through my mind, I feel physical pain. It's like a knife to the belly. Or maybe the ribs.

It hurts so goddamn much.

My phone is on the nightstand. Did *I* put it there? I don't remember how I ended up in bed last night; I have only vague memories of sitting on the sofa with that policewoman, Lina Torrero, and her male colleague. Dad and Agneta were there too. Did they ever leave? I listen for clues but don't hear anything; the house is quiet. Unusually quiet.

Out of sheer reflex I pick up the phone and wake up the screen. I realize I'm hoping to see a text from Jennifer. A shuddering sob slips out. Never again – *never, ever* – will there be a message from Jennifer on my phone. Never again will I get a text from the night bus that says On my way or Home in 5, punctuated with a heart or two.

Never again.

There are other messages on my phone. Lots of them. I read a few, one from Nina among them, but soon I put my phone aside. None of these messages mean a thing. There are no words that can bring Jennifer back to me.

Several of our friends want to know if there's anything they can do. But what would that be? There's not a thing anyone can do.

Jennifer is dead.

There's a soft knock at the door, and Dad's head pokes

through the crack. He comes in, stopping a few metres from the bed.

'How are you feeling?'

My head explodes, my throat constricts, and my ribcage squeezes my lungs. I can't produce a sound; all I do is shake.

Dad sits on the edge of the bed, brushes my hair out of my face and tries to stroke my head with even, gentle pats.

'Cry,' he says. 'Just cry.'

It's like an echo from another era.

Maybe he stays there for two minutes. Or ten. Or an hour. I have no idea. At last, I'm out of tears.

'Where's Max?' My voice is gravelly.

'He's in the kitchen with Agneta.' Dad adjusts the covers, tucking me in just like when I was little. 'We thought we would stay until the police had been here to talk to you.'

Just then Agneta enters the room. She approaches the bed, takes my hand and squeezes it.

'How are you doing?'

Before I can respond, she's over at the window, fiddling with the blinds; she raises them halfway until I can see a streak of grey January sky.

Dad squeezes my arm; then, with some difficulty, he gets to his feet.

'Jennifer's confirmation pastor just called,' says Agneta, who is back by the bed. 'He called Max, that is.'

'Anders Edwall?' I look at her. 'What did he want?'

'I expect he wanted to show his support and . . . you know, offer his help. Max took down his number in case you want to talk to him.'

'I don't believe in God,' I whisper, feeling my throat tighten again.

'I think it was more in case you needed someone to talk to.' Agneta is standing in the doorway now. 'What do you say to some coffee and a sandwich? The police were going to come around ten.'

I don't know how I'm supposed to be able to sit upright and talk to strangers about my dead daughter. It feels downright absurd. But a moment later, it occurs to me that they're coming to see us for a reason. They're going to figure out what happened. And who did it.

If that Willie Winkie killed my Jennifer, I hope he spends the rest of his life behind bars. Or rots in hell. Same goes for Petter Silvén. Same goes for whoever did it.

I have to pull myself together. Because I am determined to do everything in my power to find that bastard.

'What have they told you?'

I swing my legs over the edge of the bed. Both Dad and Agneta look surprised, unprepared for the sudden energy in my movements.

'What have who told us?' Agneta asks.

'The police, obviously. About Jennifer. Do they know how it happened? How she ended up in the quarry?'

'They really haven't told us anything yet . . .' Dad shrugs. 'They've only asked questions.'

I stare at him.

'They talked to you two too?'

He nods. 'Just really briefly. After they talked to Max.'

I'm so confused.

'But why?' I get to my feet. 'What can *you* tell them? You haven't seen Jennifer since Christmas Eve.'

'Nothing about her disappearing,' Agneta says. 'But I guess they wanted to get a picture of . . .' She hesitates for a moment, but then goes on. 'A picture of the family, the people around Jennifer.'

The floor sways beneath my feet. I try to make sense of what Agneta is saying. Then my whole body goes cold.

'They aren't thinking . . .' I take a step forward and grab her arm. 'They aren't thinking it was suicide, are they? That she . . . That we didn't . . .'

'Lollo.' Agneta places her free hand over mine. 'They haven't said what they're thinking. And I suspect they're not going to until they know for sure.'

'I'll be right there,' I mumble. 'Just need to take a shower.'

The water streams over my naked body. I close my eyes and try to ignore the thoughts that force their way in. No such luck.

Was Jennifer so unhappy that she took her own life?

Were there signs, things we didn't spot?

Should we have noticed something?

One of the poems I found on Jennifer's computer comes back to me.

I love you.
I hate you.
But I hate me more.

My tears join the water, disappearing through the holes in the chrome drain.

53. Fredrik

Malmö is painted in shades of brown and grey. To be sure, there are some signs of yesterday's storm in our neighbourhood: north-facing lawns are splotched with white, and the plough has left behind a narrow strip of snow on either side of Sallerupsvägen. But the closer to downtown I come, the browner it gets.

Hardly two days have gone by since I drove to Klagshamn, and yet the car feels strange, as though my muscle memory has been completely erased. At the intersection with Drottninggatan, I forget to put in the clutch, and the gears shriek as the engine cuts out.

There's not much traffic this early in the morning, but it's still hard to find a parking spot. Apparently lots of people have taken time off between New Year's Day and Epiphany, because the side streets behind the police station are full of parked cars. At last I find a spot after all, as well as a sign that shows me which parking apps will work here.

I've been dreading this moment since New Year's Eve, but I feel remarkably relaxed as the glass door of the massive building closes behind me. Maybe that's because most fears are worse in your mind. Or maybe I still have the ability to maintain my composure when it's crunch time.

Because I'm guessing that crunch time starts now.

I'm sure I can expect whoever questions me to be trained to recognize anxiousness or uncertainty. So I must appear calm and collected. This is my only chance. I may be under suspicion at this point, but, assuming they don't have any concrete evidence, I should be able to talk my way out of this as long as I can explain myself and keep from falling apart.

You didn't do anything, Fredrik.

You just talked to Jennifer.

And you definitely did not hide a coat in a dumpster in Elisedal.

You've never been there, you don't even know where it is.

I walk up to the glass booth and state my business. The woman in the booth hands me a visitor's badge and tells me to have a seat. The bench is hard and uncomfortable. But I suppose feeling uncomfortable is the whole point here. I look around. A young man on the next bench over is staring vacantly ahead, one foot jouncing on the floor. Is he some sort of suspect? Or is he here to give a statement? Whatever the case, he seems really nervous.

'Fredrik Andersson.'

Startled, I leap to my feet and find myself standing eye to eye with the same policeman who was at our house the other day. My heart shifts into a new gear. There's something about this man that makes me uneasy. Maybe it's his penetrating gaze. Or his quiet demeanour. It seems deceptive, like the calm before the storm.

'Wow, you're really on the ball around here.'

I groan inwardly. Maybe that phrase could be chalked up to an occupational hazard, but I don't think I've ever used it before.

'Marko Stojković,' says the hefty officer, putting out his hand. 'We met last Tuesday.'

We shake hands, and I hope that whatever's happening on my face resembles a smile.

'This way.'

Stojković walks ahead of me further into the building. The hallway is empty and desolate. There's not a soul in sight, just an endless line of closed doors. I try to hold tightly to that laid-back attitude that I had just a moment ago.

I have to do this right. I have no other choice.

For a moment I see Nina in my mind, just the way I saw her on New Year's Eve before it all went to hell. Her hairdo, the soft curls on the back of her neck, her green dress and big smile.

Darling Nina.

'Please, come on in.'

Stojković has stopped in front of one of the doors. It's wide open, and he gestures for me to precede him. The room is very small. The floor is grey, the walls are white, and the only furniture is a table and four chairs. It looks exactly the way I've always pictured an interrogation room. Cold and impersonal.

We sit down at the table; me on one side and Stojković on the other.

'The detective will be here any minute,' he says.

I nod and gaze out the window. All I can see is a dull grey sky, and I turn back to look at Stojković, forcing myself not to avert my eyes. This must be one of their tactics. They're making me wait alone with him to see how I behave.

Just then, the door opens and a short woman in her thirties enters the room. Her long, dark hair is up in a high ponytail, and she's wearing civilian clothes, just like her colleague.

I start to stand up, but the woman takes a step in my direction and extends her hand.

'No need to get up,' she says, squeezing my hand with surprising strength. 'Sorry to keep you waiting. Lina Torrero,' she continues. 'Detective.'

'Fredrik Andersson,' I say for no reason.

After all, she knows perfectly well who I am.

Lina Torrero lets go of my hand and takes a seat beside Stojković, who opens a laptop and waits.

'Okay, then . . .' Torrero flips through a few documents. 'We might as well get started.' She glances up at me. 'Do you have any questions before we begin?'

I shake my head, but my mind is buzzing with thoughts. *Should* I have questions? Should I raise hell, questioning why I'm even here? Should I make a scene because they made me come in during Christmas vacation?

Lina Torrero starts a recorder on the table and states the names of those present as well as the date and time of this interrogation. Just like in the movies.

'How are you feeling?' she asks.

'How am I feeling?'

Lina Torrero allows the question to hang in the air for a moment before she goes on.

'Your wife said you haven't been feeling well for the past few days.'

'No, I mean, yes. That's true.' Stojković's eyes are burning holes in my head. 'I'm under a lot of stress at work. And then all this with Jennifer Wiksell. I had a little brother who took his own life. He was a few years younger than Jennifer when it happened, but . . . Well, you always think . . . Those are some tough memories.'

She nods.

'You're a teacher, right?'

'Yes, upper grades. Math and gym.'

Torrero glances at the top piece of paper and then looks at me again.

'Do you have any idea why you're here?' she asks.

'Not to talk about my health, I'm sure,' I respond in an attempt at humour.

Neither Torrero nor Stojković cracks a smile.

'I assume it has to do with Jennifer,' I rush to say, adding, 'But I honestly don't know how I can help. You've talked to Smilla, my daughter. She and Jennifer had a party at our house, but I only said hello to Jennifer before we went to her parents' house, I never actually talked to her.'

Stojković's fingers fly over the keyboard. What is he doing? What I just said – was that really something he needed to get in writing?

Torrero clears her throat. 'Can you describe your relationship with Jennifer Wiksell?'

'Relationship? We didn't have a relationship.'

I don't even have to act indignant.

'As I understand it, you were close to Jennifer,' Lina Torrero says calmly. 'She liked you.'

I exhale.

'Jennifer and I got along well. She hasn't always had it easy, and –'

'Can you expand on that?' the detective interrupts me.

'On what?'

'You said Jennifer didn't have it easy.'

I pretend to consider the question for a moment, but then I recite a speech that I've been tinkering with for days.

'Well, Jennifer's parents have always held their daughter to awfully high standards. At the same time, they hardly have any time for her. I guess I'm one of the few adults who truly listened to her. To be honest, she was pretty difficult when she was little, she was attention-seeking in a lot of ways. Which was probably partly because she so rarely got any affirmation from her parents. But if you took the time to talk to her, she was like any other kid.' I settle in against the hard backrest. 'You run into that kind of thing at school all the time. Most students aren't difficult if you just treat them with respect. And give them time.'

'When did you see each other?' Torrero asks.

I freeze.

'We didn't see each other. Or, I mean, we saw each other at family gatherings. They were more frequent when the girls were little, and always for Midsummer and New Year's Eve. In recent years, Smilla and Jennifer would eat with us and then head out for their own celebrations later in the evening.'

'So you never spent time one on one, just you and Jennifer?'

'No, we did.' I relax again. 'For a while, a few years ago, she needed help with math. I would drive over to the Wiksells' to help her. It happened on a couple of weekday evenings, and as I recall both Lollo and Max were away on one of those occasions.'

'But, besides that, you haven't seen each other outside your families' spending time together?'

'No.'

I aim a steady gaze at Stojković.

Lina Torrero doesn't say anything as she gazes down at her documents. All I can hear, besides the rustling of paper, is a humming sound from a vent up by the ceiling.

I glance at the sky outside and try to imagine what it would be like to never leave this building, to be locked up in a space this small, with only a single, barred window on to the world.

'Did you ever have contact by telephone?' Torrero suddenly asks.

'Not often,' I reply. 'But once or twice she called to ask for help with a math problem.'

Torrero nods thoughtfully.

'I don't imagine it was math problems Jennifer wanted to discuss when she called you on New Year's Eve.'

This conversation has progressed just as I suspected – and wanted – it to.

'Called me?' I put on a contemplative expression. 'Jennifer and I didn't talk on the phone on New Year's Eve.'

Lina Torrero shoves a piece of paper under my nose.

'According to the carrier's records, Jennifer called you just after midnight.'

I shake my head.

'There must be some mistake. I didn't talk to Jennifer on the phone on New Year's Eve. I just said goodbye and wished her a Happy New Year at home in our kitchen.'

'The carriers' call lists are typically very accurate,' Torrero says drily. 'And the call lasted for several minutes.'

She places a slim finger on the paper between us.

I throw up my hands.

'Well, in that case she must have called me, and I must have accidentally picked up somehow. My phone was in my pocket, and that sort of thing can happen. That you call someone or answer by mistake, I mean.' I let my gaze wander between Torrero and Stojković. They don't look convinced. 'I swear. I didn't talk to Jennifer on the phone on New Year's Eve.'

'Come on.' The detective raises her voice. 'You're not

the first person to cook up a tale about pocket-phoning. You might as well tell us the truth.'

Torrero's unexpected shift in tone makes my heart start beating frantically; I can feel my pulse all the way down to my fingertips. *Remain calm, Fredrik*, I command myself. *They're trying to put you off balance, so don't give it to them. Don't give them anything.*

I sit up straight and look at the detective without blinking.

'I *am* telling the truth. Do you think I'd sit here and lie to your face?'

Stojković and Torrero exchange glances. And perhaps they're communicating in some secret code, because suddenly Torrero leans back in her chair.

'Okay, that's that, then.' She can't hide her irritation. 'But what do you think Jennifer wanted?'

'How should I know?'

The detective looks at me, her face blank. 'You could make a guess.'

I sigh, but I'm secretly delighted to be back on track.

'Well . . .' I take my time answering. 'It probably had to do with the party. Maybe she wanted to tell me it had gone off the rails. Maybe she hoped we'd come home and catch Smilla red-handed before she had time to clean up all the evidence.'

Torrero frowns. 'Why would Jennifer want that?'

'They were fighting,' I remind her. 'Maybe Jennifer thought it would be a good way to get revenge.'

Stojković's fingers dance over the keyboard and Torrero leans across the table a bit.

'Can you just briefly run us through your whereabouts on New Year's Eve? Let's say from seven o'clock onward.'

'I was at a party,' I say. 'At the Wiksells'.'

'And you never left the party?'

'Sure, when we went home. Around two thirty. But I've already told you that.'

The detective nods and gathers her documents into a neat pile.

'Thank you, Fredrik,' she says. 'And thanks for coming at such short notice.'

She looks at the clock, states the time aloud and turns off the recorder. We stand up and shake hands.

'Sorry I didn't have much to offer,' I say on my way out the door.

'I think we actually got quite a bit.' Lina Torrero holds my gaze. 'I hope it's okay if we get in touch again, if anything comes up.'

'Of course. All you have to do is call. I always pick up.' A laugh starts to bubble up in my throat and it's all I can do to hold it to a smile before I get in the last word. 'As long as I haven't accidentally put my phone on silent, that is.'

Stojković walks ahead of me down the hall and drops me off in the lobby.

On my way to freedom, I realize that Torrero's comment about getting 'quite a bit' could be interpreted in two totally different ways. And hadn't Stojković nodded when she said that?

That familiar nausea is back. I'm drenched in a cold sweat and my legs will hardly bear my weight on the short walk from the police station to the side street.

I collapse into the driver's seat and rest my head against the wheel as the dizziness slowly fades away.

54. Nina

Fredrik is at the police station. He didn't say much before he left; he seemed anxious and on edge.

I tried to make a joke of it, saying I hoped they weren't going to lock him up. But Fredrik didn't even crack a smile, just scoffed and waved me off like an annoying insect.

My laptop is in front of me on the kitchen table; the coffee-maker is sputtering in the background. Vilgot's watching TV, and Smilla and Anton are asleep. You'd almost think this was a typical Christmas-break morning. No one could tell that our friends' daughter was just found dead in a limestone quarry. There's nothing in here to suggest that I have a child who's on the brink of a nervous breakdown and a husband I no longer recognize.

I Google my way through thousands of descriptions of stress-related illnesses. It's clear that stress is a common problem. There are any number of blogs, forums and wellness websites to dig into.

The description of chronic-fatigue syndrome provided by the national healthcare site seems balanced and straightforward, in contrast to many others. I stop there and start reading.

You have no energy and experience serious exhaustion that doesn't go away no matter how much you rest.

Bingo.

You are irritable, anxious and low-spirited.

I read ever faster.

You may experience various problems with your stomach and digestive system.

The relief is so great I want to cry. Absolutely everything here describes Fredrik right now. And if the problem has a name, there must be ways of dealing with it.

Finally, some positive news.

I get up and go over to the coffee-maker. It's becoming increasingly clear what needs to be done: since Fredrik – in accordance with his diagnosis – is having trouble getting anything done, it's up to me to make sure he picks up the phone and calls the clinic. It will happen today, as soon as he walks through the door.

I take out a mug, pour some coffee and look at the window. My gaze is immediately drawn to the wilted amaryllis. It seems the sole reason for this plant's existence is to give me a guilty conscience. I go to the windowsill, grab the pot and put it in the sink. There, the de-Christmasing has officially begun.

On the internet it said that recovery from chronic fatigue can take a long time. I cling to the word 'can'. Fredrik is strong and fit, so he'll probably recover pretty quickly. And I hope he does, as much for his own sake as for mine. I don't know how long I can handle him being the person he's been for the past few days.

Smilla stands at the threshold of the kitchen. She's wearing the plaid pyjamas she got for Christmas; her hair is a mess and her eyes look narrow and swollen.

I hurriedly put down my mug and go over to give her a long, firm hug.

'Good morning, sweetie. How are you feeling?'

She squirms out of my embrace. 'Like shit.'

Her response gives me hope. There's a sharp undertone to Smilla's voice that reminds me of her usual, grumpy teenage self. Yesterday I couldn't hear anything but despair.

'I understand. What would you like for breakfast?'

She shrugs. 'Is there any cocoa mix?'

'There is if Anton didn't finish it all.' I pull out a chair. 'Have a seat and I'll fix you some.'

Smilla lands on the chair and pulls over the newspaper that's been lying on the table untouched. My first instinct is to tear it out of her hands. For my part, I got caught up in my Googling and haven't read whatever's in the news about Jennifer today. I'm fairly certain there will be at least one article about the discovery in the quarry.

A moment later, I realize that Smilla must have already read everything there is to read about Jennifer on her phone. I can't shield her from reality.

Smilla flicks through the paper as I take out bread, butter and cheese.

'It's so weird . . .' she says after a while.

I turn around.

'What's weird?'

'All this.' She waves her hand at a page of the paper and begins to read aloud: ' "Seventeen-year-old Jennifer Wiksell, who went missing early Tuesday morning after a new year's party in Malmö, was found deceased near her home yesterday afternoon." ' Smilla turns to me and continues: 'I just can't believe it's Jennifer they're talking about. *My* Jennifer.' Her voice becomes thick. 'You read about scary stuff like this all the time, about girls disappearing, getting raped and murdered. But it's always been kind of like seeing it in a movie. Now that it's someone I know . . .

knew . . . it's scary *for real.* I just can't believe Jennifer is dead.'

She collapses on to the table. I dash over and crouch down to wrap my arms around her.

'I know, honey. I know.'

We stay there for a long time: Smilla on the chair, her head against my shoulder; me crouched down, my arms around my warm and living daughter. It doesn't matter that my legs are falling asleep. She's here with me.

As Smilla grows calm again, she makes it clear that she's had enough hugging and pulls the newspaper towards her again.

'It also says something . . .' Her eyes skim the columns of text. 'Here. Look.'

I follow Smilla's index finger and read: 'The police have not ruled out foul play.'

'That must mean it wasn't suicide, right?'

She looks at me with pleading eyes.

'Probably,' I say. I can almost see a weight lifting from Smilla's shoulders.

I skim the rest of the article and read about new witness information which, according to the *Sydsvenskan* crime reporter, might shed new light on the investigation. Apparently some Danish citizen celebrated the new year in Klagshamn, drove home that night and managed to miss all the hullaballoo surrounding the case. Until now.

'You're right,' I add. 'It seems like there might be other reasons.'

Smilla stands up to get some paper towel from the counter, using it to wipe her eyes and blow her nose.

'I bet some dirty old man killed her.' She tosses the crumpled paper towel into the trash. 'If they don't catch the asshole who did it, I'll find him myself. And kill him.'

I nod. Rage can be a good motivator.

'Whatever happened, I'm sure the police are doing their best. And you've already contributed by telling them what you know.'

'But I hardly had anything to tell them . . .'

Smilla falls silent as the front door opens, and Fredrik steps into the front hall. His head is hanging, and he clearly isn't well. His movements are those of an elderly, frail man. Or someone who's lost everything.

'Hi, there!'

My voice sounds fake and hollow. I'd hoped that a visit to the police would put Fredrik in a better mood – that the fresh air and different environment would perk him up. My disappointment is so overwhelming that I can't control myself.

'Hello! Did you hear me?'

A pale face looks up, peering at me through the balusters.

'I heard you.'

'Then feel free to respond,' I say, raising my voice. 'So I know that you did.'

Fredrik holds tightly to the balustrade as he comes up the stairs to the kitchen, as if he might collapse at any moment. I immediately regret my snide comment and my anger turns to self-contempt.

Shape up, Nina, I admonish myself. *Christ, you just read a whole article about chronic fatigue. Fredrik isn't acting like this deliberately. You're supposed to* help *him, not crush him further.*

Smilla looks up from the newspaper.

'Shit.' She stares at her father. 'You *must* be sick for real.'

Fredrik forces a smile and tousles Smilla's hair.

'I'm just a little overworked,' he says. 'But it'll be okay.'

'Speaking of –' I try to make my voice sound calm and trustworthy. 'I was just reading about chronic-fatigue syndrome, and –'

Fredrik's already halfway out the kitchen, and if I had managed to muster a smidgen of patience, it's out the window now. I stand up.

'Can you stay put while I'm talking to you?'

Fredrik whirls to face me. 'Am I allowed to go to the bathroom first, or would you rather I piss myself?'

Smilla rolls her eyes and I take a step in Fredrik's direction.

'Well, why not just say so, then? That you're going to the bathroom. Why would you just walk off without a word?'

When Fredrik meets my gaze, it's suddenly back. That cold, harsh look.

'I wasn't aware I had to inform you of my every move.' His voice is constrained. 'Can I go now, or do I need some sort of permission slip?'

Steam is coming out of my ears and I throw both hands in the air.

'For Christ's sake, Fredrik, it's not about permission, as you well know!' My hands fall again. 'It's about . . . about walking away from me when I'm talking to you.'

Fredrik turns around without a word. He yanks the bathroom door open and closes it behind him with a bang. I find myself staring at the closed door.

Is this my husband? When did he become such an idiot? I have to bite my tongue to keep from screaming out loud. If Smilla weren't sitting right here, I'd do it. Scream, that is.

Goddamnit all to hell! I don't want to be in this house. I can't handle this any more, I have to get out.

'Smilla,' I say as I put my mug in the dishwasher, 'pack your toiletries and a few changes of clothes.'

She looks at me, puzzled. 'Where are we going?'

'To Grandma and Grandpa's.'

I'm pressing the lid on to the tub of butter when I realize Claudia is there with her family. I feel a split second's hesitation before I realize that I don't give a shit if they're there. I don't give a shit that I'll cause a fuss, that it will mean changes to Mom's meticulously planned mealtimes and that there will be a thousand questions to answer.

I have to get out.

My coffee date with Malena will have to be postponed. I'll text her; she'll understand.

'Today?' Smilla frowns. 'But we weren't supposed to go until tomorrow.'

'I changed my mind. And I'm sure Grandma and Grandpa will be nothing but glad to see us sooner.'

Midsummer's Eve, 2018

Fredrik

I see her as she comes walking along the road that leads up to the house. She's barefoot and carrying her shoes in one hand, setting her feet on the strip of grass between the ruts left by tyres. A small white purse bumps against one thigh; it hangs from a gold chain that crosses her chest. Like a golden seatbelt. It can't be much past midnight yet, or maybe twelve thirty. Why is she back already?

I've slouched down in the wicker chair, but now I straighten up. The world spins around me. Shit, I'm trashed.

Jennifer's only a few metres away when she looks up. At first she looks surprised – and maybe a little confused – but then she flashes a big smile and steps up on to the deck.

'Where's everyone else?'

'Ashleep. The party . . .' I realize I'm slurring; it takes effort to produce words. 'The party is over.'

She sits down across from me, dropping her shoes on the wooden planks.

'But you're not in bed?'

'No, I'm . . . I have to sober up a little first. I had –' I cough, and have to swallow down sour bile. 'I had a little too much tonight.'

'Then you have to take a swim!' Jennifer claps her hands. 'That'll sober you right up.' Suddenly she's on her feet, hauling me out of my chair. 'Come on.'

I try to protest, but it's like I have no strength, and soon I'm stumbling across the lawn like a ragdoll.

'Oh my God.' Jennifer giggles. 'How much did you *drink*?'

There's a strong odour of pine and saltwater, and something kind of spicy that must be perfume. The smells make me feel dizzy and nauseous. My feet sink deep into the soft, slightly damp sand. A pinecone pokes the arch of my left foot and I cry out.

Jennifer huffs and puffs but finally manages to tow me all the way across the sand dunes.

At last we're standing on the shore. The sea spreads before us, shiny and dark. The air is mild, with hardly any breeze.

'Nice, right?'

Her whole face is one big smile.

I gaze out at the Baltic Sea, drawing the humid night air into my lungs, and suddenly everything around me seems to have sharper contours.

What am I doing here?

'Damnit, hold on . . .' I look at Jennifer. 'This doesn't feel right.'

A light seems to go out in her eyes, but her smile is still there.

'Oh, come on, don't be such a wuss.' She takes off her purse and tosses it in the sand, quickly pulls off both dress and bra, stands before me. 'We're just going to take a dip. A little night swimming never hurt anyone, right?'

I look away, starting to fumble with my belt and fly.

'Okay,' I mumble. 'A dip.'

We walk down to the water's edge. It's shallow a long way out, and we have to wade pretty far for the water to reach our waists. I dive in, letting the sea surround me. Back above the surface, I see that Jennifer has followed my example. Her head is sticking up close by.

'You were right,' I say, blinking water from my eyes. 'Perks you right up.'

Jennifer smiles and I can see that she's checking out my upper body. I get the sense that she's eating me up with her eyes. I dive again, taking a few strokes towards the horizon. I turn on to my back and splash my feet.

Jennifer is still standing waist-deep in the water. The deserted shore and night sky create a dramatic backdrop for her. The whole scene looks like a painting. She reaches out her arms, cleaves the smooth surface and pops up next to me.

'Pretty awesome, right?'

Plump beads of water drip from her hair and run down past her neck, following the gentle roundness of her breasts.

I look away.

'That's enough exercise for me.' I'm breathing hard after the short swim. 'Not quite in good-enough shape for this.'

Jennifer grabs hold of my arm, pulls herself towards me and plants her feet way too close to my own.

'If I notice you're about to drown, I promise to rescue you.'

There's that look again, that hungry gaze. Her eyes have taken on the same deep blue shade as the sea. It's hard to interpret the expression on her face.

Completely without warning, Jennifer throws her arms around my neck. She winds one leg around my thighs and clings tightly to me, pressing her breasts against my bare chest.

'What are you doing?'

I try to hold her away from me, but it's like being in a vice; she refuses to let go.

Quick as a flash, my body reacts. I don't want it to, but it still happens. The only thing separating Jennifer's belly from my throbbing genitals is the wet fabric of my briefs.

'Fuck!'

A violent shove. She almost ends up under water but manages to stay on her feet.

I set course for the shore with long strides; I want to run, but I curb the impulse.

My mind is spinning. Should I apologize? I don't really need to, do I? She's the one who leaped at me. And what did she mean by it? Was it some sort of test? Or is she planning to use this against me? If so, why?

Behind me I hear Jennifer ploughing through the shallow water. My temples are pounding; the hangover is on its way. I have to remember to drink some water before I go to sleep.

Our clothes are where we left them. I turn around, take off my briefs and hurry to put on my jeans. Jennifer wiggles into her dress and shoves her wet panties into her purse along with her bra.

'Where's Smilla?' My jeans are sagging around my legs and I tug at them. 'Is she still at the party?'

Jennifer shrugs. 'I assume so.'

She looks angry, but I don't want to discuss what just happened. My eyes are drawn to the pine trees and I call up an image of the bed in the guest room. I imagine myself lying there already, right next to Nina.

'Shall we go?'

'Not yet.' Jennifer takes my hand. 'Come on.'

'Hold on.' I work my hand out of her grip. 'Where are we going now?'

'Over there.'

She gives me a sly smile and points at the closest beach hut. It's the last in an uneven line of little bathhouses, sunk deep in the sand and surrounded by poky lyme grass.

I shake my head. 'I think it's best if we go back in now.'

'Do you have to be such an adult?' Jennifer pouts. 'Just let loose for once.'

I button one button of my shirt, then bend down and pick up my briefs, which are now both wet and sandy.

'I *am* an adult.'

'Yeah, yeah.' She grins. 'But that doesn't mean you have to be boring. Come on. Midsummer only comes once a year.'

Somewhere deep down inside I know it's a bad decision. And I don't understand how she manages to convince me. Maybe I'm still drunk and prone to ill judgement. Maybe I want to be nice. Or maybe I can't stand the idea of seeming old and boring.

'Okay. But then we're going back in.'

Jennifer sits down along the front wall of the beach hut. She slaps the sand beside her.

'Room for one more.'

Once I'm seated, she sticks her hand in her purse and fishes out what looks like a roll-your-own cigarette. She waves it in front of my face.

'You smoke?' I ask.

'I never smoke regular cigarettes.'

'But . . .' I look at her. 'What's that? You're not into drugs and all that, are you?'

'Just a joint on special occasions.' Jennifer giggles but, when I don't say anything, she quickly adds, 'That's all, I *swear*.' She elbows me in the side. 'Haven't you ever smoked up?'

'Well . . .'

'What do you mean, "well"?' Jennifer's gaze bores into me. 'Either you have or you haven't.'

The water before me is no longer the Baltic Sea but the Pacific Ocean. The memory of a beach party, light beer and warm night air flashes by. Bon Jovi's 'Runaway' on an enormous boom box.

'Nineteen eighty-eight.' I run my fingers through the cool sand. 'I was an exchange student in the United States. It was a hell of a fun year. And over there it's a lot more common to smoke weed . . . as common as alcohol. So, yeah, I've tried it. But not since, and never in Sweden.'

'In that case, it's about time.' She lights up, takes a deep drag and slowly blows out the smoke. 'Your turn.'

I look at the joint between Jennifer's slim, tan fingers.

'You know what, nope.' I shake my head. 'How would that look? Given that I'm a teacher and all.'

'How would it look? No one can see you here. Relax.'

I hesitate for a moment. Then I take the joint, bring it to my lips, inhale the smoke and cough.

Jennifer smiles. 'A little rusty?'

I nod and take another drag. I hold the smoke in my lungs for a long time, then close my eyes and blow it out.

We lean against the hut, passing the joint between us. I gaze out at the unusually calm sea and feel my body soften, let my thoughts fly free.

Jennifer turns to face me.

'Have you ever thought about how these beach huts look like huge fucking birdhouses?'

She giggles, and my own laughter bubbles up beneath my skin. I try not to chuckle, but I can't stop it. The more I think about how I shouldn't laugh, the more I do. In the end, the two of us are in a pile on the ground, giggling hysterically.

Once our laughter dies down, we stay on our backs and catch our breath. A bank of clouds moves slowly across the grey-blue sky.

I heave myself up and prop myself on one elbow to look at Jennifer.

'You're pretty damn funny. Did you know that?'

She smiles. 'And you're pretty damn sexy.'

I bring my index finger to my lips. 'Shh.'

Jennifer scrambles to her knees, leans over me and takes away my finger. An instant later, she's pressing her lips to mine. I'm not at all prepared; I lose my balance and fall backward. Jennifer straddles me and starts to grind against my crotch.

At first I just lie there, completely paralysed. My mind is sluggish, as if my thoughts are swimming through tar. I'm trapped under her weight, an animal caught in a snare.

Only when she brings her mouth to my ear and whispers, 'I love you' can I act again.

'Shit!' I shove her off and get up. 'What the hell are you doing?'

Jennifer leaps to her feet. '*Me?*' Her cheeks flush. 'You want it! Don't you think I can tell?'

My heart pounding wildly, I look around.

'I don't want anything! How can you –'

Jennifer looks like she's about to cry.

'But we love each other!'

Oh my God. What is she saying? I take a step forward and gently tilt her head up between my hands.

'Jennifer.' Her eyes brim over with tears and I wipe them away. 'Listen. I've known you since you were born. And I love you as if you were my own daughter. But this . . .' I shake my head. 'It just all went terribly wrong. I'm drunk, high . . . You're drunk and high. It doesn't mean anything, okay? It was a mistake. And it won't happen again. The fact is, we could decide that it never happened at all.'

Jennifer turns around and runs for the house.

55. Lollo

'Thank you, Lollo,' says Lina Torrero. 'I know this must be extremely difficult for you.'

We're standing in the front hall. Torrero and her colleague, whose name I've forgotten, are on their way out.

'I had to do it,' I whisper. 'For Jennifer.' My eyes meet the detective's, and I try to keep my voice steady. 'Promise me you'll find whoever killed her.'

'Like I said.' Torrero zips up her jacket. 'We don't yet know if there is a perpetrator. But I promise we will do our utmost to figure out what happened.'

Her brown eyes are full of warmth and her handshake is firm. I trust this woman.

Once the door is closed, I hear the scrape of chairs on the floor and the clatter of dishes from the kitchen.

Agneta comes into the hall.

'Did it go okay?'

I shrug. 'I'm not sure how to tell.'

'I'm sure it went fine.' She places a hand on my upper arm. 'Lennart and I were thinking of heading home now.'

Dad looks at me. 'If you'd like, we can take Chanel with us. In case that would make things easier . . .'

'That would be really nice of you.'

I love my dog, but I don't trust myself right now; I especially don't trust my ability to keep a living creature alive. My fuzzy memories from yesterday evening frighten me.

Dad gives me a hug and my knees go weak.

'I think I need to lie down. Can you find everything?'

Dad leads me to the living-room sofa and I can tell he's struggling to keep it together.

'You'll let us know if you want us to come back, right?' he asks. 'Or if you want us to stay a little longer.'

'Take Chanel and go on home,' I say, without quite knowing what I want. 'Max is here. And we'll be driving to Lund soon.'

'Lollo, I wish . . .' Dad takes my hand. 'I wish there was something I could do to bring Jennifer back.'

Tears are running down his furrowed cheeks, and I'm transported to my pink bedroom in the house where we lived in the eighties. I'm sitting at the white desk, drawing with my new markers. There're a lot of them, and they're all lined up, a rainbow in a metal case. Dad is standing in the doorway. He says something, then turns away. He did that a lot. Turned his face away as his shoulders bobbed up and down.

I lie down on the sofa and close my eyes. My body feels weak and wrung out, like after a bout of food poisoning. The interview with the police must have taken more out of me than I was aware.

But it was a battle. I truly had to fight not to lose focus, because my thoughts kept trying to wander off in every direction. Throughout the interview, my throat was tight with tears. Obviously I know it's perfectly acceptable for someone in my situation to be sad. But I was afraid of losing control, sure I wouldn't be able to stop crying once I started.

I hear Dad baby-talking Chanel as Agneta rampages around trying to find kibble and leashes. What Max contributes to the situation is unclear, but I could not care less right now.

Our conversation with Torrero and her colleague didn't straighten out a single one of our questions. In fact, it did the opposite. It sounded like they were pretty fixed on the idea that it was an accident. At the same time, they haven't ruled out suicide. Torrero's colleague explained that they couldn't be sure yet because they were still waiting on the medical examiner's report.

'It's only on TV that they work 24/7,' he said with a smile.

As if that was supposed to be amusing. I know what a medical examiner does, but I certainly don't wish to be reminded. And, anyway, there is not a joke in the world that could make me laugh right now.

I will never be able to laugh again.

We'll get to see Jennifer today. Which means that the medical examiner's office must have worked pretty quickly after all. Torrero has promised to meet us there.

I don't know how I'm going to manage; I don't even know how I'm going to get off this sofa and into the car. Yet it's all I want to do. I need to see my little girl.

Neither Torrero nor her colleague seemed all that interested in Jennifer's alternate Facebook account. Most of the questions they asked had to do with her circle of friends. They wanted to know who Jennifer hung out with in her free time; they even asked about her relationships with our friends.

'Is there anyone in your social circle who might have wanted to hurt Jennifer?'

Now, that question struck me as pretty funny. As if Lisen or Fredrik had anything to do with this.

I don't get it. If I were a police officer, the first thing I would do is track down every soul who's friends with

Jennifer Wicked on Facebook. And I would pay extra attention to that Willie Winkie. Considering the conversation they had on Messenger just before Jennifer disappeared, you'd think that would be a matter of course. I mentioned both Willie Winkie and Petter Silvén several times, but it seemed like the message landed on deaf ears. Maybe they've already talked to them?

Torrero and her colleague were just as vague about the work to come as they were when talking about the present situation. It's incredibly galling. As family, we should be allowed some sort of insight into the investigation. It should be our right.

Lina Torrero has been our designated police contact, and, given that role, you'd think she could be a little more open. We've been given her direct line, and she told us we can call any time. But what does it matter if she can't tell us anything?

'We're leaving now, Lollo.'

I open my eyes and see Agneta all bundled up in her coat and hat. Dad stands close behind her with Chanel in his arms. He waves tentatively and Agneta blows me a kiss.

The E22 cleaves the flat landscape in two. Max takes the northern Lund exit, turns left at the roundabout and drives towards downtown. This part of the city usually sparks memories of the days when Nina and Malena were university students here. All the wild parties they smuggled me into – the Lund Carnival, and the Valborg parties at the end of April.

Today there is no nostalgic shimmer to the city. I feel sick and am staring straight ahead without seeing anything. I try to push all thoughts out of my head. Yet there they are, all the time. Those thoughts.

We haven't exchanged a single word on the way here. There's nothing to say.

The GPS voice informs us that our destination is on the right. We park outside a big red-brick complex and step out of the car. An icy wind sweeps over us from between the buildings; it finds its way in underneath pants and down coats.

My whole body is trembling, and I cling to Max to keep from falling over. How can my husband just walk along, so steady and straight? Why isn't he breaking down?

I don't notice Lina Torrero until her voice forces its way into my consciousness.

'Hi, so glad you made it.'

She holds a door open and soon we're crowded into a space that looks like a dentist's waiting room. There's a coat-rack here, a few chairs and a closed bathroom door.

Death's waiting room.

We hang up our coats. A woman with curly silver hair and glasses shows up and shakes our hands. She introduces herself as Eva-Lena, a hospital chaplain.

Eva-Lena has seen Jennifer and says that she's lovely and we'll be able to touch her if we like.

I want to ask how she can possibly be lovely after an autopsy, but I'm afraid that if I open my mouth I'll throw up, so I let the chaplain keep talking.

'I'm here for support,' she says. 'If you'd like, I'm happy to read a poem. We can also pray or sing together. But that's all up to you. And if you'd rather be alone inside the chapel, just let me know and I'll wait right here.'

I have no idea what I want. The conversation goes on,

but I don't have the energy to listen. My head is buzzing, as if that icy wind has followed me inside. I let my eyes rest on a point to the left of the bathroom door and try to steel myself for what's to come.

With each passing second, we come closer and closer to finality.

'What if they're wrong?'

My voice hardly carries, but Torrero hears me.

'The wrong person?' She rests a hand on my arm, squeezing it gently. 'I'm sorry, Lollo, but I'm afraid it's not.'

'Well, then . . .' The chaplain looks at Max and then at me. 'Shall we?'

She pushes through the swinging doors and we go in.

Max and I just stand there. My eyes sweep over brick-red walls, lit candles and blue decorations. At last I have seen everything but what I came to see. The reason we're here.

Torrero and the chaplain remain in the background while Max and I slowly approach the stretcher.

I close my eyes and pray for myself. *Let it be a mistake. Say it isn't her.* But when I open my eyes, there she is, and I have to bite my own hand to keep from crying out.

Jennifer looks like she's asleep. A blanket is pulled up to her chin, and her hair is spread over the pillow. Her skin is white under her freckles, and her lips are tinged slightly blue – but it's really her.

We stand in silence, side by side, looking at our dead child. Our beautiful daughter.

I'm holding tightly to Max's arm, and I can feel sobs rolling like quiet waves through his body.

For my part, I'm torn between the urge to howl out my grief and the desire to drop dead on the spot.

A mother isn't meant to say farewell to her child.

56. Fredrik

'Nina, please . . .' I look at her and am almost frightened. Her brown eyes are embers of rage. 'I'm sorry, I didn't mean –'

'Stop!' Nina holds up one palm. 'If I don't leave now, I will say things I'll regret later. It's just as well you spend a few days on your own.' She sighs. 'And you can think about whether or not you're going to call the clinic.'

'Why isn't Daddy coming?'

Vilgot is standing in the hall, all bundled up. He's got his Ninjago backpack in one hand, and addresses his question to his mother even though I'm standing right here.

I haven't been found guilty yet, but to my son I'm already invisible. For one horrid second I feel like this is the last time I'll ever see him, and I have to draw on all my strength to keep from crying.

'Daddy isn't feeling well,' Nina replies as she rummages frantically through a drawer. 'He's going to stay home and rest . . . where on earth are my mittens? Have you seen my mittens, Fredrik?'

Mittens?

'Anton!' Nina stomps up the half-staircase, continues to the next set of stairs and calls up: 'Are you coming or what? Smilla's waiting for us in the car!'

Anton comes thundering down with an open duffel bag in one hand and his phone in the other. He steps into his sneakers and I wait for Nina to ask him to change into boots, but she lets it go today. Instead she sends the kids to the car.

'Bye, Daddy!' Vilgot calls.

Anton gives me a nod and a furtive glance before he vanishes out the door.

Nina is still here, looking at me. She doesn't seem furious any more, just sad. I wait for her to say something about a divorce, that she's thought about it and decided we should go our separate ways.

I feel hollow.

Inert.

Drained.

It's like a thick fog has settled in and around my brain. I can't think, and my whole existence is fuzzy and unclear.

In one sense, it's just as well they're leaving. For the moment, I am a worthless man and a worthless father.

Yet this is the exact situation I was trying to avoid. For six months I was tormented by the idea that Jennifer was going to make up tall tales and ruin my life. Then came New Year's Eve, and everything went straight to hell. For all that.

But the police didn't have to come get me. My family has left me voluntarily. Maybe I should just give up.

'Goodbye, Fredrik.'

Nina takes a step towards me and gives me a hug. I inhale the scent of Acqua di Giò and am overwhelmed by a storm of emotions so intense I have to gasp for breath.

My chest is burning. I want to tell her how much I love her. I want to ask her forgiveness for having ruined everything, and I want to beg her not to leave me no matter what happens. But the words catch on my tongue, the fire is already ash, and I remain mute.

She lets go of me and picks up her bag.

'I hope you're feeling better by Sunday. We'll talk then. Please go read about chronic fatigue on the health guide. If you have the energy.'

And then they're gone.

57. Lollo

I don't know how long I've been lying on the sofa when Max plops down by my feet.

'How are you doing?'

He rests a hand on my arm, slowly stroking the fabric of my sweater. We've hardly touched each other since Jennifer disappeared. It's like everything that happened has driven us further from each other – when it really should be the other way around.

What is wrong with us? Aside from the fact that we didn't manage to take good care of the only child we had.

A vast darkness spreads through my chest, pressing against my lungs, squeezing my airways with all its might. I can hardly breathe, much less talk.

Max takes my hand. 'That was a stupid question,' he mumbles. 'You don't have to answer.'

I look at my husband. His eyes are red-rimmed and swollen; his hair is lank. He looks tired and haggard. But I can't muster any sympathy for him.

'We failed,' I say. 'We were totally fucking useless as parents.'

Max's eyebrows knit in surprise; his expression is pained.

'Don't say that, Lollo.'

I drop his hand and manage to sit up, moving backward into the corner of the sofa.

'But it's true!' My hands fly out. 'We had a daughter but we didn't know her. We cared only about ourselves.'

'You're not being fair to yourself. Or to me.'

'Fair?' Tears run down my cheeks as the words tumble helplessly from my lips. 'We're the ones who weren't fair to Jennifer. We had no patience. We . . . *we* . . . killed her.'

Max stares at me. 'You don't mean that. You're in shock. I —'

'And you.' I aim an index finger at my husband. '*Where* were you when Jennifer disappeared? Where the hell were you when I needed you? You said you were at work. And that, in and of itself, is just sick. But the sickest thing of all is that you drove out to Lindängen and beat up an innocent kid. Just because he's Muslim.'

Max is startled. 'How do you know about that?'

'The internet.' I raise my voice. 'Did you really think I wouldn't find out? And what the hell were you thinking? *Were* you thinking? You're so in love with your fucking job — what will your clients say when they read in the paper about assault and hate crimes? Did you think that would be good for business?'

Max opens his mouth to say something but I can't stop.

'And, by the way, were you even really at work?'

I hop up off the sofa and walk into the front hall.

'Lollo, what are you talking about?' Max follows me. 'What do you mean?'

I pick up my purse from the floor and demonstratively drop it on the chaise longue, then start to dig through it.

'This.' I wave the receipt in front of his nose. 'Explain this.'

'Explain what?' He grabs the receipt from me, starts to read it and then shrugs. 'What about it?'

'Well, don't you see? Read what it says!'

'Calm down, Lollo.'

'"Calm down, Lollo! Calm down, Lollo!" Is that all you can say?' Spittle flies from my mouth, and my eyes burn with tears. 'How about you explain how someone was sitting in Falsterbo eating hamburgers at the same time you were out looking for Jennifer?'

Max sighs. 'I was looking for her. All night. In town, and down in Falsterbo.'

'You didn't mention anything about Falsterbo.'

'Maybe not.' He places the receipt on the bureau. 'But I was there. And I got hungry on the way, so I stopped by Burger King at Mobilia and brought the burgers to the cottage.'

'*Two* combos?'

'What?'

'You were so hungry you ate two burgers with fries?'

Max shrugs. 'Yeah.'

'I don't believe you.'

'Believe what you want. But I'm telling the truth: I did search for Jennifer, and, by the way, I also landed a big sale. A mansion in Bellevue. Call anyone at the office.'

'It doesn't matter. You went to work even though Jennifer was reported missing. That only proves *exactly* how little you cared about her.'

Max throws up his hands. 'Talk about the pot calling the kettle black. You may have spent more time at home, but you sure as hell cared more about your phone and your fucking blog than about Jennifer.'

I know he's right, and that makes me even more furious. All the darkness that's squeezing me from the inside has to get out before I explode.

'Excuse me, but which one of us went to parent–teacher and progress meetings? Who sold hotdogs at soccer matches? Who packed lunches and gym bags? *All* you've ever done is work!'

A vein on Max's forehead bulges; it looks ready to burst any second.

'And apparently it didn't help.'

I gape at him. 'What didn't?'

'Packing lunches. Because you just said you failed as a parent. That *we* failed. But maybe lunches and gym bags aren't a substitute for love?'

What the hell!

'Haven't I given Jennifer my love?' My voice fills the hall. 'Isn't it love, selling hotdogs and packing gym bags and making food? Is it my fault Jennifer didn't want any love once she got to be a teenager? Is it my fault she slammed doors and never shared anything about her life?'

The darkness is everywhere now, all through my body. I take a step forward, moving so close to Max that I can feel his hot breath on my forehead.

'Don't you fucking stand here and lecture me about love! Because you've always loved your job more than your own child.'

Max's nostrils are flared. For a split second I think he's going to slap me, but instead it's as though all the rage drains right out of him. His eyes look tired and his voice sounds like a stranger's when he says it:

'Jennifer wasn't my child.'

58. Fredrik

I should find it a relief finally to be alone, to rest without any disruptions. But I can't relax. The moment I close my eyes, I see Marko Stojković. It feels like he might turn up at our door brandishing handcuffs and his baton at any moment.

I sit down on the sofa but immediately stand up again, pace the house, circling ever closer to my laptop. At last I open it.

I had promised myself not to read even one sentence about Jennifer's disappearance, but it's like someone else has taken control of my fingers. They flutter across the keyboard, turning up everything from sob stories in the major evening tabloids to strange threads on obscure forums.

One lunatic on Flashback Forum claims that Jennifer was selling sex online and thinks 'that little whore got what she deserved'. A medium from Småland says that Jennifer isn't dead at all; she's just on a temporary visit to the spirit world. A classmate, Samira, tells *Aftonbladet* that Jennifer 'probably would have become prime minister someday' and that it's 'so crazy that Jennifer won't be coming back to school after break'.

I feel mildly nauseous but can't stop reading; it's like I have to keep going. A variety of self-harm.

Time collapses, and, just at the point I don't know how long I've been staring at this screen, I turn up an unread article on the *Expressen* website. The headline shouts its message in big, black letters.

PLAYING CHILDREN FIND DEAD GIRL'S PHONE

I stare at the words as though they're written in another language. My heart beats like it's possessed, while my sweaty hand guides the cursor across the screen. I miss the link and have to click a few times before the article opens.

Malmö Police received unexpected help on Friday morning in the investigation of seventeen-year-old Jennifer Wiksell's death. *Expressen* has previously reported on the girl's disappearance and the discovery of her body on Thursday afternoon by Missing People. She was found in the limestone quarry lake in Klagshamn, about fifteen kilometres south of central Malmö.

The unexpected discovery came in the form of a mobile phone, which, according to *Expressen*'s sources, belonged to the deceased.

Six-year-old Belinda Bogdani, who found the phone, handed it over to the police.

'The phone was under Belinda's bed when I cleaned her room this morning,' says Belinda's mother, Edona Bogdani. 'Belinda and some friends found it when they were playing in the woods behind the bus stop on Tuesday. I guess they thought someone had tossed it there. The screen was broken, and they couldn't get it to turn on. Belinda brought the phone home and forgot about it. I immediately remembered what had happened and contacted the police.'

There goes my last shred of hope. There's a microscopic chance Jennifer *didn't* have a copy of her phone on some server. In which case, the police have only had the carrier's data to go on. With her actual phone in hand, they're liable to find a whole lot more. Texts, chats. The whole nine yards. And not just recent examples.

I resume my restless wandering from room to room. My anxiety is eating me up, and I feel Marko Stojković breathing down my neck. More than once I think my phone is ringing, but when I look at the screen it's black.

What am I going to do? Is there anything I *can* do?

No, is the short answer. I can't do a thing.

Except wait.

On my fifth or sixth circuit through the living room, I stop in front of the liquor cabinet. A little whisky might not be such a bad idea. I'm sure it's not the best plan to drink hard liquor on an empty stomach, but I'm really not hungry, and a liberal shot of whisky might jump-start my system. Increase my appetite.

I put in the effort to get out an actual whisky glass, study the available selection in the plundered cabinet and choose a middle-shelf Laphroaig that apparently didn't appeal to Smilla's friends.

I let the amber liquid swirl around the glass a few times before I take a big sip. It doesn't taste as soothing as usual, but I like the burning sensation as it trickles down my throat.

After a couple of glasses I finally feel somewhat relaxed. The fog in my mind lifts slightly, and Stojković drops into the background.

I look around the living room, taking in my surroundings in a way I don't think I ever have before. I study each piece of furniture, the books in the bookcase, the coffee table and the wall art. I decide it feels cosy here. Certainly not as elegant as Lollo and Max's home, but cosy.

Are they happier than we are? Of course they're not happy *now*. But were they happier before?

Lollo and Max have always seemed very close. I've always thought of the two of them as a united front against the world. But that could be a façade. And most people over thirty are aware that money and belongings are no guarantee of happiness. You can have a fantastic house by the sea, a bunch of cars straight off the assembly line, the latest Weber grill, and *still* be deeply unhappy.

I take another sip and close my eyes as its warmth spreads through my body.

What is happiness? Is it finding love? I read somewhere that our worship of romantic love is only a few decades old.

In my opinion, this overconfidence in pairing off as a solution to every problem leads to depression in greater numbers. Because not everyone finds The One, no matter how hard they look. And those of us who believe we've found her – how can we ever know she's really the *right* one?

I must have been happy once upon a time.

59. Lollo

'What did you say?'

My head is pounding and my fingers are tingling. I stare at my husband.

'I'm sorry, Lollo. I . . .' Max looks unhappy as he fumbles for words. 'She wasn't . . . Jennifer wasn't mine,' he repeats at last.

I leave the front hall; I'd like to run out of the house, but I don't get any further than the living room, where I sink on to the edge of the sofa.

'I don't understand . . .' My mind is spinning; I can't focus. 'It . . . how can you say that?'

Max lands heavily on the easy chair across the table from me. He leans forward and buries his head in his hands for a moment before sitting up and looking me in the eye.

'I'm sterile, Lollo. I've known that since I was fifteen and got the mumps. The doctor who examined me said I would never be able to have children of my own.'

'But –'

Max waves a hand. 'Hold on.'

I bite my upper lip with my bottom teeth. The pain reminds me I'm still alive.

'I meant to tell you,' Max says. 'But it was never the right time. And then you started going on about having a baby. When Nina was pregnant with Smilla, that was all you talked about . . .' He sighs. 'I didn't want to disappoint you. I was afraid you would leave me if I told you the truth.'

'But who –'

Even as the words are leaving my mouth, I realize that Max doesn't know. I'm the only one who –

'No idea,' Max says quickly. 'And I've never cared to find out.'

'But weren't you . . .' I gaze down at my lap, then raise my head again to look at my husband. 'Weren't you –'

'Angry at you for cheating, you mean?'

Max leans back in his chair.

I can only nod; I'm having trouble talking as my memory sifts through the time just before I got pregnant, counting the months, wondering how this could be possible.

'No.' He shoots me a crooked smile. 'The fact is, I was happy. It meant I didn't have to reveal that I'm defective. I felt like such a failure, even an embarrassment, that I couldn't give you what you wanted most of all.'

My cheeks get hot as images from a wild new year's party appear in my mind's eye. We were at Malena's place. None of us had kids yet, but Nina was hugely pregnant with Smilla, and I suppose we all felt like it was our last chance to really live it up.

Nine months later, Jennifer was born.

'But I always thought . . . I mean, I don't want you to think I . . .' My thoughts are skidding every which way, slipping out of my grasp. 'Are you sure you're sterile?'

Max nods. 'One hundred per cent.'

My fingers have stopped tingling, but the headache is still there; I rest one hand on the arm of the sofa and try again to capture one of the many slippery threads of thought that are gliding through my brain. It doesn't work.

340

'I don't think you've been unfaithful since,' Max contin- ues. 'Obviously I can't know for sure, but I've never worried about it. The year before Jennifer was born we partied pretty hard, and, well, I guess I have to confess that I wasn't exactly an angel either. When you told me you were pregnant, I figured we were even.'

Buried memories rise to the surface. I remember how Max and I would tumble out of the taxi outside our apart- ment after wild nights of partying, drunk and furious. As soon as we got in the door we would start shouting at each other. Most of the time it was because one of us had been a little too friendly with someone else in our group, or had danced too much with them. These fights typically ended with make-up sex on the hall rug. It feels so far away.

And what had happened at that new year's party eight- een years ago – I'd actually managed to completely repress that memory. You remember what you want to remem- ber, I suppose.

'I . . . I don't know what to say. It's . . . I . . .'

I bite my lip harder and taste blood as the skin breaks. Max stands up and comes over to me.

'I understand, Lollo.' He takes my hand in his and squeezes it hard. 'And, like I said, I had decided never to tell. There was no reason to, right? It just slipped out this time, and I'm so sorry . . .'

I shake my head and try to force my already overloaded brain to absorb this new information. Did Max just tell me he cheated on me? I don't even have the energy to be upset.

My eyes wander across the wall to the right of the sofa. A whole wall full of black-and-white photos of my family. I swallow, force myself to rethink it: black-and-white pho- tos of *what used to be* my family.

That gallery wall is decorative and has been admired by many. I took most of the photos myself, and I recall that I framed and arranged them based on a tip in some magazine.

Jennifer, captured in mid-air on the beach in Falsterbo.

Max, posing in front of the Eiffel Tower with sunglasses propped on his forehead and laugh lines edging his eyes. He's looking lovingly at the photographer. At me.

There is one photo of the three of us together. Agneta took it at Max's fiftieth birthday party. Max and I are standing next to each other. My arm is tucked under his, and I'm leaning on him as if he's my rock. Jennifer is standing in front of Max. He's got a hand on her shoulder and her face is turned up; she's looking at him with a smile.

That wall was proof of our happiness as a family. Now it's nothing but a sad monument to everything that has been destroyed.

I can't hold back the words. They've been on the tip of my tongue for ages, but it seemed impossible to say them aloud. Not any more. I've crossed all the lines there are to cross.

'You assaulted a child.' I turn slowly to Max. 'So how can I be sure you didn't hurt Jennifer? That you weren't the one who –'

At first, Max doesn't seem to get what I'm saying. But then his pupils expand.

'Christ, Lollo.' He drops my hand. 'For fuck's sake, give it up! How can you even think that? I loved Jennifer.'

60. Nina

Mom opens the door even before I've managed to bring my finger to the doorbell, and Vilgot throws himself into his grandmother's arms. Unexpectedly, I find myself tearing up at the scene. Mom straightens up again and looks at me. I can see the worry in her eyes, but I don't want to talk about Fredrik right now, not in front of the kids. Instead I take a step forward and embrace her.

'Thanks for letting us come early.'

'You're always welcome, Nina. You know that.'

I peer over Mom's shoulder, searching for the ivory coat among the outerwear in the hall.

'Where's Claudia?'

'They're in Lund.' Mom lets go of me and adjusts her blouse. 'Visiting an old classmate. Darya, maybe you remember her?'

'Of course.'

Darya Hosseini was a spoiled brat. Her dad was some sort of lawyer; her mom was a doctor. Darya wore designer clothes head to toe, had her own horse, and took every chance she could get to talk about her family's extensive travels.

Claudia often fell silent when Darya talked about Miami and skiing in the French Alps. I always wished I could think of a retort that would shut her up, but camper vacations on Öland didn't feel like much to brag about.

Darya seemed to have this constant need to put

Claudia down, and I never understood how my sister could tolerate it, why she kept hanging out with Darya. Maybe Claudia used her friend as a ticket to a life that was otherwise well out of reach. After all, Claudia got to play in their mansion in Professorsstaden. She got to pet the horse and see her reflection in Darya's shiny riding boots.

'They were going to have dinner there tonight,' Mom says.

As I'm taking off my coat, I discover Dad is in the living room, sitting in his favourite chair with his feet on the ottoman and a big smile on his face.

'*Hola*, Carolina!'

I'm just as surprised each time someone uses my full name. These days it happens only when they call my turn at the dentist's office, or something like that. Dad alone stubbornly refuses to call me Nina.

I wave, hang my coat on an empty hook and turn back to Mom.

'Bad timing, for us to show up right when you got the chance to rest.'

'Oh, don't worry about it.' Her smile looks a little strained. 'We'll have something simple. Meatballs and potatoes, everyone likes that.'

Smilla and Anton come through the door.

'Whoa!' Dad calls from his chair. 'That doesn't look so good.'

The kids look around, bewildered.

'There.' Dad points at the white earbuds sticking out of their ears. 'Something is growing.'

Anton's expression doesn't change, but Smilla smiles and rolls her eyes. Vilgot chortles and heads for the living room.

344

'Stop!' I shout. 'Shoes.'

It's sweaty in the cramped front hall, and, as always, I get the feeling that we're a disruption. Mom and Dad live an orderly, quiet life where everything has its place. All it takes is my big, loud family crossing the threshold for that orderliness to go out the window.

This time, at least, we're not the first ones to bring chaos. Claudia's family got here first. Pauline may be a well-mannered, perfect kid, but I can still see traces of her here. A naked baby doll is standing on its head in one of Dad's rubber boots, and in the middle of the floor is an open Pippi book that Mom hasn't yet tidied away.

After dinner, two spilled glasses of milk and a big lingon-berry stain on the pale tablecloth, Dad decides to take Vilgot outside to get some exercise. Smilla and Anton slip away as soon as they've put their plates in the dish-washer, and I let them go.

Mom and I end up alone in the kitchen, as we tradition-ally do. Sometimes I let myself get annoyed at how Dad and Fredrik always avoid the general kitchen area when-ever we spend time together. To be sure, Dad always keeps a safe distance from the stove, which is Mom's fault. She thinks he gets in the way and shoos him off if he tries to approach. But Fredrik is at least as comfortable in the kit-chen as I am; it's only when we're with my parents that he attaches himself to Dad and turns into a chauvinist pig.

Like Dad, Claudia has always managed to avoid kitchen chores. It's as if she slinks out, slippery as an eel. At first it was because she was little, and then . . . well, once some-thing becomes a habit, that's that. I can only hope she's improved in that sense. She can't just come here with her whole family, stay for days and act like she's checked into a luxury hotel. Our parents are getting old. And Claudia is an adult now, damnit.

Mom puts leftovers into plastic containers. She takes out freezer tape, writes on it with black marker and smooths the tape on the lids. MEATB + POT I S. I wash pots and serving dishes and dry what won't fit in the dishrack with a perfectly pressed dishtowel.

We work in silence. I know Mom is about to burst with curiosity, that she's waiting for an explanation for our sudden arrival. And obviously I have to tell her. The only question is, what will I say?

A few hours ago, I was just about ready to file for divorce. But the further we got from Malmö, the greater my doubts grew. An uneasy feeling in my stomach turned into cramps. I still have a stomach ache.

How could I have left a sick person on his own? How could I be so hard on Fredrik when he isn't feeling well?

What if he's suicidal?

But, no, surely he isn't. I would have noticed. Fredrik has been grumpy and out of sorts for a while now. Not depressed. But then I think about what Malena said when we were talking about Jennifer's disappearance earlier this week. That there isn't any particular type for suicide. And that people often keep their problems close to their chest.

We mentioned what happened during dinner, but as luck would have it my parents didn't want to get into any details while Vilgot was there. He knows Jennifer is dead, but that's all. Smilla's hanging by a thread, and I've hardly had a chance to talk to Anton.

Damnit, Fredrik! Why does he have to have a breakdown just when Jennifer goes and dies? I want to be there for my children right now. I want to be present while they go through the grieving process, there for their questions, there to give them helpful answers. Fredrik and his failing health are standing in my way.

I dry yet another serving platter and watch as Mom digs through the cupboard for more plastic lids. Her back is more stooped than it was the last time I saw her, her eyes more tired. But that could be my imagination. Maybe I'm just projecting my own physical state on to her.

'We had a fight,' I say at last.

Mom presses on a lid until it clicks, then turns my way. 'What about?' she says.

'Fredrik isn't doing very well,' I reply. 'Like I said the other day . . .'

'Has it become worse?'

'*I* think so. But he refuses to accept how bad things are, refuses to get help. And I'm going crazy! I can't even talk to him any more.'

I give Mom a brief rundown of the situation, and by the time I'm finished she looks horrified.

'That sounds pretty bad, Nina. Was it really such a good idea to leave him alone when he's having such a hard time?'

I glare at her. 'He doesn't want help! What does it matter where I am, if he refuses to talk to me?'

'Fair enough. But I just thought . . .' Mom hesitates for a moment. 'I guess I was just thinking . . . what if he goes downhill again?'

'Then he has only himself to blame.'

I slam the door of the china cabinet and hear the glasses clinking inside.

'You could call him tonight,' Mom suggests.

'Sure. Or *he* could call *me*.'

Mom raises her eyebrows. 'Fredrik is the one who's sick.'

I don't know if it's Jennifer's death or my anxiety about my husband. Probably it's a combination.

'What about me?' My voice cracks and my eyes fill with tears. 'Doesn't anyone care how *I'm* feeling? Jennifer is dead! My children are distraught, and my husband is going insane or something.' I sink on to a kitchen chair. 'I can't do this any longer.'

The kitchen falls silent – like the sea settling after a raging storm.

A warm hand lands on my shoulder. 'It'll all work out, you'll see.'

'But how?'

My voice is whiny, and I feel like I've travelled forty years back in time. The same kitchen, the same little girl, the same mom.

She squeezes my shoulder. 'We can't change what happened to Jennifer. But I'm pretty sure you could use a few hours' rest.'

'But Fredrik . . . You said –'

'Go lie down in our bedroom for a while.' Mom lets go of me and walks over to the sink. 'I promise to keep the kids out of your hair. And, once you've rested up, we'll have a cup of tea. There's fresh-baked Tosca cake.' She gives me a cautious smile. 'What do you say?'

Tea and Tosca cake can't solve my problems, but rest – a few hours of sleep – surely can't hurt.

'Thanks,' I say. 'That sounds nice.'

61. Fredrik

I must have fallen asleep, because the music almost startles me out of my chair. At first I don't know where it's coming from. I turn my head slowly, looking for the source of the racket.

Eventually I realize that the music is coming from my phone. 'Pour Some Sugar on Me', my ringtone. But this realization doesn't come as a relief – rather the opposite. My heart pounding, I lean over the table and look at the screen.

I don't recognize the number, so I assume it's the police. They've got Jennifer's phone. By now they'll have read whatever's in her apps and texts from New Year's Eve. Jennifer wouldn't be Jennifer if she hadn't spent the bus ride to Klagshamn spreading lies about me.

Or else it's the coat. Maybe a security guard spotted me at Elisedal and jotted down my licence-plate number. Someone might have dug through the dumpster and made a connection between the coat and the man who was driving around an industrial area in the middle of the night.

It's all over now.

The song starts over, the volume increasing a notch. I stare at the digits on the screen but can't bring myself to touch the phone.

Suddenly it hits me: if the police suspected I have anything to do with Jennifer's death, they wouldn't call me first, would they? They'd just come here and catch me off guard.

That does it.

The phone is slippery and slides out of my grasp twice before I get it the right way round.

'Hello?' I clear my throat. 'Who's this?'

'Hi, Fredrik. It's Lollo.'

I gulp. 'Lollo?'

'Yes, it's me.' She sounds annoyed. 'Can we meet up? I need to talk to you. In private.'

The hand holding the phone trembles against my ear. 'Talk?' My mouth is as dry as sandpaper. I moisten my lips with my tongue and taste sour whisky. 'Why?'

'I don't want to get into it over the phone. Are you available to meet up in town?'

I close my eyes and try to get the spinning room to stop, but that just makes it worse. So I open my eyes again.

'In town?'

Lollo sighs. 'Yes, or wherever. I just want to talk to you, Fredrik.'

'Uh . . . Nina's got the car. She's in Höör . . . I'm not feeling so well, I –'

'Are the kids with Nina?' Lollo interrupts.

'Yes.'

My family has left me.

'Well, I'll just come over, then.'

No.

No!

NO.

'I don't know, Lollo, I –'

'Fredrik, this is important. I'm already in the car, and I'll be there in twenty minutes, okay?'

An instant later, the line goes dead and I find myself sitting with the quiet phone in my hand.

What in the world could be so important that Lollo needs to see me the day after her daughter was found dead?

It *must* have something to do with Jennifer. Maybe Lollo found evidence. A diary. A letter that was never sent. She's going to force me to confess.

My fingers fumble to bring up the call list on my phone. I press the topmost number and listen to the ringing on the other end. I wait.

No answer.

Oh, hell.

My heart is beating fast. I look around the room as if I'll find the solution to my problems around here somewhere. No such luck.

I suddenly stand up; I nearly tip over and try to remember exactly how many glasses of Laphroaig I downed before passing out. Three? Maybe four.

My head is pounding and dizziness forces me back into the chair.

62. Lollo

I hang up, toss my phone on the passenger seat beside me and lean my head back against the headrest.

This new knowledge is overshadowing everything else. I get that it's temporary, that it's just a way to shift focus from the horror to something a little easier to deal with. But I let myself be pulled along, unwilling to think about death.

I drive as if in a trance. Gas, brake, indicator. Twenty minutes later, my Mini Cooper is in the driveway of the Anderssons' row house. The car door slams loudly, and I jog up the uneven slabs to the front door.

The house seems deserted, and I hesitate, looking around. It's dark outside now, and there are Advent candelabras and stars lighting up the windows of the other houses. I can see the silhouettes of two people behind the curtains of a window across the street. Two kids are playing with a dog in front of another house.

There are no signs of life at the Anderssons'. The kitchen window is dark, but I think I see a faint glow which must be coming from a light further inside, maybe from the living room.

I hit the doorbell, and there's a rasping sound on the other side of the scratched door. I cannot believe they haven't replaced that door yet. How long have they lived here? Eighteen years? They could have at least repainted it.

I give the doorbell another whirl, but nothing happens,

and I'm just about to take my phone from my purse when I hear a soft sound from inside the house. A moment later, the door swings open to reveal a narrow crack of darkness. I stick my head inside and gasp.

'My God, Fredrik. Are you okay?'

He gives a crooked smile. 'Not so much.'

I don't think I've ever seen Fredrik in such bad shape, not even when he was hung over after our binges back in the good old days.

'Are you sick?'

Fredrik shakes his head. 'Nah, just a little burned out . . .'

He stands there in the dim light, running one hand through his hair and repeating the motion several times as if he's developed a tic. His pale face is covered in dark stubble that's a little too far gone to be attractive. His eyelids droop.

My first instinct is to turn right around and run back to the car. But I'm here now, and who knows when I'll get the chance to talk to Fredrik in private again. Might as well get it over with.

'May I come in?'

'Lollo, I . . .' He teeters and grabs the doorframe. 'I'm tired. Really tired.'

I stare at him. 'You're not exactly the only one.'

'I'm sorry.' Fredrik opens the door and takes a step back. 'I'm sorry, Lollo. I . . . I'm so, so sorry. I don't know what to say . . .'

'Thanks.' I step into the front hall, hang my jacket on a hook beneath the hat rack and turn around. 'You don't have to say any more. Could we have some coffee?'

We go up the steps and into the kitchen. I sit down at

the kitchen table while Fredrik goes over to the coffee-maker. He just stands there with the pot in hand, noticeably swaying.

'Have you been drinking?'

'Just a little whisky. But I don't think my tolerance is very high right now. I . . .'

Fredrik loses his train of thought and I stand up and grab the pot from his hand. 'Sit down.'

He obediently takes a seat on a kitchen chair while I turn on the tap and measure out water for four cups. I find a filter, fold the edge and press it into the basket. The metal can of Zoéga is in the cabinet above the sink. This kitchen is almost as familiar as my own; I can find just about everything after so many coffee hours and parties. Being alone here with Fredrik, though, is a new experience.

'Lollo,' Fredrik says, his voice suddenly sharp.

I turn around.

'Why are you here?'

I start the coffee-maker and go back to the table, pull out the chair across from him and sink into it.

'I have something to tell you.'

He gazes at me curiously and my heart beats faster.

'Do you remember . . .' I say tentatively. 'Do you remember the new year's party at Malena's? The one we had the year before Smilla and Jennifer were born?'

At first Fredrik looks totally blank, as if he doesn't remember who Malena is. But then he seems to wake up and starts running his hand through his hair again.

'You mean when . . . the time you and I . . .'

I nod and consider the pathetic figure before me. How could I find him attractive? *Did* I even think he was attractive? Or did I just want to mess with Max?

A whole gang of us were celebrating the new year at Malena's that year, about twenty people. Fredrik and I sat next to each other during dinner, and he kept coming back to how boring Nina had become during her pregnancy. At first he just complained about how tired she was, but eventually he started whining about how they never had sex. Not long after that, I felt a hand on my thigh.

At first I was totally floored. What was he doing? That sort of groping wasn't like Fredrik at all, and my first instinct was to give him a good slap. But then I noticed Max flirting with one of Malena's single friends, and I decided to give him a taste of his own medicine.

The more we drank, the bolder Fredrik's advances became, until at last we ended up in the bathroom. Unfortunately, I can't say I'm not to blame – both of us had a lapse in judgement. Then again, I don't think either of us meant to go all the way. I remember that, right before it happened, Fredrik mumbled something about how maybe we should stop. But by then I had made up my mind.

We sobered up right around the time he pulled out. I was so ashamed; it all felt wrong and uncalled for. We promised each other never to utter a word about what had just happened to anyone. Then we left the bathroom one at a time, leaving a few minutes between our exits.

At midnight, Max agreed to try to have a baby. I suppose we were both feeling some regret after our respective dinnertime flirt-fests, and in a rush of new year's sentimentality he caved.

We slept together closer to dawn, and when it turned out, a few weeks later, that I was pregnant, I convinced myself there was no way the baby could be Fredrik's. As I recalled it, we had been careful.

'Fredrik,' I say. 'This is totally the wrong time to tell you this. But I still thought you should know . . .'

He looks at me, puzzled, running his hand through his hair.

After a deep breath, I tell the truth.

'Jennifer was your daughter.'

63. Fredrik

My whisky-marinated brain has a hard time absorbing what Lollo is saying.

It's too big. Too inconceivable. Too painful.

'Aren't you going to say something?'

She watches me with tears in her eyes.

I blink, trying to understand, and realize that no matter what I say it will be the wrong thing.

'Say something!' Lollo shouts.

I can't meet her gaze; I quickly turn my head to look out the kitchen window.

I don't see the streetlights, the identical houses or the candelabras in the neighbours' windows. Instead I see fragments of Midsummer's Eve: Jennifer's smile, the hair falling over her one eye, her freckles, her breasts . . . which suddenly turn into Lollo's breasts in some bathroom somewhere, a long time ago. Sweat, lust, her warm body against mine.

Oh, God.

Nausea shifts in my stomach, curling on itself like a thick, black snake. I try to breathe calmly, try to shove all my thoughts away. But they won't retreat. They crowd and press their way out. They scuffle and shove, taking up space, filling my whole head.

An instant later, it's New Year's Eve in my mind's eye. I see Jennifer's figure staggering down the narrow path. The fog, the rain. I squeeze my eyes shut but can't stop the fresh images that pop up behind the old ones. The soaked coat, the black water of the quarry.

My heart is out of control. I bolt from my chair.

'I'm sorry.'

Lollo frowns. 'What did you say?'

I'm just as clueless as she is. Who just said they were sorry?

'What did you say?' she asks again.

I know I should shut up, but I can't stop the rush of words now. They expand in my throat, making me feel like I'm suffocating.

'I didn't mean to.'

Lollo's expression is no longer curious but wary, maybe even suspicious.

'What are you talking about?'

A tiny voice inside tries to stop me, reminding me that it's not over until it's over. But that voice is too weak. My pulse is thundering wildly, drowning out everything else.

'I'm sorry, Lollo, I should have told you, but . . .'

I sink on to the chair I just bolted out of, burying my head in my hands.

'Fredrik.' This time it's Lollo who stands up. 'What are you raving about?'

When I don't say anything, she slams a fist on to the table.

'Answer me, goddamnit!'

God, if you exist, help me now. Take this opportunity to show yourself.

'Fredrik?'

I pull my hands away and look at Lollo. Louise Wiksell, my wife's best friend, our family friend for more than half our lives. Usually so in control, this woman has transformed. Her hair is stringy; her clothes are wrinkled. And there is a bottomless well of despair in her eyes.

'I should have gone after her,' I mumble. 'I shouldn't have left her.'

In the background, the coffee-maker hisses. I need to put out mugs soon. Maybe get out some milk.

'Who are you talking about?' Lollo asks. 'Nina?'

'No, I . . . she called me on New Year's Eve and I panicked, I didn't want –'

'Hang on a second.' Lollo takes a step in my direction. 'Are you talking about *Jennifer?*'

My body is being enveloped by a massive wave of exhaustion. I'd really like to lie down. Just lie there perfectly still, and never say another word to anyone. But I do manage to utter one word.

'Yes.'

Lollo stares at me.

'But what . . . Why did she call you? What did she say? What –'

'She wanted to talk,' I interrupt. 'Jennifer was disappointed in me and she wanted to chat.'

I see Lollo's confusion, watch her desperately trying to compile my disjointed words into something comprehensible. Her gaze wanders. She looks at me, then at the front door, then back at me. Suddenly her eyes fly open wide, her pupils so big that their blue irises look black.

'Was it you?' she whispers. 'Did you kill Jennifer?'

No! I want to shout. No, I didn't kill her.

But, of course, I did.

I killed my own daughter.

'Listen, Lollo. She fell down, I wanted to help her up, but –'

Lollo looks around, locates her purse and grabs it from the floor.

'I'm calling the police.' Her voice is shrill as she digs frantically through the bag without taking her eyes off me. 'Do you hear me? I'm calling them right now!'

She slowly backs away from the table as though she's afraid I might attack her.

As though I were a killer.

'It's totally fine if you call the police,' I say, realizing that I mean it. 'But, please, just let me explain first.'

'I don't want to hear another word from you!'

Lollo is screaming. She holds her phone out like she's aiming a handgun at my head.

And I wish she were. I want to die. But before everyone starts telling their truths, I want Lollo to hear mine.

'Five minutes,' I plead. 'Give me five minutes.'

She doesn't say anything, just stares at me with what looks like hatred. So I keep talking.

'I . . . I didn't hurt her.' My voice is thick; the words come out in fits and starts. 'You . . . have to believe me. I know it was wrong of me to leave her. I should have dragged her home to you, should have forced her . . . But she refused. So what was I supposed to do? I'm so sorry. I know it doesn't matter what I say, but you have to believe it was never my intention. I don't understand how she ended up in the quarry!'

Lollo seems flustered.

'But why?' The hand holding her phone drops to her side. 'Fredrik, *why?*'

I sigh.

'It's a long story, but . . .' Tears burn behind my eyelids. 'This wasn't what . . . I loved Jennifer.'

Lollo stiffens.

'Loved?'

She spits out the word like she's taken a bite of something nasty.

'Not like that. We . . . Look, you *know* Jennifer and I got along well. I tried to be a role model, tried to listen to her and be patient with her. But on New Year's Eve . . . we met up in the woods and –'

'What the *hell* were you doing in the woods?'

If possible, Lollo's gaze is even blacker than before.

'It's not what you think.'

I stand up and take a step in her direction.

Lollo recoils.

'Stay right there!' she shouts. 'Don't touch me.'

'Lollo, listen to me. We were only talking, we . . .' My cheeks are wet and the tears cloud my vision. 'It started when Jennifer and I took a swim at Midsummer. At night. She came back from that party down in Falsterbo and thought we should take a dip. I think she got it into her head that we, that somehow we . . .'

I should just shut my trap, stop digging myself in deeper and deeper here. And why would I bring up Midsummer in the first place? There was no reason to mention it. But it's like I just need to let it all out.

Lollo suddenly takes a few quick steps towards the counter, and, an instant later, she's holding one of our kitchen knives.

'You fucking paedophile!' She throws herself at me. 'I'm going to kill you!'

64. Nina

'Have you talked to Lollo since they found Jennifer?'

Smilla's question is so unexpected that I find myself inhaling sharply. I turn my head and look at her, on the sofa next to me. Her legs crossed under her, her face in her phone.

'No,' I reply. 'I sent a text.'

Smilla turns to face me. 'Isn't Lollo, like, your best friend?'

I have to consider the question before I respond. The sad truth is that Lollo and Malena are all I have. And I've spent more than two decades letting them get on my nerves, especially Lollo.

'Lollo and Malena are my oldest friends,' I say at last. 'But I don't know if that means I'd call them my best friends.'

Smilla frowns. 'If Lollo and Malena aren't your best friends, then who is?'

'Oh . . . Cecilia, maybe. And Eva.'

'Who are they?'

'My colleagues.'

'I've never met them,' Smilla says. 'They can't be your best friends.'

'Maybe not.' I shrug. 'But, you know . . . as an adult, when you work full time and have a family . . . it's hard to spend time with anyone but your colleagues and your family. At least when your kids are young.'

'You should call Lollo,' Smilla says.

My daughter is right. It's just that I don't have the courage. I'm afraid of being sucked into this any more than necessary, afraid that the wreck that is Lollo will end up in my lap. And how the hell am I supposed to glue Lollo back together when Fredrik is broken too?

'I know, sweetie. I know.'

I pull Smilla close, putting one arm around her shoulders as I glance towards the kitchen, where Mom is getting the evening coffee ready. She happens to look up and our eyes meet. Mom smiles contentedly and goes back to her kitchen duties.

Say what you like about my mother, but she knows me well. An hour of sleep has done wonders for my mood; I can finally think somewhat clearly again.

'You can always talk to me,' I mumble, burrowing my nose into Smilla's hair. 'No matter what. Remember that.'

She looks at me. 'You think Jennifer committed suicide?'

'I don't know. The police seem to have other theories.' I lean back. 'It's very possible that Jennifer was depressed . . . did she mention anything to you? Did she say she was having a rough time somehow?'

'Nah. But we hardly ever talked all autumn.'

'Depression could be one reason that she withdrew,' I say. 'Mental-health issues are increasing in teenagers . . .'

Smilla nods.

'I don't think I have a single girlfriend who *isn't* having a rough time. More or less rough, that is.'

'But that's terrible.' I put both arms around her and squeeze hard. 'How are *you* doing, by the way?'

I'm a hypocrite. How can I accuse Lollo of not paying attention to Jennifer when I'm no different? What do I really know about my daughter and her world? My guilt unleashes a wave of heat that starts on the crown of my head and stops at my toes. Sweat beads on my upper lip, and I wipe it away with my index finger.

Smilla creeps closer into my embrace. 'Aside from this Jennifer stuff I . . . guess I'm mostly okay.'

A shudder runs through her body.

'I'm sorry.' I ease up on the hug. 'Stupid question.'

'I don't think it's sunk in yet.' Smilla sighs. 'That Jennifer is gone, I mean.'

We don't say anything for a while. I watch as Mom arranges coffee cups and napkins on a tray. She still uses that ugly lacquered birch tray Claudia made in woodworking class back in school.

'There were rumours about Jennifer,' Smilla says.

She leans forward, puts her phone on the coffee table and sinks back against my chest.

'What kind of rumours?'

'Drugs and stuff.'

'I see.' I try to hide my shock, but I realize Smilla can probably feel my heart beating from her current position. 'Do you think there was any truth to them?' I ask. 'To those rumours?'

'I didn't think so.' Smilla sighs again. 'Or maybe I just didn't want to think so. But now I wonder. You know, if she was depressed, and . . .'

I try to follow my daughter's line of thinking even as my own thoughts are bouncing around like pinballs.

'You mean, she might have been having mental-health issues and the drugs were a way to ease them? That she was high and started wandering around and fell in the quarry by mistake?'

Smilla squirms. 'No, like . . .' She turns her face up

towards mine. 'You know how it said in the paper that the police couldn't rule out foul play?'

I nod and Smilla continues. 'Maybe there was some dealer who got angry when she didn't pay . . .' She looks down at her hands and twists her watch so the buckle lands under her wrist. 'Or however it works.'

I picture Jennifer. So like Smilla, in appearance. For a while, when they were around ten, the girls would amuse themselves by tricking people into thinking they were twins. They got the same haircut, bought the same clothes and practically screamed in delight if they managed to get someone to mistake one for the other. There's a photo from those days of the two of them standing hand in hand down in Falsterbo. Cheerful and freckled.

Could it really be true that Jennifer was on drugs?

On the one hand, it sounds ridiculous. On the other hand, it wouldn't be much of a surprise at all. A drug addiction would simply confirm everything I've always worried about. Her lack of boundaries. The feeling that anything might happen when Jennifer was around.

But surely Lollo and Max would have noticed if she was heading down the wrong path like that. Isn't it obvious when you look at someone to know if they've been abusing drugs for a long time? And Jennifer looked so bright and fresh on New Year's Eve.

I shift slightly to the side so I can take a good look at my daughter.

'*You're* not doing drugs, are you?'

Smilla's eyes open wide. 'Seriously, what do *you* think?'

'I'm your mother. I have to ask.'

From now on, I will always be a step ahead, instead of waiting for rumours to crop up.

Smilla pulls away, shooting me another accusing look. 'Don't you trust me?'

'Of course I do.' I stroke her cheek. 'But listen . . . what kind of drugs are we talking here? That Jennifer was using, I mean.'

'No idea. Like I said, it was a rumour. Maybe she just tried something once. People get ideas.'

Smilla takes her phone from the table. A clear signal. She doesn't want to talk any more, and probably feels insulted. But I'm not about to back off. Can't get answers if you don't ask the questions. So what if the kids feel insulted? Once they're adults, they'll realize we were asking out of concern.

I need to talk to Fredrik about this drugs business, find out if he's noticed anything. Heard anything.

Speaking of Fredrik. And speaking of mental illness. Was I too hard on him?

There's a persistent dull ache in my belly. I would never forgive myself if something happened to him now. If he harmed himself, or . . .

I rise from the sofa.

'Have you seen my phone?'

'It was on the bureau in the hall before we ate.' Smilla doesn't look up from her screen. 'Are you going to call Lollo?'

'Yes,' I say. 'But first I'm going to call your father.'

65. Lollo

My hand squeezes the black plastic handle. I stretch my arm out ahead of me, aiming the knife at Fredrik and watching the veins in his forehead throb. His eyes are wild with fear.

That cowardly, sick, pathetic bastard!

'How long has it been going on?' I shout. 'Have you been fucking her since she was little?'

Images flicker through my mind, as though I'm watching a movie in fast-forward.

Jennifer at three, sitting in Fredrik's lap with a picture book.

Jennifer at six: a smiling Fredrik takes her little hand and offers to help with the croquet set.

Jennifer at fourteen. She's sitting at the kitchen table in front of her open math book, Fredrik by her side.

Who knows where his hands were when no one was looking?

'Lollo, please . . .' Fredrik stands stock still, only his lips moving as he whispers. 'I've never . . .'

'I hate you. I'll kill you, I'll . . .' I compose myself but don't let down my guard. I let the knife dance before Fredrik's face. 'No, hold on. I'll cut your dick off. Death would be getting off easy. I want to watch you suffer absolute hell!'

My rage props me up. It keeps me upright and alive when all I really want is to disappear and leave everything behind.

But before I give up, Fredrik must die. And his death will not be quick; it will be drawn out and excruciatingly painful.

I'm just about to order that weak piece of shit to pull down his pants when a hard-rock guitar starts playing behind us. The sound distracts me. It's only a millisecond, but Fredrik sees his chance and takes it. He grabs my wrist, twists it and pushes it backward so the knife is pointing at me instead. I recoil even as I resist him with all my strength. A jolt of pain shoots up my wrist. Fredrik may look like a wreck, but he's surprisingly strong.

'You bastard,' I hiss. 'I hate you. *Hate* you.'

'Lollo, I . . . I don't want to hurt you.' Fredrik is out of breath. 'Can you just put down the knife and talk to me instead?'

'We have nothing to talk about. Nothing. Understood?' The music gets louder. Where is it coming from?

'Fuck, fuck, fuuuck!'

I roar in time with whoever's hollering in the background. Spittle flies into Fredrik's face, and as a drop splashes into his eye he starts. At the same time, I hurl myself forward, using all my weight.

Fredrik staggers backward and hits the door of the fridge with his shoulder. The sudden movement throws me off balance too.

What happens next takes only a split second. Yet all the while I have the sense that I'm seeing the sequence of events before it's actually happened. I watch Fredrik tumble to the floor with a thud; I watch myself follow him down, and I watch the blade of the knife sink into the thin skin just beneath Fredrik's collarbone.

A paralysing sensation spreads through my body; I

can't move a muscle. My gaze is stuck on the knife, and only its handle is visible.

Fredrik stares at me. His face is pale and his lips are moving, but no sound comes from his mouth. I know I should do something, but all I can think about is a black-and-white silent film.

It's only when the annoying music ends that I get to my feet and find my phone. After two failed attempts, my trembling index finger hits the digits in the correct order. *One, one, two.*

With the phone to my ear, I rush back to Fredrik. I sink to my knees beside him, but all I can do is sit there, helpless.

What should I do? Should I turn him on his side? Or is it best to leave him be?

A cool voice speaks into my ear. 'SOS 112, what is your emergency?'

'The knife,' I gasp. 'You have to come! Right away.'

'What happened?' the voice asks.

'An accident. With a knife. We fell, and now –'

'What is your location?'

The operator's calm demeanour is an affront, and my head feels polished smooth on the inside. I don't remember what street they live on.

'I don't know!' My heart is pounding. 'I don't remember!'

I'm screeching that she should fucking well be able to trace the call, even as I remember something about an app I maybe should have downloaded, when Fredrik suddenly opens his mouth and recites the street address in a monotone.

I repeat what he says and the voice continues. 'Is the individual breathing?'

'Yes. Yes, he's breathing. Should I pull out the knife?'

'No,' the voice says, sounding a little less cool. 'Don't touch it. Just wait for the paramedics to arrive. Help is on the way.'

After a few more questions, the emergency operator seems to feel the situation is under control, but she keeps me on the line.

I turn on speakerphone, sit down beside Fredrik and place the phone on the floor between us.

'I'm sorry,' I whisper, leaning back against the fridge. 'I'm sorry.'

He's lying perfectly still, his eyes closed, and each breath seems to cause him terrible pain.

It strikes me that he might die. In which case I have killed Nina's husband.

And Jennifer's dad.

My head is full of thunder. I close my eyes and wish myself far away as I listen to Fredrik's laboured breathing.

'Was Jennifer . . .' he coughs. 'Was she really my daughter?'

I nod without opening my eyes, and realize that tears are running down my cheeks.

'She . . . was alive,' Fredrik continues. He squeezes out the words, has to pause to catch his breath. 'She was . . . walking . . . on the road. Unsteady. But walking . . . I . . . searched. Went back. Couldn't . . . find her. I'm sorry.'

He falls silent.

The coffee-maker sputters.

In the distance, I hear sirens heading our way.

66. Nina

'Am I speaking to Carolina Gonzales Andersson?'

This is the second time today someone has called me Carolina. But this voice doesn't have the warmth of Dad's. In fact, it sounds extremely formal. I leave the sofa and rush to the front hall to get away from the cacophony in the living room. Vilgot is playing *Sorry!* with his grandfather, and they are, to put it mildly, highly engaged.

'Yes, this is she.'

There's rustling on the other end, as if someone is turning over a piece of paper.

'And you are the spouse of Fredrik Andersson?'

At this, my heart starts to beat double time. The blood rushes out of my brain, and my fingertips tingle oddly.

'Yes . . .'

'I'm glad I got hold of you. My name is Helga Gunnarsdottir. I'm a physician, calling from Skåne University Hospital.'

I stagger over to the stool next to the hall bureau; my back slides down the wall and I land with a thud.

'I'm calling about your husband,' says the woman on the phone.

The words I'm searching for get tangled together and nothing comes out.

'There's no need to worry,' the doctor continues. 'The situation is serious but not life-threatening.'

'What happened?' I leap to my feet and start fumbling

for my coat among all the outerwear. 'Where is he? I'm not at home. I'm . . . I'm in Höör. At my parents'. But I can be in Malmö in an hour or so.'

Both Mom and Smilla have come out to the hall. They're standing side by side, gaping at me, wide-eyed.

'Fredrik has been sedated and is asleep now.' Helga Gunnarsdottir speaks in a melodic Icelandic accent. 'And there's no reason for you to rush over. He's in the ICU and visitors aren't allowed. With any luck he will be transferred to a pulmonary unit tomorrow, in which case you can visit him then.'

'A pulmonary unit?' I stop mid-search; the arm that had been rummaging for my coat just dangles at my side. 'Why does he need to be in a pulmonary unit?'

'Your husband has suffered a pneumothorax.' She pauses briefly, then adds, 'A hole in his lung.'

'What? How . . . how did that happen?'

'A stab wound,' the doctor says. 'But, like I said, his condition is stable and, given the circumstances, Fredrik is doing well. I'm sure he'll be able to call you tomorrow morning.'

'A stab wound?' I have to sit down again. 'He was at home! He got stabbed at home?'

Mom and Smilla are still there. Mom has both hands to her mouth, and Smilla's face has gone white.

'Unfortunately I'm unable to give you any specific information,' says Helga Gunnarsdottir.

'But I'm his wife.' My voice cracks. 'I have . . . I have the right to know what happened.'

'Hmm, yes . . .' The doctor suddenly sounds chagrined. 'Fredrik expressly asked us not to release any details. Not even to you.'

My phone is about to slide from my grip, and I squeeze the soft plastic case harder.

Is Fredrik cheating, after all? Was it a former mistress who stabbed him? Or a current one?

Surely it can't have been a burglary. We don't have any valuable art or precious antiques. But maybe someone broke in to steal Anton's gaming computer. I try to imagine such a situation and conclude that it's totally absurd. Plus, Fredrik would never try to resist. He'd give the thieves everything they asked for, and probably even help them carry everything to the getaway car.

The doctor clears her throat, and I'm thrust back into reality but can't remember where we left off.

'In all likelihood, your husband will make a full recovery,' Helga Gunnarsdottir says, adding, 'We will of course be in touch if the situation should change.' There's a brief silence. 'Is that okay?' she asks.

It is definitely not okay. Not at all.

'Of course,' I say. 'Thanks for calling.'

I hang up and stare at the phone screen.

'Who was that?' Mom dashes over to me. 'Nina, what's going on?'

'That was the hospital . . . it was . . .' I look at Mom. 'Fredrik was stabbed.'

Smilla looks like she's about to pass out, and I stand up.

'It's okay, sweetie.' I pull her close. 'Dad's going to be fine; the doctor says he'll make a complete recovery.'

My arms around my daughter, I try to push aside the feeling that my world is crashing down.

67. Lollo

The lobby of the police station is almost completely empty. A guard in a glass booth nods in recognition at the two uniformed officers who accompany me. I receive a visitor's badge, and then we start down a long corridor.

'Here we are,' says the ruddy woman who previously introduced herself as Sally. She holds open the door to a small, sparsely furnished room. 'Have a seat. Lina Torrero is on her way.'

I sit down on one of the four chairs, grateful that the detective will be here soon.

Sally and her colleague arrived at the hospital just minutes after the ambulance pulled into the bay. As soon as they learned that Lina Torrero is our family's contact in an ongoing investigation, they called her.

'Would you like something to drink?' The male officer, who's around my age but still has an enormous hipster beard, looks at me. 'Coffee? Tea? Water?'

'A glass of water, please.'

He gives me a curt nod and vanishes into the corridor.

I lean into the hard backrest, close my eyes and try to breathe in the way that promotes wellness. I think of the hundreds of yoga classes I've taken over the years. I had not expected to find them most useful here, in an interrogation room. But, after a few deep breaths, the pressure squeezing my chest does, in fact, ease. Not entirely but close.

There's a clatter at the door. The Beard comes back in,

along with Lina Torrero, and we shake hands for the third time today. The Beard sets a glass of water at my place and leaves the room as the two women sit down across from me.

Sally starts typing at a computer. Torrero places a flimsy plastic folder on the table and opens her laptop. She takes a phone from her back pocket and places it on the folder.

'How are you doing?'

If anyone else had asked that question, I'd be furious. But I like Lina Torrero. She doesn't seem to be asking because she's obliged to, but because she actually cares.

'Not so great,' I say.

Torrero separates her ponytail down the middle and pulls at the two sections to tighten her hairdo.

'Hope it's okay we brought you here.' She lets go of her hair. 'It's always a little messy, trying to talk at the hospital.'

I nod, and the detective continues.

'First and foremost, we'd like to know more about the incident this evening.'

'I didn't mean to.' My cheeks flush, and I have trouble meeting her gaze. 'It was an accident. It –'

'Hold on.' Torrero turns on her phone and places it in the centre of the table. She rattles off the date, time and names of those present. 'There,' she says. 'Tell me what happened at the Anderssons'.'

'I . . .' My hands tremble as I reach for the glass of water. 'Max and I had . . . we fought. And I . . . I needed to talk to someone. About everything that happened . . .' I take a drink, manage to miss my mouth and capture the stray drops that trickle down my chin with my free hand. 'Nina wasn't home, but Fredrik invited me in anyway. He put on coffee, and . . . And then suddenly he started babbling about how he saw Jennifer that night, on New Year's Eve . . . and I . . .' I put down the glass and look at the two women in front of me. 'I saw red. I wasn't thinking!'

Torrero asks for more details as Sally takes notes.

'From what I understand, Fredrik doesn't want to press charges,' Torrero sums up when I'm done.

I nod, and the detective informs me that, even so, they are required to draw up a report for causing bodily injury.

'As long as Fredrik doesn't change his mind, that's probably as far as it will go,' she adds.

'What about Fredrik and Jennifer, though?' I look at Torrero. 'He *admitted* that he saw her on New Year's Eve. You have to look into that more, don't you?'

'We'll certainly be questioning Fredrik further,' Torrero says. 'But he says that Jennifer was alive when he left her on Gads Väg.'

'That's what he *says*.' I throw up my hands. 'But do you really believe him?'

'I tried to contact you and Max after we saw each other in Lund.' The detective looks at her laptop and then at me. 'And at least now I know why *you* didn't answer.' She gives me a crooked smile. 'Do you have any idea where Max is, by the way?'

An uneasy feeling in my belly. What the hell is he up to?

'No, I took off with the car and haven't heard from him since.'

'I see.' Lina Torrero tries to make eye contact. 'The reason I wanted to talk to you both is that we've received quite a bit of new information in Jennifer's case, information to suggest we're not dealing with an accident.'

I open my mouth, but Torrero beats me to the punch.

'From this point on, we are investigating this case as a homicide.' She doesn't avert her eyes. 'And I would like to point out that the new information docs *not* implicate Fredrik Andersson. We suspected that he'd had contact with Jennifer on the night in question, and now we have confirmation of that. But we don't believe that Fredrik is the one who killed Jennifer.'

I look at the detective, perplexed, trying to make sense of what she's telling me.

Homicide.

Was Jennifer *murdered?*

'It may seem that Fredrik was in the wrong,' Torrero continues. 'That he should have convinced Jennifer to come back home. But that he returned to the party without her is not a crime in and of itself.'

'But . . . but what happened, then?' I look at the two officers. 'Are you saying she met up with someone else after that? Was it Willie Winkie? One of those men on the Facebook list? Petter Silvén? Have you looked into him? He lives right nearby, he –'

I fall silent as I realize that I'm babbling, and Torrero's friendly brown eyes have me suddenly on the verge of tears.

'Unfortunately, we can't discuss who we have or have not looked into,' she says calmly. 'Nor can we tell you what we're working on for the moment. The primary reason for contacting you this time was to advise you that we have upgraded the incident to homicide. We also need to ask a few more questions . . .' Something about the detective's expression changes, and there's a brief pause before she gets to the point. 'The autopsy report is complete.'

My mind paints a picture. The stiff body of a girl on a

bare, stainless-steel table. My stomach ties itself in knots. I look around for something to throw up in, but in the end I manage to swallow what was rising in my throat.

'What's the matter?' Sally asks. 'Are you okay?'

I nod and take a sip of water. I search my memory for other pictures, ones that show Jennifer alive – with a gleam in her eye and a smile on her lips. Instead I see a pale face, silent lips, closed eyes.

'So . . .' Torrero seeks my gaze again. 'According to the report, Jennifer had traces of both cannabis and tramadol in her blood.'

'That can't be right,' I whisper. 'There must be some mistake.'

'Unfortunately, there isn't.' Torrero looks at her screen. 'It wasn't a great deal, but in combination with alcohol –'

'Someone must have forced her to take it.' I aim pleading looks at the two women; my voice regains some of its strength. 'Jennifer wasn't on drugs! We would have noticed.'

Even as the words ricochet off the bare walls, my doubts start to grow. How can I be so sure Jennifer wasn't into drugs? After all, I had no idea what she was up to online.

'It must have been someone at that new year's party who tricked her into it.' I hear the hesitation in my own voice. 'A . . . one-time thing.'

'Well.' Lina Torrero starts to skim through her folder. 'Perhaps you've heard that someone found a phone belonging to Jennifer?'

She places a photograph on the table, turning it around so it's right side up for me. The photo is of a tiny, old-fashioned cell phone. It's blue, and it looks like my very first one, which Max gave me for my birthday sometime in the early 2000s.

'That's not Jennifer's phone.' I point at the photo. 'She had an iPhone. The latest model.'

'Jennifer had two phones.' The detective takes the photo back. 'We haven't found her iPhone. But we were able to download a copy of her calls. And this one' – Torrero looks at the photo – 'this one wasn't on contract; it was prepaid.'

'But . . . what was it for, then?' I look at the dark-haired woman in confusion. 'Were you able to see who she called?'

The detective puts the photo back in the folder.

'She mostly texted from it. The prepaid phone was a burner, a phone she used to call dealers and clients. And, yes, we were able to trace some of Jennifer's contacts. But that's all I can say, for the time being.'

I lean over the table, bury my face in my hands and let the tears come.

Murder. Drugs. Willie Winkie. Fredrik. Max. Should I call Max? Do I *want* to call him? Could he be involved in all this crap somehow? Should I air these thoughts to Torrero?

I'm so tired. So incredibly tired.

When I eventually lift my head, there's a box of tissues next to my glass of water. I take a tissue, blow my nose and dry my eyes.

'You must think I'm the world's worst mother.'

The delay in Torrero's response is just a smidgen too long. 'Don't think that,' Lina Torrero says. 'This could happen to anyone. All sorts of people, from any social class. We can do everything for our children, and they still end up in trouble. Trust me, no one is immune.'

Epiphany Eve, 2019

Saturday

68. Fredrik

Lina Torrero is watching me.

'You're one hundred per cent sure you don't want to press charges against Louise Wiksell?'

'Yes,' I say. 'It was an accident. Lollo was upset, and I . . . I'd had a lot to drink.'

The detective leans back in her chair, crosses one leg over the other and regards me with an unreadable expression.

'You were lucky in one respect.' Her eyes go to the tube that's sticking out of my right lung. 'It could have ended a lot worse than this.'

The oxygen machine responds with a long, protracted sigh, and I have nothing to add. Yesterday I was convinced the end had come for me. The pain was indescribable. Each breath burned like fire, and my life seriously began to flash before my eyes like in a movie. I was surprised at how panicky I felt. I thought I was prepared to die, that it was my only way out. But at that moment – with a knife in my lung and my back on the kitchen floor – I knew.

I don't want to die.

I want to live.

Lina Torrero stands up. Her colleague, a redhead whose name I don't remember, closes her notebook and pushes the two chairs back against the wall. She gives me a curt nod, quickly shrugs into her jacket and disappears into the corridor.

Torrero stops in the doorway. 'We'll be in touch, in one

way or another.' She gestures at the drainage tube. 'At least I don't have to worry about you running off.'

When calm has settled again, I close my eyes and try to make sense of the tsunami of information that's just washed over me. But it doesn't really work. Maybe that's down to the nature of the information. Or maybe it's because of the medication, all the painkillers that are being pumped through my body at the moment.

Torrero said that Jennifer was murdered.

Murdered.

It seemed she had been doing drugs too. Tramadol. Marijuana. Possibly more.

I immediately confessed that we smoked up last summer; after all, I had to explain why I'd kept quiet about seeing her on New Year's Eve. But I swore up and down that I'd never heard Jennifer mention any other drugs.

Apparently she was selling to kids in the area. It wasn't big business, but still.

Shit, Jennifer. How could everything go so fucking sideways?

My head falls back against the pillows. I take a deep breath, only realizing my mistake once it's too late, and groan loudly.

A passing nurse sticks her head into the room. 'Are you in pain?'

I shake my head.

'Just press the button if you need anything,' she says, rushing on.

I return to my conversation with Torrero, trying to recall the details.

If I understood the detective correctly, I'm not a suspect in the murder. I don't seem to be suspected of anything – except poor judgement, maybe.

Torrero was awfully tight-lipped, but she claimed they're close to a breakthrough with the investigation. She hoped the case would be concluded before the weekend was over. Today is Saturday. That must mean they already know who the killer is.

Jennifer was murdered.

It's absurd. What could she have done to give anyone a reason to kill her?

A young girl.

My daughter.

All at once I'm back on the beach, seeing Jennifer on that blue Midsummer night. I don't want to think about it. Don't want to be reminded of what a close call it was. Although that wasn't *me* reacting to her overtures. It was my reptile brain.

My fingers fumble across the bedside table and I manage to grab my phone without moving my torso. The screen shows me a new text.

Driving now. N

The message was sent almost an hour ago. I drop the phone on the yellow blanket and turn my eyes to the ceiling. There are no cracks here; instead there's a grid of white ceiling tiles in perfect symmetry.

Nina.

What the hell am I going to tell Nina?

We had the briefest of chats this morning, right after they moved me here. She was completely hysterical, and hadn't had a wink of sleep all night.

I told her I didn't want to relate the story over the phone and asked her to come to the hospital as soon as possible. And I am dreading my wife's reaction.

It strikes me that if I had just kept my cool, most of the stuff about Jennifer and me could have remained a secret between me and the police. But now . . .

Lollo knows I took a swim with Jennifer at Midsummer. She knows we saw each other the night Jennifer disappeared. And it's pretty clear that I could have prevented what happened later by dragging her home to the Wiksells' after our encounter in the woods. Or at least I could have stopped it from happening right then.

If that was when it happened.

Lollo will never forgive me. And I doubt she'll keep her thoughts to herself.

Which means Nina has to hear my version.

69. Nina

'But I don't get it! What was Lollo doing at our house?' I'm standing in the centre of the room. My heart is thudding against my ribs; tears and snot are running unchecked down my face. I feel like my whole body is about to dissolve into a puddle on the shiny grey floor. 'You have to explain . . .'

My voice dies out as a loud ringing starts up in my head. White spots dance before my eyes and I grab a chair, landing on its hard seat. Bent over, my head in my hands, I wait for the ringing to stop, then look up again.

The head of the bed is raised and Fredrik is slumped heavily against the pillow. His face is the same shade as the pillowcase. Next to the bed is an IV stand. He's got a tube stuck in his side, and more ports in his wrists and elbows. One screen is measuring two different values; one must be Fredrik's heart rate.

'Why?' I whisper. 'Why was she at our house?'

'No idea. She said . . .' Fredrik gulps and continues, his voice strained. 'She said they had a fight. Lollo and Max, I mean. Lollo got in the car and just drove. Wanted to get away. And she just ended up at our place.'

I take my phone from my purse, blink away the tears and glance through the list of received calls.

'She didn't call first.'

'Well, like I just said . . .' Fredrik sits up straighter with a groan. 'It wasn't planned.'

I close my eyes again, rubbing my temples and trying to

digest what I've just learned. About night swimming. About lies. About shame and guilt.

'So . . .' I open my eyes. 'You lied about New Year's Eve to keep from revealing what happened last summer?'

Fredrik nods. 'Although nothing happened,' he's quick to add. 'You have to believe me, Nina. All that happened was that we smoked weed. But you know how Jennifer is . . . how she *was*. She could have made up absolutely anything. And after #MeToo and everything . . .' He looks at me with puppy-dog eyes. 'Who would have believed me? No one! I would have been a middle-aged creep. Everyone would have taken Jennifer's side. She was disappointed and angry. She could have had me fired, turned my family and friends against me, she . . .'

Fredrik trails off and looks up at the ceiling.

I don't know what to say. I've suspected all along that something was wrong, and not just the fake work situation he'd cooked up. I'd even touched on the idea that Fredrik's behaviour might have to do with Jennifer. But I never could have imagined this. It's beyond all reason.

'I understand . . .' Fredrik inhales sharply and grimaces in pain before he continues. 'I understand if it's hard for you to trust me at this point, but I swear to you –'

'You mean,' I cut him off, 'what you're saying is that Lollo stabbed you because she thought you had killed Jennifer?'

He nods again. 'I thought *myself* that I'd killed her. Not, like, with my hands, obviously. But I thought what had happened was my fault, that I was going to prison for it. She hit her head, it was bleeding, and I was afraid she had a concussion. At first I thought maybe she just lay down and froze somewhere. And then, when they found her, I was convinced she had fallen into the quarry because of her injury, that she was dizzy or confused. There is such a thing as reckless endangerment. As in, if you walk away from someone who's in danger —'

'Shut up!'

I do what Vilgot usually does in stressful situations: clap my hands to my ears and close my eyes. It's an effective way to block out the world. Everything goes dark and all I hear is my own heartbeat pounding between my ears.

My thoughts are out of control, impossible to capture or stop. I open my eyes and consider the man in the bed in front of me. I let my eyes take in his limp, unwashed hair, his salt-and-pepper stubble, his sunken cheeks. The tears rolling down his face.

Who is he? What has he done? Can I trust what he's telling me?

'I'm leaving now.' The arm of the chair strikes the bed as I get up. 'I need to think.'

With my coat balled up under my arm, I head for the door.

'Will you come back tomorrow?' Fredrik whispers behind me.

I turn around.

'Maybe.'

70. Lollo

A sob rises in my throat and I try to distract myself by looking at Chanel. Dad dropped her off early this morning. I couldn't stand the house being so quiet and wanted to hear paws on the parquet; I needed to feel her shaggy fur between my fingers.

Now she's walking alongside the path with her nose buried in last year's leaves. The poodle seems completely unfazed by everything that's happened. Although maybe Chanel understands more than we suspect; maybe she does feel the loss but has the good sense to focus on those of us who are still here.

We're on our way out to the point, and I'm huddled behind a scarf, hat and big sunglasses. The sun is conspicuously absent, but I want to avoid looking people in the eye. I would have preferred to avoid other people altogether, but I had to get out of the house.

Away from Max.

My husband has been lying to me for over seventeen years. How the hell am I supposed to tell truth from fiction, if he chose to lie about what should be the most important thing of all: our child? *My child.*

All the times I've called and he hasn't answered. All the times he's worked late, played golf, gone on business trips. What was true? What was lies?

Can I really trust that it was Max – and only Max – who

ate hamburgers down in Falsterbo early that Wednesday morning? Can I trust that he wasn't with Jennifer?

Max swore up and down that he has never hurt her. He seemed honestly dismayed that I suspected him at all. And, deep down, I don't think Max could be involved. But that the suspicion was there in the first place . . .

This morning I got out the school directory again. I flipped to the class photo and took a look at the boy Max beat up. Ali. He's pretty handsome. And he must be decently smart besides, or he wouldn't have been accepted at Petri. How on God's green earth could Max have attacked a seventeen-year-old? What a goddamn coward. A pathetic, immature coward.

Can I live with a man I believed – even for a moment – was capable of killing someone? Do I want to live with a man who is probably going to be convicted of assault?

Max is the one who's done wrong, but his bad reputation is going to hit me just as hard. We have the same last name. What if he has to sell the agency? Because who wants to trust the most important purchase of their life to a criminal? Not me.

In which case, we'll probably lose everything. Our life and our friends. I haven't heard a peep from Lisen and Ivanka since the assault was made public. Not one of the papers has published the name of 'the successful Malmö realtor who beat up a defenceless boy'. But people aren't stupid. Everyone knows who they're talking about.

One strange factor is that Max hasn't shown any remorse. He claims the police were too lax, and he would have left Ali alone if they'd taken the information about him seriously. Which is some interesting logic. Because it seems that Ali has nothing to do with this.

My husband scares me. Who is he? Who has he been, all these years?

Chanel lets her nose guide her on and she zigzags down the path. My thoughts are moving in a similar pattern, and they land on Fredrik. The man who was Jennifer's father. *Is* Jennifer's father.

Because I'm still Jennifer's mother, right?

A stab of pain in my chest. The knife that punctured Fredrik's lung seems to have drilled itself right into my own heart. Someone twists the handle, again and again.

I can't stop the tears from coming. They pour forth behind my sunglasses, and the world around me blurs into a brown haze. I unconsciously lengthen my stride. I'm dragging Chanel by her leash like a puppet on a string; she must have been whining for a while, but before she can catch up her protests have grown much louder.

I stop, let the poodle do her business and march onward. It's like my legs are trying to flee from my head and everything inside it.

I'll never be able to look Nina in the eye again. *Never.*

And Fredrik, that fucking idiot. Can he really be trusted? He says Jennifer was alive when he left her. But can he prove it?

Torrero maintained that Fredrik is innocent. But I'm sure even the police can make mistakes. Maybe she only said that to protect Fredrik from me. Is Torrero afraid I'll stab him again?

And then there's that stuff Fredrik was babbling on about . . . that he and Jennifer took a swim together at

Midsummer. What was that about? It's all such a mess . . . a fucking can of worms!

Chanel yaps suddenly. I look up to see a baby rabbit further down the path. It's trembling, hypnotized. Staring death in the eye.

Did Jennifer know she was going to die? Did she have time to feel scared when she met her killer? Did she cry for help? Did she plead for her life?

The knife in my chest twists again and a sob finds its way out between my lips. It's a strange sound. Eerie. I don't recognize my own voice.

The rabbit wakes from its temporary trance, gives a start and scampers in among the trees.

71. Nina

I storm down corridors, not bothering to read any signs; I let my inner GPS lead me to the exit. I have to get out of here, I need oxygen and daylight. I need time to think in peace and quiet. I need to try to understand. If it's even possible to understand any of this.

It's a relief to escape the nauseating hospital smell and the sighing oxygen machine. I fill my healthy lungs with raw, cold January air and hurry down the sidewalk towards the parking garage.

Just before the crosswalk I meet an old man who's struggling to push a wheelchair. In the wheelchair is a shrunken woman with a purse in her lap. The sight of the old couple makes me want to cry. Will Fredrik and I grow old together? Do I want us to?

A mental image of my apathetic parents-in-law flickers through my mind. Their silence, their wordless accusations.

'Nina!'

At first I don't realize that someone is calling to me. But finally the penny drops and I turn around. A woman in a white coat is jogging along the sidewalk. She's short, with medium-length blonde hair, and is holding a snack cup of rice pudding in her hand. The woman seems vaguely familiar but I can't place her.

'You don't recognize me, do you?'

She's standing in front of me now. Purple socks in white Birkenstocks, a big smile on her face.

'Um . . .' My already overheated brain is going a mile a minute. 'Maybe.'

'Victoria.' The woman puts out her hand. 'Vicky.'

'Oh my God! I'm sorry.' I take her hand and shake it. 'Vicky. Now I see. How are you?' My other hand automatically comes up to my eyes and their smeared mascara. 'Do you work here now?'

We let go of each other's hands and Vicky nods.

'On the same unit as Malena, even.'

It's clear that Malena and I have drifted apart. Ten years ago, I definitely would have been aware of something like this. Vicky hung out with us a lot back in our school days. Pregaming in Malena's shared kitchen, coffee at Lundagård, studying at the university library.

Vicky looks the same, but just like me she's put on some weight. For some reason that makes me happy in the middle of all this mess.

'How long have you been working in Malmö?' I ask.

'Since last summer,' Vicky replies. 'I was in Lund for years. And then I was in Eslöv for a bit, at a clinic there.' She smiles again. 'You're still in touch, I hear. You, Malena and Lollo.'

'Well . . .' I try to smile but it feels like my skin is too tight, that there somehow isn't enough of it. 'Maybe not like in the good old days. But we usually celebrate New Year's Eve together, at least . . .'

The sentence hangs in the air and Vicky suddenly leans in, lowering her voice.

'It's terrible, by the way. This Jennifer thing.' She shakes her head. 'It must be the worst thing that can happen to you. To lose a child.'

I just nod, fervently hoping that Vicky needs to get

back to the emergency department soon. I don't want to open up about my inner chaos to someone I haven't seen in over twenty years.

But Vicky doesn't seem to be in any rush; instead she moves in even closer. She's so near that I can tell where she must have spent her break – in one of the glass shelters where patients and staff stand around and puff on their cigarettes together. Like an incubator in reverse.

'I can hardly believe it's real,' Vicky continues. 'First Theo, and now this . . . I mean, it makes you wonder . . .'

'Theo?' I take a step back and look at the woman before me. 'What do you mean?'

'Oops.' She brings her hand to her lips but immediately moves it again. 'I thought . . . I mean, you're close. I thought you knew.'

'I know Theo's had some problems and changed schools. But, from what I understand, he's doing better.'

'I mean . . .' Vicky hesitates for a moment but soon finds her stride. 'Maybe I shouldn't be telling you this, but . . .' She looks around, as if she's afraid someone might be eavesdropping from around the corner. 'But I'll do it anyway. No need to mention you heard it from me.'

I try not to look too interested, afraid she'll change her mind.

'It was last fall.' Vicky glances over her shoulder again. 'Theo came into the emergency room one night. Convulsions.'

I stare at her.

'What? Why? What was wrong?'

'Tramadol.' She lowers her voice another notch. 'And pot.'

My stomach flutters.

'Theo?' My voice is high and shrill; I can't control it. 'Marijuana?'

Vicky looks at me gravely. 'He could have died. We were this close to losing him.' She measures a tiny space between her thumb and index finger. 'But luck was on his side.'

I try to absorb what Vicky just told me. I'm both shocked and a little insulted. Why didn't I know this? And all this talk of drugs, out of the blue.

'Shit,' I say.

Because that's the first thing that comes out of my mouth.

'Deep shit,' Vicky echoes. 'I was one of the ones treating him, and it wasn't a pretty sight. Malena and I have talked quite a bit about it since, so, I mean ... I didn't think I was violating anyone's privacy.'

'No worries.' I wave one hand. 'It's fine. I won't say anything. I'm sure Malena will tell me about it when she's ready.'

'I'm sure,' Vicky repeats. 'By the way, do you know what's wrong with her?'

'Wrong?'

I suddenly get the sense that I'm living in a parallel universe.

'Yeah ...' Vicky hesitates before she continues. 'She's been off sick since New Year's Eve.'

I look at her.

'She hasn't mentioned anything, but –'

'Maybe you partied too hard?' Vicky smiles but at the same time there's a haunted look in her eyes. 'Look, I need to get going now. Otherwise my colleagues will have my head.' She gives me a quick hug. 'But it was nice to see you, Nina. Take care, and say hi to Lollo for me.'

I stand there and watch her go, a white-clad woman hurrying down the sidewalk.

72. Lollo

'Chanel is home now!'

I unhook her leash, herd the filthy dog into the hall and turn back out into the cold. I kick the door so it closes with a satisfying bang.

In the car, I get out my phone again. I open 'contacts', type an *m* in the search box and select one of the names on the list. Then I wait.

Hi, you've reached Malena Lagergren. I can't answer the phone right now, but . . .

I toss the phone on to the passenger seat and feel tears burning behind my eyelids.

I suppose I should really just be patient and stay home until she answers. But it feels totally impossible to go back inside. The very thought of being in the same house as Max makes my body seize up.

Jennifer's belongings have the same effect on me. Her shoes in the hall, her toothbrush in the bathroom, her workout clothes on the drying rack – every object seems to scream my name. It doesn't help if I close my eyes or look away; traces of Jennifer are all over the house. This morning it was a pair of earrings on the kitchen counter that made my legs give out.

I have to get out of here. I have to relieve this pressure, let it all out. And I need something to do. I can't just sit still and let my thoughts take control.

One option might be to knock on Lisen's door. Or to

walk over to Ivanka's. But they don't seem to want to have anything to do with us any more. Plus, we don't know each other that way. We party together; we don't cry together.

Now that Nina is no longer an option, Malena is the only one left. She's seen me cry before.

I back out of the driveway as I try to convince myself she'll be home. Didn't she mention something about being on vacation over Epiphany weekend? I'm sure she just has her phone on silent. Or else she's in the bath.

It doesn't even take ten minutes to drive to Malena's condo on the outskirts of Tygelsjö. I drive down Gessie-vägen, watching the Öresund Strait open out past the wet meadows. The water is always close by in Klagshamn; that's why we chose to move here. And because, at least at the time, the people who lived down here were good folks, financially secure.

We wanted Jennifer to go to school with like-minded people, wanted to avoid all the problems that inner-city schools have to deal with. But the village has grown, and in her last two years of school the neighbours grew ever more mixed. I'm sure it was some of those transplanted welfare cases who got Jennifer to try drugs.

Fuck! Fuck! Fuck!

I bang the steering wheel with my right hand, and the car swerves. A minivan is approaching from the other direction. For a few tense seconds, I lose control and picture the head-on crash. The driver of the minivan leans on their horn, but by then I've managed to correct my course; I'm back on the right side of the road. My heart pounding, I turn off towards Tygelsjö and try to calm my panicked breathing.

In the midst of my relief at avoiding an accident, a wave of distaste sneaks up on me. At first I can't tell what's bothering me, but an instant later I realize what it is.

There's been radio silence from Malena since New Year's Eve. She hasn't said a word since she and Adde hopped into their taxi and headed home. No 'Thanks for the party' text on New Year's Day. And not once has she expressed any sort of concern – or sympathy – about Jennifer's disappearance.

I could be wrong. I might have missed Malena's attempt at getting in touch among the hundreds of comments that have come pouring in. Or maybe she did text, but it never arrived because of poor coverage or some other technical problem. Yes, there could be a thousand different reasons why I haven't heard from her.

Still, I have a hard time letting go of this thought.

There's an open spot across from Malena's driveway, and I find myself sitting in the car, taking in the world through the dirty windshield. The neighbourhood was built relatively recently, lots of two-storey buildings with brown façades. Malena's condo is stylish, with a small garden, and is close to Theo's school. But I suspect they'll soon settle down at Adde's house in Vellinge. Malena has never lived in one spot for very long. New guy, new address.

A woman in a long cardigan emerges from one of the houses a little further down the street. Her cardigan flutters in the breeze. She jogs down the flagstone path, a knotted garbage bag in hand. Once the bag is in the bin, she pulls the cardigan tightly around herself and hurries back into the warm.

Just as I place my hand on the door handle, something

in the rear-view mirror catches my eye. It looks like a police car. I always get butterflies when I see a police car, especially when I'm behind the wheel. But there are no butterflies today – today I feel a huge fucking punch to the gut.

I turn around and discover, to my horror, that it really is a police car – and it's coming my way. My hand slides off the door handle, and my heart leaps into my throat. I watch the garish Volvo pass me and make a U-turn, until at last it parks across the street.

Two uniformed officers step on to the sidewalk, just a few metres from Malena's mailbox. The female officer points at the house where Malena lives, even as she spots me and says something to her colleague. He crosses the street and approaches my car, knocking on the driver's side window.

I roll it down.

'Hello.' The officer smiles but I have the strong sense that I'm being scrutinized. 'Are you waiting for someone?'

'No . . .' I've been holding my breath for too long and have to suck in fresh oxygen to go on. 'No, I got lost. Just stopped to check the address again.'

'Where are you going?' His eyes land on the passenger seat, where my phone is upside down where I tossed it. 'Maybe I can help you out.'

'Thanks. But I'll be fine. Just need to make a call first.'

He wishes me a good day and goes back to his colleague, who by now has advanced to Malena's door.

I hardly have time to exhale before the door opens. The cops block my view, and it's impossible to tell who's standing in the dim light inside the condo.

I try to make sense of the scene that's playing out

before my eyes, but I find myself fumbling in darkness. It's like trying to figure out a TV series by watching the beginning of the final episode. I see people playing various roles, but I have no idea what they're doing.

What are the police doing here? Did something happen to Theo? Or are they after Adde?

A moment later, the officers vanish inside, and Malena's face appears in the doorway. She catches sight of me and freezes, but then, her expression unchanged, she closes the door.

15 April 2019

Monday

73. Nina

I'm freezing. The waistband of my pants is too tight, and I can't button my blazer any more. In the sharp morning light I discover that this scarf is entirely the wrong shade of blue. It clashes with my suit. Why didn't I pick out clothes that would be warm and comfortable?

People line the walls. Most of them look relaxed, as though trials and dead seventeen-year-olds are run-of-the-mill in their lives.

Lollo doesn't seem to be here yet. Deep down, I hope she won't show up until I've taken my seat inside the courtroom.

We've exchanged a few polite messages on Messenger but haven't seen each other face to face since the funeral. And, to be perfectly honest, I don't think either one of us wants to get together right now. That Lollo lost her daughter is bad enough. But the circumstances have made everything vastly more difficult.

At the start of the year, I was questioning the value of our friendship. Someone with a sense of irony and black humour must have heard me. Now I don't even have to wonder what we'll be doing next New Year's Eve. And I doubt we'll be getting an invitation to Midsummer in Falsterbo.

Lollo and Max have separated, but I'm not so sure it'll end in divorce. Is Lollo prepared to give up the money, the house and the summer cottage? Grief can certainly take its toll on a marriage – just look at my in-laws. And, personally, I'd have a hard time forgiving Max for assaulting Ali. Yet they're a united front: Lollo and Max have always stood up for each other.

I could use a trip to the restroom; I've had stomach cramps all morning and couldn't get down a bite of my breakfast. The clock on the wall says there're only five minutes left before it's time. Will I make it?

Suddenly the hum of chatter quiets down and all eyes look in the same direction. I turn my head to see Lollo and Max walking in, accompanied by a woman in a tailored suit and high-heeled pumps. The latter sends nods and smiles of recognition left and right. Max and Lollo are both looking at the floor, moving single-mindedly towards the door.

I want to flee, but I realize I need to stay put. It would look awfully strange if I moved now. If only Fredrik were here so I could hide behind him.

The door of the courtroom opens and the crowd begins to move. Out of the corner of my eye I see Max and Lollo again and force myself to stand up straight.

Lollo glances up. For a brief, breathless second I meet her gaze and goosebumps pop up on my arms. It's like looking into a bottomless well.

Max pretends not to see me. He was charged with assault; that case was heard a few weeks ago. Neither Fredrik nor I attended, but the rumour is he'll either get a month in prison or ankle monitoring. I don't know which I'm hoping for.

'Well.' The chief judge, a woman with short grey hair and bright red glasses, turns to Malena and I start to listen again.

'We will now hear from Malena Lagergren, who will tell us in her own words what happened on the night in question.' The judge nods in encouragement. 'Go ahead, Malena.'

My friend must have lost ten kilos in jail. Her shoulders look sharp, as if her black blouse were draped over a giant hanger. She rubs her hands together nervously, her eyes on the table. In the silence that follows the judge's words, I'm sure that Malena is about to fall apart. But then she finally starts to speak.

'I was at a party at the home of Jennifer's parents, Lollo and Max Wiksell. We've known each other for a long time, since our high-school days.' Her voice is weak but collected when she goes on. 'We had dinner, and . . . well, my boyfriend and I had an argument. It was nothing, really, but both of us were pretty intoxicated and it got out of control. Just after midnight I went out to the garden to cool off, and I caught sight of Fredrik Andersson as soon as I walked out the door.'

I freeze. I've got the sense that, from now on, that name is mud, that it's sordid and ugly.

Fredrik Andersson. The man I once loved more than anything on earth. The man I promised to love for better or for worse.

The 'for worse' part is hard. Sometimes it feels impossible. Still, I'm leaning towards the idea that we have to try to find our way back to each other, if only for the kids. I simply have to trust Fredrik's version of the story. Or else I'll go insane.

Malena's voice reaches me again.

'He was walking down the sidewalk in front of the house, and he looked like he was in a big hurry. So I got curious and followed him.'

She stops talking and takes a drink from the water glass in front of her. The sound is amplified by the microphone; otherwise, the room is dead silent. It's like everyone is holding their breath.

'I kept my distance,' Malena continues. 'I was hiding in the trees. And I was just about to turn back when Jennifer came out of the woods.'

Malena recounts the argument that ended in Fredrik returning to the party while Jennifer wobbled in the opposite direction.

'I couldn't hear what they were arguing about. And, once he'd passed me, I ran after Jennifer . . .'

For the first time all morning, Malena looks up from the table. She turns her head and looks at Lollo.

'I wanted . . .' Her voice cracks and she starts over. 'I wanted to *help* Jennifer! I didn't think she should be out on her own in that condition. But she was totally beyond hope. She kept screaming that she hated everyone and everything.'

I glance at Lollo. She's sitting perfectly still, her back straight and her hands resting in her lap. How can she look so indifferent? For my part, I'm having palpitations and freezing one second, sweating the next.

'I tried to get Jennifer to come home,' Malena says. 'I followed her down the path, begging and pleading. But she just kept going. Even though she could hardly stand up straight, she ploughed on, crossed the road and started down the path that leads to the diving platform. And when we were all the way to the quarry, that was when she started talking about Theo.' Malena addresses the chief judge directly. 'Theo is my son.'

The defence attorney leans over and whispers something

in Malena's ear. Malena waves her off, turning back to the short-haired judge again.

'So there's Jennifer, looking me in the eye and telling me *she* was the one who got Theo into weed and tramadol. She even admitted that *she* was the one who sold him that shit. *Because he seemed down*.' Malena's voice has gained strength now, but tears are flowing freely down her face, and I can see snot glistening on her upper lip. 'I was furious. I shouted at her, told her to apologize. Didn't she realize what she'd done? Theo could have died!'

The chief judge asks Malena to clarify, and the defence attorney makes another attempt to tell her something. But Malena just shakes her head and keeps talking.

'Theo *protected* Jennifer. All fall, he refused to say who had sold him that junk. And she laughed at me! My son had hovered between life and death, and Jennifer was just grinning in my face. She said it wasn't her fault that he was "such a fucking sissy".'

My scarf feels like a noose. I loosen its knot, tug it down and don't care if it reveals too much of my chest. Just let this be over soon.

'Jennifer was unsteady on her feet,' Malena sobs. 'So I was holding her by the arm. But she kept trying to pull away, and eventually I didn't feel like helping her any more.'

Malena is thoroughly absorbed in her own tale, and the defence attorney shoots her client a look of resignation.

'I was just furious.' A shadow crosses Malena's face. 'And Jennifer was running her mouth off. She was so disrespectful, so rude . . .'

She stops, closes her eyes. The seconds tick by, and a mild wave of confusion runs through the crowd; people fidget in their seats. The chief judge is just about to say something when Malena suddenly opens her eyes and looks at Lollo again.

'I shoved Jennifer.' A buzz of voices rises from the spectators, but the sound ebbs out as Malena continues. 'She fell into the water. But . . . but it wasn't a hard shove! And I was sure she would be able to get out. I didn't mean for her to die!' A whimper escapes Malena's lips, but then she collects herself and whispers, 'I'm so sorry, Lollo. Forgive me.'

She buries her face in her hands and her body shakes with sobs.

74. Fredrik

Nina gazes out the window.

'How long will the sentence be, do you think?'

She asks the question without looking at me. That's what she does these days, avoids looking me in the eye.

'Not a clue,' I say. 'I don't think she'll be found guilty of murder. It wasn't like she planned it. Maybe manslaughter . . . Or negligent homicide.'

'Poor Theo.' Nina sighs. 'I wonder what will happen to him now?'

I know that whatever Malena did, she did because of Theo. Or maybe even for him. But I don't say a word. Because Nina wouldn't understand.

She's never been there. On the edge.

'And Max?' Nina cups her hands around her mug and blows on the steaming coffee. 'Have you heard anything else?'

I shake my head.

'I assume his sentence will be handed down any day now.'

You'd think we were discussing court cases we'd read about in the newspaper or seen on TV or Netflix. I wish we were. Sitting here talking about homicides and sentencings in the context of our friends is totally bizarre.

'It's just so . . .' Nina takes a breath, then exhales shakily. 'Tragic. All of it. Malena . . . And Jennifer, just gone. I can't . . . I just can't believe it.' She puts down her mug and undoes the top button of her pants. 'It's crazy. Unreal.'

Nina falls silent and my gaze follows hers. Outside, the sun is shining on the dusty sidewalk. The tree next to Lykke's driveway is exploding pink and white; the beechwood hedges are shades of green. That delicate foliage gets on my nerves.

'I'm so glad I went, though,' Nina says after a while. 'To court, that is. It feels like closure somehow. Or whatever.'

She's recounted the information that came out in the courtroom while I was sitting outside and awaiting my turn to testify. And I agree that both of us needed to hear Malena's version of the events of New Year's Eve, if we're to have any chance of moving on. Malena's story doesn't diminish my own part in what happened, but it does clear up some questions.

Was it fate or coincidence that made her follow me? She could just as easily have gone back to the party, made up with Adde and danced to Max's crappy music until the wee hours. She never would have run into Jennifer that way.

When did the police realize Malena was involved? I'm guessing that the old phone those kids found in the woods contained text messages that led back to Theo. But apparently there was a witness as well, someone who had seen a woman in a sequinned dress acting strangely near the quarry on New Year's Eve.

According to Nina, Malena panicked after the incident and decided to walk all the way home to Tygelsjö. But then she came to her senses, realized it was too far and that she couldn't just leave Adde and Theo at the Wiksells'. Maybe it was Malena's extra lap of the neighbourhood that meant I never ran into her when I went back to look for Jennifer.

Anyway, the prosecution's trump card seemed to be the physical evidence, because Malena's DNA was recovered from under Jennifer's fingernails.

I've spent a lot of time trying to figure out why I couldn't find Jennifer when I found her coat. Now the picture has become a little clearer.

Her body was in a relatively inaccessible location, not far from the open area where the home-made diving platform stands. From what I hear, Malena claimed, when questioned, that she and Jennifer walked past the platform and eventually ended up where the body was found.

My theory is that Jennifer fell in somewhere in the vicinity of the diving platform, landed badly and died on the spot. I think Malena must have moved the body out of the open and that Jennifer's coat came off while she was being moved. Then it must have floated away and become caught in the tree where I found it.

Or else Jennifer dropped her coat on the path; some kids could have tossed it in the water the next day. Either way, I intend to keep these theories to myself.

'That must be why she had that cough,' Nina suddenly says. She seems to have forgotten the unspoken rule about not looking at me, and I notice that her brown eyes are glistening with tears. 'When we spoke on the phone . . . I think it was the day after New Year's Day. She coughed the whole time. Must have caught a cold when she was out in the middle of the night wearing only that sequinned dress and nylons.'

Maybe that sequinned dress was a tiny stroke of good luck for me. Without it, Malena probably would have flown under the radar and all attention would have been on me. I assume her DNA wasn't in any database, and it was Jennifer's communication with Theo along with the witness statements that led the police in the right direction.

'Oh, God.' Nina wipes a few tears away and lets her head fall back. 'I mean, I just don't know what to think about Malena. She never meant for this to happen. But she should have stayed to make sure Jennifer wasn't hurt.' Nina looks at me. 'How could she just walk away?'

I wait for my wife to realize that she's asking the wrong person. But she seems to think my role in this drama has been resolved.

'I do actually get it, though,' she continues. 'That Malena was so enraged that she went mad. I mean, all that stuff Jennifer said about Theo. At the same time . . . Isn't it pretty disturbing that she was able to keep up that façade for so long? We talked on the phone twice, and both times she sounded perfectly normal. Or maybe I was too shaken to notice anything. It all just feels so unsettling. I thought I knew Malena, knew who she was.' Nina sets her mug on the table. 'Did you see how she looked, by the way? Malena, I mean. I could hardly bear to look at her. So pale and gaunt . . .'

Apparently Nina is haunted by her hours in the courtroom and needs to vent. I'm shaken myself, but it wasn't Malena's appearance that made the biggest impression on me. It was Lollo's.

Throughout my testimony, Lollo sat stock still, staring straight ahead. The set of her jaw was firm; she wore an expression I'd never seen on her before.

Louise Wiksell will never forgive this, that much is clear. Nina gets up and goes over to the coffee-maker for a refill. On her way back to the table, she stops at my chair and strokes my cheek slowly.

'Are we going to get through this?' she asks.

I have been asking myself the exact same question for almost four months now. And, from the start, it's all I wanted – to get through this. But now I don't know any more.

What price am I prepared to pay to keep our marriage from falling apart?

Nina doesn't have a clue what happened in that bathroom eighteen years ago. Still, she'll always have the upper hand, something to rub my nose in. And I can't blame her for that. How is she supposed to trust me?

We've given Smilla and Anton a sanitized version of what happened on New Year's Eve. Anton seems to have swallowed it hook, line and sinker, but the way Smilla looks at me has changed.

'Maybe,' I reply. 'I hope so.'

Nina smiles and bends down to kiss my forehead.

3 May 2019
Friday

75. Lollo

'How are you feeling today?'

As usual, the question throws me off kilter. I have to concentrate to keep from hyperventilating.

'I'm sorry, I . . .'

'Lollo,' Anders says gently. 'Don't apologize. You have every right to be sad.'

Anders Edwall is the pastor who baptized, confirmed and buried Jennifer. He's one of the few people I trust. With Anders, I can show all sides of myself, even the ones that might not match the image of a grieving mother.

I spent most of our first conversation being furious. With Malena, with Fredrik, with Max, and with life in general. Anders's calm demeanour only made me more furious. I wanted him to be just as angry as I was.

With a little perspective, I can understand the point of one of us retaining our good sense and composure. Anders *is* upset by what happened, I know that. But he's also someone who comforts others professionally – and clearly that was the sort of person I needed.

After a few meetings in Anders's office, I realized that some of my rage was aimed at myself. And that has been tough to handle. It's still tough.

Our attorney called this morning. I'm still not quite sure why; she really had no new information to share. It was probably because she wanted us to lower our expectations when it comes to Malena's sentencing. The punishment probably won't fit the crime. Not by a long shot. And that's just not right, damnit! My daughter is dead; everyone knows who killed her – and still we have to be lenient.

Anyway, I doubt Malena Lagergren will be able to live a normal life after what happened. I guess you could say that will make up for a mild sentence.

The question is whether she'd told the whole truth. That 'little' shove might have been something else entirely. Max says I have to let it go and move on, but I hate not knowing. I hate that Malena knows while I have to take her word for it.

And I don't.

We're living together again, Max and me. The number one reason is that I couldn't stand living with Dad and Agneta. But I've also had time to think. About Max. About us.

All the things I accused him of in connection with Jennifer's death – in hindsight, it was unfair of me. Max has always worked around the clock, has always been hard to reach on the phone. It wasn't a behaviour that began when Jennifer disappeared. Besides, I'm guessing that his job functioned as a coping mechanism during those days. When Max was at the agency, he could focus on his deals and shut out everything else.

He has apologized to Ali and his family. That was one condition I set before I agreed to move home again. And he swears up and down that he – and no one else – ate two hamburgers at the summer cottage.

It's all give and take. After all, I slept with his friend. His *former* friend.

'Do you know what the worst part is?'

I look up at Anders and he shakes his head.

'That I turned out just like my mother.' Suddenly there's a lump in my throat and I have to swallow. 'Mom never told me she loved me. At least, not that I can remember. And I don't know if I ever told Jennifer I loved her. I mean, face to face. Maybe I just wrote it' – I glare at my phone, which is on the small table between us – 'on that fucking phone.'

I'm crying now, and I let the tears come; I don't care that it makes me ugly. Anders hands me a plastic sleeve of tissues. They all come out when I take one; they spill on to the table and I curse under my breath, then pick up the top one and blow my nose.

'When someone dies . . .' Anders collects the unused tissues in a pile. 'When there's an unexpected death, that's often the part survivors find most difficult. Not only do you grieve for a beloved family member or friend – you also grieve what you never had time to say.'

I nod. We've talked about this before, but it's something I need to dwell on. Anders seems to understand, or at least he's never complained that I'm repeating myself.

'At the same time,' he continues, 'at the same time, we can't walk around thinking that every day might be the last. We don't have that kind of energy. No one does. We have to believe we have all the time in the world, or we'd be lost.' He pushes up his glasses, but they immediately slide down again. 'And remember that words aren't everything. We can also show love through our actions. I'm guessing that your mother did all kinds of nice things for you. Just like you performed acts of love for Jennifer.'

'I just don't know . . .' I take a deep breath and slowly blow out the air. 'I just don't know how I can live with it. All the things I never said. All the things I never did.'

Anders leans forward and places his warm, dry hand on my own.

'You've been through a lot, and it will take time to heal those wounds.'

'Are they going to heal?'

I sound like a stubborn child, but he just smiles his gentle pastor smile. At first, I found that smile infuriating, but now I like it.

'Maybe not entirely. But time typically settles like a protective layer around things we find difficult. You're still seeing your psychologist, right?'

I nod, and Anders smiles again.

'Talking about what happened is a big part of the healing process.'

The fact is, he's right. Talking is important; it helps purge your system. And the more I think about it, the clearer it becomes what I have to do.

On my way out of Anders's office, I take my phone from the table and bring up the number.

76. Fredrik

Nina's on her way to the front door, her arms full of bags and suitcases. Vilgot, who is supposed to be helping her, has found a ball and dashes out to the lawn.

'Fredrik.' Nina turns around. 'Can you grab the stuff from the backseat?'

I open the car door, take the bag of Thai food in one hand and gather up all the bank documents in the other.

We've been downtown to meet with our personal banker. He's not actually that personal; he rather lives up to the stereotypical image of a slick salesman. But after some careful calculations – and more or less forcing me to sign up for a new private retirement plan – he allowed us to remortgage the house for another couple hundred thousand kronor.

It's time for the big renovation, the one we've been putting off all these years. True, that's mostly because of money – and our not having any. But time and energy have been roadblocks too.

I didn't exactly jump for joy when Nina suggested, a few weeks back, that we should take out another loan and start looking for a builder. But, oddly enough, her enthusiasm was infectious. After everything that's happened, it's nice to have something concrete to focus on, and, besides, it's good to have a project to work on together. Redoing our house could be a way for us to make a fresh start.

The scent of curry and lemongrass rises from the bag

and makes my mouth water. Smilla and Anton will be happy when they see tonight's dinner. They're always complaining that we don't eat enough takeout. 'Everyone else' does it 'all the time'.

Nina's phone starts to ring just as I step into the front hall. She finds it quickly but hesitates for a second when she sees who's calling.

I just hope the banker hasn't changed his mind.

She gives me a pointed look and brings the phone to her ear. It must be my mother-in-law; Inger has a special talent for always calling right when we're about to eat.

'Hi, Lollo.'

My wife sounds unnaturally cheerful. I can make out Lollo's voice only as a dull murmur, and yet I know exactly why she's calling.

'What did you say?'

Nina, who is about to hang Vilgot's backpack on a hook, freezes mid-reach. Then she slowly turns around to stare at me.

The floor drops out from beneath my feet.

Acknowledgements

Without friends and friends of friends who are willing to step up and talk about everything from the workings of the judicial system to models of boats, life as an author would be much more difficult. This time, several of you even read the whole manuscript – many thanks.

Viveka Smidvall and Martin Eggert answered my questions about police work; Pernilla Qvarfordh contributed her knowledge of emergency medicine; and Daniel Krona helped with my inquiries about forensic medicine. Maria Lundberg gave me insights into her experience of saying farewell. Thanks to all of you for so generously sharing both your time and your knowledge.

Lena Sanfridsson's sharp reader's mind gave my fledgling manuscript wings. Thank you, Lena. You are a star.

Anette Eggert, Mattias Edvardsson and Mårten Melin read the manuscript several times over, gave me valuable feedback, and were also tireless cheerleaders from start to finish. You are gold.

A book is a team effort, and behind *Happy New Year* is a dream team: my publisher Helena Ljungström and editor Katarina Ehnmark Lundquist at Albert Bonniers Förlag, my agent Christine Edhäll and her colleagues at Ahlander Agency. My warmest thanks to you all. It's an honour to work with you.

Mom and Dad, thank you for supporting and encouraging me always. You are my role models in so many ways.

Micke, Lukas and Elvira. Thank you for your patience, love and unending support. I love you.